the single dier

the single soldier

GEORGE COSTIGAN

urbanepublications.com

First published in Great Britain in 2017
by Urbane Publications Ltd
Suite 3, Brown Europe House, 33/34 Gleaming Wood Drive,
Chatham, Kent ME5 8RZ
Copyright ©George Costigan, 2017

A CIP catalogue record for this book is available
from the British Library.

ISBN 978-1-911331-20-9
MOBI 978-1-911331-23-0
EPUB 978-1-911331-22-3

Design and Typeset by Michelle Morgan

Cover by Michelle Morgan

Printed and bound by CPI Group (UK) Ltd, Croydon, CR0 4YY

urbanepublications.com

The book is my love-letter to the people of Latronquiere, who so very warmly welcomed my family and other animals when we took the risk of moving our lives there.

a prologue

THE CHILD STRAIGHTENED.

Her mother worked.

Zoe picked a handful of raspberries and crushed them in her mouth.

"Hey, mademoiselle, weeding."

"He's late," the child replied, searching up the lane towards the village square.

Her mother worked, back bent, trowel busy.

"No." Zoe ran to the wall. "Look."

Sara stood long enough to see the cow take the corner.

The cow pulling the cart laden with another day's work.

Stone, again.

And walking beside his work, the man, wearing horse-blinkers.

His clothes grey with embedded dust, his beard and hair too.

His pace never changed. Slow.

"Jacques!" Zoe called.

"Leave him." Her mother's tone was sharp.

Blinkered, the man kept his sight directly in front of him, though he surely heard Zoe's whispered, "Jacques, Jacques."

Every evening.

The metal rim of the cart wheels ground into the rough tarmac.

Passed the child.

The clopping dwindled away and Zoe watched him descend the lane to the little bridge.

"Mamman?"

"Weeding."

"What will he do when the cow dies?"

"Pull it himself I shouldn't wonder."

Zoe returned to their vegetable plot and fiddled at a weed.

"Is he mad? He is – isn't he?"

"No. He's working. As you should be. And he's sad. So there's a difference."

Ten minutes later when Zoe straightened again, there, silhouetted against the evening sky, walked the cow, the cart and the man now without his blinkers.

And if she woke early enough she would see him returning tomorrow morning, the cart empty and by the time he trudged past her window the blinkers would be back on.

And she would eat her breakfast and go to Maternelle.

THE SINGLE SOLDIER

THE SINGLE SOLDIER

THE SINGLE SOLDIER

Jacques

one

THE CAT SCRATCHED AT THE WINDOW. I must fix that volet so he can't open it. Might get another half-hour. He rose, the dog shook itself awake. Softly, so as not to wake mother behind the thin wall, he dressed. Then, clogs in hand, he let the cat and the morning in and himself and the dog out.

Down the dozen stone steps and into the warm shit-stench of his barn and his meagre herd. He forked hay down to their feeders, whacked the first upright, wiped the hay from the nipples and, scraping yesterday's drowned flies from their buckets; sat to milk. Six adults, two with calves and all female. One male next time they need coupling, please Lord. In the first of the sunlight the dog gnawed at his flank.

Half-an-hour later he had carried the warm liquid to the caves beneath the house; found the dog's tic, crushed it, and loosed his herd for the day.

The dog led them blundering out, great clumps of manure splattering the lane and the flies would be gorging by the time he walked back. Right at the corner of the house and into the first of his three fields. One grassed, one fallow, one crops. Maize.

He stretched. Looked back.

The three farms. His, Arbel's and Duthileul's.

Puech.

As he washed at his well the sun cleared Duthileul's oak, and he could break his fast and his mother's sleep. He took some kindling and two eggs and the chickens bitched, outraged, again. The dog yawned, followed. Clogs left outside. The door-latch stuck, you had to jiggle it just so.

The grey ash pile, seemingly inert, snarled yellow teeth around the kindling and he set the big pot with water and fed it the eggs. Rolled a first ciggie while he waited for it to boil.

Back in his room he pulled the sheet and blankets straight, silently. Still she slept. Took some bread from the crock, cut two slices, buttered both. Two plates, two spoons. Her tray. Salt and pepper. The water began to dance and he sat on the bench Arbel had made him and lit his cig. The first deep haul laid his back into the wall and thoughts of Arbel. And Ardelle. Married now.

The cat wound round his legs till he gave it milk.

When the fag died he spooned the eggs from the water and enjoyed the cooling them in his leathery palms. He made coffee, laid her tray, then tapped and opened his mother's door.

Her room.

He placed the tray on the single chair whilst he opened the windows and volets and the north-facing room took the light softly and spread it along the wall, across the big armoire cupboard, the cobwebbed crucifix and down to her, a twig of steeling hair caught at the corner of her gaping mouth.

Her eyes flickered, a hand jumped and she woke.

"Sleep well?"

"Dreaming. Of your grandfather."

"Breakfast."

"He built this house..."

"...with his own hands. Eat, the eggs'll go cold."

They ate, mother and son.

The dog waited for crusts.

"He was a fool."

They finished and he stood, piling the tray.

He turned at the door.

"It's to be warm - you could sit in the garden."

"Perhaps..."

He threw the dog the crusts and they left her.

The fire bothered him, he shouldn't keep it in. But he knew she wouldn't sit in the garden. He fed it some of the wetter wood.

"I'm in the garden, mamman."

A late cuckoo called.

The tomatoes needed water or this spring sun could strangle them. He pulled water from the well and spread it. And would need to again tonight. He weeded. His mind drifted to Sara and the sex she shared with Jerome and that thought hardened him till he opened his trousers and pulled his tension out. Hoed it into the earth thinking, it was half a child. Half his child.

Market tomorrow, swap my bread tickets and buy candles, oil, matches.

Wash-day Friday and fishing. She'll eat fish, mother...

His mother sat in the silence. A random spit from the fire. Her room inert but for flies. Through the window Duthileul's farm yard bulged with ploughs, cutters, pigs, ducks, wealth. Her feet dangled short of the boards and she watched the veins fill. The rhythm of work had left her. She had raised him to run their lives alone and that was good, good for him; but now she had no forward motion.

She had lost that, and Faith, when she'd lost him, her dead man. She swung back into the bed.

He came up the stone steps, kicked off his clogs. Pick a salad for dinner, weed the vegetables, buy canes for the mange-tout tomorrow. Plough the second field, harvest the maize in the third much later. And his eyes lifted to the extent of their land, his beech-copse. And behind and beyond that - a thin strip of faraway blue - the hills of the Cantal; and behind and beyond them, as remote as the moon, The War.

A silence had taken root with the defeat, the armistice and Vichy. Shoulders had shrugged when The Requisitioning began but argument or opinions were as rare as motor vehicles. It mattered not one sous that the war would surely never come up the lousy D roads to conquer St.Cirgues – a bar, three shops, the post-office, the church – no, it was dread of collaborators that had strangled chat. The old men, hunched under their flat black berets, sat in the Café Tabac, their efforts of 14-18 wasted, The Bosche triumphant at last. The people had been told to "Wait and see - Attentisme", and they did. When they were told that France was 'A favoured nation in the new Europe' some approved and some didn't. Silently.
Everyone knew they were to report any Resistance activity, or anyone tuning their radio to De Gaulle, or any communist, unionist or Jewish activity. But everyone knew Feyt the tailor was a Jew, their Jew, and the months had passed and he still dressed the men and lived his bachelor life. Everyone knew Jerome Lacaze said he was a communist, but he still walked between his mother's huge house and the bar to drink.

Mignon had been made the Vichy official in charge of the requisition, giving out bread-tickets when he came for meat, milk and vegetables for the Bosche. He had played full-back in the village team, but everyone knew that even if there were enough to make a side, and there wasn't, and even if there were another team to play, which there wasn't, he wouldn't be picked.

In the café the official press was read and when Maréchal Petain spoke on the radio Herrisson the Gendarme stood with folded arms to ensure Patriotism was seen to be observed.

Grivault cut his meat thinner, Jauliac watered the wine just a little and the women hoarded what they could; thinned the soup and mourned their sons, dead or deported. Fabien Cantagrel wrote every month from some place called Dachau, the same letter, unchanging. The Curé rode in on his Sunday bicycle and hid behind his Latin, sticking to the scriptures like a leech.

St.Cirgues, like France, was bowed.

They sat outside the Café Tabac, the last three boys of Allibert's class of '33. Jerome, Jacques and Arbel. And drank.

"Your mother?" Jerome began their catechism.

"The same. Yours?" Jacques squinted in the fresh sun-light.

"A cow."

"Still?"

"Once a cow..."

Jerome turned to Arbel. "Ardelle?"

"On form." Arbel, nearly toothless at twenty-two, grinned and poured wine down his throat.

"Sex," Jerome leaned back, "is obviously good for a body."

"No no no." Arbel wagged a forefinger sideways.

"Sex is not good?" Jerome raised an eyebrow.

"Marriage," Arbel poured his third, "is good."

"And the sex?"

"Well..." Arbel grinned, flushed, drank.

"Do you ever think of God watching you?"

Arbel's mouth straightened.

"'Mm, there's Arbel and Ardelle banging away. 'Me Almighty, but that looks good.' D'you spose he gets a stiffy? Like Jacques here?"

Arbel's face whitened. "Don't take His name, Jerome."

"Only musing - no offence. You don't think He bothers to watch? No. He's asleep, isn't He?"

"Don't take His name."

"Where is He these days, Arbel? Berlin?"

"Shh." Jacques looked round but the old ones were slumped over their pastis like broken playing cards and only Duthileul Pére, sitting in his window seat, nodded at Jacques.

Madame Carnac, the one two generations of small boys had called The Witch, strode past to gather her wood and grass. She lived with her chickens, trading them and their eggs for everything she needed, so living outside the system of money. She ate no bread, drank no wine, never went to Mass, and it was said she was bald beneath the wigs she washed in the Lavoir on alternate weeks.

Louis cycled across the square. The village idiot who invited all the women to come mushroom picking with him. None went anymore.

"Where's Sara?" Jacques wondered aloud.

"Talking of sex?"

"No." Jacques frowned at Jerome.

"She's coming."

They took another mouthful of wine. Younger playing cards.

Sara could see them from her kitchen, where Chayriguet was washing his hands.

"Does your mother know?"

"No."

"Does his mother know?"

Sara laughed. "No."

"Does he know?"

"Not yet."

He dried his big hands on the towel and picked up his bag.

"You're three months gone. No charge."

"Thank you."

"Will you tell the Curé?"

Sara looked at him,

"You know Jerome."

"I do."

"Thank you, Doctor."

He turned at the door.

"If you reconsider - I'm not a Catholic, Sara."

They stood, the big oak table between them.

"I am."

He nodded and left. She watched him drive away, stood there a second longer and looked. Jerome and Jacques and Arbel.

Thought it would be Jacques. No. Jerome. From The Big House. With his mother.

She'll disown him.

He'll be so happy.

What will we call her? Our secret. When was the last time I had a secret? Funny. She's a secret now. And when she's not a secret she'll be a scandal. With a pagan for a father.

And how do I know it's a girl?

Because I do!

She walked across the square. Arbel and Jacques rose and kissed her welcome. Jerome lounged back and took her in again. Wide face, wide shoulders, wide grin, good hair, bad teeth. A woman

since childhood. Sara. His paysanne.

She was pregnant.

That was why Chayriguet had called.

Oh my God, he'd done it this time...

And all those prayers, all that disgusting midnight pleading debasement at the crucifix, all that hypocrisy and feebleness - dead. Gone.

Good!

He was glad.

My mother will go mad. Or die. Or to ice.

Yes, ice. Ice'll suit her.

He reached for the big hand and the strong fingers knuckled into his, sharing the secret and its fears.

"Drink? Oh, yes, I think so."

Jerome looked round.

At Jacques, who'd become a man before he'd even been a lad. At Arbel, all bone, muscle and red wine; with his grin, His Lord and Ardelle. At Sara, my earth. Pregnant. And this café, full of fossils and Duthileul. And Russians dying as I sit here.

"Russians are dying as we sit here."

"Shh." said Sara, automatic.

"I don't understand what my response should be."

Jacques and Arbel, recognising this tone, reached for the tobacco.

"I'm humbled."

"Drunk, more like. Again."

"No, Arbel. I'm excited."

"You're excited?" Arbel looked mockingly around.

"Yes. Here. In silent Cirgues. What do I do?"

"You? You talk. Do about what?"

"Arbel," Jerome gripped the hard arm, "Arbel, men are dying, babies are dying, now. What is my response?"

"You? You gab."

"Do you know - of course you don't - do you know one thousand French Jews," he turned briefly and lowered his voice, "...died last year? No. You didn't. Because the papers you don't read wouldn't tell you. Because they died in France. In French concentration camps. Under French Government orders."

Now all of them looked round and Duthileul Pére's cold watery eyes rose.

"Encore." Jerome raised the bottle.

Janon the hunchback barman shuffled out, wiped the table and stood there, puffing.

"No work to do?"

The old one had limited conversation with anyone under sixty-five.

"Raising a glass to Vichy and victory."

"Good," he nodded, dim.

"Petain is France..."

"...France is Petain." Janon grunted, took the empty bottle and shambled back inside.

"Catechisme," Jerome sneered. "Must be all that Catholic practice, eh, Arbel?"

"It's their hope."

"It's their disgrace."

"And what's yours?" Sara nudged at him.

"That I don't know what to do. For the Jews, for the Russians - for my baby. For all the babies. French, Russian. German, even. Eh?"

Janon re-appeared with a bottle, went back.

Arbel stared at Sara. Filled their glasses.

"You're pregnant?"

"Yes."

"Name of the Father the Son and the Holy Ghost."

"Thank you, Arbel."

"Oh my God." He poured his glass down his throat.

Sara laughed.

"You're pregnant?" Jacques looked at Sara.

"Shh!" Jerome mocked. "Yes. What is my response, Vermande?"

"I don't know."

"Get married." Arbel grinned.

Jerome's smile was beautiful. "No-o."

"Get very drunk, then."

Jerome turned back to Jacques.

"You're jealous?"

"Yes."

The silence grew quiet and thoughtful.

Like St.Cirgues.

Jacques walked past the cemetery. Michel Pinot and Silvane Galtier asleep now after their brief war. The woods began, the road rose and a brilliant-blue dung-beetle waddled across in search of the morning's droppings.

Yes, he was jealous.

A jay swooped across the lane. Another followed, chasing.

Someone had left one red sock on a branch of a tree. He hadn't noticed it this morning. Had it been there this morning? It was good. One red sock. Why? A sign for the Resistance? Here? In Duthileul's woods? Surely it wasn't him - that greedy unsmiling prune. Were there really Maquisards? Jerome talked, but it was talk, wasn't it?

The Germans were two hundred kilometres North, and the war was in Russia, even in Africa, some said. There were no Germans here. Why would they be? What is here? Us and our farms.

Duthileul's herd stared as he strode by.

Where was this war? Not with the birds, or his cows, or in the dancing leaves. It was in his mother. As if she were pregnant with it. A cancer of grief. Started when his father was gassed in the last push of 1918. The father he'd never seen. And she'd lived and raised Jacques to be the father everywhere but in her bed. But when this new war had started it had laid her down like a floorboard. And he knew she was dying of it and would die unless it were stopped. His stride shortened as the lane rose sharp to meet the house.

Another truth was, Mamman had made herself weak in order to protect him, to prevent him from being called up, two years before. But that was over. They were safe now. They had less, but they had enough to live. And she wasn't living.

He knew, suddenly, like a farmer, as he came into her room. Like looking at a sick cow; she had six, perhaps nine months left.

He was five, in primaire class, when he'd first realised he had no father. He asked her and she told him. The War. In an onion field. 17. She had a photograph, in the pocket of a dress. Him, in his uniform. Just a big grinning lad.

Jacques was nine when he first noticed the village women muttering. In church or on market day, he saw the way his mother withdrew from them. Away from their belief that she should snap out of it, as they had had to do, and had done.

He learned the land, the moons, the seasons and their tasks in a way that made school books remote. Like all the first-born boys, he knew his future and Allibert lacked the humility to teach through the land; he retained a snobbery, a rigidity in his methods that failed his warm nature.

By thirteen he was the farmer. His mother had worked their three

fields, fed them from the vegetable plot, and once a year had even dragged a beast to cut the hay on Janatou. Their fourth field.

The folly her father had won that night he lost everything to Duthileul Pére. He was a famous fool. Never play with land. And he'd played cards and made Duthileul's great-grandchildren secure by losing eight hectares. Everything you could see from the front door, except the three fields and the copse. And he'd won Janatou, a sharp sloping hillside field, four kilometres the other side of the village, facing the Cantal Mountains. He never went there and the field was hardly worth the effort she expended to reap it. But she had walked with a cow and cart, every year, and done it. Baled it and brought it back. The winter feed. He was thirteen when she asked him to do it.

It was the furthest he'd been in his life.

Wednesday, first light, he yoked the strongest cow to the cart, took the scythe, the strong string, his knife, cheese and bread, and left. September. Always cut between the September moons. Down through Duthileul's woods, up past the cemetery and its high walls, past the village wash-pond and into the town square. Janon the hunchback nodding from wiping his tables outside the Café Tabac as Jacques Vermande took the Maurs road alone for the first time.

In twenty strides he passed Sara's house and was walking alongside her land. She looked up from the vegetables, straightened, grinned.

"Leaving us?"

"Janatou," he said, self-importantly.

"Pff," she rubbed at her back and bent again.

As the road turned back to face the morning sun, suddenly there was St.Cirgues, all toy-town simplicity as though God had copied the classroom bricks from Primaire. All he'd ever known right there. He laughed and the cow flicked back its ears, and they walked.

There was a spring, a source, there for him and the animal, she'd said. He passed the rusted iron crucifix and the three houses of Poutiac. An old one came to a balcony and watched the boy and cart all the way past, then went back inside.

He thought of the girls in his class and their chests. Sara and her chest. Sara, who laughed. Who seemed to know what he thought. About her chest. And Jerome, who made her laugh in a different way. A way that somehow made him hard when he thought of it, like now.

The cow walked, its huge shoulders a tireless see-saw.

He almost missed the postboxes and the turning.

Overgrown with a year's nettle and hawthorn the path led him down to his work, his land. The track was lined with blackberries, red berries and raspberries, all bursting with juice, all his. He stopped by the shell of an ancient oak. Hollowed dark by time, dead longer than his mother's life. An eerie standing corpse. Saplings sprouted in a circle around it, acorns that had fallen and taken.

Now the trees seemed to gather, waving castanets of dry leaves as the beast brushed past and finally Jacques pushed a last low branch aside and saw the diving, impossible field.

And then his eyes lifted and took in the hundred kilometres of valleys in layers and ridges all the endless pastel colours of an Auvergne Autumn, leading his heart and soul to rest on the peaks of the Cantal mountains.

The next time he would experience a similar emotion was when Simone came round the corner of his barn with Chibret the Mayor. And he would be twenty-four.

He made a leek soup and brought it in to her, the dog following.

"A little pepper?"

In the kitchen he took down the mortar and the grains and ground enough to cover the bottom of an egg-cup. The dog followed and slumped down to wait.

"The village?"

"Normal. Less of everything."

"War."

"I suppose. The Requisition."

"The black market, more like."

Her face registered nothing more than experience. Two bluebottles battered against her windows.

"Sara's pregnant."

The woman looked up.

"Who?"

"Jerome."

"Lacaze?"

"Yes."

"His mother will freeze over."

Like you, he thought.

"The fool."

"Sara?"

"Him! Head full of spiders. And his politics."

"That's all talk."

"Is it? Is it? When the Bosche come - what will that fool do? I'll tell you! He'll leave her and he'll fight for his talk and he'll die with his talk and she'll be left."

She seemed to physically shrink, yet at the same time her eyes widened and filled, and when her legs kicked out at her helplessness the soup spilled, the bowl rolled from the bed and broke neatly and she slapped at her tears, furious.

The dog looked hard at her and then to the fallen crusts. She fell back, blasted, into her pillows.

He took the corners of the eiderdown and swung the mess to the floor. He pulled her blanket up and looked into her prematurely old face.

"Men have no imagination," she panted, "The future is nothing, because men die in the present for Glory. And death is not Glory, it's final."

Her son didn't know what to say.

"He wanted to fight. 'For France', he said. And he did and he died and don't go, son. Don't ever go."

Her fingers clawed round his wrist.

"Don't die for France, or for today. Don't fight. Don't kill, my son. Don't kill."

The lines on her neck, the crow's feet, the sweet faint motherly smell. And his face touched hers, their cheekbones nestling, warmth yet in her tired skin. Nothing feels quite like blood on blood.

He gathered the broken bowl onto the tray, the eiderdown in the other hand, said, "Washing," and went out. The dog hesitated, followed.

She thought of a picture in a school history book. There had been some war between Catholic and Protestant. She couldn't remember when, or which, but the picture had shown an army of men attacking a church. A monastery, something. A soldier had scaled a statue of the Virgin and was decapitating her with a mallet. At his feet a comrade had been shot, through the neck, by someone with a gun inside the church. This meant it must be at least the sixteenth century, since she remembered Allibert insisting they understand the importance of the moment hand-rifles had

appeared and how history altered for ever. She had remembered it then and she knew it now. Had lived this little life ruined by guns. But it was men's history that changed with the gun. The history of women stayed the same. Raise men, lose them, grieve. And what was the point of women's grief in the weight of history and all the world? All through that book, every other page had a picture of men dying. To rid France of the English, the Germans, the Austrians, the Spanish, The Moors, The Cathars, the Protestants, the Kings, the Bourgeoisie and men still dying till today when that Lacaze fool would make another baby fatherless, another peasant woman grieve, when he died 'for France'.

And she? Another widowed peasant woman. What place had her grief in this world? With him. Jean-Luc. With her precious sexy lad. His son, Jacques, older now than the boy-father who had shaken every drop of him into her and then gone and died for an onion-field.

Her head drooped sideways and she prayed again for death. Still she prayed, though now she knew, because she lived, God was deaf.

At the lavoir Jacques squatted on the sloping stone ledge traversing the two pools, slid the eiderdown into the water, took the soap from his pocket and washed.

Both his shirts, his Sunday trousers, socks and underwear. Rinsed them in the smaller pool. Squeezing, wringing, his hands stinging red with the cold. Then back on the barrow, the soap re-wrapped in his pocket and home to milking, the fire and food.

LaCroix was felling wood for Duthileul in the valley field. LaCroix. The family of incest. Him, her, a mother, no one sure whose, and two sons, no one sure whose, simpletons. Jerome had joked once about Jacques and his mother. He had thought of it

too, once. Jerome changed the joke to calves' mouths. Then loaves of damp warm bread. Then he must have fucked Sara because he had dropped the joke abruptly, and took to urging Jacques to the dances and village fetes. He had gone, felt gauche - and now...

He stopped at the iron bench, rolled a cigarette and let the smoke at his thoughts.

"Don't kill."

But if a Bosche came, and would kill her, then he would kill the Bosche, wouldn't he? Yes. He would defend her time.

And if the Germans threatened any of his friends and he could save them, he would. Jerome, Arbel, Ardelle. Sara.

Duthileul, then? Yes...

Does that mean everyone French?

Collaborators?

But, aren't we all collaborators? Our food is feeding them. We're not fighting them.

So was it wrong to obey the Government? They'd met Hitler and they'd stopped him invading the south, and they said Resistance was wrong. Why say that?

Because, Jerome said, the Government was collaborating.

But what was their choice? Invasion.

Rather than that, wasn't it better to collaborate?

So,

what about the Russians?

Were they wrong? The Bolsheviks. Fighting Hitler for him? Well, they weren't fighting for him or for us French, they were fighting for their mothers and friends and homes. So, who was wrong? Us, for not fighting, or them for resisting? Because shouldn't they fight to defend their land, their homes? The French had. And lost. Had it been wrong to fight in the first place then?

No. Because he would defend his land, his mother, and his friends. So, he should help them, the Russians.

But, this was mad - hadn't the Russians helped Hitler at the start? Hadn't they invaded Poland? Wasn't that why everyone except Jerome hated the Communists? They hadn't helped when France was invaded. They had helped themselves.

Who should he help?

And how? He had nine animals, three fields, Janatou, his beech copse and his mother.

And in the end, because of the Requisition, the only people he was helping were the Germans. Who, twenty-odd years ago, had killed his father.

He hauled hard at the tobacco, sucked it down, let the smoke and his confusion drift up and out.

What was his mother saying?

Turn the other cheek.

But when Christ turned the other cheek it was to a slap. Christ's action required eyes to meet and shame be turned to love. This war was fought at the range of a rifle or a tank or a Stuka. Not a slap. Rifles had sights, but they were instruments of the blind. It's easy to kill if you can't see the eyes. He killed flies easily, and weren't we all just so many flies to a bomber-pilot? Bullets couldn't be shamed. Bombs were indifferent to Christianity.

So how would Jesus deal with Hitler and his armies? He wouldn't. He would be killed. His own people had killed Him easily enough... Jacques' chest heaved hard and he didn't understand.

If Our Lord couldn't have saved even Himself...

No. That's not right. He accepted His death. He accepted God's will. Then what is God's will?

Thou Shalt Not Kill.

A last drag. His head lolled back. How can a painter paint those

trees so they move? How could they paint the wind? How would he ever be loved? When? Two more jays swept across.

The cows, heavy with milk, late by their day, gave gladly. The swallows cleaned their metal-blue wings. He closed the barn doors and pulled a salad supper from the garden. His house-swallows dashed out to the trees and back. They were smaller than the pair in the barn. Cramped by the eaves of the house?

He cut some ham, washed the garden insects from the lettuce, sliced a little cheese. Gave the cat cheese rinds and milk. Gave the dog ham rinds and water. Wondered how the cat purred and drank at the same time. The dog gathered itself by the fire, rested his head on his legs, looked at him once, closed his eyes and went to sleep. Fast, easy. The cat washed and groomed.

The dart of an evening wind drying his washing. He took his mother's meal to her. The dog woke and followed.

"I made you break routine."

He shrugged. Gave her the tray. Paused at the door.

"Mass on Sunday?"

"No."

Their ritual wash-day conversation. Three days early.

He ate at the table. Another ritual, he ate his evening meal alone at the table. From thirteen, when he had first come back from Janatou, from his being the farmer, she would place it before him and then leave him, the man, at the table.

He threw crusts to the dog. Finished. Another day. Lit a candle and took it to her. Closed the volets. Took the tray and her bed-pot. Looked at the first stars. Clear sky, the chaleur had begun. Felt her eiderdown, nearly dry. A cow vaired in the barn as he passed. The dog waited at the top of the stairs. Trudged up, kicked off his clogs, took her pot back.

"Nothing you want?"

"No."

"Call..."

"I would."

"Night mamman."

"Night son."

That last ritual over he fed the vegetable cuttings to the fire, sat on Arbel's bench, undid his trousers, stretched his toes to the edge of the ash and reached for his tobacco and papers. Best part of the day. The last fag.

One of the cows was mounting today. She'll need the bull. Have to talk to Duthileul. The bastard had the best one, no question. His hand gently rolled at his balls and his gaze rested on his mother's door.

His Mother. Old, and like the century, killing itself at forty-two.

two

TWO YEARS BEFORE, Simone, her mother and father, and the civilians of Peronne, where the Somme meets the Oise North-East of Paris, waited, listening to the shared radios and prayed. That the French Army would hold. That the English would come, that the Germans would not. As in all wars God is deaf to the defeated and on and on through the brief glorious summer, like a plague, came the Bosche. Why, argued the people, would they want their town? They could pass it by, it had nothing. A ruined sandstone castle where Charles the Bold had once held Louis XI. Good fishing; but nothing else of virtue, except it was their home.

Should they leave, should they stay? They stayed. And like dawn the Germans came, winning.

First a trickle of refugees; Belgian, Dutch, Flanders French begged food and a bed and told of bare chested young soldiers running triumphant through the fields, rifles over their heads, singing; then in the morning wrang their hands and left. The Bosche were two days away. And still people stayed. The trickle burst to a flood and lastly came the bewildered young hopeless of the French Army; riding, striding, limping through and ordering them to evacuate and still father stayed. So mother stayed. So Simone stayed. Father

called the soldiers and the south-bound neighbours cowards and the neighbours called him a fool and left, on bikes and carts and cows, with sacks and suitcases and mattresses, and Peronne's four thousand became a few dozen.

Mother dropped Father's gun down the well and packed Simone's case. Simone took out one of the coats and put books in its place as the first planes strafed the town and the first shells broke up the Mairie. From the radio De Gaulle called for continued Resistance. Simone cried when her father struck her mother, finding the gun gone, and as a June Tuesday broke, the tanks came. Blew up the church, sprayed destruction and passed. And still he stood, as the jeeps and armoured cars spat out men.

Two teenagers advanced on him and he cried "Vive La France!" and nothing more as four bullets ripped his chest apart and sent him sprawling back into the kitchen, his life running ruined over his tiled floor. The boys stepped past the mess, kicked round the house and one went back outside to see if there was time for rape. There wasn't. An officer ordered the women taken to the rubble-strewn town square to wait. The tares of the village gathered. Mute. Female or old. It took a silent half hour for the handful of men to be found and removed and then the women were marched to the station.

As the soldiers crammed them into trains with rifle-butts and laughter her mother spat in a young, clean face and she was hauled off the train and Simone never saw her again. Orphaned in an hour.

The train left for Paris, but at Crepy she got off and walked away from the station. She had her suitcase and her hate and with the refugee exodus she marched herself through Reims, Chalon and Troyes, racing the future gathering behind her. She was forty kilometres outside Dijon when capitulation came and Hitler took sweet revenge for the humiliation of 1918.

France was halved.

And with the others she strode south.

Because she was young, twenty and pretty, she was befriended and abused more than most. A lorry driver took her virginity in return for a seventy kilometre lift and others more shards of her dignity for a bike or a night out of the rain and it seemed to mean only that her descent through France was quicker.

She buried her dreams of teaching, of Paris, alongside the memory of her parents.

She slept in beds, barns, ditches, rain; with cattle, sheep, fleas, tics, farmers and fellow refugees. From her suitcase the dispossessed stole her clothes and then stole those she stole to replace them. Her books no-one touched.

Christmas 1940.

She was placed with a family in time for their threadbare celebration. He was 57, she a year older, childless now, and they never spoke about anything. Her father had argued politics, religion, the weather, anything on which he could exercise his curiosity. These people were cowed and only too willing to trust Petain and Prime Minister Laval, to accept the defeat and "Attentisme"; to do nothing more than survive.

Food was scarce, these prematurely aged people wouldn't deal on the black-market and so it was scarcer still. France was like her family. Two-thirds dead and one third mute.

Germany invaded Russia. She'd been so very much younger when her father had seethed with shame that Stalin should ravage Poland's back, unprotected, as it fought Hitler at the front. She'd understood only a betrayal of his Socialism, a concept she hadn't grasped. Now this news was greeted with pride. Prime Minister Laval said so on the crackly radio. He desired the victory of

Germany because he believed Bolshevism to be a greater evil than Fascism. The man and woman nodded at the meagre dinner table and Simone asked herself what her thoughts were. She didn't know. She'd only been thinking survival.

But when the Legion of Honour sent a battalion to fight with the Bosche, to fight with her parent's killers, to fight in German uniforms, and the couple grunted their hopeful approval, Simone began to search outside their bare house for a response. In the silent streets, in the hunched shoulders, in the darting eyes, she needed to believe in, at the very least, a confusion like hers.

One Sunday after Mass she shook hands with the Curé and he invited her that evening to talk. She didn't know what to expect. Anything was possible. Be cautious.

They sat by the cold iron stove in his study, the walls loaded with books, and drank weak coffee. She talked of her past and her journey. He nodded, patient. A drip of her pain leaked out. He greeted it with his. At a government bankrupt of Christianity. The radio played jazz quietly and he told her of Pére Chaillet and an escape route south to Spain for orphaned Jewish children. An hour had passed when he gave her his blessing and she walked home.

Bad joke - she had no home. Half a country away her roots lay wasted.

Could she put down new ones here? With those people? In that house?

Well, what else had she? What else was she?

And what did the Curé want? Was any of what he said true? Was all of it? What did he want? She trusted him, that's all she knew.

No, she wanted to trust him.

The following week Maréchal Petain, the hero of Verdun, Saviour of France, worker of the miracle - Freedom, walked the same streets and a hundred and fifty thousand greeted him with religious ecstasy. Her 'family' at their windows, crying. Roads solid with hope, as real as hers, and just as desperate, and this too stirred her, to stand tiptoe to see the white moustaches and the straight back. Joan of Arc grown old and male. And it was for this man the Curé had revealed his disgust. Was this man a disgrace? Were all these people fools, traitors?

He shook her hand after Sunday Mass and she went to his rooms that evening. They talked, drank thin coffee and he tuned the radio to listen to Laval.

"All communists are in the pay of the Jews..."

He switched it off, disgusted, tainted, and gave Simone two broadsheet printed pieces of paper. "L'Humanité." Warned her to let no one see it. Warned her again at the door.

In her cold cot under the slope of the roof she read of unionists and communists being rounded up and sent to camps or deported, their wives imprisoned for protesting. She read of the vile Statute of Jews, of a synagogue in Nice ransacked whilst the police stood arms folded outside. She read it all and read it again, a void in her life filling with the anger of the writers, and with their search for like minds, for revenge, for Resistance, for Dignity. For a Response. It was the first she'd read since Peronne.

The following week there were six already round his stove.

A teacher, as she had dreamed of being, a butcher, a gendarme and three older ones, who identified themselves only as "French". She sat, distrusted for her youth, her sex, her Northernness and her newness. At nine o'clock the Curé checked the quiet streets through his curtains and turned the radio on, tuned it minutely and faintly, and through the night London spoke and then De Gaulle spoke. Immediate interference. Military music. Vichy's orders. The men cursed, apologised to her and then cursed worse.

Still, De Gaulle was talking, and somewhere he would be heard. They turned it off to talk themselves. At last, she thought, talk.

There was a blur of figures from the butcher. Arrests of French men and women denounced by French traitors, the scale of the requisitioning, proof of the black market and the ultimate economic deceit of Vichy, that four hundred million Francs a day was being paid to Germany. That was the price of their freedom, that was the price of being a favoured nation, that was why the cities were starving and that was a war crime itself.

"Can't eat figures," one of the men grumbled.

"They're facts."

"Can't eat them, either," said another, shifting.

"Then why pass on the newspaper?"

"I don't. I wipe my arse with it."

"Then why come?" the teacher asked.

"The Hun."

A silence.

The butcher spoke again. "They're not our only enemy."

"They're my only enemy," said the first.

"That and your ignorance."

"Not needing to be communist is not proof of ignorance my patronising friend. I want the Hun out of France."

"Why is he in France? Economics. Why is he not in The South? Economics. He doesn't need to be in the South! We're paying him to stay out!"

"I know. I accept. But economics won't get him out. Economics is not the issue, Liberation is the issue. I'm poor and land is the only wealth of the poor."

Murder members of the local Gestapo, that was a response that would be understood. The teacher counseled non-violence and two of the men snorted. The Curé told them a German soldier had been killed, in Bordeaux. And two in Paris.

"Good."

"In Bordeaux twenty-seven were killed as a reprisal. In Paris fifty."

There was silence.

The Curé added, "Vichy selected the fifty. Communists, unionists, Jews. And their wives."

The teacher asked what would be achieved by the murder of even one collaborator.

And one of them said, "I'd feel French."

"And we'd all be vulnerable."

"You mean this group is going to do nothing?"

"This group doesn't know yet what it should do," said the Curé softly, "that's why we're talking."

"But you won't mind what I might do, so long as it doesn't affect you? This? This coffee-evening. This blather of theory. A wash-tub of women."

"Don't reprisals matter to you?" The teacher seemed genuinely shocked.

"People are not all the same. Not blessed equal in God's sight. Some are scum. No use. All Germans, some French. This is no time for education, just remedy. You cut when the sickness is so bad nothing else will work. How bad must this get for you?"

"And the slaughtered innocents - martyrs?" The Curé asked, sad.

"Yes. Right since Herod, don't patronise me. The world is changed by action. While wankers sit to talk. Call it politics and economics."

"Then you must act and may God guide your conscience."

"He will. And may He pity yours."

"He does."

The man stood and left. Before the week was out he was dead. Found in his room, shot.

The silence the following Sunday spoke loudly of suspicion.

Then there were twelve, including two from the University who wrote the paper. And they brought other papers. "Le Coq Enchainé" and "Liberation". They were not alone.

Each week she took her newspapers, folded inside her vest, and wondered what to do with them. She left one in the lavatory of a café, two in the library, one on a pew after eight o'clock Mass. It was weeks before she dared pass one directly to the friendly barman in a café. Her heart raced, then raced more as the man took it, nodded, and left her. When he came back with a different paper to give her she had fled, frightened, and that frightened him. He burnt both papers.

The couple became afraid of her movements, and she toyed with which lie to tell them. A man? The church? She even considered telling the truth till she saw their horror when someone painted a cross of Lorraine, the symbol for a Free France, on a neighbour's wall. So she said nothing, which frightened them more. At Mass each Sunday she prayed for Hope and they prayed she would go away.

Each Sunday evening the group fragmented a little more. Action, action, how long will we do Nothing?

In March their world spurted forward. The Berlin Philharmonic were coming to play Beethoven. In their town hall.

Now the talk warmed.

Police and collaborators would both be there.

But they could surely be silent no longer. A line had been drawn. Demanding a response. They voted on slips of paper put in the Gendarme's cap.

Unanimous.

The night of the concert they each made their separate ways to the town hall square. And found people gathered and gathering.

Looking in each other's eyes.

It became a hundred. Another hundred. Still coming, gathering. More. A thousand now, surely. Standing behind a line of police and waiting. Silent. And as more came so they all caught the idea of Silence and it solidified. Two thousand, three, more; all of them keeping the night mute. Watching their town hall fill with fellow citizens, fellow French.

The orchestra arrived, walking from wagons up the steps of the hall and stopped, facing this mass. Fifteen strings, eight brass, six woodwind, timpani, a harpist, a thirty-strong choir to sing "Ode To Joy" and they stopped, held by the harmony in silence, and faced three thousand. So these were the French. No wonder they were so easily beaten.

The Mayor's car drove up. Hands were shaken. And now one man ducked calmly under the linked arms of the police, crossed the cobbled square, up the steps, disappeared into the hall, came out with a leather and chestnut Louis Quinze chair, raised it over his head, and smashed it. The silence shattered into cheers. He was arrested. Sent to a camp.

And the orchestra played, but Simone believed Beethoven would have been with them, listening as only a deaf man could, to the silence of hope in the bitter night.

And now she allowed herself to believe in a future. If not for her, at least for France. That night in her cot she tasted it, rolled it round her body, couldn't sleep. Couldn't wait.

From the radio Vichy banned celebrations of the fourteenth of July. At their next meeting the jubilant group could hardly believe its luck. Who in Lyon now would not protest at such a strike against French history? The butcher urged the Curé to preach Revolution the following Sunday. The Curé urged him to come back to the church.

Laughter.

THE SINGLE SOLDIER

But, the following Sunday the Curé preached shame and disgrace and his congregation slumped in their pews, avoiding the arrows of his pain and anger. Outside he shook her hand tightly and she felt paper passing palm to palm. In privacy she read that nine had been arrested, and the communists, the butcher and the two from the university sent to a concentration camp outside Bordeaux, and that she must leave. There was the name of a friend, another Jesuit in a mountain village, Souceyrac, three hundred kilometres south-west. Part of Pére Chaillet's escape route. And under "God Will Be With You" he had added, "If you have to make a pact with the Devil to drive out Germans - you make a pact with the Devil, every time."

That night she became a refugee again.

April 1942.

Snow. In Clermont she was placed with a family who ignored her and she left after one silent meal, heading for the escape-route. How would she pay? With sex? What else had she? Unless she stole. She would certainly beg.

She walked.

Farmers took brief pity, a barn some nights, some nights their beds, some nights of her periods she accepted, then stole food and walked away whilst they slept from the sex. Rattled Mayors crowded stragglers like her into the school rooms of the smaller towns; perhaps a blanket, perhaps soup and always the same stories to listen to.

She walked.

She stole a bike and rode half a department before she woke one morning and found it stolen. She walked. Towards the Curé's friend. What rumours she heard she discounted and then Pére Chaillet was arrested. That she believed. Would the escape route exist without him? What else could she do but hope? What else

kept her walking?

Into the Cantal.

Open country beneath a brutal, icy sky. She found a plough, slept under it with ants in her hair. What am I? One crawled up her nose and she got up and walked.

Le Rouget - six kilometres.

She walked.

She walked. With her case. Who am I? Who am I now? On this road, God knows where, going God knows where. I'm no resister, that's for sure. I'm no hero - no Jeanne D'Arc. I'm nothing. I'm No-one, surviving.

She walked, amazed at her own strength. She'd had one cold in two years. She hadn't eaten meat since before Lyon. The cold seeped into her bones and she walked with it, accepting. I'll accept anything now. I'm a non-person. Can't remember if I was ever proud but I'm not now.

I'll find this Curé. Get to his village, find him and ask to help, help others to escape.

Father would be proud. A freezing tear scorched her cheek.

She walked into Le Rouget. Begged bread, got the previous day's, a rare delight, and waited for the Mayor. He drove in and she waited in his outer office. Her eyes no longer took in the walls, the notices. Two, three hours passed. As hunger roamed her stomach, the door finally opened.

"In. Sit." He offered the last knuckles of a fat red hand. "Yes?"

"I'm from the North."

"Who isn't? Yes?"

"I need to get to Sousceyrac."

"Ohh?" He leaned back.

She sat back too. Mutual distrust. Natural now.

"Why Sousceyrac?"

"A friend there."

"Who?"

There was no point in lying.

"The Curé."

"Mm. His name?"

She told him. He folded his hands across his waistcoat.

"No."

"No?"

"Gone."

She aged suddenly. France gaped before her. Where now?

"Need to get anywhere else?"

"No."

"No more Curé friends?"

"No."

"Wait outside."

She listened to him phone and mutter. Monosyllabic, deliberate. Fool she was. The Curé was a Jesuit and the Jesuits alone of the Catholic hierarchy had been vocal against the war. Chaillet had been arrested as a traitor. She should get up and walk out of here now. Where? The next village? The phone would catch her.

"In."

She stood.

"There's a dormitory for refugees at the Gendarmerie."

"And tomorrow?"

"Tomorrow..." he shrugged, blew a dismissive breath and stood half out of his chair and was back to his papers by the time she turned to go.

She slept in an unlocked cell, with three others.

Next day she waited. He didn't come. She slept in the cell again. With two new silent men. They were given black bread and dandelion soup. This Mayor, he didn't have to find her a place, he

could shrug her away. For the fun of squashing her hopes.

Next morning she took her case and walked up the main street, past the railway station, the exhausted shops and sat on the stone steps of the Mairie. His car drove in and she followed him into the cold building and sat in his outer office for two more hours.

"In. How did you know the Curé?"

"My family."

"Balls."

She thought of the Curé in Lyon, the teacher, the butcher.

"No. Where is he?"

"I told you."

She wanted to say "Balls", but nodded, practiced now.

"I'll drive you to a place. Tomorrow."

"Thank you."

His finger ends extended and she walked back to her cell in the Spring sunlight.

Jacques stretched his legs forward, his eyelids drooping to counter the glare from the water. His float steadied. Two trout and home. Wiped his knife, sat, waiting. As still and quiet as the surface of the Roc.

Had Jerome told his mother? No chance.

But if Ardelle had told hers then Madame Lacaze would know soon enough. Or if Sara had dared tell hers. I told mine and the secret will die in her room.

His mother will cut him off. Sara is scum to her. And then what about Sara? Jerome will never marry her.

In an hour he had two carp and one of the trout. The sun said nearly noon and with no wind in the pines sheltering the lake he

THE SINGLE SOLDIER

had less than an hour now before the water heated enough for the fish to seek the shade beyond his rod.

He gazed hard at the float, willing the fish to strike.

Can you wish a fish? And is that a sin? Is that Covetousness? And if he could, if, say, he had one wish, would it be for a fish? One wish. What would I want? A bull.

No. Mamman well. Yes. And laughing, happy. Yes, that. Or Peace? A car approached. Can only be Chibret or the doctor. Chibret. Where had Mayor Chibret been?

And what would he wish for himself? His eyes lifted away from the float. Stupid. Wish your life away. 'Iffing is close to sin,' his mother always said. Stupid to wish. Don't they say that with every wish comes a curse?

The line moved and his hand tightened. The float edged right, stopped, moved again, sank and he struck. The rod bent. Trout. Struck again to bury the hook and played it in. Big. In you come. His rod arched and his mother's dinner slid and scrambled kaleidoscopic across the water and out. Sharp club with the knife handle, done.

He packed up, ate his cheese reward and walked back to the village. This half-kilometre of lane was bounded on both sides by Jerome's family land, and there, a separate two hundred metres from the bottom of the village, the Big House. Purple volets and sandstone pastel walls. The too-neat garden, its late spring flowers regimentally erect, the orchard behind. The big crucifix. Wrought-iron railings. Old Money. He saw no-one as he passed the Gendarmerie, La Poste and the Mairie, came into the square and there, outside the café, feet up on a chair, Jerome. And with the big glass window between them, Duthileul Pére.

The old money and the new.

Inside, in the cigarette smoke silence, two old ones and Valet, the

retired garagiste, scowled beneath their berets and gulped pastis until the papers were read.

Janon shuffled out with Jacques' beer. Shuffled back.

"Fish for mother?"

"Fish for mother."

He rolled two cigarettes and they smoked. Jacques nodded at Duthileul, the old bull, waiting. Looked at his friend, the father to be.

"What's she going to say when you tell her?"

"Moo."

"You are going to tell her?"

"If she asks. When she asks. I'll need some of the money now."

"She'll find out. Everyone will."

"I know. I'm expecting De Gaulle to congratulate us tonight."

De Gaulle's broadcasts. Illegal to listen.

"Want to listen?"

"Shut up."

Jerome looked steadily into Jacques' face.

"I like you, Vermande."

"Marry me then."

Jerome lifted his drink.

"Remember when I said Vichy had sold everything French? Eh? And you thought - 'that wanker Jerome, what does he mean?'"

"Yes."

"Laval has banned celebrations of July the fourteenth."

Jacques couldn't stop himself snapping a glance at the old ones, and him, Duthileul, fixed in his chair.

"Why?" And then, whispering, "How do you know?"

"And which question," Jerome smiled, "is the more important?"

Jacques felt a flash of irritation with Jerome's patronising. "Why."

"Yes sir. Why would our Prime Minister do such a thing, Jacques?"

Jacques looked at the fire in his friend's face. The same fire as he'd had at school and it had burnt nothing yet. Unless, Jacques thought, you count Sara.

"To please the Bosche?"

"Voila. And what do you feel about that?"

"Not much."

Some music, a high piano with a cello beneath wound out of the café radio and into the early afternoon.

"What do you feel?"

"When all else fails - get angry."

"And do what, Jerome?"

"Gather. Resist."

Jacques leaned forward onto the table and watched Duthileul while he whispered, "I won't talk here."

"Scared?"

"Of you, yes. Do what you must do but don't sit here hoping for a fight with one of those ancient turds. Act. Stop talking."

They looked at each other and again Jacques thought of Sara.

"You have a child coming. Is this your response? To fight?"

"Yes! He must be proud of me - I must be proud of me. I must resist. Or your father died for nothing, eh?"

"Resist?" Valet had turned in his chair. He barked again. "Resist what?"

"Don't, Jerome."

"The enemy."

"Ahh. The Russians?" The old ones cackled.

"Russia is fighting Hitler."

"Makes a change." More laughter.

"More than Petain does."

"Petain is France, France is Petain."

"Catechisme." Jerome snarled.

"Enough."

Duthileul silenced them all.

Jerome gathered his glass, went inside, paid and leaned his back into the fixture of the bar.

"Fine. In Free France I will not speak, I will be free only to be silent."

"Like all of us," said Duthileul.

"'To live in defeat is to die every day.'"

"Who's that?" Valet sneered, "Stalin?"

"Buonaparte," said Duthileul.

A silence.

Jerome nodded to Jacques and strode home. Jacques re-lit his cigarette, pinched one last drag from it and downed the beer. He took his glass back and Duthileul turned his chair to face him. Jacques waited. The old man smiled.

"I have to charge a little more. The War. You understand."

"Yes."

"Everything costs." He even tried to look a little sad.

"Yes."

"Bring her when you wish. Only a few sous, a few francs more. You're a neighbour."

"Aha."

Chibret bustled in, shook hands, refused a drink, exchanged brief words with Duthileul, who nodded sharply. Chibret took Jacques' arm and led him outside.

"A word, in my office, Jacques?"

"Yes..."

He gathered his rod and fish and they walked down to the Mairie, into the cool. Through the big hall piled with corn and eggs, potatoes, milk, meat, hay even; the requisition from their farms, into his little office where Chibret hung his jacket on his

chair, gestured at the one opposite, and settled. He cleared a space by elbowing paper left and right, leaned forward and looked at Jacques.

"An evacuee. The Prefecture demands we find accommodation, do our bit blah blah blah. From the North, was in Clermont - etc etc. Jacques?"

"One?"

"It's why I thought of you. No room for families, have you?"

"No."

"Squeeze her in?"

Jacques' mind jumped.

"Er...yes."

"Good man. Thank you."

Mayor Chibret leaned over the desk and shook Jacques' hand, business done.

"Bloody paper. Mountains of it. Triplicate. Who reads it? My secretary, Severine, she's ill. I never liked the miserable cow. Now she's ill for three days and I know why she's miserable and I miss her. War for you. Changes you."

Jacques rose.

"Your mother?"

"Fine."

"Don't see her at Mass."

"No."

"You'll find room?"

"Yes."

"I'll bring her tomorrow. First of many, eh?"

A woman!

Oh God, how old? He laughed. First time I've done that for a bit. Where will she sleep? In my room. I'll sleep in the barn. Like when

the day-old calves need feeding. No, make a bed upstairs in the grenier. Warmer. Nearer Mamman. He noticed his bag, the fish, swinging. And he heard his whistling as he passed his neighbour's herd and the bull, good big bull, pray it gives me a male calf.

Is this woman going to meet a boy or a man?

What makes a man? I'm six years older than my father ever was and I've never done what he did - fought, killed, had a child, died. I've never had sex...

I must cook the fish, milk the cows, take the beast over the lane and tell mother about our guest.

They ate, the trout sweet.

"Butter tomorrow."

"I know."

"I know you know."

They ate.

His mother said, "She could be older than me."

"I know."

"Good."

Next morning when he brought her bread and egg she said, "I'll do the butter."

He nodded slowly. "O.K."

"Have you made a bed upstairs?"

"I will."

"For you?"

"Yes, of course."

She ate. The dog sat up.

"We've only two chairs," she said.

"Mm."

"And she's from the North?"

"Yes."

"I hope she's Catholic."

I hope she's fun, he thought.

He found weeds he'd too long ignored, so as to be there to greet her. Should he pick some flowers? He blushed at his crudity. His mother, dressed, came to the door, and stood shading her eyes from the noon-light.

"Bring me the milk then."

He ladled it into the big pot and thought, she's done nothing for so long, she'll be too weak for this. Butter is hard work. But, if it means she's coming back to life...

As he came up the steps there she stood, pale and thin - sell her if she was a beast - but she was trying. Good. Good. Is this the wish?

"This is hard, mamman."

"Oh, really."

"Fine."

He took down the paddle, wiped the cobwebs off it and left her to it, bathing back into the heat. The ploughing. Oh shit, the bull. Was that a car? No. Calm yourself.

Simone waited. Le Rouget knew her story. They hunched past her, the latest gossip. At noon he appeared and went into the Mairie. Two hours later she climbed into his car and they rose into the hills. The silent man, driving with one fat hand, the car hugging the sharp corners in the lowest gear, endlessly up and away from the war.

Up into the store-cupboard of France; pasture, cattle, farms, wee clusters of houses. Le Fern. Le Martinet, La Vitarelle, the roof-tiles changing from the slate-grey of the lowlands to rounded terracotta orange speckled with mosses, the roofs angling less sharply against the winter snows. Then a sandstone chateau with one crumbling tower, a sore thumb of ancient opulence in all this practicality; and still the road turned and rose and then, as the car came through La Bouyogne, a panorama spread in front of her, an upland plateau rolling and tumbling for ever.

He hadn't made his bed. Blankets. Strode back into the house and there she sat, the paddle adrift, her arm fallen, asleep in the chair. His shadow darkened the milk. Blankets first. Walked heel first into his room, took one from his room, one from the wardrobe in her room, went upstairs and laid them against the south wall for warmth. Old sacks beneath for a notion of softness against the boards. Went down for his clothes, leaving the empty drawers for her.
This 'her'.
He draped his mother's wasted arm over his shoulder and lifted her easily, less than the milk, laid her in bed, covered her.
Sat to the milk and the paddle.
The butter, cheese and the white cheese. He churned. As it thickened and pulled at his muscles he remembered Fridays at the wash-pond when his ears had burned at the piss-taking; but washing was as hard as sawing, churning as aching as digging. He worked, the dog licking up the few splashes and the separation came.

THE SINGLE SOLDIER

The car rocked now, at speed on the flat, the sun bright, and on through another clump of maybe ten houses, Lauresses. Still on, another long high bend, a single farm and now St.Cirgues. The car stopped and so would she. Whatever this was, whatever this took, this was a stop. This was high enough, far enough, to stop. A road sign said Sousceyrac 7 kms, but no. This, St.Cirgues, this would do.

A smaller, slightly less fat man, with mottled hands greeted them. Chibret.

🐏

The dog cocked its head, went outside and barked. He checked his sleeping mother, pulled her door closed and went outside, his heart booming. Heard the car stop, heard one door slam and the other close and then round the corner of the barn came his Mayor and Simone.

three

THE TRIANGLE SHRANK, he shook his Mayor's hand and Chibret christened her.

"Simone."

"Jacques."

Dirt-weary legs, her whole frame pared. Veins standing angry on her forearms, chest as flat as his, hair straggling round a face once pretty, but weathered now, worn. Warred. Not a face of these hills. Thinner nose. Different eyes. She was a town-girl. Small. Not made and raised for his work. Her forehead was long. She was plain and she was beautiful.

The dog sniffed all round her and she let the back of her hand drape over its nose.

Chibret shifted his weight, rested a hand on his belt and puffed a little.

"I must go - paper..."

He shook hands in the silence, his thoughts back with his sickly wife. The silence waited till his car left, then began again. A man, a girl, a case and a dog, waiting, in bright light.

Jacques thought.

"Come in."

"Thank you."

He took her case, then, not sure he'd said the right thing, stopped. She waited. He moved again and led her up the stone steps and into the cool. He put the case down and looked at his house with her eyes.

"It's brown," he said.

"Yes."

"Sit down. Please."

She sat at the table.

He looked at his fire but saw nothing.

She placed a hand, an arm on the table.

He turned around.

Here she was, holding herself. Here. To stay. In his house. In his life.

She was young. She was here. Simone.

She looked up at him, staring, his mouth open, stupid. Their eyes met. His brain threatened to choke. Time stood still. When Time moved he saw a hungry animal.

He reached down ham, unwrapped the muslin, sliced it thin, twice, re-wrapped it, got bread from the earthen crock, cheese and a plate, a bottle of wine, rinsed a cup in the bucket and placed it all before her on the table. Took a pace back to the fire.

"Thank you."

He cut the bread and left the knife for her.

"Eat."

"Thank you."

She sat a second and looked at the food. As she reached for the ham he moved to change the cup for a glass. Poured her a glass of wine and moved to the door. The dog stayed, all eyes.

"I'll - be a second."

He went outside.

Her back kissed the chair.

Her mouth stopped smiling, her bones relaxed, a hand flapped flat on the table.

"Ohhh," like sleep.

Not carrots, she's too tired. Lettuce. The first strawberries! Found three good sized ones. He could feel his teeth, the very bone of them. He could taste the blood in his cheeks. He could hear it warm and running. I want to scream!

Looked up at the time. An hour to milking. Milk. I gave her wine. He marched into the cold of the caves and filled the metal cup, took it carefully up the steps and back into the house. He washed the lettuce and the fruit, placed it all before her and backed away to watch.

"This is - I needed this."

"Good."

She drank the milk. Ate the strawberries, one exploding too big in her mouth, she hiccuped forward to catch the drips.

Then the hard, clear cheese. He watched, enchanted, till she'd done.

"Cigarette?"

"I don't."

The cat strolled in and froze. It gawps like him, she thought.

"Simone," he introduced her, his voice dry round the word.

The cat looked deep into her eyes, held them, then padded to her.

"What's your name?"

"Doesn't have a name. It's the cat."

"Oh. The dog?"

"Dog's called Tayo."

He rolled a cigarette, concentrating for a second. She took a mouthful of the wine. The alcohol sank, and she shivered.

"Cold?"

"No. The wine."

"Ah."

"It's good."

"Good."

And now he saw how much she needed sleep. Pecking the cigarette he took her case and opened a door behind her. Took a pace into the room and waited. She turned and saw the bed. The bed.

"Come."

One window, a chest with a bowl and jug and a towel, and the bed. A solid oak box raised two feet off the ground. Blankets and a pillow. A pillow.

"Sleep. Wake when you wake. There's a pot under the bed. Meet Mother in the morning." He stood, hand on the door.

"I will, if you don't mind."

"You will - and I don't."

He closed the door.

She heard him pick up the plate and wash it in the bucket, cross the room and then she saw his head descend the steps outside her window. And she was alone. The mother. The little fat Mayor had said, but tomorrow would do. The light halved. He'd closed one volet. His face appeared.

"Sleep."

He closed the other and the light cut to two white streaks of sunlight through old knot holes in the pine. One touched the end of the bed. Her bed.

She sat on its edge and scraped the boots off her filthy feet. They stank. Poured a little water into the bowl and sank the black toes. Ancient hay drifted free. She sat. She just sat.

She dried her feet white. Laid her jacket over the bed end, a decrepit sleeve catching a stripe of light, unbuttoned her dress,

laid that rag down too, her vest she left and now, listening to the precious sounds she made, pulled back the covers. She slid one leg in and then both and down oh down into the cold deepness and her back and her shoulders just kissing the peace and now the pillow folding around her head and she lay. She just lay. The ceiling, broad oak beams, cobwebbed nails, hooks, a shelf over the door, a rosary. Floorboards above, solid as the century, and her bottom spread, her arms spread, her thighs and ankles crossed each other in hugs and her body believed - at least for now.

Her mind asked what and why and what next and who and she shut it off, selfish sleep consumed the woman and laid her to rest like a child.

He milked, took it to the caves, came out and stretched high in his garden and wanted to shout and didn't know what. He strode to the compost and opened his trousers, and loosed himself hot, clear, long and strong. A grinning pleasure.

He went to make the evening meal.

He woke his mother gently and ate with her. The mother arched an eyebrow.

"She's asleep," he said.

They ate.

"She'll sleep till morning."

"Will she?"

"Yes."

Finished, he quietly put things away and came back to sit on her bed as evening walked by.

"She's young."

"Oh."

"Simone."

"Simone...?"

THE SINGLE SOLDIER

"I didn't ask."

"Where is she from?"

"I didn't ask. The North, Chibret said."

His mother nodded, tired, and then said,

"She's been a long time coming."

"Eh?"

"Two years."

"Yes. Yes."

"Well - she's here."

They sat a while longer. Then he rose, closed the volets, took her pot and emptied and cleaned it. Returned.

"Goodnight, Mamman."

"Goodnight, Jacques."

"Call. I'll be upstairs."

"I will."

He shut her door. Kicked the fire into the smallest space and sat to look at Simone's door. What a last cigarette!

Everything beat faster. A grin had taken root. He smoked round it. Why had this happened? There was no answer. It was just simply Wonderful.

He lit a candle, closed the kitchen volets and padded upstairs to the grenier. The dog looked at him, looked at his bedroom door, and followed.

Sacks of flour, sacks of last year's nuts, a pile of spare tiles his grandfather had left lest his roofing prove inadequate. It hadn't. Stooping to avoid the two A shaped oak beams, he moved his pile of blankets to the far corner. Above her.

He stood out of his trousers and lay between his blankets and pecked out his candle. The room shrank to black and he just lay. He imagined everything, just everything, for one mad second.

Love, marriage, children and unending joy. He rolled onto his stomach to press his glee-kiss into the floorboards.

Next morning early he milked and hurried them to their field, dawn just breaking as he got three eggs, three, and scuttled inside to breakfast his women.

The tiny fire had died and he lifted the ash with his hands, not wanting the scrape of a shovel to spoil sleep. He fetched kindling and bigger pieces, lit it, poured fresh well-water into the pot and waited, watching her door. Don't wake yet. The water moved, the bubbles rising to boil. Fed it the eggs, rolled his cigarette, lit it, cut bread, got both plates - I need to buy another - prepared coffee and when his smoke finished he spooned out the eggs and cooled them in hands warm as his grin. He poured coffee and everything was so.

He pushed at his mother's door. Placed her food on the bed, opened the window and the volets and the day slid in.

"Sleep well?"

The light was low and thin by her routine.

"Did you? This is early."

"Yes, I must have."

"Where's yours?"

"Out there."

"Oh."

"Eat, mamman."

And he left her and went back to taste the thrill he'd imagined himself to sleep with. The tray laid, he pushed open her door and her eyes met him.

"Breakfast."

"In bed?"

"Yes."

"This once. Thank you."

"You've slept."

"I have."

"Good."

"Thank you."

The mother listened through the thin wall. Then saw her son appear and sit at the table to eat where he could see both his women. Like a man, thought the mother. Sweet like a boy, thought the girl.

He gave her one of his shirts and a pair of trousers in return for the dress and her socks and the ragged wool cardigan he took to the wash-pond. He was half-way down the lane when he stopped. He hadn't introduced them.

"Come here," the mother called.

Simone stood in the doorway, his shirt falling huge.

"Sit."

She looked and sat in the only place, the bed.

"My son is naive."

Simone waited. The woman almost smiled.

"Find a dress." She nodded towards the wardrobe.

Simone waited a second, unwilling.

"You choose, please."

"Well. One of mine, not his."

Simone opened the wardrobe. One black, one cotton with pastel flowers; one obviously for best.

She said, "It's pretty."

"Mm. Later, perhaps."

Simone took out the flowered one, stood out of Jacques' clothes and buttoned the dress.

"It fits."

"Good."

Pockets on the thigh, there was a piece of paper in the left one.

Simone sat. "This invasion, I'm sorry - "

But the woman shook her head and dismissed the apology. "War."

A minute passed.

"Where are you from?"

The mother watched Simone's eyes scour the room for a security.

"Later... tell me later."

Simone, grateful, nodded.

A bird called, two notes, endless.

A fly burst in, ransacked the air and fled.

The dog came in, slouched in the doorway.

Across the lane activity. Curiosity either hadn't time, desire nor need enough to show its face.

Simone searched for conversation, for a starting point.

Then saw the woman didn't need talk.

She simply sat, propped, her mouth almost smiling, taking in the two years that had stripped the bloom off this child and replaced it with defences. Like an armoured calf.

Outside an old woman's voice screeched. A weary young man replied. The bird still called.

"Your parents?"

"Dead."

The women sat sad.

"Your - his father?"

"Gone. Dead."

How old was she? The boy was twenty, maybe a little more. Why was this woman in bed? She belonged there. She looked weak and worn but not ill. Later...

He barrowed back up the lane and the dog stirred.

"He's back," the smile feebled around her mouth.

He beamed stupid at them, his tired mother and this girl.

"The washing."

He strode out to the garden, hung it, trowelled a salad, pulled a bucket of water and came back to feed them.

He ate off the wooden board.

He ate exactly as he always ate, at the same speed, the same pauses, the same as ever, except when he looked up Simone was there.

And now he heard the silence he always sat in.

I must talk...

"It's warm," he said.

The women waited.

Simone looked toward the mother's door. Silence.

So Simone said, "Mm," and waited.

Silence.

"Cheese?"

"Yes. Please."

"Mother?"

"No. Thank you."

When he went in she was asleep.

Will this make her live? Will this change save her? She hadn't eaten much. He put her tray on the floor and rubbed the cobwebs off her crucifix and rosary. Please, God. The dog sniffed past the lettuce and looked huge cow eyes from him to the ham. Jacques flicked his head, and draping it over his teeth, the dog took it to the garden to savour.

He washed away. Simone sat at the table.

"She's sleeping."

"She's tired."

He nodded, agreeing.

He sat and smoked. The dog returned, circled and slumped in shade.

A bird sang. He finished the smoke and could sit here for all

Eternity with her, silent.

He rose, stooped in the fireplace. "I must work."

"What can I do?"

He looked. Looked at her shoulders, tight.

"Rest. It's warm outside."

And he was gone, the dog following.

Simone sat on the steps.

Looked at this new Life.

Wild flowers, crocuses, a burst of parched daffodils. A bush, something she didn't know, was it elderflower, married with the hawthorn draped around the well. Behind that the orderly vegetable plot, flourishing. And hollyhocks, tall and swaying, as full of life as the swallows. The sun was sweet. Flies zipped close. Stukas. Two, three, four separate bird calls, another. The dog lay in the shade, nose rising with the feeble breeze and watched her and dozed.

What was Peronne now? A German town.

When he came back with the herd she had been there one day.

The girl sat and watched Jacques move ordered and unflurried through the preparation of their meal. For the time it took to prepare the mother's tray and their table, she didn't exist. He was working and that was all he was doing. Neither hardship nor effort, as natural to him as it had been to her mother, only he did it without distraction. Once he had the soup simmering he relaxed with a cigarette and came back to the room, the house, his dog, and her.

The mother ate slowly and listened and they sat at the table, silent like a married couple, until she complimented his cooking and he looked up at her, this magical marionette, eating his soup at his table in his house.

Time, freeze, please.

She watched the routine of the well-water, the vegetable peelings to the fire, the bed-pots and the volets, the candle and then heard the mother and son and heard it as it was, a ritual. When he sat to smoke again she felt intrusive to his rhythm and wished him goodnight and went to her room. His room. She took the paper from the pocket of the dress. A photograph, a young man, in First War Uniform. She placed it carefully at the bottom of the drawer and took the dress off. A day.

Jacques smoked. Tomorrow Saturday. Plough. Sunday. Mass.

Outside a three-quarter moon cast his shadow sharp as he pissed against the barn. The dog sniffed it, covered it, and they went back inside. Candle lit, up to the warm smell of grain and to lie in sleep again, above her. He rolled onto his back, to imagine Sunday and what would be said and thought. And what he would feel.

But in the silence he thought about rain for the vegetables, or he would have to carry well-water. A douche, Lord. And he'd missed the cow's time, would have to wait three weeks now.

In the morning Simone watched.

Whilst he milked, his routine with the beasts, the chickens, the wood, the fire, watched him prepare and make the breakfast, take it and wake the mother and then return to eat with her. They sat and ate and the mother through her door watched them both and her coffee cooled and the dog ate her bread and egg.

"I'm not hungry," she told it, and smiled.

Simone watched him wash and tidy the few things and he felt her eyes and wondered how long this would last. Being watched. Nobody had watched him, as though either he or his labour were interesting, not since childhood. His mother had been patient and

practical, and Allibert, with the faint smell of his lunchtime pastis, strict and rigid. Her watching wasn't either of those. Why is she watching? What does it matter why? Because it makes goose-flesh, it makes me want to shout, like everything about her. He looked round.

"I was thinking..." he began.

"I could tell."

Could she tell what I was thinking?

"Could you tell what I was thinking?"

"No." A breath of a laugh.

"Oh. Good." Then he smiled, young and scared. "Do you want to know?"

"Do you want to tell me?"

"No."

"Well."

Her mouth twitched to a smile. He went to plough manure into the fallow field.

Was that a conversation?

My God! We can talk. To each other. About Things.

What things?

He ploughed.

Nothing could ever be the same again.

Nothing could return to normal.

The only normal there can be now is normal with her. And how long will it take to become normal? This isn't normal. This is 'if' come alive. This is wonder. How long does wonder last? And is there long enough to reach normal before the war comes over the mountains? And will it? And what then? He bent his back and ploughed. Just work and let it be. There's nothing to be done but by letting it be. You plough and sow and let it be and if you're lucky, you reap.

Washing his hands at the well he heard footsteps. In the house. In their house. She stood at the door and called him. Called his name.

"Jacques. Food?"

That mad grin charged round his face again.

Her soup was thin and spicy with more pepper than his and more delicious for his having neither thought of it nor made it. He complimented the cook and she thanked him. In her room the mother sneezed at the pepper and drank a little.

The afternoon he saw Ardelle appear briefly in her doorway across the field and they waved but too far and too busy to stop to discuss the girl. She would know everything Chibret could tell by now. So would they all. And he knew nothing more. He hadn't asked anything.

As the sun blushed toward evening he brought the cows in, tethered them, forked their hay and fetched his stool and bucket and felt Simone in the doorway as he sat to milk. He smiled and turned, but he was wrong, she wasn't there. He milked. He heard his mother saying, "Iffing is close to sin." And he turned again and she was there, small and hard, hands on her hips, watching again.

"I thought you were here. Before..."

"I was. Au toilette."

"Ohh."

The image of her squatting to shit momentarily demolished Romance.

"Supper soon," she said and went.

He was alone again - but oh so different from a whole minute before. From the day before, from all the days, all the weeks, all the years of his life before. Suddenly he wanted this war to last forever. To stay lingering on behind the hills, to become a part of his life.

He closed up the barn, took the milk to the caves, came out into

the evening silence of crickets and Arbel's meagre herd echoing in their too-big barn, some electrical machine at Duthileul's and he was glad he'd missed the cow's season. The bastard'll think I'm a fool. And he'll charge more. Don't care. I'm glad. Why? Why be glad about that? Because I had something better to think about!

He pulled a bucket from the well, and washed, wanting to be clean for her supper, walked up the stone steps, left his clogs outside and there she sat by the fire on Arbel's bench, the food cooking, her knees together, his mother's dress falling round her.

This grin began at his toes. He pulled a chair from the table and sat. She looked up.

"Pass me my tobacco, please."

"I'm in your place."

He shrugged and she reached his papers and the leather pouch from the tiny shelf hacked into the fire-wall, watched him roll a perfect cigarette, and then watched his back hit the chair and the smoke wrap around his thoughts. She stirred the food.

The fire, this soft-eyed man, his frozen mother, their blessed uninquisitiveness, the distance from the village, the scarcity even, the silence of oblivious nature, this would do. No threat, yet, in these hills. Only, in this first breathing, an active Christianity. A place to be, a place to breathe, a place to believe. Her mother's face suddenly came to her and she blinked it away, and when it rushed to return Simone hastened to distract herself.

"Good day?"

He shrugged as he did when his mother asked that question, but this was different. This was her, sitting in his space, leaning forward, asking. Asking him. This was Talk.

"You look better," he said.

"I am."

"Good."

A squall darted down the chimney and the smoke and stew-smell mingled.

"You don't mind that I cook?"

"No." He smiled. "No."

The cigarette lit up his face; the roman nose, the wide mouth, work-thick fingers closed around the fag and taking it to rest on his knee. Her eyes stayed on his face and how long had this boy been the man?

Jacques felt her eyes and his gaze rose to meet hers. There she was.

"We stare at each other," he said.

"We do."

And he felt that she had lived so much more than him.

And she could feel his excitement.

The eyes were hot but he would not burn. Not her.

Their eyes broke contact and that moment passed, but was accepted in the way she stretched her legs forward and in the flick of his finger at the ash-end of his cigarette.

"Are you Catholic?"

"Yes."

"Good."

"Good?"

"Tomorrow. They'll all be waiting for you in church. If you didn't come..."

She nodded.

His first question.

Simone stirred, tasted, and waited for another question and none came. She sat back. This was living without a past. His father must have died long ago. It was like sharing a space with another woman. Like the kitchen in Peronne, with mother making coconut-ice pudding, her mother making lemon juice drinks with sugar, her mother nodding as father said they should stay; her mother on the train, spitting and the uniformed hand snaring her throat, so strong she couldn't turn for one last eye-kiss with Simone, a rifle at her rib-cage, hauling her out of the carriage. Her mother. Pray God she didn't suffer. Pray God they shot her quickly.

The first tear sizzled on the stone and Jacques could see it came from her body since it fell from a still face. She pulled at the tiny sleeve, wiped at her eyes, and looked up.

"War."

He poured the last of the wine into her glass, and went down to the caves for a new bottle and a piece of wood for the fire. He'd forgotten the chicken's bowls. Spooned them grain, left them in their pecking order and went back to eat.

He cut the bread, she ground pepper, he cut a little cheese. She poured wine for them and water for the mother and he took it in.

"I forgot the cow."

"Needs the bull?"

"Yes."

"Duthileul?"

He said nothing.

"More?" His mother asked.

"A little."

Her head shook. In these days, in these times, the man was making. All his trust in money. He needed to shake hands with death and drop soil on a child's coffin.

"Eat, please."

"This is hers?"

"Yes."

He felt gauche, just gauche all everywhere. "You like her?"

The mother looked into her son's eyes.

"Yes."

"Good. Eat."

He turned and nearly trod on the dog.

He wanted to lean his body back till it was afloat in the air and howl this happiness.

"I never shout," he said, sitting at the table.

"No?" she smiled.

"No."

The silence was as warm as her stew and he ate hungrily. Took more and wiped the plate clean with bread. Cheese and then he put water on for coffee. He leaned in to his mother.

"Coffee, Mamman?"

"At night?"

"Oh. No? Tisane? Anything?"

"No. Thank you."

"You haven't eaten much."

"I enjoyed what I had."

He picked up her tray, tipped the bread to the dog, left her room and came back to their room.

Simone made coffee. When he reached for his tobacco she took the chair to the fireplace and their eyes met.

"The bench is yours."

They sat aside the slowing fire, he smoking and her staring into the ash. The dog lay, looked once from her to him, and settled.

Time strolled oblivious past.

Time spent with her.

Time spent easing.

When the cat came in she poured it milk. She lit a candle.

"What time is Mass?"

"Eleven."

"She won't come?"

"No."

"Sleep well."

"And you."

She went to her room.

He lay above her and his thoughts descended. But when they reached his desires he didn't imagine her, Simone; he thought of Sara and her big breasts and pulled quick and quiet as he could to get it over with.

Simone heard the thin voice at the wall and rose, his shirt falling around her, and went in to the woman's room. The smell hit her.

"The pot?"

She lit the mother's candle and took the pot out to the night, emptied it and came back quiet as the fields in her bare feet.

"Do you want anything?"

"A glass of water."

She returned with it and the woman nodded.

"Shall I close the windows?"

"The volets, thank you."

She reached out and pulled them to and the woman watched.

"Take the black dress and a mantilla for Mass."

"Thank you."

"It's nothing."

Simone took the dress, blew the candle out and left her.

He forgot, they both thought.

Sunday.

Mass. It had rained, as he'd prayed. Only a day late. He took the cows and looked back at Home.

This could never last.

This can never last.

Simone dressed and he went upstairs and sat on his blankets to pull on his Sunday shoes.

She'll go.

Live with me and a dying woman?

And what when mother dies?

If.

If Mother dies.

'Iffing, Jacques'.

Yes, yes - but, alone with me?

The two of us. She wouldn't.

No, Normal will be alone. As it was always going to be.

So, there is just this Time to pass with her.

She was waiting.

In his mother's black. Her hair combed and tied, with a fringe.

He opened the mother's door.

"You'll be late. They won't trust her. Don't blame them, we're only peasants."

"But you trust her?"

"I think so."

"Then that's enough."

He left her and stepped out of the house. Simone was waiting for him. They strode down the lane to meet his village and their God. He would have been ashamed if he'd noticed how quickly he forgot his mother to taste the walk with her.

"I'm nervous," he said.

"You're nervous?"

"You must know already - how they'll be."

"That's true."

The trees gathered at the bend and they turned into the nave of beech and oak.

The villagers gathered in front of their church, waiting for the stranger. Curious. Suspicious. Some even fearful. War rumours

were as abundant as food and good sleep were scarce. She could be anything from anywhere. Chibret was a weak fool, he should have said no. As the men shook hands, the women nodded shortly to each other, as though some Pope had once decreed it sin to smile on the Sabbath before taking the sacrament.

The bell rang and Madame Lacaze walked inside to pray alone for her son's soul. The men stubbed out their cigarettes as Arbel and Ardelle came into the square. Everyone loitered. Arbel shook hands and he and Ardelle shrugged their ignorance.

Duthileul's car came to a halt and though he was Jacques' nearest neighbour, and they all shook his hand, no-one considered asking him or Dominique, his son, nor the old Mother about the girl. The bell stopped. The village funnelled forward into the cool of their church. As Curé Phillipe came to the altar and Mass began Jacques and Simone came in at the back. Curiosity won easily over Christianity. In ones and twos and then whole families, they turned to stare. Jacques, beetroot, nodded. The children were droll, the parents' impulse undiluted. Serious eyes, locked. The priest coughed and the heads turned back, the younger needing a prod. Simone knelt with them.

Since Peronne, she and God had drifted apart. She had rejected the idea that the slaughter of her parents was part of some design she was too naive to grapple with and had come to the belief that God was a by-stander. And if that was so then prayer for action, prayer for Him to take an active part was pointless. He could not. He might want to, might ache to, but it was not possible.

And so, for what should she pray? Even if all of us, everywhere, prayed for the same thing - peace, now - it wouldn't happen. Hitler was stronger than God, at the moment, obviously.

So she prayed for His recovery. He would need all His strength to rid His world of Hitler and the killing.

"Have some of mine. My life is stronger. Take."

Beside her Jacques prayed to understand if this was part of His plan. This miracle. And that mother might live and grow to share it. Chibret prayed for his sickly wife who would live another forty-eight years and see him to cataracts and the shakes. Mignon prayed for the war to end and his vile requisitioning job with it, that he might return to his friends. Grivault prayed for the war to end and the Jew's money to be shared. Duthileul prayed that God should please Himself, since God's will suited Jean-Louis Duthileul. Arbel prayed for guidance when the war came, and Ardelle prayed hardest, that it wouldn't ever come. Sara prayed for the nerve to tell her mother and her mother prayed Sara wasn't pregnant. Louis prayed for mushrooms, and someone to go with him that he could touch. Madame Lacaze asked Almighty Forgiveness for whatever fault might be laid at her door that had led to her son and his absence of character. Madame Cantagrel begged for the return of her son. And whilst they all sincerely asked God to end this war some left it up to Him to decide who should win. The Curé preached from Isaiah and Simone waited for its relevance to conflict. It had none.

The hour passed, the sacrament was shared, and it was noted that she was wearing the mother's dress.

In the sharp sunlight women Jacques only knew from the backrooms of their husband's shops came forward to wish his mother better, shake Simone's hand and make their judgement. Those who dared a pleasantry were able to return to the flock, whisper 'Northerner', and fold their arms. Chibret wished them both well and she stood in a whirl of staring people till Jacques finally moved to rescue her, guiding her through a knot that separated as though they were leprous royalty, to introduce Arbel and Ardelle. He was touched when Ardelle placed three kisses on

Simone's cheeks and eased some weight from her day. Sara too, greeted her with touch.

"Jerome's at the Tabac," she laughed, and heads turned.

She laughed again.

"D'you suppose the Lord counts the bars while we kneel? Come Simone, come and meet my heathen!"

The village spread out, men to the Tabac, women to cook.

"I thought you were his mother at first. That would be a miracle. How is she? What do you think?"

Simone paused. "It's only three days - she's weak."

"She's a ghost, my mother says. Here! Look, this is mine."

Sara led Simone forward to bring Jerome to his feet, shake her hand, and the six of them sat.

The old men of the village nodded past and into the cool, the Vichy press and their hopeless talk.

"Don't ask him about religion." Sara said loudly.

"Don't ask him about the war either," said Arbel, "or politics."

Jerome shrugged into his glamour.

Janon grouched out, wiped the table pointlessly and flicked his chin up for an order. Went back inside to report she drank red.

"How was the opium?" Jerome looked at them all.

"Good. Pagan." Sara punched his arm.

"What?" Ardelle looked to Arbel.

"Religion Is The opium of The Masses." Arbel would need a serious drink before he rose to such feeble bait. "One of his masters taught him his Catechisme."

"Lenin," said Simone, surprising herself.

"Marx," said Jerome and toasted her with an empty hand.

"Who?" Ardelle turned to Arbel.

Arbel and Jerome laughed. Ardelle looked round at them all and set them all off.

"Well, who is the mec?"

Arbel laughed again, young, and a voice from the cafe ground into their nerves.

"Respect... no respect."

This time they all laughed and a hand slapped hard at a table inside and they stopped, Sara's hand on Jerome's arm, instinctive.

"You should farm sheep," Jerome called.

"Don't know sheep."

"Look in a mirror."

And he turned back. Too pleased with himself, Jacques thought.

Janon came out and paused long enough in his serving to defuse their laughter. Cigarettes were rolled, and the men leaned back and smoked.

"Salut." Sara touched Simone's glass. "Welcome."

"Salut."

Arbel didn't drink, he poured the wine straight down. Taste was not the point. It was taken as a fire-extinguisher. Simone watched, fascinated. Ardelle caught her eye.

"I know. An hour with God, a good wife, no war, and he drinks like loyalty. Eh?"

"I've always done it."

"And that makes it all right?"

He considered the question. "Yes. And you knew I drank when you married me."

"We knew at school you drank!" Ardelle said to stifled laughter.

Arbel sat forward and smiled, two-toothed, at Simone.

"Did you feel like a Bosche in church?"

"A stranger, yes."

He sat back, to think of something else to say.

Jacques looked from Sara to Jerome and knew neither had said anything yet.

Now he too sat back into the chair, and tasted an entirely new sensation.

She's with me. She came from the sky and she's with me.

And when this drink, this talk is over, she will come home with me.

He had no impulse other than to pass the time.

Simone absorbed the bare and dusty square of this St.Cirgues, this café, these people, his friends. These were his boundaries, now hers.

"Where are you from, Simone?" Sara prompted the talk they all wanted.

Simone told it slowly to control the tears, Jacques noticed. They all crossed themselves when her parents died, Jerome strangling the gesture. When her story reached Lyon Jerome came bolt upright.

"L'Humanité? Did you read it?"

"Of course. We distributed it."

"And then?"

"Collaborators. A denunciation."

He settled back. Nodded, hard. Simone wound the story sharply up into their hills, with no talk of Souceyrac or escape routes and the church bell signalled an hour since Mass.

The walk home again.

The common had become blessed.

The basking lizard scuttling, panicked; the jays a riot of moving colour, a stag beetle he identified and when it rose, huge in its sudden flight, she jumped back and laughed at her fear and he was charmed, charmed to death.

"And how are your nerves?"

He grinned. "Fine. Yours?"

"O.K., thank you."

Puech came into view.

The dog ran down the steps, its whole hind-quarters wagging. Jacques went to his mother's room.

"They stared."

"Only natural."

"Yes."

"I did. You do."

He pulled the door closed.

"Yes, but I love her."

A chasm of Silence opened.

"No, son. No. Not yet."

"I do, Mamman."

"Don't tell her."

He laughed. "Why not?"

The woman dredged at memory and found the words easily.

"Because Love is to be shared. Wait till she shares it."

"You're sure?"

"Oh yes."

"And you'll eat?"

"I'm not - Yes."

He left her.

It was his joy.

Her laughter and her loving-time had been so fleeting and so crushed. And in her son's passion she saw how far hers had passed and how she was holed deep by the shell she'd become. A Death drummed in her ears, pulled at her heart now that, of course, her son could be complete without her.

She was neither sad nor glad. She thought of July tomatoes. Ripe. And you either pick them or they fall. Rot. Leave a seed. And here he was, grown and glowing with the same joy that had been drowned in the cankered well of her life. Time to die. She drank some of the soup and ate a piece of bread and slept exhausted by that effort.

Soon, soon.

Simone sat and he smoked.

He could hear the moments passing. Each one a memory.

'Don't tell her. Wait till she shares it.'

But will Love wait here for her to love me?

He smiled, warm as the fire, breath rushing through his nose and she looked up for a second.

Love me? Love me like this? Never. No.

But I'll wait and as long as she's here Love will wait too. Why would it go? And hers might come? He smiled again and shook his head softly. No.

I'm no-one.

four

HERRISSON STRUGGLED with his conscience. Was he a Gendarme of France or Germany? And the nights he concluded Germany he beat his wife silently in their sex and she turned to no-one.

Mignon bought Grivault a black-market bottle of his favourite pastis and apologised but the Prefecture demanded more meat. Gestapo in Cahors now.

Feyt tailored, and the village fretted about Simone.

When Chayriguet called to see Sara the secret was finally shared with the mother.

"He won't marry you."

"No."

"Fire and destruction. Fire and damnation!" Then, "She doesn't know?"

"No."

"Oh shame and damnation! You fool."

And now the tears.

"How can I hold up my head?"

"He doesn't believe. I can't make him. I wouldn't want to."

"Shut up. You oaf! You don't do that. You don't do that."

"I wanted to."

"Of course, yes, sex, yes, there are no saints here. But you marry."

"Or..?"

"Disgrace."

"Not in God's eyes."

"Oh? And how would you know, miss? Eh? I don't meet God every day. I don't speak with Him. I speak with them."

"And?"

"I can't now, can I?"

"Wasn't worth much then. He loves me."

"Does he? Get him to prove it."

The talk would cycle endlessly - nothing words could mend.

A kilometre off the road between Senaillac and St.Cirgues, in the endless pine hills, men gathered.

Phillipe, a geography teacher from Cahors, Serge, a mechanic, Michel, a barber, Bernadie, a squat iron human, ex-Mayor of Senaillac, Fred, who'd been the school chef and big Jean-Luc, the second-team football captain in Latronquiere, an electrician.

They met with knives, hunting rifles and shame. And they talked. Of patience now and the struggle to come for Liberation. Then Vengeance and Justice and finally, Revolution and a new France, pure and hard. They spoke of De Gaulle and France Combattante and of themselves, France-Tireurs. And how they must train. And recruit the soldiers of a new France. And build a chain of safe places. Of safe friends. Places to shelter and places to hide. To hide weapons. And money. And food. A constant supply. And radios. For when the Time came. When The Germans came, as Phillipe promised they would. And they spoke of Vigilance.

She milked, learning quick, and they took the herd. Coming back one morning Dominique Duthileul, the son and heir, paused to nod.

"Salut."

"Salut."

They stood there, three humans, two dogs and his forty-odd meat, waiting. The dogs circling, as unneighbourly as their humans.

"Eh beh," he finally said and led his animals away. Simone watched him go. Jacques watched her.

A week later there were ten. A Basque, Roger, who'd left Spain after fighting Franco, a bank-clerk, Henri, and Fred brought Jerome, whom he'd met at Feyt's one night at nine o'clock. Jerome listened. Excited. Then, too anxious to be accepted, he promised some of his mother's money and the men could plan to buy weapons and ammunition. From the corrupt clerk in Figeac who knew of the stockpile from the surrender. Hidden till now, when it could make him a profit. He would be assassinated less than a year later for the key.

"What is this money for?" Madame Lacaze asked.

"Guns."

"Thou shalt not kill." And she walked out of the kitchen.

"Sara is pregnant."

She turned at the door. Mother and son looked at each other, neither faltering.

"Marry her. If you want money."

"I'll spend it on guns."

"You? You won't spend it."

"And you'll come to my wedding?"

"There'll be no wedding. You can't marry. You're too proud. And

what will your Maquisards say then, Jerome? Shall I tell you? 'Get married.'" She laughed.

"And will you come to my funeral?"

"Of course."

"And weep."

"Of course."

"What did you ever want of me? Ever?"

"That you might better this family."

"I have. I've introduced good peasant stock into our haughty blood."

"Poisoner."

And he drank for the rest of the day and walked the back fields to the camp with empty pockets and his talk was tolerated till one of the men pushed a pistol at him and told him to go and kill the village collaborator. Spittle gathered at the corners of his mouth as he lost his feeble credibility.

"I'll do it."

The men laughed.

"Who is it?"

"Who is it?" Ugly mockery. "The bourgeois communist! Who is it? Marry the girl and bring us money. Know your place."

"Fuck you."

A knife appeared in Bernadie's hand.

"As long as you provide you're worth a risk. Just. You're a windbag. This isn't talk, Lacaze - this is the time to die. And kill. For France."

"I know that."

"No," said Phillipe, "You say that."

She cut back the hawthorn, dug out nettle roots, raked them into a pile, cleared the paths between the vegetable plots and she'd weed them tomorrow. Sweat. Salt. Nice.

"Good day?" he asked, after food.

"Lovely day."

He smiled and so did she.

"Market tomorrow."

"Aha."

"Come?"

"No. Thanks."

"Fine." He nodded.

Jerome spoke to Sara's mother and she borrowed a bicycle and pedalled to St. Hilaire to see the Curé.

Jacques bought one plate and Jean-Jacques gave him the cup and cutlery and winked. Jacques blushed. The women smirked and rubbed at their ration tickets, glad of the distraction, and the precious gossip.

"She's pretty, they say."

"Yes."

The two men nodded at each other, eyes elsewhere.

"Lucky bastard."

"I am."

"Already?"

Jacques frowned.

"No."

"Tricky with Mother?"

"Some candles, please."

"Uh."

The walk home had become blessed. Everything she had looked at he saw afresh, adazzle. The simple majesty in the spread of the hawk's tail feathers as it rocked into the air, one huge beat to find a

thermal and then soar slow over it's table. And at home, mine will be laid. By Simone.

"How was the village?"
"Same. Less."
"The war."
"The black-market."
The mother listened and slowly, and against her will, she came back to life. To their life, yes, a borrowed life, but her son didn't care as long as she knew some joy, for he had a harvest to spare. She set her emptiness aside, for the moment, for their sakes, and as the summer shone on, for the warmth outside her cell. She sat in the garden, walked a little and felt the heat.

The two women cooked one night, the mother making a salad dressing with mustard and Simone dipped her finger in it to taste and the mother slapped at her hand and both froze and then all three laughed. Short but oh! a symphony to him. Simone was more than welcome, she was a blessing, and that night she lay in his bed and allowing herself one moment of immodesty, believed it.

The commune assimilated Simone like a shared cold-sore. On Sundays they stared and nodded. Him they read, fallen like an axe-head, hard and deep. Her they simply wished away, break his fool heart, like his mother, and go. But when the Curé read Jerome and Sara's marriage banns the congregation forgot Simone and watched Sara's mother holding her head just straight. And Madame Lacaze, for whom this was news, clenched her jaw and focused hard on the bottom of one of the altar candle-sticks. Jerome had said nothing to her. She used the rest of the service to steel herself for the public kissing with that woman, pregnant with her grandchild, and her mother, before she could escape home.

"July 14th, what is it?" Jerome was drinking already, and had a bottle and five glasses ready.

"My mother's birthday." Arbel sat. "Cheers." He raised his glass to Jerome.

"And Bastille Day."

He looked round.

Jacques wouldn't meet his eye, but watched Herrisson and old George Gley, the mason, talking with Duthileul. Gley, whose family had got all the work of the commune when his grandfather sank into alcohol after the card-night. Ardelle looked at Jerome.

"What about it? Is this a history lesson?"

"What do we do, Ardelle? On that day?"

"Who's we? I work. You drink. He works – and then drinks. Men get drunk."

"We celebrate, exactly."

"Any excuse."

"Not this year."

"Why? No wine?"

"Oh no. It is illegal. Unpatriotic. Forbotten."

"Shh," said Sara.

"No."

"I'd like another drink, then, husband."

"Banned. By the Germans? Oo no. By we French."

The men smoked and the women turned their glasses in their hands and waited.

"Am I depressing you? Uplifted by Jehovah as you all are. And the glad tidings of my marriage. It's just, you see, there's a war going on," he leaned forward, "and we're losing it. Us. The French. Which we all are. We're losing. Sorry."

"I thought we'd lost." Jerome was getting on Arbel's nerves.

"So what are you going to do?" Ardelle asked.

"Celebrate."

"And I'll work. So it'll be just like normal." And she drank a little and flushed a little and Arbel was proud.

"Will you celebrate?" Jerome turned to Simone.

"I won't."

"Why not?"

"I'm tired. And I've slept in cells."

"Tired? Oh dear."

"What will you do?" Jacques asked.

"I don't know yet."

"No."

By the second week their evenings stretched to another cup of coffee, the end of the bottle of wine and the first time she read a book.

"It's Zola."

"Zola."

She looked up at him. Dumb. Might be talking to the cows.

"Jacques - can you read?"

"Yes."

"I'm - I apologise."

"Why?"

"I didn't mean to offend."

He smiled.

"You didn't."

"Good. Would you like to read it? Or another?"

"No."

"Oh."

She smiled.

"You like it," he said. "It grips you. You disappear when you read."

"You do, too. When you smoke."

  THE SINGLE SOLDIER

"Do I?" He smiled. "Would you like a cigarette?"

"No."

"There we are then," he said and she laughed.

Bent her head and read.

She and Jacques' mother darned one rain-filled afternoon. Spoke not at all, but sat mending his socks, her cardigan. The mother silent in confusion at her pleasure, Simone silent because the mother's pleasure was tangible.

He made a stool and one evening within the first month the mother broke all the rules by coming to eat with them.

She told the tale of his first loaves, how they'd been harder than the barn wall, and Simone smiled and Jacques watched his mother smile, the flush rising in her cheeks, the blush of the young woman she still was. He pushed his food past the knot of thankfulness at his throat.

This was the wish. No. In truth, Simone was the wish, and this, this was both. Both. Why?

The cow's cycle came round again and he led it across the road and Dominique penned it with the thick male for an afternoon. Jacques stood there watching the bull take the air and his beast taste the new pasture. He went into the kitchen of the farmhouse and the old deaf mother looked up from her Bible.

"Do I have to give you change?" she shouted at him.

"No."

He left the money and her by the window. In the field the bull waited.

June shone into July.

The three of them evolved in a slow dance. The mother turned again toward her own death, thinking this is what the boy must want; if I'm gone he'll be alone with her and I'll be at my peace.

But the summer birds she could name by their song. And she

worried at the tomatoes, hauling an evening bucket from the well. And she made the butter, her muscles hurting, hurting, but she finished it. In the still evenings she watched the girl returning to her fuller bloom and her son's love deepen with patience.

"Mother..."

"Jacques?"

"You're better."

"I'm stronger."

But out in his fields he did wonder what life would be if she died. If she had.

Alone with Simone.

He stood the plough slack and fell forward. "Almighty God - forgive me my sinful flesh weakness."

The dry earth bit his knees.

He waited.

"I meant it. But it's weakness. Truth and strength want your will. Not mine."

He waited.

Nothing.

He rose and worked on, hurt.

At supper Simone gave him silence till his eyes rose.

"What?" she asked softly.

"Shameful, Simone. Not for sharing."

She nodded, accepted.

"What is it?" His mother asked. He looked at her. Thought, 'I wished you dead.'

"Iffing," he said.

"Close to sin."

"I know."

"What will be will be."

"I know."

"Goodnight, son. Goodnight, Simone."

She went to her room.

"Goodnight Mother. Call."

"I will."

He watched Simone making their tisane, the hard thin body in his mother's dress, the hair tied snap in a tail, the sun that had caught her legs and arms a little. No. He didn't desire her, naked, no. He only wanted her here for ever.

When she sat he was afraid she would ask his thoughts and he would tell her. But she looked at the flat chest and strong shoulders, black curls dusty with earth, big nose, big mouth, his cigarette, and thought, this is the brother I never had.

Sundays passed.

The staring diminished. They thanked God for his mother's recovery and Simone dared pray the German Hell might pass these people by; though she remembered she'd prayed that before, with her own mother. Of all of them on their knees before their God she knew there was nothing that could not be swept away. People, towns, countries blown to dust. So what could they do? Pray. And hoard. Why hoard, she wondered. Because it was the only practical way to hope.

On July 5th Jerome and Sara married.

The ceremony was as bare as Jerome could have it. He asked Arbel and Ardelle and Jacques and Simone to stay away from the hypocrisy - which they did - but the rest of the commune poured into the church. Too good to miss, this. No best man, no bridesmaids, no flowers, her pregnant. What a feast! And Madame Lacaze! She must be humbled, ashamed, furious, but she'll never show any of it - not her.

Jerome looked round at the tight smug faces and knew now what he would do on the fourteenth. His mother fed Sara's family and her son left her to live with them. She gave him no gun money. She had given it to Fred, demanding his utter secrecy.

As his plough sliced and his earth parted so Jacques' life filled. He would sit of an evening and smoke a little and talk a little and drink a little and taste each crumb of Time. He would have changed nothing and, to his ecstasy, nothing changed.
The repetition of the days, the weeks, were all he wanted. To stop and sometimes see her, and more and more the two women, filled his cup. He thanked God with a true heart every day and Sundays were not special any more. God's house was his.

On July 14th Jerome went home, to the cellar, found his father's sword and tricolour, marched back up to the square, and sang "La Marseillaise."
Silently the village gathered and Sara's eyes filled, and he sang it again and again until Herrisson arrested him and he spent the night in the cold Gendarmerie. Some wanted to laugh but didn't. Some wanted to sing and didn't.
When he next went into the hills the men had moved camp and he was rejected. Sara held him in the crook of her shoulder and bullied him to his tears. He kept them till he heard that one hundred thousand had marched through the streets of Lyon, seventy-five thousand in Clermont and he in St.Cirgues. Then he wept.

St Cirgues' War became the Requisition. Mignon's orders lengthened and rumours and anger about the Black Market deepened and the women of the village acted. Seven walked in on

Chibret in his office and demanded eggs and flour to feed their children and when he gave it he confirmed a Black Economy. Either he didn't need all the Requisition or he could replace what he'd been forced to give. When more women went next day the cupboard, they were told, was bare. It was not, it was sealed with the gleaming padlock Chibret had driven to Aurillac for. The village shrugged, self-serving politicians were nothing new, and their reaction was to hoard more.

Jacques too hid eggs and stored vegetables in the bread-oven and wondered about his maize.

Mignon drove up to Puech one day with a truck and Regis Garceau, the village slaughter-man, and took one of Jacques' nine beasts, one of Arbel's dozen and one of Duthileul's, and Arbel came round late that evening with two bottles. He poured them each a glass and drank the rest of the first bottle. He and Jacques sat on his bench, rolled cigarettes, smoked and stared at her.

Arbel nudged Jacques, "Mother?"

"She's - better." A grin warmed him.

"I've seen her," Arbel registered the miracle.

"Yes, she is."

He tasted it. Tasted true. Arbel looked at Simone.

"This is you."

"I don't know why."

"Because he's happy!" Arbel laughed at the obvious and then again as Jacques' cheeks coloured.

"Well," she looked at them both, "that's good."

"I like it," said Jacques.

Arbel started the second bottle.

And he hunched forward a touch. "What if it comes, eh?"

"What?"

"The War."

"Oh. That. Yes."

"We'd be called."

"Maybe it won't come."

"It will," said Simone, "and you'll have a choice."

The boys looked at her certainty. Arbel stopped drinking.

"What choice?"

"Fight or refuse."

"Refuse the Government? Can't be right." Arbel shook his head.

"Then your choice is theirs. Your choice is made."

A silence grew.

"You'd resist?" Even here, Arbel lowered his voice.

"I don't think so," said Simone. "I'd run. I want to live. I feel I've died once."

"Vermande?"

"I'll defend Mother. That's all I know. And I'll defend Simone and I'll defend you. What else can I do? Nothing."

Arbel, reassured by Jacques' confusion, sat a little further forward on the bench, emptied his glass, refilled all three.

"No. But Duty," he said, "is good." And he drank. "To Duty."

Jacques raised his glass and the girl just smiled.

"Jerome, eh?" sniggered Arbel.

"I heard, yes."

"Lacaze the flag."

And they laughed, feebly.

"At least he did something." Simone said.

The boys nodded, silenced.

Then Arbel shifted and spat into the ash.

"He's got twice our cattle put together and Mignon only takes one!"

"Jerome?"

"Duthileul!" Arbel coloured.

"Well he paid him off," Jacques said, "I suppose."

"Bastard." Arbel was cold.

"Thou shalt not covet thy neighbour's cattle."

"No. I know."

A different silence.

"But it's not just," said Jacques.

"No. It is not."

Simone wished them good-night and went to her room. She heard one of them descend to the caves and return. She heard wine pouring and them talking. Then Arbel left. Then he came back.

Jacques went to his mother's room.

"One of Arbel's cows. Sick. Just going to look."

She nodded through her sleep. *She does look stronger. Needs a beef-stew though,* and they left.

It was half-past midnight.

Jacques and Arbel walked. At the rise to the church square Arbel stopped and took his shoes and socks off, put the shoes back on and hauled the thick woollen socks over them. Jacques copied him, a tightening beginning in his stomach, a drought in the corners of his mouth.

A dog barked.

"Can you pick a lock?" Jacques whispered as they approached the Mairie.

"No. Can you?"

"No."

"Then we won't use the door."

Arbel produced a wrench and wrestled the volet hinges from their concrete setting, laid the shutters silently down and looked at the window.

"Your turn. I've done my bit," he winked.

The village slept like a children's book, the moon-shadows sharp and beautiful.

The window.

"I don't know," said Jacques, "how you break glass silently."

"You don't. You take the whole pane out."

Their pen-knives ripped out the ancient putty, scraped the inset where the glass sat, took out the wee pinning nails and with both knives at once they levered one pane. It moved, resisted, then came complete and fell past their frozen grasping fingers, dancing through acres of air, reflecting for a spinning instant their village at night, and then shattered.

They froze, eyes bigger than their mouths, ears wider than both. The silence healed. Nothing.

The window opened and they swung in, lit Arbel's candle, and found the double doors and Chibret's padlock.

"Smash the bugger," Jacques looked at Arbel's wrench.

"Right."

Jacques wrapped his jacket around the offending article and Arbel venomously left it ruined. They listened. Silence. In the big room there were at least ten muslin-wrapped carcasses.

"Which is his?"

"The biggest."

Arbel cut the muslin open and lifted the stiff back legs. He put them down and spat on his hands. Looked behind him, where he was going with the beast. Spat again, picked up both hind legs, took the slack the dead muscles allowed him, braced himself, took a good lung-full and pulled.

His back moved.

A centimetre.

Breath screeched through his lungs. His hands fell to his knees, his strength wasted in an instant. He gulped enough air to straighten his ravaged back. There was a long silence.

"You know what?"

Arbel's eyes were locked on the beast.

"What?"

"You can't steal a dead cow."

Ever so very slowly Arbel began to shake. The shake took a hold. They both shook. Shaking to hold back a tide. They dared one tiniest glance and both surrendered, into helpless laughter.

Arbel fell on the carcass and howled noiseless and neither dared catch the other's eye again. It began to feel like the nicest possible way to die.

"We should have known," Arbel said in gulps, "we're fucking farmers!"

"And," Jacques tried twice and finally managed, "where did we think we were going with it?"

The laughter slowed and stopped as Crime and Punishment slid into the room. Sobering.

Half a kilometre away sleep was not disturbed by the faint single peal of the church bell. In their candlelit Mairie its boom demolished humour.

"What do we do?" Jacques said, his ears humming.

Arbel looked at the crammed provisions. "Organise a fete."

"Now?"

"For tomorrow."

He stood, all action now, and cut muslin from four of the animals, sliced it into large squares and tied each into a make-shift bag. Eggs, cheese, fruit, vegetables, nuts, wine, bread, everything light enough to carry. Pockets stuffed, jackets weighted, hands full they turned to go.

"Who's this meat for?"

"Germans. Or the black market..."

"Fine."

Arbel went back into the room and Jacques heard splashing. They

clambered back through the window, passed out the booty and clanked down outside.

"Put the volet back?"

"Let him. Wait here," and he disappeared inside again.

Jacques waited two endless minutes in his village square, surrounded by broken glass and bags of crime. What would he say if someone woke and looked out? And how could something so serious be funny?

"What?" he said, when Arbel finally re-appeared, sweating.

"Insurance." The mad grin and he'd cut clumps of meat.

They threw every guarding dog a bone as they left food at Sara's, Jireau's, Jauliac's, Feyt, the mushrooms at Louis', something at the door of everyone they liked.

"I feel like Father Christmas," said Jacques.

"Hang on - brainwave." Arbel scooted down to the Gendarmerie and left a dozen eggs for Herrisson.

They had one bottle of wine left. Arbel ripped the cork out with his penknife, drained a throatful, smacked his lips, and looked at Jacques.

"Well?"

"What?"

"Shall we go back? Feed everyone?"

Two of the dogs found them, barked with delight and the boys took one look and fled.

They had half the bottle left and Arbel cheerfully drank it.

The silhouette of Duthileul's farm set Arbel off laughing again.

"No, no. Sh! If they wake they'll know it was us."

"It was a great night."

"Sleep best, friend."

The church bell struck the half-hour and in the black lane they

shook hands, tight, strong.

"Jacques. Do you and her...?"

"No."

"No, that's what Ardelle said."

He came in, shushing the dog as he climbed the stairs, jiggled the door, climbed to his bed and laughed himself to sleep.

Next morning the village divided sharply between the outraged and the well-breakfasted. No-one gave a fig about the Mairie, but speculation about those who'd received manna was all-consuming. Jealousy fed Suspicion.

In the dawn at Puech Simone knew something for she woke to hear his snoring and she had milked the herd and taken them to pasture before it stopped.

"Sleep well?" She poured coffee.

"I did."

She smiled.

"You did."

Herrisson ate sumptuously, hid the remaining eggs, pulled his uniform tightly together, promoted himself to Detective, noted the means of entry, scoured the urine scented room for clues, couldn't find any, and wondered what to do. If it was someone outside the commune they were gone; if it was someone in the commune, then, obviously, fresh omelette for breakfast, it was a friend. And if he arrested anyone they'd be shot. There was no-one he particularly wanted shot, so he flannelled Chibret who muttered about the Gestapo from Aurillac arriving to do his job. Herrisson whitened. "Don't tell them. Get it back."

"You can come with me."

"Oh, fuck."

"Exactly."

And they went to each house, where it was either denied, or had been eaten.

"We thought it was you," said Jireau's wife, "I was coming to thank you."

"You stand for Mayor," said Chibret, sour.

"You love it," she laughed and closed her door.

The village enjoyed Chibret's squirming.

"Fat pig. Sell a suit. Buy the food back. There's a market somewhere..."

Chibret called Herrisson off and never mentioned the affair again. The following Sunday, in the sun outside the Tabac, Arbel kicked at the two dogs circling his feet and Simone looked sideways at Jacques and thought, 'Well, he did something.'

His maize ripened.

"What will you do when it's over?"

"Believe. I don't know. I'm not thinking about it." Simone said. Truth was easy here.

"What did you want to do?"

"Teach."

"Teach?"

"German." She snorted a wry breath.

August blazed, the lane dusty all month, and two-hour siestas while Russians, English, Americans, Poles, Australians, Italians, German and Japanese died. The cows were besieged by flies, straw hats the order of every day and Simone felt repaired, and at last, young again.

"Where can I swim?"

"The Roc. Where I fish."

She walked with him, the village twitching and nudging and

sewing this tit-bit into the patchwork of distraction that was Simone's saving grace.

She took off her dress and plunged, knickers and vest, in, surfaced, threw her hair away from her face, spat, laughed and called, "It's horrible, come on!"

"I can't swim."

"You don't have to!" She stood, water just above her waist. He looked at her. Took off his clothes and stepped in. Mud rose between his toes, slugs of earth.

"Ugh!" He fell forward and swallowed half a lung-full.

A yard apart, his chest dripped thin mud and it was firm and strong and her vest clung to her tiny breasts and flat waist and he said, "We're staring again."

On baking day, the first Monday of September, she went up to the grenier for flour and saw his blankets. She took one from her bed to make his softer. He lay that night and thought, I have a wish now. For her to see Janatou, and for me to see her there.

Jerome worried Jacques. Drinking with him and Simone on market-day he produced, in broad daylight, a copy of "Le Coq Enchaine".

"No, no, my friend. Quite safe. My mother-in-law is cousin to some prefect, somewhere."

And he toasted himself with pastis. Jacques sipped his beer, Simone left her wine.

"And you two?"

They looked at each other and back to him.

"We're friends." Jacques said.

"Sara and I, we're friends," he said, "and we fuck."

"We don't," she said.

"Maybe you should."

"To be like you?"

"To be what everyone says you are."

"I don't want to be what anyone says I am."

"And Jacques, my old friend?"

"They said Mother and I did. I don't care what is said."

"I like you, Vermande. I do." He raised the thin glass and drained it.

"You're drinking too much."

"I'm a married man! It's what we do. All us married people worry about you sober young things, you know. 'They should be like us,' we say. Normal. Dying. Or dead."

"You under-value yourself, Jerome. You always have."

"That's true. I do. I expect more of myself and I am always disappointed."

"Poor little rich boy," said Simone.

"Ah, c'est moi. J'accuse."

"Why are you drinking, Jerome?"

He leaned right forward, "Because I hear rumours from The War..." he said, waving the paper.

"No, no, Jerome. Not here. I'll be at home. No more talk here."

Jerome laughed, lurched to his feet and saluted.

"I'll bring it, shall I? When it's fact. Eh?"

"Yes. Do."

The walk home was quiet.

It lay between them. He hated it. He sat on the iron bench and she stood in the lane and looked up at the trees and he looked up at her.

"Fuck is a bad word," he said, slowly.

"For Love, yes. For loving."

"I don't want to fuck, Simone."

"I don't want to make love, Jacques."

"I know that."

"Do you?" And she'd said it.

"Yes. Of course."

He smiled. "I was asleep Simone. You're my wakening."

She said nothing.

Then, "And you're my peace."

Harvest came early and Mignon's truck with it. Took the Germans' giant greedy share of his maize. He and mother shrugged; they had enough and he'd hidden more, but Simone felt anger. When her eyes dripped towards sleep that night she was still angry, only now with herself, because she'd suffered at the hands of this war and she'd been granted a recovery and it must be time to stand again.

five

A JEW WAS SEEN eating the brains of a German soldier at nine o'clock. This was wrong on three counts. Jews don't eat pork, Germans don't have brains and at nine o'clock everyone is listening to De Gaulle.

Herrisson pinned a poster behind the bar.

How To Recognise Vermin.

A crude cartoon of a Frenchman and a Jew, the Jew with a huge nose and a rat's body.

Jerome sat in the Figeac bars for a week, in Bagnac for a week, in Maurs for four days before he recognised a face. Michel the barber. The man left the bar. Jerome followed him, got a time and place for a rendez-vous and met them two nights later.

"I can get a barn, I think."

"Think?" Bernadie growled.

"At Puech. It's perfect, isolated."

"And money?"

"I might be able to get it."

"Get both. And no more singing."

"Will you come with me today? To Janatou. To harvest the grass?"
He waited. "Simone. That's a lie. Will you come just to see it. Please."

She steeled herself.

"No. I have somewhere else I have to go."

She watched his face fall, waited for "Where?" and saw it didn't occur to him.

"Today?"

"Yes."

"Then you must."

They sat, egg shells, crusts, cooling coffee and the mother, all ears.

"Another day. Next time?" she said, his disappointment blatant.

"It'll be there next year," he managed.

Her eyes faltered from his.

Surely she could wait one day, after all this time, fulfill his simple pleasure? No, no. Begin. Today.

"I hope," he added.

"I hope the War is over."

I'm not sure I do, he thought.

He yoked a cow to the cart, loaded his scythe, string, food for them both and they left his mother in the garden, looking at the Cantal and frightened.

Alone.

Clear sky, sharp heavy weather North.

They walked.

"Can't we ride on the cart?"

He laughed. "I've never thought of that."

The beast took their weight and moved on, down, through the woods. Where was she going? Why? He didn't have the right to ask. She would tell, or she would not. But he saw a change in her.

She looked straight ahead.

They rode into the village, the curtains gaped and she got down in the church square. Took her food from him.

"Take care, Simone."

"I will."

And he took the Maurs road, past Sara, thickening with her child, bending to her vegetables, and Simone took the Sousceyrac road.

The village wove these events into the quilt of their imaginings about Simone, Jacques and his mother.

Seven kilometres.

Long walk. Long time since I walked. How long? Months. Of peace. Recovery.

This is right, then.

Arbel was right - Duty is Good.

A rabbit crossed her path, followed by three others. She walked through Senaillac; a school, a shop, a tiny spray of houses, no-one. The road rose through a brief wood and there, again, was the endless roll of forested hills. This was surely unconquerable, or impossible to police. Too vast, there can't be that many Germans. Naive, Simone. Collaborators, remember? And, this was France - some people will sell anything, certainly Patriotism - for Land.

The escape route. Had that fat mayor lied? Even if the Curé were not there, the route might still be. I feel it is.

I feel better. I feel good.

She walked.

He was scything when, "Vermande!"

"Lacaze."

Here? Jacques leaned on the long oak handle.

Jerome was alight, galloping down the hillside, and he looked sober.

"Sara's thrown you out?"

"It's come."

"The baby? Jesus, has it lived? I only saw her this morning..."

"The Reléve."

"The what?"

Jerome paused for effect, Jacques saw, with irritation.

"The Reléve. The War! We have to go. Three of us for one of them."

"What?"

"Three of us go to Germany to work and they say, they say," he snorted, "they'll send one French Prisoner of War home."

Jacques' heart iced. Jerome laughed.

"Aha! At last, eh? Oh, Jacques, at last!" He whooped, loud, and hooked a punch into Jacques' shoulder.

"But... when?"

"It's voluntary. Now. But they'll make it law - they'll have to."

"Voluntary? Voluntary? We don't have to go?"

"We're not going! Go? To Germany? Are you mad?"

"But if it's law... we'll have to."

"Or?"

The word hung while Jacques thought.

"Don't go?"

"That sounds better. Stay and fight."

"Fight who?"

"Well, the government for starters! God you're dim. They're the bastards who'd send you to Germany!" He laughed, the obvious beautiful.

"Fight the government. Now who's mad?" He took a breath. "What about mother?"

"How will she be if you go to Germany?"

"What about Simone?"

"She'll fight."

"Fight what? Herrisson when he comes to enlist us? The Gestapo he'll bring with him?"

"We won't be there when those rats come."

"Oh?"

"We'll be in the hills."

"With mother?"

"Jacques, this is War. Not with Mother, no. Nor with Sara and my son. And definitely not working in an enemy factory feeding his killing machine. We'll be with friends, comrades. Jacques, we are France now. Me, you, Arbel, maybe. We are France. Not Vichy and Laval and his deals. There is no legitimate government. We are the conscience of all you can see and everything you can imagine."

He swayed a little, the light in his eyes fierce. Jacques looked at the scythe in his hand. The winter feed around him.

"When?"

"Soon, my friend."

"Oh my God."

Jerome took a breath. He searched Jacques' furrowed face.

"Will you help?"

"Who? Help who? How?"

Jerome looked round, even here and lowered his voice.

"Help France. Your barn. Hide things there."

"Things, Jerome?"

"Weapons."

The world heaved. His ears rang. Jerome waited.

The silence answered him.

"All right. Will you come and listen to De Gaulle tonight?"

Jacques looked at his anxious friend.

"Yes."

"Good man. A quarter to nine, the Tabac. Bring Simone."

"I'll ask her."

"She'll come."

"Will the Germans?"

"Yes. Not while they're winning. But this Reléve means they need. So, it's turning. Can't you feel it?"

"I feel fear."

Jerome looked at the honesty and slid an arm round the hard shoulders.

"Me too. I want to live to be a father."

"Me too."

"Well I was always faster than you."

"You were."

"Still am I bet."

"You drink too much."

"Top of the hill?"

A hundred metres sharp rise to the crest.

"Go!"

Jacques lost a clog, then the other and the new hewn grass-clumps ripped into the soles of his feet as he pushed his weight through his knee-caps. His lungs turned to brandy, tearing air in and out and he won.

"You're right." Jerome, hands on his knees, gasping, gasping. "I drink too much."

Jacques raised himself upright and there was his constant, eternal view, reaching forever to the blue.

Simone. I love this and I love you. And this bastard Reléve must part us. Why, God?

The fat mayor had lied, the Curé was there.

And he'd been expecting her. A letter from Lyon, some months ago from his comrade Curé, dead now, God rest his soul. He had kept the faith that she would reach him.

And the escape route was there, too. Faint. Feeble. Under threat from Vichy, the Germans, collaborators, and, shamefully, the neutral countries; that ageless rite of passage, greed. What had begun as evacuation of persecuted innocents had thickened into a grubby gravy train. North Africa or North America - if you could pay.

It needed whatever her help could be. She had a barn? That would be a perfect last staging post before Sousceyrac. Ask. Ask and let me know.

"Your Curé, Phillipe, has a bike. I'll speak to him. Gently. He's timid. I'm glad you're not. I'm glad you came, very glad. Ask your friend, Jacques. And money. We need money. Charity and human fellowship don't last long enough. We have to pay. And we must - these are the children of the world. Bless you, Simone."

Jacques walked the cow and the winter feed home.
If I go.
When I go.
If I have to go.
Wherever I'd go - she'd be left. Would she want that? And if she didn't what about Mother?
I can't stay in the house if I desert or refuse this whatever-it's-called.
And now guns and barns...
It's harvest. Everything grown is cut.

Oh, but I want her to stay.
I want it all to stay.
What can I do to keep her?
He snorted, joke. What can I do to save her from war? Nothing! On earth.

Tell her tonight, then?

Tell Mother? No!

Have this one last night of peace. One last evening by the fire.

Oh, no. De Gaulle. Everything has changed. So quickly. Why? The summer has gone, today.

Where did she go today?

She walked home.

It was home. Will he give the barn?

And the mother? I'll ask. What else can I do?

The evening flickered through the woods, the red sky spreading deep and deeper over the land. Life was changing. She walked.

Jacques and his mother sat at their table and he ate. When he avoided her waiting eyes she said, "Did you see Lacaze?"

"Yes." He looked up. "Did you?"

"Came here. He went to Janatou?"

"Yes." Dread slid up his spine.

"Why?"

"News."

"Of?"

"The baby." A tiny silence.

"No Mamman, that's a lie. The War. The War."

"He walked two hours to say what, Jacques?"

"I can't lie, Mother."

"Good."

"There's to be a Réleve..."

She sat back, stone.

"Both of you, both of you, both of you..."

"No, Mamma, no."

"All my life. Stolen."

"Mamma, not Simone. Only men."

"What?"

"Not both of us."

"You and your father."

He looked straight into despair. "I won't go, Mother."

"You will." She caved inwards. "You will, you will, you must you will..."

"Mamma. Mamman! It's voluntary. I don't have to go. It's not law."

"Yet."

"Mamma, that's iffing."

"War is close to sin, boy. It's as close as you and I can get."

"Which is better? To help the enemy, or kill him?"

She laughed, cold. "Neither. They're both final."

"Life's final."

"Life's a fraud."

Some flies walked undisturbed over the plates.

"And where is she?"

"I don't know."

"You didn't ask?"

"No."

"No, I wouldn't have either."

"She'll come back. Tell us."

"I don't want to know."

His mother went to her room and lay down.

The September evening bathed St. Cirgues in ochre as she walked past the curtains and came up the lane to Puech, tired and strong, the dog leading her in. Jacques, alone. Good.

"Food?"

"Please."

She waited for his questions. None.

She wanted his curiosity. If only to enjoy how much she trusted.

"Your mother?"

"She's - asleep."

He made tisane to go with the salad and waited for her to talk.

She waited for him to ask.

Why didn't he ask?

"Simone?"

"Yes."

"Will you come with me tonight. To the village. Meet Jerome."

"Why?"

"To listen to De Gaulle."

His eyes met hers. He would give the barn, he would.

"Yes."

At half-past eight there were two old ones and Valet, Grivault and Duthileul. Jacques and Simone took their drinks outside.

Jerome walked past, mouthed "The Church," and was gone.

They finished their drinks and his cigarette and he took the glasses back.

"Nearly nine," said Valet, fat.

"Need a lift home?" Duthileul growled and Valet smirked. Fat and cold.

"No, thank you, we have friends to see."

"Friends? Ohh."

"Good night."

"Enjoy yourselves." Laughter followed them, faded.

Jerome stood in the arched doorway.

"Feyt's. You know it Jacques, I'll take Simone. Go the back way, by the football pitch."

"Feyt?"

"Feyt. Hurry."

"Good for their gossip," laughed Jerome as he and Simone took the Figeac road. "I dare you to hold my hand."

"Is this all a game?"

"No. Hasn't Jacques told you?"

"Told me what?"

"Then he hasn't."

He waited for her to ask what, and she didn't.

Feyt's house stood back, detached, and Jerome walked her past it, then looked back to the silent village and took her hand as he turned smartly up a slope of grass and across Feyt's vegetables to his door.

Feyt. Small and stocky, his gait tired, a flat cap over no hair and sad eyes that crinkled a welcome into their corners as he shook her hand. Jerome walked past Jacques, to the window, moved the curtains and stood there. Watching. Checking. He looked insane.

"No-one see you, Vermande?"

"No."

A long padded table with a two metre metal rule embedded in one edge, scissors, chalks, needles, pins, cottons, rolls of strong cloth, tape measures and a sewing machine and its box. A canvas torso stood in a corner, naked. Nothing else, one chair. And Jerome twitching at the window.

The little man made tea and gave them each a cup and Jacques stared. His only Jew. This made no sense. How did you know he was Jewish? He didn't speak Jewish. What was Jewish? His trade? His nose, like the poster? Jacques stifled a laugh.

"What? What?" Jerome was stressed.

"My nose - " he stopped, reddening.

"Yes?" Feyt asked.

" - is bigger than yours!" And blushed.

Feyt laughed.

  THE SINGLE SOLDIER

"I read a poem once, an Englishman. He said that to the blind all men are equal. Perhaps, since blind men can't fight, it would be better if we were all blind instead of German or Jewish or French."

"There'd be no need for a tailor," said Simone.

"Good, I'm tired. But," he raised a finger, "would we sacrifice our sight for peace? I fear we'd rather see the mess we make of existence."

The church bell sounded. Feyt lifted the sewing-machine box and revealed a radio. He switched it on, the valves warmed and the metal speaker crackled and he tuned it minutely, just as the Curé in Lyon had, and La Marseillaise could be heard. Jacques gawped.

"They're playing my song," Jerome laughed from the window.

"This is London. Ici Londres."

The four of them placed their cups down.

De Gaulle, confidence in every enunciation, spoke.

"I refuse. I refuse to accept the military verdict of 1940 as final, I refuse to accept the Armistice, I refuse the policy of collaboration, I refuse to accept Vichy as the legitimate voice of France.

At this present hour, all France understands that the ordinary paths of power have disappeared. In the face of the confusion in French hearts, in the face of the liquefaction of a government that accepts servitude to the enemy, in the face of the inevitable incapacity of our institutions to function, I, General De Gaulle, am conscious of speaking in the name of France.

Everyone has the sacred duty to do everything he can to help liberate the country by casting out the invader.

There is no way out and no future without Victory. But this gigantic effort is already revealing that the danger menacing the country is not just from the outside. Victory will be no victory unless it brings courageous and profound re-birth from within.

The French people are not only waiting for Victory - they are

preparing for a revolution. Vive La France!"
Some music began and Feyt switched it off, covered it with the box, gathered his scissors and no-one spoke. Jerome came away from the window, his fists clenched, his eyes red with tears. Jacques felt the vivid taste of an entirely new excitement. Simone shone.
They shook Feyt's hands, his warm eyes crinkled and they left him cutting Valet's new jacket.

"Not alone, Jacques," said Jerome as they parted. "Not alone. We have a leader, eh?"
"Uh-huh." Jacques didn't want talk.
"Talk about things on Sunday?" Jerome searched his friend's face for the barn. The barn.
"Mm." The guns.
The danger.
The sky was dark. No moon. Just stars.
They walked, two young people. Nothing was said - there was too much to think - and then as the woods cut the night to black their pace slowed and he felt her nearer and for the first time, they touched. Simone placed a hand into the crook of his elbow. Jacques felt the exact detail of her skin and heat rushed around him, his breathing deepening, the grin exploding into his face and the urge to shout again. She stumbled on something and the fingers gripped tighter and he shook his arm free and took her hand and hoped the woods would stretch to Doomsday. His huge hard paw swallowed hers, the softness of the palm, the thin fingers gripping at him. He turned to look and saw nothing.
"Are you looking at me?"
"I am."
They walked.
"How are you?"

"I'm fine. Fine." She squeezed his hand and the hairs under his balls uncurled and he squeezed back.

"And how are you?" she asked.

"Full. This has been - a full day."

"Mm. It has."

The road turned to meet Duthileul's pasture and there was starlight enough not to hold hands. Fumbling, they parted.

But they had touched and he had survived. He longed for his solitude now, to go through the day and think and then savour its greatest thrill last.

Simone was baffled.

She had no experience of gentleness in men. Some fumbling at school, an excursion or two into Love's suburbs in her teens and then brutal necessity and soul-less degradation on her journey South. But everyone, all men, had wanted. Something. A touch, a kiss, a feel, to claim some moment of her life for theirs. Either that or nothing. Undesiring and therefore indifferent. And this man wanted something too, but it was so gentle, a butterfly's wing. She felt unique in his sight.

"Talk tomorrow?" she said as the dog came to meet them.

"Yes."

When they came in, before he lit the candle, she rose on her tiptoes to kiss him, as she would her father, or any good friend, and feeling his utter unpreparedness for such a gesture she spun away to her room.

They lay a floor apart.

Jerome and his guns. Resist this Reléve? Suppose they called tomorrow? And De Gaulle and my mother - they oppose each other. How do I help him and protect her?

The dog scratched and slumped against the chimney-breast.

He will give the barn, she thought, hoped - but have I the right to ask, to expose him and his Mother to the danger?

I won't go and I won't take Jerome's guns. Not yet.

She held my hand.

And we'll talk tomorrow.

Arbel snored. Ardelle lay awake. She knew only that he had lied to her. Lacaze had come, they had talked and Arbel had come back and lied. Denied the lie and now there was nothing to say. She could ask Lacaze but did she want to know? It was The War, coming with the winter. France had no army, but somehow they would take him. Why else would he lie?

Simone leaned into the mother's room. Still in bed. Odd.

"Shall I do lunch, or you?"

"You."

"Any ideas?"

"None."

She closed the door and sat on the bed.

"What is it?"

The mother faltered.

"Where did you go last night, you two?"

"To the village. A drink."

"Aha." Her eyes lowered, sad.

"It was my birthday," Simone smiled.

The mother took another breath. "I'm flattered you would lie to me, my dear."

"To listen to De Gaulle," Simone said instead of blushing.

"Oh no... oh no..."

"It must come."

"I know that."

"And we must prepare."

"Order a coffin."

She walked out to where he was turning maize roots over.

"Jacques."

"Simone."

He straightened. Saw purpose in her face. "Come to the copse."

He led her through the maize tares and into the shade of the beech. Quieter even than the faint buzz of the fields. Only Time, creaking.

"Girolles soon. And ceps. Next rain. Tasted ceps?"

"Yes, Jacques. I'm from the north, not another planet..."

"Oh. Yes."

They sat.

"What did Jerome mean when he said 'had you told me'?"

"We're to be called. It's coming, like you said. And I have my choice. Like you said."

"And you told your Mother?"

"Yes."

"I see. I understand."

"She never taught me to lie."

A half a minute passed, while he thought, 'And will you stay - and will you stay?'

"Yesterday, Jacques."

"Yes?"

"The barn - " she began.

"Yes?"

"Yesterday I went to Souceyrac. There's an escape route. For orphans. Jewish children, out through Spain to Portugal, and beyond, I think. Can they use the barn? As a resting place."

War. Nearly here. I have to face it. But - it must mean she'll stay!

"Yes," he said and her heart jumped once.

"What about your mother?"

"We'll see."

And there they sat, Simone warming all over, looking at him. Rooted in his environment, rooted as his trees. The paysan. No pays sans paysans. And he wants nothing I do not care to give.

"You're a treasure."

"Am I?"

"You are."

It's a pity I don't want you, she thought.

They told the mother.

She nodded, this was their life, she'd had hers. She was not afraid.

"Tell no-one, Jacques."

"No."

"No."

They made a cot in the calves' stall, a crib, and stood back, proud. Joseph and Mary.

Hitler's armies met their second Russian winter and froze outside Stalingrad. The Luftwaffe flattened Coventry, London, Portsmouth, raising an implacable hatred with the dust. The Japanese slaughtered young Americans as they sliced and swathed through South-East Asia. And the events that would govern the lives of Jacques, Simone, his mother, St.Cirgues and Free France gathered in Africa, as Rommel dug into the endless sand at El Alamein.

THE SINGLE SOLDIER

The Sunday Morning air, clean and fresh, mocked Ardelle's leaden and desperate heart. In the clamour of hope reaching for God's attention she raked her fingernails into her flesh, believing her pain must command His attention, and in His Benevolence, He would relieve it.

But as they sat outside the Tabac, Duthileul and the others glassed in behind them, she knew. Knew in her husband's slumped and silent shoulders that this next conversation would feed her nightmares for the rest of the war. The wine dribbled from the corners of her mouth, swallowing beyond her.

Jerome's grin, irritating all of them, was the face he set against the fear that Jacques would withhold the barn, and Phillipe and the men would reject him again, and this time finally. And then what? Jacques felt Jerome reaching for him across the silence. As he also felt Simone's new contentment at his side. Sara rested her hands over her widening Christmas-baby growing.

Ardelle turned to Arbel.

"Tell me. Now."

Silence.

"Tell me."

Her soul lifted into the thin waters of hysteria and she gripped her glass to steady herself. In the quiet she turned from Arbel to Jerome.

"You tell me." Her face, fierce.

Silence.

"Pair of cowards."

Jerome sat up, stung, moving past Sara's warning arm.

"It's a Reléve. A call. For volunteers. To work in German factories. Why haven't you told her this?"

"Because..."

"You'll go?" Jerome exploded. Heads lifted.

"Yes."

Silence. A sudden tablecloth of it.

"Your duty?" Simone said quietly.

"Yes."

"To who?" Jerome leaned forward.

"France." Arbel met Jerome evenly. Challenge in his eyes, too.

"Ardelle is France, too." said Sara.

"Not to him," Ardelle shook her head hard so as not to cry here. Now.

"Arbel," Jerome ransacked his brain, "if we three went, they would, they say, return one French Prisoner Of War. Right? A Frenchman. Captured and imprisoned by The Germans, for fighting them. And now, should we three go and help a nation that invaded and killed and imprisoned our people? Help them? Willingly? Arbel?"

"I'm a peasant Jerome. I raise cattle. I am cattle. I answer the biggest stick. The Government's."

"Over the top. Cannon fodder."

"If that's what I am."

"It's voluntary," Jerome said to Ardelle, and sat back. "Now."

"I'll go." Arbel said.

Ardelle looked at him, stood and walked home alone.

Arbel finished his cigarette, crushed it under his foot and walked home a hundred metres behind her, his conscience neither consolation nor company.

"Husband." Sara punched at him.

"Wife."

"Take that smirk off your face please, I want to slap you."

"Jacques?" Jerome faced his fear.

"Yes?" Jacques faced his.

"You've thought...?"

"It's not possible Jerome."

Jerome's face fell as his anger rose.

"Afraid?"

"No."

"Sure?"

"Quite."

The four of them drifted. Apart.

"They say," Jerome drained his glass, his throat scorched, "single women'll be called, too." Jacques' dilating eyes saddened him. He ignored it. "But you could solve that problem, Simone."

Jacques blushed and Simone sat forward.

"I won't be any part of your bright shining future Jerome, since it has no regard for the feelings of friends."

"Only a joke. Christ!"

She stood. "At whose expense?"

"Oh mine! Mine. Forgive me. Please."

"Forgive yourself."

His mouth dropped a little. "For what?"

"Exactly. For what?"

They walked where they had held hands. A metre apart.

"What did he want? Jerome?"

"The barn. Hide guns. For the Resistance."

"Why did you say no?"

"The children..."

"Couldn't we do both?"

His mouth drooped. "I never thought of that."

"What's the difference? Two dangers?"

"I never thought of that."

He stopped. She stopped.

"I'll go back," he said.

"I'll go back. I'll tell him."

"All right."

He turned for home, turned back and asked.

"We won't marry, will we?"

"No, Jacques, we won't."

"No."

He walked home and Simone strode back.

"Lunch? Mamman."

"Where is she?"

"Talking. To Lacaze."

"Oh, God."

Jacques scoured the room for simple conversation.

"Lunch?"

"Nothing. Water."

He made a soup.

Simone found Jerome drinking. Sara had gone. Duthileul Pére grudged his head a millimetre as their eyes met. It was the first time they had. She sat next to Jerome, their backs to him.

"You can have the barn."

"Eh?"

"You heard."

"Why?"

"Because you can pay."

"What?"

"I need money. You can have the barn if I can have money."

Jerome's brain struggled to clear, to sober. It needed another drink. He waved a hand and Janon came out.

"Drink?"

"Coffee." Simone nodded.

THE SINGLE SOLDIER

"Another," he gave the old one his glass.

Janon lumbered away.

"I have no money."

"What?"

"My mother has money. I don't. Not since I wed 'the slut'. And she had said no money unless I married her. A liar, my mother. Dishonourable."

"Oh."

"That's why I need the barn."

"It's all you have to offer?"

"And my life."

"Yes. But no money."

"No."

The drinks came.

"Why do you want money?" he asked.

"A good cause."

They sat there. At dinner-tables starved imaginations would serve up this morsel to chew on. Her and Lacaze...

"He's got money. Shit-head. Behind us."

"And what would he want me to do to get it?"

Jerome enjoyed the stench in his imagination for a second.

"Nothing! If he masturbates he comes in centimes. Can I still have the barn?"

Simone thought.

"Can I speak to your mother?"

Jerome leaned forward.

"If I get half of anything you get out of her."

"I can speak to her?"

"Go ahead. My mother's weakness is her Christianity. It's pious. My mistake has been to not play along with her charade. That's the key-hole."

"What's her name?"

"Quasimodo."

When the broth was simmering he remembered the water.

"I forgot. Sorry."

The mother nodded, left the glass. He looked again for conversation, didn't find it and went back to the food which was ready when Simone came in. He took a tray in to his mother.

"I'm not hungry. I said."

Jacques closed the door. Put the tray down.

"This is not right."

"Not feeling hungry?"

He took a breath. "Starving yourself."

"God's will."

"No, it isn't. It's yours."

She barely shrugged. He came and stood by the bed.

"Suicide is a mortal sin."

She looked away. He sat on the bed.

"It's not forgiven, mamman. It's not forgiven."

With horror he saw she was passing beyond religion's blackmail.

"Was it God's will Father died?" he asked.

"It must have been."

"You don't believe that."

She looked at him.

"No."

"I have a future, mamman."

"What is it?"

"I don't know."

"No."

"And neither do you."

"No." She nodded. "I don't know."

"Don't you want to see it? Share it?"

"I'm tired."

"You're frightened. And iffing."

"I'm tired, Jacques. I'm sorry."

"But - won't you stay long enough not to frighten her away?"

A quiet followed as mother and son looked sad and selfish at their lives.

"Oh, mother I ..."

She looked at him again.

"You're a good son."

"Oh mother."

Their lives clouded.

The mother ate less, rose less, did less and talked less and Jacques was helpless.

This woman is dying because I've come. So, am I to take this woman's place? Why? Because the woman imagines something ordained in me? Because, like him, she thinks I'm some form of miracle? Because, even if it was so, and it isn't, why wouldn't the woman stay for the son's pleasure? Because she meant only to entrap? To shed her responsibility and not stay to see any failure? She went to speak her mind.

"This weight is too heavy," she told the mother. "You may do as you wish, you must, but not because of me. Either you eat or I must leave today."

"Then I'll eat."

"Thank you."

Simone needed more time before she dared Madame Lacaze. She borrowed Arbel's bike and rode to Souceyrac to give the Curé the news. He blessed her and Jacques and asked about money. She shrugged. He understood. All she could do now was wait. For the first child. He wouldn't tell her more. Ignorance was a profound form of safety.

Jerome's guns arrived.

Jacques levered up six huge cubes of his barn floor, dug out beneath, buried four cloth-covered weapons, replaced the stone, earthed in the cracks, shook hands once with the silent man, Roger the Basque, and resolved to forget about them. This was insane. No-one could get those weapons in a hurry. No-one but him and the silent man could even find them in a hurry. He wondered if people weren't making this war up as they went along.

Rommel began his attack on Montgomery's Eighth Army. Five days later he was back where he started. Montgomery waited.

Curé Phillipe shook hands outside Mass, leaned weakly towards her and she heard, "Tuesday."

I'll see one of these children and then I can ask Madame Lacaze.

At the Tabac the villagers drank in silence. The Reléve was now news not rumour and some of the old ones looked at them with pity. Some. When Valet raised a glass and winked Jacques felt an entirely new impulse, the desire to maim. He and Simone walked home, the beauty of autumn irrelevant.

"Tuesday. The first child."

"My God. How long for?"

"I don't know."

"Will someone come for them?"

"I don't know."

"Are we supposed to take them?"

"Jacques - I don't know."

She turned to him.

"Are you afraid?"

"Er - yes. You?"

"No."

"O.K. Then me neither."

Montgomery talked and talked to his troops, day and night, waiting till he was sure they had all heard his voice, till he was sure they knew he believed they were invincible.

On Tuesday night they sat and he smoked and she read and they fed a tiny fire and waited. Drank coffee but still her eyelids fell and the book sagged and dripped in her hand and he reached across and silently took it and leaned back to watch. He wanted her so asleep he could lift her. She slumped right forward; jerked, shocked upright, smiled unseeing at him and he took one hand and lifted her to her feet.

"What? Wait. What?"

"You're asleep."

"Is he here?"

"No. Bed."

"Wait. We must wait, Jacques."

"I'll wait. You sleep."

"O. Sure?"

They weaved across the room, her weight sliding into his chest, and he opened the door. His bed.

"Bed, Simone."

"Wait."

"I'll wait."

She looked at him.

"Good."

He closed the door. He heard the brief bed sounds and waited. He heard nothing, then a fly, then her breathing, long and deep. It was almost cold.

He went back to the fire and smoked.

The cat washed and bit at her spine. Now she suddenly looked up, eyes dilating, body lowering. A house-cricket fell. She missed it with her paw, leapt after it, the dog following. She cuffed the dog away and bit at it again. She had a mouthful, a wing, and spat it out. It lay motionless between her and the dog and she spat twice and padded away. The dog trapped it against a wall and ate it. The cat washed itself.

His cigarette finished. Black outside, surrounding a three-quarter moon yellower than his cheese. Sleep, no-one coming now. A moth circled his candle all the way upstairs. He lay and watched it, then put the flame out before it killed itself.

No-one came the next day.

Evening found them by the fire again.

"She's dying." He thought aloud.

"Yes."

'And will you stay?' he thought silent. 'Will you stay?'

There was a knock at the door.

The dog barked itself awake, angry and ashamed and he shushed it.

They looked at each other and he went to the door.

The latch stuck, his hand not steady. Now it was.

And there stood Herrisson.

"Vermande. Salut."

"Salut." Jacques' mouth dried.

"Mademoiselle."

"Monsieur." Simone throbbed.

Jacques' face whitened. "Come in."

Herrisson took his Gendarme's hat off and stepped in.

"Storm coming."

"You think so?" Jacques blurted.

Herrisson looked at him, surprised. "Don't you?"

He put his hat on the table and stretched his shoulders. Jacques closed the door. One glance at Simone - if they should come now.

"Reading?"

"Mm."

Simone stood in the fireplace, Herrisson by the table, Jacques at the door. He knows. He knows. Jacques walked a kilometre to the fire. Stood there eyes fixed on the metal buttons. No. It's the eggs. He knows. No! The Mairie. It's the Mairie.

Herrisson sat, flattened a big paw on the table.

"I might have to move."

"Eh?"

"Toulouse. Posting."

He looked at Jacques.

"I hate Toulouse."

"Oh."

"Been there?"

"Me! No." He knows.

"Hell's kitchen. But Duty calls, eh?"

Duty. It's his duty to arrest me. Oh, Mother of God - it's the Guns! I'll be deported. Put in a camp as a Maquisard.

"Maybe not. Hope not."

Jacques' mind failed him. He looked at Simone. Since she came I've robbed my own Mairie, hidden guns, listened to illegal radio - De Gaulle! - he knows about that, too - Feyt - and now I'm waiting for a Jew. Me. Vermande. Which crime has he come about? All of them? I'll be shot.

"A drink?" Simone asked.

"Please. Wine." He unbuttoned his great-coat. He leaned back in the chair and looked at Simone and Jacques, side by side in the fireplace.

"No-one likes me. Why? Because everyone thinks I know something; no-one believes I know nothing, so they all stand like you two, frozen with fear. What have you two done? Eh?"

He laughed, a pistol crack, and they both jerked in shock.

"Look at you. Guilt all over you. That's all I ever see. I'm sick to death of it."

Simone poured a glass for him.

"Thank you." He downed it. "Shit! Jauliac's? You know he taps it from his toilet. Wait."

He went outside.

They stood, looking at the empty doorway and listening to his footsteps go around the barn.

"What does he know?" Jacques whispered, "Which?"

"I don't know. The guns?"

"Or the radio. Feyt."

"Course. Oh, yes. I meant the child."

"Which is worse?"

"Are you thinking of bargaining?"

"I can't think. I'm frozen. Or the Mairie..."

"What Mairie?"

"Oh nothing, nothing. What do we do?"

"Pray they don't come now."

"Why has he come?"

"I don't know Jacques! Stop asking me stupid questions."

Her fear shocked him, his ears reddened. Herrisson clattered up the stone steps.

"Voilà!" A bottle of red, labelled, and the label lined with gold.

"Corkscrew?"

They looked at each other. He was drinking good wine with them. Was this Iscariot kissing Christ? Their last supper together. Had he a macabre streak?

"Yes," Simone passed the corkscrew.

"Where was I? Yes, you two, a perfect example of my view of humanity. It says - you're saying now - 'You could possibly be a half-way decent human being, but please, fuck off.' All day, every day."

He pulled the cork and Simone, half hypnotised, washed glasses.

"And so why did I ever want to be a Policeman? Forgotten. I looked it up the other day in a dictionary. 'An organised force of civil officers to preserve order!' My life's a very bad joke. There's no organization, no force, no officers, no civility. Order to preserve, oh yes indeed, sir. But, when that order is broken, what can I do?"

There was a silence. Simone and Jacques wondered whether they should respond, and if they could.

"Chibret." He hadn't seemed to notice their reticence. "When the Mairie was broken into, he expected me to find someone. Why? Because I've got the cap. I'm the flic. But all a policeman sees that a Mayor can't is people looking guilty. It's not good for the soul, believe me. Here."

He poured them a glass each.

"The summer of '36. Peace, glorious weather, just married, posted here - taste it - its reality."

Jacques stopped breathing the first time Herrisson said the word "Mairie" and now he had to consciously inhale to gather the strength needed to reach the glass and then hold it. Herrisson toasted.

"To reality. Six fucking years ago - pardon me."

"To Peace." said Simone.

"Yes," managed Jacques, and they drank.

The grape took them through taste into after-taste and then warmth, reaching from the vines' roots to theirs.

"Ahh. Eh? Softly now. It won't last. 1936 didn't. Make it last."

What does he want?

Simone's fear shifted enough to see this man was drunk. Drunk because he had to arrest her and Jacques?

"Can't have children."

Jacques' glass froze half-way to his mouth. What? Can't have children? Jewish children?

"Chayriguet says I'm firing blanks."

What is he talking about?

"So I'll be no use to the Super-race. What use is a flic? Eh? And a flic in War? Not even a finger in the dyke. I'm a puppet. You're a puppet, Vermande. And you too, Miss."

"I know."

"Do you? And how long have you known that?"

"Since I decided to do something."

What is she saying?

"Cut the strings, eh? Feel good?"

"Feels better."

"How does a policeman cut the strings, eh?"

"I don't know, sir."

"Me neither, Miss."

"Simone."

"Me neither. Toulouse! Why not? Who am I? Pull the puppet's strings - there I am - in Toulouse. New streets full of guilt and 'fuck-off-flic'. Strangers. How can you police strangers? I know you. I can police you - whatever it is I do, can't think just now - but strangers?"

Police us? Know us? Jacques was a statue. The room was too quiet every time Herrisson stopped speaking.

"What do I do, Vermande?"

What do you do? Oh Hell on Earth, talk sense, man.

"I don't know, Monsieur."

Herrisson heaved heavily and fixed Jacques slowly, securely.

"What do you know, Vermande?"

This is it.

"I - "

"I don't know you," he went on before Jacques plunged into confession, "What do you know?"

"Nothing."

"Nothing?" His tone veered towards anger. "You farm, your animals, you know them - ?"

"Yes. Oh, I see..."

"You know there's a storm coming. Don't you?"

"Oh yes..."

"Do you know who's going to win this war?" Eyes like ball-bearings.

"No."

"Germany. Say. Let's say. What about you then?"

"I'd farm."

"And if France won? Ha! If the Americans and the English won..?"

"I'd farm."

"So - you know your future."

"Do I? Oh, yes."

"No. You don't. I know your future."

Jacques aged.

"You're to be called for The Reléve."

"Ohh."

His eyes flew to his mother's door, back to Herrisson. "Not the gu... Ohh."

"To go to work in Germany."

"Yes."

"You're to be called to volunteer. I'm going to call. On you. To volunteer."

"But - " Jacques' mind stalled like his plough in bedrock.

"When?" asked Simone.

"Tomorrow."

"Ohh." Jacques sat, fell, onto his bench. His glass spilled. Herrisson looked at the wine, poured enough to replace what Jacques had spilled and then re-corked the bottle.

"Black market. Chibret gave it me. Thinks he's bribing me. He's no idea what for - just thinks he ought to. Good form. Black Market, blackmail. So I won't report him. Who would I report him to? The SS?"

He turned to Jacques, the ashen stone-man.

"Ever met one? An SS? I have. Incomplete. No heart. Should've killed it. At birth."

Simone saw Jacques leaving and her left with his mother and her dying for sure and then what? Her, left in their house?

"The ultimate Policeman. All your worst nightmares in a leather coat. Vile."

Jacques tried to speak. "My mother..."

"Your mother? Ah! Yes, tomorrow..."

A silence.

"If I refuse?" Jacques dared to splutter.

"You won't refuse. You won't be here. You'll be out."

"Out?"

"Be out, Jacques. I'll call at two. Be away."

A new silence.

"On your file, in triplicate, it will read 'Unlocated.' Not 'Resister.' O.K? My Duty will be done, seen to be done. And my conscience? Well, that rotted away years ago. Pickled by Chibret's bribes."

"Not so, monsieur," said Simone, warmly.

"Oh, sweet. But this is a good day. A French day. I have other days, bad days, German days. Can't stop being a policeman; can't cut the strings."

Jacques body unknotted enough to think - he wants nothing. He's a Saint. He's ignorant. He knows nothing. He needed a cigarette.

"Arbel now. Can't give him this." He pocketed his bottle. "He'd drink it! No notion of taste. Lunatic."

He rose and Jacques wanted him to stay - now he was human.

"And Dominique Duthileul?" Simone asked.

Herrisson raised an eyebrow at her.

"Bold, Mademoiselle, bold." He gathered his hat. "None of your business I should say."

"No, it's not. Exactly."

"No such thing as an even playing field."

"I know."

"Could make you ashamed if you thought about it. Night."

"Thank you, Monsieur, thank you." Jacques wrung the hands; cold, damp, sweaty - or were those his?

"There's no safety, Vermande. The world is ill."

And he was gone.

The door closed.

They looked at each other. Younger and older. He blushed, grinned, giggled and she laughed and he laughed and they stifled it and it burst through their fingers.

"I thought..." Jacques couldn't speak, shook his head, and just laughed.

"I could hear you thinking!"

"What? What!" His mother called.

He flung her door open. She blinked in the light and saw two silhouettes, laughing.

"I'm not going, Mother. Germany. I'm not going."

He danced a daft jig and Simone laughed.

"Not yet."

"God! Be happy, Mother! Herrisson called, I'm not going. I'll be here. We'll be here. Together. Duty IS good - and mine is to you."

At Arbel's table Herrisson's tone hardened.

"I'll go," Arbel said, again.

"You won't. If I find you here tomorrow, I'll arrest you."

"For what?"

"Oh, I'll think of something Arbel - I'm the law. Drunk and disorderly, deserting your wife? I'll arrest you and you'll eat my left-overs for a week. Mule-headed goat. You can go when it becomes Law and it will, Ardelle. Till then - you can be a husband."

Arbel opened his mouth.

"Shut up, Arbel. Or I'll thump you. Ignorance isn't charming. It's lazy. Damned peasant. Don't you dare take easy choices. You can damn well stay here with the rest of us and think and struggle. Bloody cheat!" He rose, angry. "Be out, Arbel, or be very cold for a week."

Arbel dutifully froze for a week.

Ardelle too, and everyone recognised a reprieve when they heard about it.

And on the eighth night as Arbel and Ardelle held each other again, Montgomery finally launched his attack at the pride of Germany.

His mother ate enough to keep his caring and the girl's threat to leave at arm's length. She and Simone sat a different kind of silent afternoon together. Simone sewed, the mother watched. Soon.

This child is ready. Soon.

Still the orphan didn't come. Jacques dug manure into the vegetables and laid straw to protect the plants from the coming frosts. So did Sara, and Madame Lacaze, Duthileul, Feyt, the fat Mayor in Aurilliac, the prefect in the Auvergne, and every gardener and every farmer in the Northern Hemisphere, whichever side of this war they were on. His swallows went south. The robins would arrive soon.

Montgomery shelled Rommel for a week, day and night.

Jacques and Simone waited. Nothing. Curé Phillipe's eyes avoided hers and her dread of Collaborators re-surfaced. The Curé? Possible.

Phillipe talked. Jerome and the men listened.

"Hitler cannot beat Russia. Napoleon couldn't. So, this war must turn because History demands it. And we are answering History's demands on us. We refuse. And our refusal will allow us to look at a Russian, a British, or an American soldier without shame. Perhaps this is absurd, but only by such absurdities can we retain and restore our dignity as men. Our ideals must be Liberty, Justice and Peace. And those who put Peace first often wind up as collaborators. The times that are coming will be hard."

After ten days and nights of shelling Montgomery drove a hole two miles wide in Rommel's belief and the Seventh Armoured Division and the New Zealand Division poured through and the tide of the war changed. Any tidal takes Time to wash up around the world and that much longer to roll up foothills three hundred kilometres inland.

When Jacques answered the door there was a woman he'd never seen before. She gave him a tiny case and the hand of a small boy. "Here. Luther. Good luck." And she turned to go.

"How long for?"

"I don't know." She turned to go.

"When will they come?"

"Who? I don't know. Good luck." And she was gone.

The child stood. Boots, no socks, short trousers, jacket, eight year-old eyes swollen with memories.

"Hungry?" Simone smiled.

A nod.

"Stupid question?"

A smaller nod.

"No more questions. Not tonight?"

A warmer nod.

When he slept Jacques asked, "How do we get him to Souceyrac?"

Rommel counter-attacked, failed, fell back, and retreated. Two nights later, as a freak desert rainstorm halted the Allies' hounding of their prey, Simone waited for twilight and then crossed Duthileul's barbed wire and his big fields, avoiding the village curtains, and came on Madame Lacaze's door from the Roc road. She knocked and heard someone. She knocked again. The door opened.

"Madame Lacaze? My name is Simone."

"I know."

"I want to ask you something."

"Money?"

"Yes..."

"For my son?"

"No."

"Half a truth is better than none."

Simone looked up the road, looked at St.Cirgues. Licked her lips and looked back at the woman. At her thin mouth.

"I want money for children. Jewish children."

A beat.

"Souceyrac?"

"Yes."

"Why should I?"

"I can't answer that. But as you know about the escape route you must know why you haven't given." A beat. "Or perhaps you have?"

Nothing changed on Madame Lacaze's face, nor in her eyes.

"Why should I trust you? With my money?"

"Don't. I wouldn't."

"No?"

"Of course not. Only come and see the child, please."

The desert rain lifted. Rommel ran, and the news reached the Café Tabac. Sara kissed her husband on the mouth, licked his pastis from her lips, put his hands over their child and said, "Don't. Speak. Don't."

The café was full and the village listened as Premier Laval promised France that the Bosche, their protectors, would turn at Tobruk and defeat the English once and for all; those same English who had run like rats from Dunkerque.

The next night the clouds were high and Madame Lacaze walked. Those in the village who noticed assumed she must be going to talk money with Duthileul but why walk; why not drive, why not dig her car out? And why talk money? Because money talks to itself, of course.

She stood with them in the oil-lamp light of the barn and Luther was impeccable in the peace of sleep. She walked back without having said a word, stood in front of the crucifix in her garden and waited.

The Allies landed in French North Africa to trap the retreating Germans and drive them from the continent. They expected no resistance, but the French army, loyal to Petain and Vichy, fought the Americans and the English, and the press and the radio celebrated their heroism. Premier Laval called for the way to German Victory to be upheld. The radio replaced conversation and in every commune tensions bulged.

Her car was seen driving to Puech. People sat by their curtains to await her return, but the car took a back road through Gorses to Souceyrac with Simone and Luther on the floor all the way there and Simone on the floor all the way back.
"Good night."
"Good night, Madame."
"Don't tell my son."
"What has he done to you?"
"He doubts me. Don't tell him."
Simone didn't mention money. None of her business anyway.

To the Allies' horror the Vichy French Army continued to fight. According to the plan General Giraud should have stopped the fighting. When he failed to do so the Americans did a deal with Admiral Darlan, in Africa at his sick son's bed-side, and he took command and ordered a cease-fire. Darlan was Vichy's man.
De Gaulle wrote to Roosevelt.
"I understand the United States buys the treachery of Traitors, if this appears profitable, but payment must not be made against the

honour of France."

Phillipe's anger, too, was calm.

"Our allies trade with Vichy. Pragmatism, not honour, is the rule. But all things must pass. These are the death-rites of disgrace."

Laval was incensed. On Sunday radio, with the congregation of the nation gathered to hear, he damned Darlan for failing to do his Duty. The cease-fire was a felony. From this moment he took command of the French Armies. He re-issued his order to fight the English and the Imperialist Americans and to make the way clear for the Forces of the Axe.

"Who was that?" Ardelle asked when the music began again.

"Prime Minister." Arbel had respect in his voice.

"Ours?"

"Theirs," Jerome nodded over his shoulder, "The Gathering Swine."

"Who's ours then?" Ardelle asked.

"De Gaulle." He said it softly.

The air stilled. Jacques looked to see if they'd been heard.

"Oh. And where's he then?" Ardelle asked the table.

"London." Jerome answered.

"England!"

"Shh!" Arbel and Sara were too slow.

"What's he doing in England?"

"Shut up, woman!"

"What about England?" A voice from the bar. They froze.

"It's cold," called Jerome.

"Murderers."

There was a silence.

"Does he mean Jeanne D'Arc?" Arbel winked at them.

They all heard a chair scrape along the floor.

"El Kebir is what I mean."

It was Galtier, the postman. He came out and his cold watery eyes

fixed Arbel. "Remember Silvane, my son? Uh? Good player, eh? Quick, brave. Remember?"

"I remember the funeral."

"Exactly. 1940. Died when his ship sank. Died when his ship sank in harbour. Died when the English sank his ship in harbour! Allies they call themselves!" He spat. Sara's hand tightened on Jerome's arm. Simone took the man in. Gnarled at forty-five.

"Eighteen he was..."

"War is cruel." Jerome said kindly.

"Is it? How cruel is it Lacaze? Mers-el-Kebir, June 1940. How many French sailors died? Under English fire? Guess!"

"Twelve hundred."

"Twelve hundred is correct. And should I trust the English now? Trust Churchill now? Churchill's orders killed my son. Should I trust him now, eh, Lacaze?"

Sara's nails dug into Jerome's arm.

"Eh? Vermande?"

"Do you trust the Bosche?" Jacques heard himself say.

"They didn't kill my son." Galtier turned, surprised, on Vermande. "Killed my father." Jacques gestured to Simone. "Killed her father and mother."

"Didn't kill my son." His eyes wandered, weakening. "English killed my son."

Arbel lowered his eyes.

Someone moved in the bar. The moment was passing.

"No honour for him. Not even killed in action. That's the English." He turned back towards the bar.

"All honour to him," said Jerome, "he was prepared to die for France."

"Like you, Lacaze?"

There was a silence. Don't speak, Jerome...

"Yes."

"Then you're the fool they all say you are. It's over. The Bosche rule Europe."

"Not while I live." Jerome's neck grew scarlet.

"Ohh! Go on, then!" Galtier snarled. "Go on then, fight! Join! Who would you join, Lacaze? Let's all guess."

"The French."

"Which French?"

"The Free French. France Combattante."

"The Terrorists? The traitors?"

"Patriots."

"Traitors! Herrisson, arrest him! No, don't. Go on then, Lacaze - fight. You're a big stupid strong lad. Fight the Germans. They're in Africa. Or you could walk North, find yourself a Hun. Paris is full of 'em. Go on. No? No - you're sitting here, drinking and waiting, aren't you? What are you waiting for? Uh? Shall I tell you? A call-up. Oh yes. A call-up is necessary for Lacaze. Something to rebel against. Not something to stand up for. Where is your free-will, Lacaze? Go on - go and kill his father's killers. Do it because you believe. Eh?"

Jerome froze in shame.

Into the silence Simone said, "And will you fight to kill your son's killers?"

"Stranger." The word spat.

"You mean, no?" Her tone was even and even gentle.

"Stranger."

"I wonder if you won't wait for a winner and then ride home."

"My grief is real. Whore-bitch."

Arbel, Jacques and Jerome all stood and Herrisson appeared at Galtier's elbow.

"Foreigner."

"I'm French."

"Foreigner."

She sat back and her eyes dropped and Galtier stood ten long seconds more looking at them and then went inside. The bar absorbed him silently and Herrisson fitted a glass into his hand.

"Hitler will drive you back," he called, "you and De Gaulle and the Americans."

But Hitler read the writing on the African wall and in order to cover the now vulnerable Southern coast of the Mediterranean he swept into Free France, trampling Vichy's credibility to scraps of shit, stormed down to Toulon, too late to stop French Admirals from scuttling their fleet.

And in the mother's room that night she heard the sound of the German Army, the roll of the wheels, the clatter of the tanks, the symphony of invasion; and she lay and called their horror on, and when they passed her window she leapt aboard and Jacques found only her body next morning.

six

IT RAINED, OF COURSE.

Curé Phillipe, like all but one of his thin congregation, hadn't known Jacques' mother well enough to be able to speak of her, so he spoke of Christ and His sufferings and how Jacques could take comfort from them. He clipped the longer prayers to their nub, but only the pious noticed, and, it proving their piety, approved. Simone wondered if Christ would have talked about himself, but shook the thought away.

Arbel and Jerome, Ebro and Jean-Francois took a corner each of the cheap box and Simone turned Jacques to lead the few mourners into the rain. They walked behind him, the men with their caps in their hands, the women paired under their umbrellas.

The dripping procession stopped at her plot, where what had been brought back of her husband waited for her.

Some flowers were put in his hand and then taken and placed on the box and Arbel and Jerome were straddling the hole, lowering the box, laying her flat. It made sense she be laid flat. To rest. To sleep.

"Good-bye, Mamman," and the words took gulps of oxygen to say. A hand on his wrist encouraged him to cry for her waste, her grief, her happiness now, and for his aloneness - and he wiped his dripping face on his wet sleeve and started to roll a cigarette but the rain washed it from his hands and into the mud. The hand turned him now and he followed, happy to be led. People he passed nodded. He caught the habit and nodded back.

"Where are we going?"

"For a drink," said Jerome.

"Oh." Then, "The cows..."

"Done," Arbel said, "all done."

"I can't think."

"Don't."

Simone squeezed at his arm.

Respect removed the caps and berets of the old ones gathered in the bar, and raised them to their feet. Respect not especially for her, but for motherhood and death. They watched him led to a table and a cognac fitted into his fist.

Everyone he knew crammed into that bar. Any excuse for community.

All of them thinking "Him and her, now..."

It took half an hour for the first laughter. Sara. Eight months huge now.

Jerome shushed her. Arbel bought another bottle.

"What's the joke?" Jacques stared at his glass.

"This lot," she said, "waiting for you to go so they can talk about you."

"And Simone."

"Yes."

"They can wait." Jerome said.

"They will." Arbel re-filled their glasses. "To her."

"Mamman," said Jacques and sloshed the drink down.

He couldn't think. He daren't think. There was only one thing to think about.

"Simone?"

"I'm here."

"We're orphans."

"Yes."

A cigarette was lit and fitted into his fist. The smoke rose straight. The bar waited, a thin mutter.

"Jacques?"

"Jerome?"

"What was her name?"

Jacques looked up at his friend.

"Denise."

The bar silenced. Who'd remembered, who hadn't, who'd never known, who'd never known her, who didn't care. The rain fell outside.

"To Denise," Jerome raised his glass. "Bon voyage and bon courage."

The bar shifted with his atheistic piffle but said nothing. Just warmed itself from the inside. Pastis, gut-rot red wine - whatever. It was November 1942, and the commune was happy to use whatever excuse culture defines to drink together. Baptism, Christmas, an invasion, a funeral.

Another drink, a pastis now, was pressed into his hand.

He looked up. Allibert, round now and white-haired, his old headmaster.

"Thank you, sir."

"To her past and your future, Vermande."

"Thank you sir. Where's my dog?"

"Home," said someone, gently.

Home.

Without her.

With Simone. If...

He poured the hot pastis down his throat.

"If I felt every moment - like this - I'd be dead, too."

He's talking. Let him talk.

"To live so long in grief. That's to die."

"She was tired," Ardelle said.

"She was mine."

The bar fell silent again.

"I want to see her."

He stood and felt an arm on each shoulder, another at his elbow and then someone stood close and wrapped both arms around him.

"Close your eyes." Jerome. "Now - look - you can see her smiling. I can see her smiling. Leave her be, Jacques."

"The cows..."

"Done," said Arbel, gently.

"She'll be hungry. She'll be worried."

"She isn't." said Simone.

He looked at her. "Shall we - will you - can we go home?"

"If you wish, yes please."

The bar gathered itself to be relieved.

Hands on hats, glasses on the tables. The Curé pushed through to him.

"Her work was done, Jacques." A nod. "Yours isn't. God still has work for you to do." A nod. "May He go with you always."

"Thank you, yes."

Chibret took the hand the Curé dropped.

"For the best, Jacques. For the best."

"For the best?"

"You know..." His eyes tried to lift Jacques', fixed on his waistcoat.

  THE SINGLE SOLDIER

"All for the best. Really and truly. Anything you need - now - ask."

"Thank you."

As he lurched into the fresh wet air Duthileul appeared.

"I'll drive you back."

"No. I'll walk."

"He needs the air," said Simone, "Thank you."

"You'll be drowned."

"No-o." Jacques looked at him, "We'll be wet."

The café waited a whole three minutes before a game of belotte began.

They passed the cemetery.

"Mine. Mine."

Simone waited.

He stopped walking - there was nowhere in this wet world to go without knowing.

"Will you stay?"

She stood, drenched, in the lane. "If I may."

Snot and joy and remorse exploded into his mouth, his nose, and his stomach heaved alcohol past his clenched teeth and he fell over his locked knees, her hand on his back till it was done.

"More?"

"No." He wiped the yard of spittle away. "No, done."

He straightened.

Rain.

What had she said? Had she said?

"You'll stay?"

She smiled, yes.

Jacques Vermande laughed.

Duthileul had to brake hard to avoid hitting the bereaved son, laughing. His mother in the back was thrown to the floor. Jacques laughed.

"You'll stay?"

"Yes."

They took their first steps homeward.

"But…"

"Fuck what is thought, Jacques. Life's too short and definitely getting shorter." She seemed like a rock of certainty. "You know that."

"I don't know what I know."

"No. So, let's go home and light a fire."

They came up the steps, the dog barking welcome home. As he opened the door to a home without his mother he let her misery and grief and pain pass him and out of the door and into the rain to be washed into his earth; he had grieved enough for her when she was alive. Simone moved to the fire and he watched the back of her, bending.

"Jacques, take those clothes off - get us some blankets, something. Where are the matches?"

They began this new dance - this pas de deux.

He lay awake much of that night feeling his guilty way around his excitement. Simone wondered how long this next life could last.

🐑

"You bastard! Oh, you big-boned Bolshevik bastard!"

"Fine, Sara, you're doing fine." Chayriguet smiled at her mother, all pursed lips and concentration. "Really, all you need in this game is patience. A cup of coffee, madam?"

She bustled around Jerome, banished in the kitchen, listening.

"Ohh, here he comes again - ohhh you big shit, you fat shit, ohh,

get out of me!"

"Fine, that's good."

Eight hours later Sara's obscenities climaxed into purple and bloodied perfection - their daughter. Jerome was allowed in now to wonder at the wonder and heard himself think, "I've made something." And he thought of his mother and how she would have preferred child and Sara to have died.

No.

No. I don't know that...

In bed that night, their child in the crook of Sara's arm, Jerome Lacaze stared at the knots in the ceiling oak as though the answers of the centuries might unfurl from there and wisdom and peace, fulfillment and eternity would be visited on him.

On them.

St.Cirgues tutted.

Simone hadn't left. Shameless. She'll be next with calf - in a month - good luck to them.

No-one would have wanted to believe the truth.

That she waited for him to speak, and he waited for the courage to speak.

Finally, after three days...

"Speak."

"I'm ashamed."

"Why?"

"I wanted this. Her dead. And - just you and me."

"She did too."

"Did you?"

"No."

"What sort of man wants his mother dead?"

I can't answer that, she thought. Not out loud.

"I wanted this. You. And me. I wished for this."

"Yes. You said." She waited. "And..?"

"I'm glad."

He'd said it.

And she smiled. "Good for you, Jacques. Good for saying."

The church, bare for Denise's funeral, was packed for the christening. There were true stories that Sara had said the child was to be called Hazel and both the Curé and her mother had refused to allow the child to be named after "a bloody nut" and so Sara had had her way - the babe was baptised Zoe. She carried the child from the font to Madame Lacaze who kissed the crying life and almost smiled at Sara but forced her eyes back to the altar. Jerome stiffened and Arbel punched his arm.

"Grow up, you prat," he whispered in God's hearing.

"Red hair, red heart!" Jerome was tanked.

"Red arse!" The men guffawed with Valet. "Like father like daughter - full of red shit! Laval's got a Christmas present for you, Lacaze. A christening present, sorry." The men cackled. "S.T.O."

Service Travail Obligatoire.

Ardelle's heart quailed. This time Arbel would go. Obligatoire.

"De Gaulle's got something for you..."

"De Gaulle! The runaway?"

"That pompous streak of piss?"

"What's he got? Apart from an English microphone?"

"He's got the soul of France - and you are the arse-holes of France."

"Hark at the atheist - in church one week to be married, another for a christening! Your beliefs are hard to believe Lacaze!" More cackling.

"Husband - shut your mouth, please." Sara jiggled the swaddled life. "And drink to our child."

"Or?" Jerome blustered. "Or what?"

"We'll take you for more of a fool," said Arbel, "than we usually do."

"Coming from you..." Jerome turned to launch into Arbel.

"Shut up, Jerome."

"Ahh, the noble Vermande." His attention swung to Jacques. "I'm a father, Jacques. Me! This idiot."

"We all pity her her father; but like you - she's got Sara."

"Not for long now. No, sir. S.T.O. Eh? Monsieur Valet?"

"Best thing for you!"

"You'd go, wouldn't you? You'd serve The Reich, right?"

"I would. And you will too, come January."

"I will not!"

"Please?" Sara said, "One day's rest?"

Jerome was silenced by her reproach. For a second.

"You love-sick mush, Vermande."

"What?"

"Jacques, you're the cat. Simone's the cream. It's a dream. When you wake it'll be this S.T.O., this war, that knocks you up."

As Jacques' face fell so a childish venom entered Jerome. "Meanwhile - how is paradise?"

"Don't you know?" said Ardelle, "You bloody ought to."

And she toasted the new life.

Their wee table stilled.

The old men sank back into the polished chairs.

Jacques walked down to his beech copse. To think.

S.T.O. Working for Germany in Germany. Guns in the barn. Talk of Germans in Figeac, in St.Céré, approaching their valleys. War coming up the hills. Gestapo in Souceyrac they said.

Pity Mignon.

Pity the German Youth freezing in their ice-grave tanks outside Stalingrad.

Pity the children coming to sleep in the barn.

He looked look back at his house.

His to share with Simone. Theirs.

Till? Till the war separated them. January? This obligatory work?

I won't go. I don't know what I will do but I won't leave her to go there!

He laughed out loud.

I feel better than everyone else in this war at this moment. Someone must feel best; it must have been Hitler once, well, now it's me. It didn't last for him and it won't last for me. It can't, can it? But I am happier than I have ever been before in the whole of my life. God! It is Christmas.

She looked at him over their slow fire.

His eyes had cleared.

I can hardly look at him so happy.

Jerome is right, I'm a living dream. I fell from The War and now we're almost man and wife. And he won't hurt me - not if we were here forever.

And we haven't got forever.

Ardelle clung to the bones of her man, her stomach and chest pressed into his sleeping back. How does he do that? How does he just sleep? Why can't I? I don't want to be alone. Be left alone. I can't.

She punched hard on his shoulder and he grunted and flattened onto his front. She wanted to pummel at him - beat him incapable of leaving - tether him like a goat in a shed - till this S.T.O. passed. "I'm helpless," she cried, turning away from him. She rolled straight back and thumped again and again into his shoulder blades.

"What - what? Ow!" He turned to see her.

"I hate you."

"Oh. Ohh." His eyes closed and he lay flat with the thought. "Right."

The sad shops set up their thin spruces, decorated them with paper presents and offered their customers a plate of cheap boiled sweets.

He moved down from the grenier to his mother's bed. Only the thin wall his grandfather had built against his wife's reproaches between them now.

New Year's Eve dawned cold and they rose and she dusted the whole house, opening all the windows, hanging the bedclothes to freshen in the winter air. He watched.

"Staring?"

"Staring."

Phillipe could smell something in the cut of the German Officers' steps as they strolled around Cahors. They walked tighter. And now they looked around. Nervous, then.

He and Marco Garceau talked in the room behind Marco's bar.

"Virginie?"

"She's fine - your mother?"

"O.K."

"Your thoughts?" Garceau lowered his urgent voice.

"The Ratier Factory in Figeac is making Focke-Wolf parts. Yours?"

"The garrison here?"

Phillipe grinned.

"Good to know we're both mad, then. We need to be an army for

that. We're groups."

"Unite us."

"I'm planning to."

"Good. Target practice on collaborators?"

Phillipe nodded. "For now…"

Garceau lowered his voice further. "How? The Ratier - how?"

"Dynamite."

"Dynamite?"

"That's why I'm here Marco."

"Take me three months, at least."

"And enough so when we start we can sustain it."

"And ride the reprisals?"

Phillipe nodded. "And till then?"

"Train. Train them hard for what's to come."

"They'll need some theatre, too."

"Theatre?"

"Ah oui, theatre."

Marco raised an eyebrow. Phillipe raised one in return.

Garceau said, "I'm finding the RAF. Slowly."

"Drops?"

"When we're organised. Only then. The English and Americans are scared shitless we're all communists."

"Don't tell them we are then."

"I won't."

New Year's night.

Arbel and Ardelle came with a bottle. They drank and listened for the church clock. Ardelle looked from Simone and Jacques and her blurring gaze settled on her husband.

"When it comes…" Ardelle began.

"If…"

"No, Arbel, when," she was drunk enough to insist, "you'll go, won't you?"

"Yes! Drink, woman, drink. This is none of their business."

Ardelle looked at her man. "Ohh. I see..." she said, nodding her head.

"You see what?" Arbel almost snarled.

"That you drink to get to where you can't think."

Arbel said nothing.

"And I," she said, "drink so I can say things I'm too afraid to think sober..."

She nodded her frightened head at this truth. "And there's another difference between us."

Silence.

"And, I'm sorry, Jacques, Simone, but we've - well I've come here so I can say things and he won't silence me like he would in our house."

Arbel, shamed, turned to Jacques. "What about you?"

Ardelle almost laughed. "He won't go!"

"No, I won't. Not willingly."

"Not a hope. Ha!" She turned back to her slouching man. "And what can you hope for when you're full of dread? For a miracle? Ha! All used up."

"Hope for good luck, woman, what else is there?"

"Hell."

This camp was in the hills between Souceyrac and St.Cirgues, a mile off the D road at the Pas D'Aubinies. High point. Clear day - see forever.

On this New Year's Eve as a frost started Phillipe led them 14 miles South-East to the ridge of the hills at Labastide. Through birch and pine forest, frozen fields and muddy fields, barbed wire fences, streams, bogs, great carpets of drying leaves; how do 10 men deal with that silently? They learn. Fast.

Within sight of Labastide they came to a barn. Watertight roof, a haven. They clattered in.

"Ten minutes. Use it well."

They cleaned the hunting rifles and knives, boiled water, made coffee and ate in the ten minutes before red-faced Alain, the butcher's brother from Latronquiere, took the lead. He headed South-West.

"The next safe house. Lavabre. We're invisible, mes gars."

Simone stood on the front step.

Clear. Stars. Wind turning to The North.

Shouldn't they all just run? Now?

Would these Germans be any different from the ones she'd already met? No.

Then why wait? Because I want to live and have my life.

She turned. Jacques looked up.

The Mairie bell tolled faint.

"New Year in now?"

"Yes. 1943."

"May we survive you."

"Everyone," said Ardelle.

"Everyone, yes."

As Ardelle and Arbel faced each other Simone and Jacques touched cheeks, once, twice, three times, their eyes lowered.

"Happy New Year, Jacques."

'May this war never end. Whatever keeps you this near,' he thought whilst he said, "Happy New Year, Simone."

Arbel and Ardelle kissed hard and almost brutal, her hands clawing at his bony shoulders.

"I love you," he said.

"I know. I wish I didn't love you."

Jacques and Simone looked at each other.

Two days later Herrisson cycled to every farm in the commune and ordered the people to gather in the Salle De Fetes that night.

The place was packed like a wedding-day church. A screen had been set up, there was to be a film. Babes in arms, Zoe included, the old men, the young, all the women. Chibret, sweating even in winter, his pinched wife, Jean-Louis and Dominique Duthileul, Madame Lacaze, everyone was sitting, standing, perched somewhere.

A man none of them knew set up the projector machine, the lights were extinguished, there were a few childish screams, mutterings of would it be Charlie Chaplin, and the film crackled into life.

Rain.

Pouring rain. And the camera followed the rain down onto a roof, down the roof to the guttering, along the gutters, down, down the grid into the sewers and into a colony of rats. Big rats. Ugly. Hundreds.

Now one rat, ripping at a dead body dressed in French uniform. The Salle stirred. The rat looked up for a moment, the frame froze and its face slowly changed to an archetypal male Hassidic. Ringlets, the yarmulke, a huge nose. The picture widened and he was seen to be stealing money from the corpse. A German-uniformed paw reached into the frame and stopped his hand.

Now the camera showed rows of such men, sitting, waiting for their noses to be measured by a German civil-servant.

Now a lorry over-full of such men. The camera going close into their faces.

And from that back to the tumbling sewer-rats.

To the water.

To the rain, the sky, some martial music and it was over.

Someone clapped. Once.

In the silence the commune thought of Feyt, though no-one turned to look at him. Might give him away. Who was this projectionist anyway?

A new film began.

A newsreel.

Petain shaking hands with Hitler.

Laval at one elbow, Goering the other.

Now Petain being greeted by ecstatic crowds in Lyon and Simone sat upright, foolishly scanning the ant-crowds.

"What?" Jacques whispered.

"I was there."

Three people turned to look at her.

Now a railway station. Happy young men getting into trains, kissing proud young women good-bye. The station sign. French. Men playing cards on the train. The train arrives at a German station, the Gothic writing. The men get off, shake hands with welcoming German officials. Are shown to lorries.

A factory. A meal-time. Smiling well-fed workers.

Then a clean, airy factory-floor. Men building trains, cars, rifles, clearly proud of their work. The same men now relaxing, playing cards, chess. Music, martial and positive, played.

Now Laval, seated behind a desk, working. A picture on the wall behind him of Petain and Hitler. Sara's hand almost drew blood through Jerome's coat so fiercely did she forbid him to speak. He turned to Ardelle.

"Laval, Ardelle."

"Looks like a pig."

"Voilà."

The film went back to the men, now getting ready for bed, each

with a wash-stand next his single bed. Lying on their beds, writing letters home.

Now here was Marechal Petain himself, addressing the camera.

All men of working age were to report, in one week's time, for work in Germany, where as they had seen they would be fed, clothed and housed and paid for their noble contribution to the new Europe in which France was Germany's honoured partner.

S.T.O. Service Travail Obligatoire.

It would be hard for the women left behind he understood that, but this was one of the last necessary sacrifices to ensure the defeat of the twin powers of Bolshevism and English/American colonialism.

Petain reminded them all, and himself, of their duty to France, their beautiful France and closed by wishing them all a successful conclusion to all their shared troubles in the New Year. The film ended with the Tricolour and La Marseillaise and Herrisson stood and so did the commune.

As the last bars played their flag changed to the swastika.

The lights were turned on.

People stood, silent.

The projectionist began to pack away his equipment.

Chibret went to the door, to shake hands.

He would stay and do the German's office work.

The commune shuffled into the streets.

All the men looked at each other, as if printing faces in their memories.

There was nothing to be said. There was only choice.

Duthileul and his son drove home. The Marechal might well believe what he had been saying, but he, Jean-Louis Duthileul, would be a fool to do so. Obligatory? Duthileul had heard the tide of The War turn. Now it was a gambler's game. All he had to do

was pick the right horse and protect his own.

Jerome kissed his daughter and his wife and her mother and went to the camp, at least until this call passed. Ardelle and Arbel walked home, her three silent paces behind him. Simone and Jacques, silent, ten yards adrift. January 1943.

Simone watched Jacques. What will he do?

The Time left with Simone is this.

One week.

What do I do? Hide? How? Where?

Go? Leave her willingly? No, never.

Join Jerome? That's not me.

Leave her with the farm? That's mad.

Then what, fool?

He found no answer in the days and woke having found nothing in sleep. He spent two days pointlessly turning over the rock-like earth where raspberries and strawberries might be planted, because it was so hard it distracted him.

The German Commandant in Cahors took a phone-call; it was the Mayor of Cardiallac. His village was surrounded by Maquisards, shooting from the hills, approaching fast.

Within forty minutes the astonished Mayor and his Mairie were surrounded by heavily armed German soldiers and officers. Clearly telling the truth, he denied all knowledge of everything, assuring them the commune of Cardiallac was Maquis-free, and they were all the victims of a hoax; but what a boon for the commune to know their protectors were so vigilant. A million thanks for your trouble. The Germans scoured the village, cheerfully terrifying, and, suspicious, left.

Half an hour later, in their best attempts at uniform and behind

Jerome bursting with pride with the Tricolour in his hands, Phillipe marched three groups, 58 men, into and around the village to the Monument to the dead of the First War. When the commune had gathered they sang La Marseillaise, tears everywhere, and Phillipe thanked them for their support, suggested their only obligation was to France, and marched the men away.

A little coup de théatre.

Simone waited four days, watching Jacques' silence and fear solidify, and then went to see Herrisson.

"Mademoiselle?"

"How does Jacques avoid it?"

"Why should he?"

"What's the point? His farm will rot."

"You'll run it."

"I won't."

"Then, yes it will rot."

"How does he avoid it?"

"What do you think I can do?"

"That's what I'm asking you."

"What are you telling me?"

"That I will do whatever I could."

"Whatever?"

"Yes."

The afternoon Madame Herrisson went to her mother Simone and Herrisson spent in bed. It was good for no-one but Jacques.

"Can I spank you?" the breathless policeman asked.

"No."

And he pumped disappointed onwards, her hands round his broad hairy back, her legs wide, trying not to touch him; till he came, when she held him like a child.

For Jacques and Ardelle the week had run laughing by. Galloping, devouring, that heartless, oblivious, bastard - Time.

Each passing meal and hour and minute he wondered so hard why he still did nothing - why he came to no decision - why he couldn't think - why he waited for a miracle; and suddenly the truck was coming up the lane to Puech.

And Ardelle screaming.

Jacques simply froze.

Too late to decide. Too late to run. Too late to hope.

Simone, breathing so shallow, waited for the truck to pass.

It stopped. Footsteps. The dog barking.

Herrisson at the door latch. You had to jiggle it just so.

Simone, cold round her heart, opened it and Herrisson nodded and took Jacques' arm.

"Why?" was all he could stupidly offer.

"Say 'au revoir', Vermande."

Simone had not taken her eyes from Herrisson, who looked blankly at her.

"Mademoiselle?"

"How is your wife?"

"Fine. Do you want to say 'au revoir'?"

Simone put her arms around his neck, kissed him on both cheeks and then hard on his mouth and he was taken to the transport.

He was gone.

She was gone.

Home, dreams, everything. That happiness, that Christmas joy, rubble.

Simone stood.

Alone. The dog looked at her for an explanation.

Would she tell Madame Herrisson? Oh, yes. She would take revenge for Jacques.

But to have slept with that man for Jacques' sake and not to have slept with Jacques..?

And now what?

I don't know. Cold fear lay in her. Empty.

At Maurs station the men answered their names on the huge lists the Germans had and went to join a train.

Jacques, numb, looked at his first ever German. Younger than him. He signed against his name, officially now in Germany, and as he moved down the platform looking for Arbel, Herrisson took his elbow.

"Come with me, Vermande," he said, loudly, officiously.

He walked Jacques to the head of the train, jumped them both down in front of it, crossed the tracks and pointed to the bicycle against the wire fence.

"Leave it in your barn."

Jacques cycled home. When he got there he saw Dominique Duthileul. It had cost his father dear – but of course he had paid. False papers. T.B. Too weak to go.

Simone heard footsteps.

She ran to the door and raced the dog to be first to touch him. She almost knocked them both down the steps as she hugged him home.

"Herrisson," said Jacques.

"Good," she said. "Soup?"

His body hummed with the touch of her arms, her chest.

"Why? How?"

"Ask him."

"Why?"

"Exactly," she smiled and he smiled too.

Simone forgot about Herrisson.

But the kiss and the hug remained alive in him and in the house.

And the thought that she had made love for him and not with him.

St.Cirgues, stripped of its young men, pieced together a reasonably correct version of why and how Vermande and Dominique Duthileul stayed. Duthileul was easy and, they said, the first time he'd ever used money well. But the village that had nominally grieved with Jacques now resented him for his escape and for his whore.

Only Mignon was glad. Rotting farmlands and increasing demands were his new nightmare. He had been spared the STO but it was a delay against his assassination and he knew that. Unless The Germans won. He had to hope for that. God.

Laval issued an order that all guns, including men's favourite and precious hunting rifles, some of them, he knew, family heirlooms, were to be handed over, lest they fall into terrorist hands. And all ammunition. Anyone found possessing either after Mignon and Herrisson called would be suspected of Resistance support and arrested. Herrisson and Mignon gathered three ancient double-barreled rifles and some useless shot.

Both Herrisson and Mignon were on the lists Phillipe's men compiled. In the barns and camps they endlessly moved between. Learning their terrain, building the chain of safety. Jacques' included. Jerome came one night and asked and for two nights ten men slept with the cows, and spent the days learning the terrain around Puech. He fed them what they could spare and was glad to do it. And the next time a month later. They didn't ask about the guns and Jacques didn't mention them.

Fred, the school chef, was charged by Phillipe with organising a constant supply of food for an indefinite period at no cost and

with no trail of information leaking behind it.

"Ah, the easy job?"

After that first S.T.O. round-up his task eased. More were prepared to give. And should they refuse they were to understand their names went on a list. To be judged implacably. When the time came.

Laval legalised, named and uniformed the collaborators. The Milice. That made the vermin easier to spot.

Pierre the bank-clerk forged papers so Phillipe could travel the canton legally as a junior official in the department of Lotoise transport, but it had to be stamped and approved. Laur Garceau walked into the German battalion headquarters in Cahors, promising information, was taken to the Commandant and hurled herself on his desk pleading to be sent to Berlin to be nearer her Fuhrer and was thrown out as a mad-woman; having stolen two stamps from the desk-top. Phillipe made contact with all the other groups, restlessly criss-crossing the department, all through late winter and spring. Talking, arguing, persuading the autonomous units of the necessity of uniting. Real Politics. For some the fear of being branded Communist, others the shame of not being branded Communist. For all the wrench of giving up the little tribe to join a bigger one. To be subsumed, to be less important. To become part of something, Phillipe urged, that would then and only then, have the power and the moral force of a Liberation Army.

He needed them all to have radios, not only for contact to plan the larger actions when that time came, but so they could hear De Gaulle. He was their unifying force. He had Marco in Cahors print and distribute De Gaulle's broadcasts till the radios came. He brought them all word of the setting-up of the C.N.R. - the Council of National Renewal - in Algiers and of De Gaulle's first vow: the promised purge of collaborators. He, Captain Phillipe, understood and totally supported the urge for action against the Germans but he argued that they deal with their own first. Whilst they united. Then The Hun and damn the reprisals, eh?

For the moment - the traitors. Be sure, then eliminate them. Frenchmen.

A civil war in a World war.

seven

ARBEL WAS PLACED in a lime-mine. The Kalkwerke Gruschka in Ludwigsdorf. After a beer each on the first night they were woken at seven, greeted by the Director and his electric "Heil Hitler" salute and put to work. Behind the professional miners at the face. A spade each. Fill wagons. Push the heavy wagons from the lime-face to the factory. There others shovelled it either into paper-bags or in the five metre-high oven.

At mid-day potatoes, a thin meat soup and an hour's rest.

After lunch they swapped jobs and Arbel's team of six were in the giant furnace building, emptying the wagons, feeding the oven. Hard, hot, hideous work. At six work stopped. Arbel registered his first word of German - "Fairhan."

They slept in a communal dormitory on wood beds with a single blanket each, and a tiny cupboard for their possessions. Arbel wrote home.

"There are prisoners here from Italy, Poland, France and the Ukraine. The Ukranians are treated like scum, Ardelle, like slugs. Worse. Dupuy, from Souceyrac, is here and Claude, the boulanger from Latronquiere. Also Jean Landes, from Senaillac. We get Sundays off for Mass and can go to the local village, they say. I'll be fine. You too, please. Arbel."

A first week passed.

Landes was appointed "Vertraussman" - Trusted man.

The work was hard. The tiredness stayed in the muscles, rooted. Rooted ache. The men played cards of an evening. Each nationality separated in the dormitory by language. And they were paid enough to drink on the Sunday. Which they did. Religiously.

Only two Jewish children came that winter as February, dripping and grey, dribbled into March. Simone and Madame Lacaze took them and drove back and had nothing that needed saying. She went to the village once a month with her coupons - Jacques' were cancelled, him being in Germany - for their essentials. When she walked back and saw the house, it was Home.

Arbel went to Mass and the ritual survived German. Outside, the youth of Ludwigsdorf, "Der Jungenfrau", marched and yelled insults at them all, especially the Ukrainians. The woman who ran the little bar Arbel drank in had lost her husband in the 14-18 war, two sons on the Russian front and her third in Africa. In the bar sat another peasant, a German peasant, and the two men recognised enough of each other to nod. The other men urged Arbel to the whore-house but he wouldn't waste his money. Alcohol was a faithful Lover, never disappointed, always offered oblivion. No whore could compete.

At the mine his body adjusted to what he did and what he got. Some stole from the Germans and ate a little better and some sold it and made a little money from their country-men. Who were grateful for any break in the torpor of digging a mine by hand.

Ardelle's first letter arrived after two months. He put it in his little pile of possessions. As she had when his had arrived. The work was the same hell. One day a wagon ran off the line and trapped Landes' ankle. He was taken to the hospital in Gorlitz, the big town, and stayed there for two days. When he returned, clearly refreshed, other men immediately inflicted similar injuries on themselves and got taken to the hospital. That lasted a week. Then a doctor came every Wednesday, saw the injured, issued pills, but there were no more hospital rests. An Italian had his eye burnt out as a pocket of air in the flowery lime popped. He had to wait four days till the doctor came. Landes, as 'Vertraussman' hobbled to the director to complain.

"Weil wir Krig haben," he was told. It's the war.

Two Miliciens; one in Latronquiere, the other in Souceyrac, were isolated, accused and assassinated. Phillipe's men re-gathered at the safe barn in the Black woods and shook hands. They had acted. They had begun. On!

Spring.
Simone lay in bed and behind their thin wall still the man waited. Was he waiting for her? Yes. Was she waiting for him? No, because he won't come. It's my wait. I'm waiting. For what?
Would it be vile? Not possible.
Would she get pregnant? Possible.
What change would it make? He couldn't love me more. It couldn't change this life for the worse. Then why not? Why wait? When tomorrow might not exist.
Yes.
Now?
Yes.

She swung out of her bed and groped in the black to her door, opened it, found the handle to his, turned it and pushed it open. His hard breathing.

Fine. That's correct. You can't decide, Simone. Not if it's not shared.

But the shadow of her action joined the hug and that kiss in the air of their house. Next day they rose and worked and ate and waited for children and none came and the faint spring evening light lingered in the window and the fire twinkled.

She had a book but he sat with his cigarette and said, "You're not reading."

"No, I was thinking."

"Ahh." He smoked.

'Ask me what,' she thought. I want him to recognise this moment. She looked up at him and he did. He had.

He stared.

She looked.

He dropped the cigarette into the grey.

She lay the book on the floor.

They stood.

In her bed he lay trembling as he listened to her peel off the vest and come into his heat. He heard and felt the sheet lift. Now her hand was touching his chest and their naked legs were touching. He shook uncontrollably. He took great breaths to calm himself. She lay her head on his chest and his hand touched her back and he grew huge and they lay for a time like that. The hairs on his chest sensed the shape of her breasts, her thighs sensed his heat and moved nearer him. Their hands moved. New. All new. Slowly down his ribs. The bones of her spine. His tight torso. His hand dared lay on her arse. Now. To his balls to hold her breasts as she

slid her knee across him and they kissed, they kissed while she placed him in the mouth of her and they were together together together together riding one horse one train one him one her one kiss one sex deeper and deeper into each other till she broke away from his mouth and knelt up and took his hands to her breasts.

"What?"

"Milk me, Jacques."

He teased the breasts forward to her nipples, through his fingers as their bodies crashed into each other - the bed the world the noises as animal as they were animal, one moment in eternity one memory one one one one act of love.

He gasped, astonished, gasped.

Gasped.

Gasping.

Tears filled his darkness.

Simone squeezed the him inside her. Locked at the waist they folded together to lie in their beautiful shock. They heard the dog at the door. As their silence grew so did his.

Simone lay on his chest listening to their hearts slowing. And a trickle of her sweat fell luscious into his mouth.

The dog woke them desperate.

The sun two hours past milking. They looked at each other wedded in sweat and sleep and sex.

The night Mussolini fell he walked with her wrapped over and round him naked to the door and stood on the stairs to let the night kiss them. It did.

They farmed and milked and stored and took children to escape and fed the men of the Maquis and Ardelle and summer came in a blaze and one midnight they made love on the grass behind the tomatoes and she knew she was pregnant.

eight

THE ALLIES, dragging the Communist-fearing Roosevelt with them, finally recognised De Gaulle's government in exile. The Italians surrendered and the Germans hastened to secure Rome. Laval could see his execution squad ahead and tightened his bond with Hitler. De Gaulle mounted a putsch against his old comrade Giraud, and ousted him. The R.A.F. dropped The Resistance the weapons Churchill judged his Home Guard no longer needed. They dropped money and of course it corrupted. They dropped agents, too. A Scot, in his kilt, joined a Maquis group near Capdenac and Marco's group in Cahors assimilated an Englishman. A Tommy. His skill was radio and he made them out of anything, it seemed - biscuit tins, old telephones, dead car parts - but they worked and were distributed, bringing the Liberating Army slowly together. Phillipe's group joined a group from Assier, disconnected a truck from a goods train at Figeac, stole the rice, drove it to Lacapelle and distributed it.

This new war was the sharing of every match, every razor-blade, every cup of water; the endless recruiting, the lists of where food and shelter were available, where traitors lived and lurked - the manna of Information. And raids and executions of known collaborators and Milice. Laval called them "terrorists"; and De Gaulle on their radios promised them that they, and only they - the Resistors, the True French - could re-build the New France. And that a New World was coming to the survivors. For now - a purge. And then - a New France - pur et dur.

Now came rumours the Italians were fighting the Germans! And the retreating Hun executed eighty Italian Policemen and twenty civilians for the death of a single German soldier. Bad Losers was the message and it was heard loud and clear across occupied Europe.

Arbel received one of Ardelle's precious letters every two months. Telling him to live. He lived. The work ground on, weakening the men's lungs. The shifts extended by an hour. Lunch became three-quarters of an hour. Sundays he went to Mass and he began to hear the priest's sermon speak of the fraternity between men of all races, all religions. That was the first Arbel had heard of such a concept for four years. Lothar, the peasant he drank and spoke pidgin German with, like a few of the older Germans, treated him with the respect due an equal. It was the marching, screeching uniformed youth, infected with The Party, who were truly chilling. Lothar told him tales of children ratting on their own grand-parents.

Zoe was eight months old when she woke one night to find her father in her mother's bed, making her a sibling.

Duthileul thought about sending money to the Maquis, decided not yet; but appeared one night so he and Dominique were seen to help at a parachute drop at Labastide Haut Mont.

Jacques looked up from his plough as Chayriguet drove into Puech. Duthileul's mother? Ardelle? Find out at lunch.

When Simone told him the world span.

Time took a picture of her, standing with one hand on the table and painted it as deep as Janatou's paradise into the soul of Jacques Vermande.

"Are you happy? Are you sure? To have it? Are you?"

"Yes."

"Oh God. Oh God."

"I thought you might be pleased."

Roaring laughter and joy swept through him and he burst across the space between them to take her in his arms and froze a pace from her knowing he'd crush her and their child.

She took his hand and said, "We've done it now Jacques."

He felt his whole life behind him and everything, everything had been leading only to this.

"When?"

"April - May."

"I can't speak."

"It does that - doesn't it?" She reached for their bowls.

"I'll do that."

"Cut the bread?"

"I'll do that."

They sat and ate. She watched the heaven in him.

"Why has this happened? Why - when others die? I can't..."

"We may all die - who knows? I don't. You don't. You're a good man and we live in insanity. And now we've joined in!"

She laughed and he said, "Does this mean we get married?"

"I hadn't thought of that."

"I don't care, Simone."

"Can we think about that later?"

"Oh, yes."

Phillipe's group, the ten, were eating when a voice called through the quiet dark, close.

"Milice. You are surrounded. Completely."

It was over, then. So briefly.

"Give yourselves up. You have thirty seconds," the voice intoned. "One..."

Phillipe said, surprisingly loud, "Load the bazooka and the stens."

"Already loaded." Bernadie called, quickest to re-act.

"Ten seconds to leave, or be destroyed," Phillipe called, calm.

Silence.

"Nine," said Phillipe.

Some motion.

"Five..."

A scramble. A rout. Men galloping back the way they had come. As Serge stood, laughing, Phillipe hissed, "Tomorrow at Black Woods. This camp is done."

He called, "One!" fired a single precious bullet into the night, and they ran.

Jacques started to do Everything and she stopped him saying, "later" - and later, to his astonishment, they made love and it was possible. More Love. He overwhelmed God with thankfulness, as Ardelle did with her dread. And she privately withheld her judgement on God's mercy till Arbel be delivered home; while her neighbour walked in living proof of His wonder.

Too old for war, Galtier, Valet, Jauliac and Grivault grumbled round the dead bar. Duthileul distanced himself a centimetre more. Sara, pregnant, toiled with Zoe on her back, weeding, sowing, watering. Soon she'd walk. Soon, please. This baby hurt. Chayriguet doctored and Chibret cursed his foolish ambition that six years ago he'd wanted so much to be Mayor he'd walked his wife and her stupid poodle right round the village the Sunday of the Vote. Now no-one much saw his wife, the damned dog was dead and his life was paper. From the Prefect, the canton, the Germans and this damned bloody endless war they were now losing.

"Are we in love?" Jacques turned from his cooking.
"Why?"
"I wanted to know."
"Don't you know what you feel?"
"I want to know what you feel."
"About you? Blessed."
She was cutting bread when, "It moved. It moved!"

The next child on its way to Spain and survival was six, and Jacques and Simone watched him eat, put him in the mother's bed, and wanted to keep him by the time Madame Lacaze came and the women took him on. Madame Lacaze noticed a change in the girl, and, like always, said nothing.

Jerome introduced Jacques to Phillipe, while his men dug up the guns.
"Thank you."
"It's not enough."
"You could join us," said Jerome.
"She's pregnant. Simone." Stupidly he pointed to her, sitting there with them.
"Congratulations," said Phillipe, "you look thrilled."
"I am. Thank you. But I can't fight. My place in this is here."

"You're right - and we're grateful." Phillipe left them in the kitchen.

"Vermande! What a father you'll make!" Jerome enveloped them both in his arms. "Better than me."

"She'll know. Zoe - she'll know you. I'll tell her."

"I'll tell her."

"Well then - I'll tell her the truth."

"What sort of a friend is that?"

"An old one," said Simone. "Wine?"

"Wine? Yes!"

They sat, Simone and Jacques on Arbel's bench, Jerome opposite, shaking his head at them, laughing and wishing Sara was there.

"Not long now, you can feel it. You know Badoglio's ordered The Italians to fight the Kraut?"

"Who's he?"

"New Italian Premier."

Jacques asked, "Won't Hitler surrender?"

"Never. He's mad. Infected with Hate."

"Aren't you, too?" Simone asked gently.

"Yes. I have to be. I don't know how else to do it."

He drained the glass.

"Sara lost the baby. The brother."

"Jerome - no - "

"It was a boy..."

"I'm so sorry, Jerome."

There was a silence.

"Sara?"

"She's Sara," said Jerome. "I want to live to be a proper father. Here's to you three."

He smiled at them.

Arbel dug. Went to Mass. Drank. Played cards with Lothar. Amazed himself with his German. Went back to his bed, slept, woke, dug, ate the thinning rations at lunch and tea-time, played cards with his comrades, slept, woke, dug, ate, worked, ate, slept, woke... He lost Time. He had no need of it.

The September Moon came and Jacques must go to Janatou before the next. He hitched the cart and cow, prepared food, string, scythe, knife and then asked for his wish.

"Will you come?"

"Where?"

"To my paradise."

Something in his smile alarmed her.

"Don't make a saint out of me, Vermande. That's not real."

"You won't come?"

A dark cloud. This man-boy, this soul, I will hurt him so bad one day. But, I promised myself a year ago that I would go. She looked at him and said, "You go. I'll see paradise when all this is over."

When he left she asked the room, "Why didn't you go? I don't get you."

He passed Sara.

Bending as she had since he was thirteen and had first passed her. Only now a daughter sat behind her, chewing at an apple.

"Janatou?"

"Yes."

"Pff."

"I should have come to say sorry."

"I should have come to say congratulations."

At Poutiac the same old one came to his steps, watched him past, went back inside. Jacques turned the beast at the letter-boxes and led them down into the dry copse. He went to the bottom corner

of the field with the scythe and the string. He worked. The cow ate. At lunch he filled a bottle with spring water and sat. This view, this day, September '43.

"I love this place, and I love you, Simone."

When they sat together that evening at Puech he said it again.

"I know. I see. I can feel."

"And marriage?"

"I don't want to, Jacques..."

She waited for his face to fall and ask 'Why not?' and she should have known better for his face never faltered; he simply took her hand and said, "Fine."

"But..."

"Fuck what is thought, Simone. If God can't see us here, He's blind."

There was another call for the S.T.O. Jacques hid in the birch copse, pointlessly, since he was officially in Germany already and Herrisson looked at Simone, saw the bloom on her, thought, "Well, it's not me," and went away and filled in his papers and Chibret stamped them and The Prefect passed them to the German Commandant in Cahors.

Once the meagre harvest was in and stored, or hidden, their needs and priorities changed. Jacques made a tiny cot for their child, Ardelle knitted boots and sleep-suits; Simone bought rough towelling for nappies, Zoe's old clothes arrived with Sara and a carrying basket, a bottle, a rattle and they assembled for their future as Autumn rushed by and Winter approached.

The German battalions in Cahors, in Aurillac, in Figeac, all over Europe and home in their Fatherland pulled their winter coats and belts tighter and their Fuhrer watched "Gone With The Wind" with his mistress. Christmas 1943.

In Ludwigsdorf Arbel was made 'Vertraussman'. Landes' ankle hadn't healed and he was sent to lighter work. Arbel was given a stamped paper to prove his exalted status. At his pleading one Frenchman, an epileptic, was sent home. Another with kidney failure and collapsing poisoned lungs. He didn't make it. As Christmas came The Director called Arbel to see him, presented him with an accordion for the men, gave Arbel and Claude an hour off work on Christmas Eve to erect a huge Christmas tree in the canteen building and on Christmas Day the officers and men of the factory sang German Victory songs at their assembled prisoners. Then gave them all ten Marks and twenty cigarettes each and said they could start next morning at 7.30. That night none of them could coax anything but painful discordant wheezing from the accordion. But two men had stolen three chickens from a nearby farm, so there was something to mark The Saviour's Birth.

On Christmas Day they went to Mass. Their first time since Zoe's christening, since the S.T.O. The congregation gasped at her bare-faced blooming. To bring their bastard into God's house and to take communion and no talk of a wedding, it stretched Christianity to breaking-point. Madame Cantagrel snarled as Curé Phillipe shook their hands and waited for them to ask him to come to discuss and announce the banns, but they did neither. The village was filling with fear and dread. The Rumour was the New Year must bring the Allied invasion, and that re-assured no-one. France was to be invaded, again. At best it would mean The Hun would retreat. At worst they would come here, pass through. The war would come up their hills. They prayed, gratefully distracted by Simone and her stomach. Jacques felt the fear though. And began to think.

Phillipe had contacts with every Maquis Group in the Department and for now he kept them armed and fed, joining them in twos and threes to make the execution raids that kept spirit and purpose high; and to protect each other at the RAF drops. They had safe barns and food stores dotted all over their endless geography, a limited supply of explosives, they had talked and raided and argued and eliminated all that year and with all their differences they were finally a united, if ramshackle, army. Waiting for the call to attack, and clear their land of its weeds.

And there were men named as Milice who were nothing of the sort. Old scores settled under cover of conflict; and almost always for the currency of the peasantry; Land. By no means all honourable men.

As there were Germans who doubted their orders without ever daring to question them, knowing that a leather-coated sadism awaited any wavering.

Arbel wrote.

They came to Ardelle only every three months now, but they proved he survived. He'd been digging and shovelling and bagging lime for nearly a year. Claude, cutting his hair, showed him the first white hair. He was not yet twenty-five. He pared his body to its needs for survival, his soul he washed each Sunday in Mass and cheap wine, and his mind he exercised with German and card-playing with Lothar. And when he left the bar he closed mind and soul down. He would have closed his ears, too; for still the accordion defeated the men, and still they tried.

Ardelle wrote, never knowing whether he received her letters, he never said so. Were they censored, intercepted? She never knew - she simply wrote.

The men of the Maquis snatched what days and hours they dared at home, because the time to leave permanently and fight and die was coming. And vigilance. Vigilance. An incautious group listening to the radio one night were surrounded by a squad of well-armed Miliciens and six died. A weak lad from their group had been tortured for the location of the camp-site. He died too.

Then it snowed. A metre and a half fell in one night, froze, and some of it was still there, in the shade, greying, in April. Too dangerous. Trails. The Maquis war went on white hold.

It snowed in Germany too and with it wind from Siberia. The men fashioned extra make-shift socks out of lime-bag paper. Tacked bits of wood to the bottom of their shoes. Were almost grateful for the shifts near the oven. Almost. The food got worse. No potatoes now. Beetroot and courgettes. They don't fill.

Jacques thought.

"How will it come?"

"The baby?"

"The war."

"When the Germans retreat."

"When will that be?"

"Jacques - what if it comes tomorrow? What then?"

"I - don't know."

"You go to the hills. I stay. You come back when you can."

"You stay? Alone!"

"I can't come with you." She stood there, five months pregnant.

"I'm not going."

"Then you'll be killed defending me."

"Us."

"Like my father."

He pulled on his cigarette.

"Or..."

"Or? Or what?"

"You go." His head was down, eyes on the floor.

"I go," she repeated. "I go where?"

"On the escape route for the children."

A beat of Time.

"I can't."

"I think you must."

"I'm not Jewish, I'm not a child, it's not for me. Us."

"Simone - you are my blood. We pay."

"Pay?"

"Find out next time - find out. They need money. You said so. You take our child in you or in your arms and you give him his life, Simone. That's sacred. Not tomorrow. But when it's Time - you'll go. And until then I'll pray it never comes."

"I'll think about that, please."

Now he looked up at her.

"And if it never comes - what then? Will you stay?"

Another beat.

Simone said, "I see why your Mother said iffing is close to sin."

"Would you stay?"

"Jacques - I didn't want to be pregnant but I'm not sorry I am. You healed me."

She took one hand into hers.

"I dreamt once of A Blazing Love. I've never felt it. But I've felt This Love, and I've healed in it, and this is not that blazing Love. So I've learned Blazing Love is not all Love."

"You love me?"

"I love being loved by you."

"You love me?"

"Yes. You're staring."

"So are you."

"I'm looking, you're gawping."

"You said it. You said 'yes'."

Simone laughed.

"We make Love!" She patted the child. "Beautifully. What's special about words? Does it make it truer?"

"Makes the best memory."

"Better than making love?"

Jacques thought.

"Yes."

"Better than making Love? Better than kissing? Better than naked? Words are better than naked! No. You're mad, mister."

"No, not words. But those words. There's a flame. Now... "

"That's your dreams coming true."

"Yes! Yes. Yes."

"But I'm not a dream, mister. This is not a dream."

"It was a second ago."

"This baby isn't."

"I know. I know."

Silence fell between them.

"How hard can you pray?" she asked.

Silence.

"Not that hard. I already did." he said.

Silence again.

"But you'd stay?"

She looked up. "Of course I would."

Warmer silence.

And another night.

Another night together.

Another New Year's Eve waiting for the church bell to toll. Ardelle come and gone. Another fire. Another fag.

And when they lay in bed.

"Your breasts are bigger."

"Mm."

"Is it nicer? For you? When I..."

"Yes. Is it nicer for you?"

"I like the idea of more of you. I love the idea of more of you."

Simone turned him on his back, took his hands and placed them underneath his head.

"You can't move - you're tied in that position."

And slowly and then in a wonder his mind exploded with her kissing mouth on his chest, his stomach and now kissing him in her.

Gasping.

Wonder-shocked.

Simone lay on his chest.

"Making love hurts now, Jacques. But..."

"Can I do that to you?"

She looked at him.

He said, "You're staring."

"Go on then."

As January crawled snow-bound past their windows Jacques and Simone lived in white peace.

"You have the best of me," one of them said - and the other agreed.

Three men made a break from the factory. One, they later heard, made it back to France but the other two spent three months in a forced labour camp. As 'Vertraussman' Arbel was taken to Gorlitz, to a big building and interrogated all day about what he knew, what he might have encouraged, what his politics were, had been. Half-way through he realised that they would do nothing to him.

He was too good a worker. They needed him. He was sent back.

"I live in a state of shock. Why?"
"Because," she sat up big and grinning in their bed, "I'm here! The fairy at the top of the Christmas Tree. You're blessed, oaf! We both are. It won't last. It'll all be blown away. All change."
"I know that."
"Good."
"I made you a rocking chair."

The war was on ice.

nine

THE GERMANS posted larger units in all the market-towns: Figeac, Maurs, Bagnac, St Céré - all the valley towns and from there they rode up into the hills to sporadically terrorise the villages. They talked with the men of The Milice, identifying them deliberately, publicly, so there could be no possibility of their changing sides. Drank in the bars and went back to their barracks, their bunks and their letters home.

Razor-blades went scarce.

A beard was taken to be a sure sign of a Maquisard and everything and everybody froze till Chibret accepted, at Bernadie's gun-point, that he go to Aurillac to buy blades. He flushed crimson with fear, shame and impotence, buying five in every shop, but he knew this might just save his neck. The men shaved and so Chibret was brought into their web. Blackmail was currency. There was but one rule now - By Whatever Means.

Ardelle gave food, Duthileul gave money, taking care to gain in return information about the RAF drops and even more care to be seen there with his son.

In the village Galtier and Valet were marked to die for their refusal to feed, to help Fred; Jauliac and Grivault watered the wine and cut the meat thinner, Chibret bustled and blustered and Herrisson lived in fear now his move to Toulouse was cancelled. He had done both - he had helped Jacques and turned a blind eye to Feyt but mostly he had obeyed German orders. He thought of joining the men but believed they would kill him on arrival so he waited, and hoped it would pass somehow, somewhere down on the A roads it would all pass by. Madame Lacaze gave money to Fred who kept his end of the bargain, that her son never know.

Phillipe told the men over and over that everyone would be called to account - either at the gates of Heaven if you believed in them - or now, for a Free France and its future. In his opinion the laws of Christianity no longer applied. This was their shared Destiny. Fail it and freeze for eternity.

Marco came through with the explosives. Phillipe picked the best ten from three groups and planned the attack on the Ratier Factory in Figeac.

As far as possible everything had been tested. The bombs and grenades, the bikes, the lorry, the guns and the men.

"We engage the Germans as of tonight. There will be reprisals. But we will fight on now till the end of us or the end of them."

They rode and drove down all four approaches to Figeac - the devices shared should any three be stopped - none were, and they gathered in the hillside facing the Ratier. Two o'clock, no moon.

Two bombs on the railway line into and out of the factory, timed to fire three minutes ahead of six more in the factory walls. At two-fifteen the first bombs of their war worked, and as the night-shift ran out to see, so the factory walls exploded, a whole section of roof fell, fire caught and spread and Phillipe and his men went back home to their camp. No shots were fired, no bullets wasted.

"This next week will be the hardest yet. Reprisals. Then we blow up the Toulouse rail connection."

The local papers and the radio would call for them to be denounced in the name of France. Hollow sound. Falling on deafening ears.

Simone and Jacques woke knowing neither had slept well and that he must move back behind his wall.

He fed the cows the winter feed, took them to mill in the snow-mud mess of his pasture, came home, fed the chickens, lit the fire, made breakfast and looked at her stomach as she sat upright in the chair.

He asked, "What more should I want?"

"What more do you want?"

"What you want. You see more."

"I did."

"What should I see?"

"You ask the stupidest questions. What do you mean - 'should'?"

"What should I see?"

"I don't know!"

"You're cross?"

"You think because I read books I know something. I know nothing."

"No-o. There's something you've seen - you would have been a teacher."

"Don't." Her voice was sharp.

"Why not?"

"It's the past and I won't think about that." Her hands on her stomach.

"I've never had dreams like that."

"It's not a dream. It wasn't..."

"It won't be," he promised.

"You don't know that."

"Yes, I do." Jacques didn't recognise this certainty in his voice, nor

did he know if he liked it. But he went on, "I do. I know. You'll teach, I can see that."

"You can't. No-one can."

The Germans cut the lunch-break to half-an-hour. The food got worse, and less, so the robbing from local farmers increased. Correspondence got scarcer. Arbel sensed the war must be turning. He didn't rationalise, he smelt it as a farmer smells rain a week away.

Another refugee child was delivered and when Simone and Madame Lacaze took him to Souceyrac Simone asked the Curé the price of her escape. She told Jacques and he thought for two long sleepless nights in his mother's bed.

Then he went to see Jean-Louis Duthileul.

"If..." Jacques faltered, standing in the warm kitchen, turning his cap in his hands.

"When."

"Then 'when' - what would you buy?"

Duthileul looked up. The girl was pregnant, what was this?

"I could lend..." he began, but Vermande cut him off.

"I could never re-pay a loan."

"No. Then let me think. How much do you need?"

Like a fool Jacques told him the figure.

Duthileul thought. Waited a day, letting Jacques think, too - and then offered just enough - for Jacques' barn, herd and the three fields.

Jacques tried to think hard and quick.

"Janatou?" he asked.

"Jacques - please..."

"I need to consider."

"Of course. But The Maquis attacked the Ratier Factory in Figeac. There'll be reprisals. Soon there'll be no time to consider."

"I know about time. Don't bully me."

"It's your need, my friend."

"We're neighbours."

"As you wish."

What choice do I have? None. If I were to only sell him the fields - where would my herd go? And if I give him the herd what use are the fields or the barn? And I must have that money. For the choice. Of Life. For them.

Jerome told Sara the news of the Ratier strike as a cause for elation and celebration; but when the village heard they finally understood the horror-rumours from Figeac. That 25 men and women had been executed whilst the old ones played boules in the church square. A lorry had driven up - unloaded twenty people randomly ripped from their breakfast tables and five road-working men the patrol had passed and picked up; the soldiers waited for the game to stop and a crowd to gather - then shot all twenty-five in the stomach and the throat. Left them for Figeac to deal with.

Went back to their barracks.

One German soldier deserted and was welcomed by a Maquis group near Carrenac and he lived out his war killing his own. The rest patrolled the towns, and the vast forested land surrounding them as far as Germany it felt, knowing the invasion battle to come would settle the course of the conflict. And some longed for it, hating the dumb insolent pompous French, Churchill and his damned island fortress, Stalin and his suicidal serfs and Roosevelt and the wretched cowardly Americans; hated the feeble fucking Italians and read avidly the reports of the Japanese - but a world

where Hitler united with Hirohito was for serious dreamers only. And some wished Hitler would stop now; and some wished him assassinated - but all of them followed orders.

There was food and drink, whores, a game of football once or twice, and as the Spring came - well hell - they could have been in Russia, in Africa, Italy. All they had to deal with for the moment were these gnats, groups of gnats in the hills. Fleas.

Tics.

Jerome's group and another from Labastide waited two starlit nights for ammunition from England and on the third night, when the clouds came, so did the planes and the boxes on parachutes. It was gathered and distributed. And some was pilfered to be sold back later to the Maquis themselves, some to the Germans, even. But re-armed, the group provided cover for Charles Arnac's men from Issendouls as they planted three bombs inside the Figeac-Toulouse train tunnel. Two went off as the early morning coal train triggered them and was devastated, the driver and his plate-man killed and as much of the coal as possible was distributed as thanks for food, shelter and support. Everyone knew by lunchtime and everyone waited for the reprisals.

The Germans consulted with The Milice.

And took revenge on an isolated farm near Tauriac. The wife was held to watch as her son, daughter and husband were hung in front of her from the barn roof, then burnt, then the whole farm razed - and she was left hanging outside the smoking wreck. They had been farmers. The Maquisards knew for sure that they hadn't been members of the Maquis - but the point the Germans wished to make spread like malaria. Only contagious.

When Jacques heard he crossed the road again.

"I agree."

"I've written it," Duthileul showed Jacques a paper.

"Why?"

"Because that's the way it's done."

"If my word isn't enough..."

"Fine. Here is your money."

A big roll. String round it. Jacques stalled.

"Do you want to count it?"

"No, I want to wait."

"Vermande," he was almost impatient, "one day soon there won't be time to cross the road and knock on this door. Take it. Bury it - but have it."

"When will you take the barn and the land?"

"Not till it's over. And perhaps you won't use the money. Won't have to use it. I hope not."

"Do you?"

"Yes." He almost snarled the word. Then his tone softened. "For you and her and the child I hope not. For me - I'll buy your land when you shake my hand on the deal."

"Right."

And he took the roll of paper that was his family's future.

And what of me, then? Don't think about that.

Duty. Duty's good.

He buried the money in the caves of the house, wrapping it in muslin. But as he took one last look he thought it looked like cheese. So he wrapped the muslin in an old shirt and tossed it on a pile of old rags down there. No. Finally he put it blatantly in a jar on the mantelpiece. Simone never mentioned it.

At the end of February Arbel saw his first Jewish prisoners. He had thought the Ukranians were badly treated but the state of these men was heart-stopping. They were marched through the town

one Sunday, on their way to somewhere Lothar wouldn't speak about, and the youth of the town hurled hatred and stones at them.

The stream of refugee children began to rush. Another child. Two one night. One March evening Madame Lacaze drove up with Herrisson in his civvies sitting with her.
"You're too far gone. Stay here."

The thaw turned the fields to slush and the men struggled to dry clothes on fires they ought not to build. A group had been attacked by Milice for their camp-fire smoke and three killed.
Valet toasted the terrorist's death and everyone wished he'd shut up. The March rain set in, boots rotted, coats sodden, impatience and discomfort a deadly mix. It was hard everywhere now. Churchill told the English that the hour of greatest effort was at hand. As Hitler had Goebbels tell the German people. De Gaulle told the French the same. So did Captain Phillipe.
He targeted fifteen Miliciens across the department and one night fifteen executions were committed and fifteen uniforms taken. Next morning, as The Milicien of Latronquiere, he called the Germans saying the village was under attack from the Maquis. He and his group stood in the woods bordering the road into the village to wait and watch. A battalion - 30 of them came down the road in three sidecars and a lorry and piled into the village - the astonished Mayor denying everything and while the German investigation went on Phillipe's men hacked down a lime tree across the first sharp corner out of the village and waited. The Germans returned, rounded the corner and ploughed into the tree. They killed six, set one side-car ablaze, had no casualties, and left.
A week later the trap was repeated near the village of Senaillac

and four more Germans killed and after that no-one could call the Germans for help - they wouldn't come - and The Resistance could press the Mayors for clothes and food and shelter. Breathing space.

The days lengthened, and the garden and their child grew. Simone bore her back-ache better than Jacques' attentiveness.

"I'm not an invalid, I'm pregnant."

"Sorry."

"And stop saying that - just let me cook till I tell you I don't want to - or can't."

"O.K. Sorry."

"Oh, shut up - stupid caring fool."

Then came a day Jerome had both longed for and dreaded.

"St.Cirgues," said Phillipe. "Milice?"

"None that I know of," said Jerome.

"Valet! Galtier. Duthileul?" Bernadie spat. He'd been Mayor of Senaillac, St.Cirgues' neighbouring commune. "Herrisson, Chibret, Mignon - collaborators all."

"Lacaze?" Phillipe looked at him.

"It's true of Valet. Galtier just hates. Mignon's a coward..."

"Doing Germany's work."

"Yes."

"And Herrisson?"

"I know he's helped some people."

"For sex - the shit," said Bernadie.

"Oh, yes?"

"So," said Phillipe, "Herrisson, Mignon, Valet. Duthileul?"

"Gives money," Bernadie again, a concrete block of man, "money he can afford - he's a chancer."

"Ask your friend Vermande."

"I will."

"Chibret?"

"A puppet."

"Whose strings?"

"Whoever's."

"If we kill the Mayor, the Gendarme and the requisitioning officer," said Jerome, "what state will the village be in?"

"Rejoicing," said Bernadie.

"Chaos," said Jerome.

"Good," said Phillipe, "out of chaos comes the new order. Tonight." Jerome had disliked these men all his life. He supported their execution - but he saw their wives' eyes - and he saw his mother's eyes and Sara's and what if revenge was foisted on Sara and Zoe?

"I want to be a part of this," he said to Bernadie.

"Who?"

"Valet."

"Good. Up close - what will you do?"

"Two shots - head and heart."

"And if his wife answers the door?"

"Ask to see him?"

"No! You shoot her and find him before he reacts. You can't leave her, can you?"

"She was my teacher from Maternelle."

"Any good?"

"I can read. And you?"

"Oh, Chibret - indolent time-serving careerist shit."

At ten that rainy night as he approached Valet's house with his revolver in his great-coat pocket Jerome's heart beat ice.

He was amazed he moved forward at all.

He was going to kill.

To take life. That Thou Shalt Not.

He was going to kill. To purge France of one of its boils.

Him - Jerome Lacaze...

He watched his hand knock.

His Maternelle teacher opened the door. A cardigan pulled over her big chest, a plain skirt and in her slippers and he stood calm and still, his hand on the cold metal.

"Jerome! What? You're drowned. Come in."

"Thank you, Madame. Is Monsieur Valet at home?"

"He is. Gaston - it's for you."

"Who is it?" Valet from the room at the end of the hall.

"Come and see! Lazy bugger," she muttered to Jerome, dripping by the door.

"Putain de merde..."

The door to the living-room opened and Valet saw Jerome and the gun and the flash and heard the boom and his stomach burst open and air and blood seethed out of him and the second shot smashed his eye-socket as Madame Valet's screams started and Jerome closed the door quietly behind him and ran.

Madame Valet stood screaming as her husband expired as quickly and as finally as a popped football before her eyes. She went to kneel by him and couldn't. She just looked at the mess. Brain and blood clotting on the door he sprawled against. Her body backed away. Someone must clean that up, and clean that carpet. Wash it. With salt? Vinegar? Maybe. I don't know. Just lift him out of here. Lift him out of my sight, out of this house. Out.

"OUT! OUT!"

Madame Vigne, who'd heard the shots and cowered in terror, recognised Madame Valet's voice in the crazed screaming. She threw on a wrap and crossed the road and knocked hard on the door. Madame Valet fainted. Madame Vigne heard the slump on the floor, the silence, knocked again and pushed. Nothing. She ran home, dressed, and strode off to the Gendarmerie, where from a hundred yards through the rain she could hear Madame Herrisson's howl. She stopped. Chibret must be dead, too. Mignon. Galtier. Duthileul? She hoped so. She forced Valet's door open to find the fat woman wheezing and saw her dead wretch of a husband and heard herself think, "Good," before kneeling to help Madame Valet.

Jerome ran hard, stumbling in the dark, round the bend in the lane, up the rise and up to Puech and in on Simone and Jacques.

The dog barked till Jacques shushed it, then sat a yard from the invader, growling, threatening. Jacques pressed a cup of wine into Jerome's shaking frozen sweating paw, Simone made coffee and he talked.

"Duthileul," he said, "Watch him, please. We need proof - proof of his loyalty - proof of his motives. Yes?"

Jacques and Simone both managed not to look at the jar of money.

"Jerome, you know him - he's for himself."

"I know. But he quoted Buonoparte once. And he sends money."

"He would," said Simone.

"I killed a man tonight. I've fired at Germans but I killed tonight." Silence.

"You always said..." began Jacques.

"I know! I know what I spouted! My God. Ha! His eyes. And I left her. What will she do to Sara and Zoe?"

"Who?"

"Madame - his widow."

"Killed a man here? You killed someone here?"

"I've said too much. You shouldn't know. I shouldn't have come. It's just - I killed, I'm a murderer."

There was a silence. Even the dog caught its weight.

"Jerome," said Simone, "what you did was assassinate."

"Perhaps." He poured scalding coffee down his throat. "It's kill or be killed. This isn't civilization - it can't be."

"It isn't - it's War," she said. "Go back to your men - they understand how you feel. They are your family."

He looked at her. Big. Looking right in his eyes.

"I've risked my family's life for a life with another family? This was never meant, surely?"

"Go. Take some food."

"Got a bike?"

"Arbel had."

"Fuck it - I need the walk."

And he went.

Chibret and Galtier had been in Aurillac; Mignon had cried, Herrisson was shot reaching for his revolver.

"I told you to shoot her," said Bernadie.

"I couldn't."

"So? She knows. Your mother is in the village - your wife, child; my God but you are a humanistic dangerous cretin."

"I couldn't be judge and jury on her."

St.Cirgues reeled and keened with the shock. Duthileul shivered. Chibret whitened and did truly thank God for his deliverance, as, later, so did Madame Herrisson. Mignon's mother had always known this day would come - he had told her so - but the sight and touch of his cold ruined stillness laid itself in her heart for always. At the funerals Madame Valet had still not spoken. She looked no differently at Madame Lacaze or Sara than at anyone else. The Curé spoke of tragedy and redemption and it was meaningless mumble to a village corrugated with shock. Duthileul sat in his house listening to the church-bell pealing its droning call to come and share the grief and he stayed where he was. To pay respects to those men would be repeated - to deny that respect would be reported. He'd picked his horse.

The villagers prayed. That Mignon's job would not be given to them or theirs. They wondered who or what or how many would replace Herrisson and they didn't give a flying fig for Valet and if Madame Valet had any sense she wouldn't either. She was in shock - and for that brief state she was even envied - but it wouldn't last - and then what?

The German reaction was to settle two of its men in Chibret's office, ten soldiers in the Gendarmerie, and their officer, Paul, a 20 year-old ambulance driver from Stuttgart, was ordered to police this lawless village and find and eliminate its Jews and Maquisard terrorists.

He walked up to the bar, straightened his uniform in the window, had a coffee, walked past the Mairie where Chibret was nodding agreement to every word he didn't understand, walked round the Church - he'd been a church-goer - walked down to the cemetery and back, to the football pitch at the top of the village and back and wondered how the hell to fulfil his orders.

He couldn't speak French, what was he supposed to do? But he must do something or the leather wasps in the Mairie would report him and he would be moved somewhere infinitely worse, and everywhere was worse now. Better this than any of the front-lines.

He piled his men into their truck, pulled up the tarpaulin and drove them rattling and visible round the village. Then up to some of the outlying farms including Puech. Jacques, seeing them from his field fled to the wood copse, the dog following, amazed at this

game. The men fired some pointless bullets into Jacques' barn wall and Simone held her stomach to calm the babe against her shock. When there was quiet Jacques hugged Simone as tight as he dared and crossed the road, shook Duthileul's hand and Duthileul said, "I'll take it when it's over, eh?"

Jacques looked hard at the older man, trying to find the right words to be clearly understood.

"Where is your heart?" he asked.

"In lineage," Duthileul lied.

Arbel was given a different pass, a 'masbefhel', which allowed him to go into the big town, Gorlitz. There was a cinema, occasionally showing French films and he was permitted, as 'Vertraussman' to take five with him. The maximum number allowed in any group of non-Germans. He and Claude watched the films, the others tried the new whore houses.

The young officer, Paul, knew what would happen. The Gestapo would wait then order a random reprisal. Or reprisals. Enemy people, but civilians. We're killing innocent flies. It's obscene. Dishonourable. It was four years since he'd heard Hitler speak and he'd lost that passion and certainty. Now all that was left was Duty. Whatever that was conceived to be.

Jacques stalled and prayed. That the baby would be born tonight. Eight months, isn't that enough? If I could just see it, meet him, hold her, feel it. Please. I've pleaded for so much and been granted so much how can I be this selfish? But it's real. Let me meet my child.

But when he looked at Simone, he saw his Duty and said, "Simone - you must go."

"Like this?"

She was big.

"Don't you think you should go?"

"Jacques - you're demented."

"Am I? Because I want to see you safe?"

She waited. There was more.

"Yes, I want to see him. Her. But if I can't have both, if I have to choose - then you should go."

"What about what I choose?"

He gawped.

"I hadn't thought about that..."

"No. I know. Our child will be born in this house."

"And then you'll go?"

"Then we'll see."

St.Cirgues settled into the rhythm of the Occupied. Stripped of dignity. The German Commanders in Cahors and Toulouse realised, too late, that if they manned these mountain villages they could starve the Maquis into need, recklessness, and open combat. So the market town battalions were broken up and each St.Cirgues got its quota of death-police. It made the outlying farms like Puech more vulnerable. The Maquis demands for food were not sugared now with any philosophy; it was demanded as a right, taken gratefully or with violence were it withheld, and dreadful threats were it to be withheld again. Duthileul finally got his chance to demonstrate his loyalty. He gave two cows to be slaughtered. Telling himself he'd have Jacques' soon enough.

One night towards the end of April the RAF dropped 3,600 tons of bombs on German occupied France and everyone waited to see what their reaction would be.

ten

MAY 1944 in the department of the Lot and Hell gathered.

On May 1st - German National Day - the men were given a barrel of beer, half the day off, some jam, ten cigarettes and ten marks each. Arbel heard his first American and British bombers flying over to bomb the heart of Germany. It was changing. No letter from Ardelle now for months - but this war was turning. The first air-raid siren. The first time work was stopped. Not long, not long, oh God, not long.

German information solidified. The Allied invasion would be in the North. All units to prepare to move North, leaving enough to secure the towns. The High Command issued papers calling for the final push to settle with the powers against the Fatherland, to secure the future for their children and their children's children and the Beauty of The Reich. The great gains in land and dignity the Fuhrer had given the people must be held for now and for a better world. It was Time.

It was Time. Simone knew. Jacques went to Duthileul and asked to use the telephone.

"Why? Who?" barked the old woman.

"Chayriguet."

"The bastard is coming? Phone him."

"I'll drive you to him," said Duthileul not moving from his chair.

"I'll phone if I may."

Chayriguet came.

Bringing Sara who sent Jacques for Ardelle and the three waited round Simone's bed; Jacques left outside with the dog.

"Lie down. Lie down on your back, my dear," said Chayriguet.

"I want to kneel."

"She knows best," said Sara, helping the gross child to squat.

"I want Jacques," she said as another contraction began.

"Vermande!" Ardelle bellowed. The dog cowered.

Jacques' face appeared at the door and Simone laughed through the pain.

"Your face! Come here and help me, mister."

Jacques stood staring at the bed.

"Kneel behind me, sit behind me - take my weight."

Chayriguet moved to a chair by the door. Sara held Simone's right hand, Ardelle, on the other side alternately mopping at the sweat and running to check the water on the fire. Simone, groaning against the contractions, then with the contractions, gasping for air; and behind her, his eyes dilated into black snooker balls, Jacques took her weight. And the sweat. And so wanted to kiss her and didn't and she went into another and screeched a little and Ardelle was there with a towel and the place was ready for the child and now they called for her to push to push and she pushed and Chayriguet came to cup with his hand beneath her and feel the head which waited whilst its mother gasped and grabbed at air

and will and filled her lungs and pushed him, ripping her a little, out. Chayriguet looped the cord back over the tiny head as all of it came and Simone mooed with the movement and collapsed back crushing Jacques into the head-board and held her arms out for the child Chayriguet placed purple, intact, blood-spattered, male and perfect at her breast.

Ardelle wiped at the child and mother with a fresh damp cloth and Sara said, "What will you call him?" and Simone said, "Jacques," and Jacques Vermande's heart burst light into every moment of his history.

The cord, the afterbirth, Chayriguet's stitches, the weighing, the paper - it all passed in a golden blur and suddenly there was Sara kissing them, all three, and she and Ardelle would be back in the morning and Chayriguet drove home and Jacques and Simone breathed slower - and slower till they could believe the life mewling in her arms would survive if they tore their eyes away long enough to look at each other.

"What can I do for you?"

"Sleep with us. I'm tired and I'm sure he is."

"Sleep on me. I won't."

She leaned against his chest and he gazed at the minute fingernails, the tiny lines on the minute thumb, the wizened ancient face.

"He'll leave me one day," said Simone.

"Don't."

The eyelashes, the hair, some tufts springing up as the birth-liquids dried, the mouth - look at it! - it was a kiss - that was a kiss! Jacques. Their son.

I'm doing better than my father then, he never even saw me. Jacques - born into war - welcome to this peace. The two-hour human made a noise from somewhere within that tininess and his mother and father smirked with wonder. When he sneezed their laughter spilt over the edges of human reason - Joy.

Maquis groups now raided banks, La Poste, tabacs, the bigger grocers and the fear of German reaction grew.
Still the Gestapo and the soldiery waited. Gathering information - true or false - about the whereabouts of the Maquis groups - waiting for the moment to strike.
A raddled cobra.
The Das Reich division based in Toulouse; tanks, lorries, armoured cars, motor-bikes and sidecars, moved up to Cahors.
People believed it meant the invasion in the North - The Debarquement - was imminent and the Germans must be headed there.
They would pass.
They would pass.
It would pass.
Wrong.
The army rolled into the Lot en route to surrounding every village, every commune on the eve of their solution to the problem of the Maquis and its collaborators. How you deal with terrorists. The great convoy spewed out groups of men in each and every village square.
6.15 in the morning.
A unit of twenty soldiers arrived in St. Cirgues to supplement the ten in the Gendarmerie. Chibret was ordered to round up every single member of his commune. By eight the villagers were in the church square. Jauliac had been beaten to a pulp in his kitchen. He was dragged into the square and thrown down in front of them all.

Madame Jauliac went to help him and was fired at.

Chibret was made to kneel in front of the crowd too, a gun at his head. He pointed on maps taken from his office to all the outlying hamlets - all the Puech's, and then to the names on the list that ought to be there. The young officer who'd arrived here a month before shrugged - he'd been and his men had searched all these places. Nothing. Perhaps he hadn't searched hard enough - what did Monsieur the blubbering Mayor think? Monsieur the blubbering Mayor thought it was unlikely both his lists and the officer could be wrong. Monsieur the Mayor was made to understand what would happen to him and the young officer should the lists or he be wrong. Everyone watching - and everyone was watching - understood the barking German language fluently.

Jacques, Simone, Duthileul, Dominique, the grandmother and Ardelle all knew.

"If we survive today - you leave with Jacques."

"If. Go to the copse. They won't take me and the baby - but you must go now. And Pray."

The last thing Duthileul said to Dominique as he bustled him out to the woods was the money was buried in the wall of the well. Now he and his senile mother sat. To wait and pray. Ardelle, too. Jacques took the dog, scuttled as low as he could down to the copse, and lay and fixed his eyes on his home and he really prayed.

In the village the hell continued as a hot day rose. Houses were ransacked and any money found was taken, any jewellery, anything. Then Galtier was pulled from the crowd and ordered to denounce anyone. He didn't understand and was beaten. Chayriguet was beaten for moving to help him. But no-one denounced old Feyt, their Israelite, shivering in the morning heat. Now riders went sent out to the surrounding farms.

From the square they could see plumes of smoke rising in the distance. Whose farm had been fired? Would they all be shot? Fear. You could touch it and it touched everyone.

Jacques heard and then saw two side-cars swing up the lane to Puech.

His heart froze.

What of his talk of protecting Simone? Of fighting for his? Defending his wife and child. Here was the attack and they faced it - he was on his dreadful empty stomach, cringing in hope. For shame. Here he was - here It was - and he was protecting what? His dog. For shame.

His son slept on the bed and woke with Simone's terror as boots clattered up the steps and the door was bashed open. She picked him up, bawling, and faced three men. One went straight upstairs, kicking the cat dead against the wall, another to the barn.

"Where is he? The man?" the corporal asked in awful French.

"What man?"

"The father of that noise."

"Dead."

"Liar," he said.

"No, I'm not," she replied in German.

"You speak German?"

"Yes."

One came clattering downstairs. "There's no-one here."

"You learned German?"

"I studied it, yes."

"You speak it well."

The second came in from the barn, shook his head, looked at her and said,

"She's fuckable."

THE SINGLE SOLDIER

"Shut your shit-filled brain," said the corporal. "She's just had a child, hasn't she?"

The first man went into Jacques' room.

"Why did you study it?"

"I wanted to teach."

"You probably could."

"Sir, there's another bed here and it's been slept in."

A beat. A heart-beat.

"You lied?" asked the corporal.

"No. I slept there to get a night's peace. The baby."

"She's lying - come on - a quick fuck."

"Ohh - give me the baby."

The infant was passed to the corporal and the two men dragged her to Jacques' bed.

"I've got the clap," she screamed as they ripped open the dress.

"Not yet," laughed one and hit her on the jaw with his rifle butt and they stripped her and burst through Chayriguet's stitches, one sucking at her milk whilst the other waited. It took them both three minutes. The baby cried and the corporal jiggled it. The men emerged, grinning, sated, and the corporal placed the baby next to the wreck of woman, bleeding from the mouth and vagina, and left.

Two other soldiers raped Ardelle, Duthileul's house was looted, he was beaten up as a useless old article and his mother frozen in the trauma and the war left Puech.

Jacques waited ten minutes and then ran low as he could home.

He asked no questions, said nothing as he bathed her mouth and washed her breasts and crotch, oh so deeply shamed by and oh so gentle with the teeth-marks round her nipples; found a clean shirt and placed her in her bed with her child, made a drink, fed it through the swelling lips and stroked her forehead, trying stupidly to iron horror away. She lay there numb, watching him but not seeing him as she deliberately re-played the whole scene over and over again and again. Every minute detail every pain every detail every scrap of the humiliation till she was sure she'd missed nothing, till she was certain she'd utterly assimilated her degradation.

"They won't come back," she said.

"Sleep. You won't be here when they do."

"They won't."

"You've risked enough."

He buried the cat, came back and sat with them.

At four o' clock, no-one having eaten or drunk a thing under the blazing sun all the men were loaded into wagons - save Chayriguet to doctor the useless pulp of Galtier and Chibret - and, irony of ironies, old Feyt - and as the women howled their despair, they were gone.

Forever.

As evening fell on the shell of St.Cirgues Jacques walked the back fields to Madame Lacaze. She agreed to come tomorrow at this time. He had one day left as he walked back.

Everywhere; Gorses, Gréze, Roqueyroux, Souceyrac, Senaillac, Lacapelle - at every inhabited dot on the map of the Lot, men were rounded up and piled into lorries, and taken to Cahors. The Germans filled commandeered schools with them. Tongues were cut from the first few who shouted defiance, others tortured for the fun of it, all that night and the next day, until the cold and un-fed men were sent on to Germany and their many deaths. The

villages were left to the women, the children and men too old to use. Or abuse.

Jacques boiled water for tisane. The last supper.

Tears mounted and he quelled them. No place now for anything but action. They ate and put their son to sleep and he packed her suitcase with clothes and her books and she watched him. He lit the candle and they took it to her bed and lay, their blood breathing between them in a peaceful sleep a thousand miles away. He woke at midnight and Jacques changed the nappy and Simone fed him, his hunger hurting her bruised breasts. His father nursed him and laid him in the cot and they lay again, both hurting. She dozed on his shoulder and he, who had prayed so often that Time would freeze, and it had, knew now it hadn't, and it couldn't.

The babe woke five hours later as a beautiful last day came and they rose.

"She'll come tonight."

"They won't come back, Jacques."

"Simone - don't. I beg you. It's 'iffing."

He took his herd from the barn to their field; by tonight they would be Duthileul's - but she and the child would be on their way to Life.

He came back to the house where she sat in the rocking chair, her face swollen and coloured, playing with Jacques.

"Let me."

He put a cotton bonnet Ardelle had made on his child's head and took him out into the bird-song and the light. He walked him round the barn, the fournil, the garden, the well, out to the field, the cattle, the copse and the view of his home "Your heartlands," he whispered to his son; back into the garden, showed him the delphiniums Simone had planted, the vegetables he'd sowed and back up the stairs to Simone, asleep like his mother in her chair. He stood in the doorway keeping his shadow from her and counted the hairs falling across her forehead, the lines at her eyes, the purpling welt of her bruised lips, the mouth he had kissed, the mouth that had kissed his, her neck, her chest rising shallow to the thin dress, her bronzed forearms, her hands, all of her - her ankles - all of her, all of his Simone he printed one last time in his heart's photo album and then he laid the child on it's back in the cot and moved around her sleeping, aching to breathe one last time the heat at her neck - but that was all done now. He had been to paradise, lived in this heaven and now it was the day of departing.

She slept till the child woke her, and saw her man sitting, smoking.
"Staring?"
"Yes."
She fed the child and he watched the tiny fists open and close as her milk thrilled him and he sat with them, his family, and the tiny hand grasped his little finger as it guzzled. Silence. No, not so, birds and baby and breath.
He burped his son and handed him back. But the action distressed him so much he took the child again in his arms, nestled him on his shoulder and walked the room as Simone tidied herself.

Lunch. Every common-place thing drenched in anguish. Talk too painful for words. Nothing to do but watch Time pass as he had done so often in joy - now it was all to be wrenched through the dreadful rightness of what must happen.

Simone didn't, wouldn't, argue.

With the babe in her arms she knew Jacques was right - but somewhere she guessed she also was right - that the war had passed St.Cirgues and Puech and would not return.

And she dared ask herself what she wanted.

Life here, with Jacques and their child - or more?

Was this enough?

Had she even the right to think such a thing?

What of her dreams? The past and the future she'd buried?

No!

No, selfish Simone - that was not the question.

The question was the child. If the Germans retreated and the child was injured or worse - what reparation could she ever make when his future had been promised, and paid for, by his father?

None. She looked at Jacques as he went to bring the beasts in and she accepted she didn't know the future - she couldn't - she could only take this chance.

They ate their last meal. Only their son had an appetite.

Jacques checked her case, rolled a cigarette and dreaded the dying of this day and the sound of Madame Lacaze's car.

"I can't speak," he said.

"I know. What can we say?"

"That you'll return?"

"I can't say that."

"No, I know. But - that you would?"

"Jacques. Please don't make me say false things. False hope - false everything."

"That you would. That would be false?"

Say it - say it for him. Say those words, Simone.

"Jacques, I don't want to go. Neither of us know where I'm going

- how far, how impossible; so there is no future. Yet. No peace. Please. I agree to go - to save our child - and that's all the future I have."

He nodded, hurt. She hadn't said it.

But she did say, "Did you never consider coming with us?"

"No."

A gulp of hope.

"They wouldn't take men."

"They might. I never asked."

"It's for children. Not men. I have to stay."

"How much money is there?"

"As much as you said."

"Then come tonight and see if it's enough. What's to stay for? What did you sell for the money? Don't tell me. But what's to stay for? Come. To see. Or to say good-bye."

Half an hour more with you, he thought, is reason enough; to hold the child in the car, to breathe his smell, and to hope.

"They won't let me go."

"I don't think so either, but come. To say good-bye. No, come for me."

"I'll come for me."

She smiled.

The last hour.

Madame Lacaze came.

"Will you pack clothes?" Simone asked as he stood.

"Simone," he almost laughed, "all I ever had of value is in your arms."

"And in my heart."

"That's all I need."

He took the money from the jar, the carry-cot and her case and

they crammed into Madame Lacaze's car. She drove off.

"If we're stopped Vermande, then we are all dead."

"I know."

"Thank you for risking my life."

"Thank you for risking yours."

As they drove into Souceyrac, silent as the moon, Jacques' heart hatched a hopeless last hope. Surely the Curé could have been taken? The escape route gone? The Germans had shattered it. Oh, please. We could go home. Give the money back. Live. Hope Simone's right. The Germans won't come back.

The Curé was there. And the money warmed his heart.

"Bless you. I won't ask how - but God Bless you."

"Can he come?" asked Simone.

"No."

The Curé was surprised by the question and Madame Lacaze shook his hand and went to wait in the car. Jacques stared at the Curé, beaten.

"They'll leave for Spain tonight."

He left them in his vestry to their good-byes.

"One last stare my brother-man. You saved my soul, you know that."

"You made mine."

"And his."

"And his."

In the square Madame Lacaze parped the horn.

"I love you, Simone."

"Good-bye, Jacques. I loved you. If it's ever safe and I can return - I will."

He kissed his son's head and Simone's bruised lips and turned and left. He shook the Curé's hand. The man looked into his desolation and told him God had work left for him to do.

Jacques heard himself say, "I'll bring the children now."

"Thank you. Bless you."

He climbed into the car and she let out the hand-brake and it was finished. Finished.

He knew.

No doubt anywhere in his mind.

Madame Lacaze let the silence engulf them for a few minutes.

"War," she said.

"Hell."

"Yes."

They drove through Senaillac, another clump raped of men.

St.Cirgues - 3km.

"My son killed."

"No!" Jacques sat bolt upright - Simone forgotten in that shocking instant. "No! When?"

"He killed. Valet."

"He's not dead?"

"No. He killed. He took Life. He murdered Valet."

"But he's alive?"

"His body is."

Jacques' spine spread back into the leather seat.

"Valet would have rejoiced at Jerome's death."

"Two wrongs don't make a right."

"I don't know what is right."

"What you did tonight was."

"It doesn't feel like it."

"That's selfishness."

"I know."

"You're a good man, Vermande. A simple fool but a good soul."

"Am I? Why did Jerome hate you?"

"You'll be spared that - your children rejecting you."

"But why?"

"What did he say?"

"He never forgave you for looking down on Sara."

"He only had her so I would."

"I don't believe that. Sara has heart."

"Yes, and years ago you should have claimed it."

"Eh?"

"Oh yes, Vermande."

"That was years ago."

"We live in the consequences of years ago."

"That sounds like Jerome."

"Does it?"

When they drove into the village Jacques asked her to stop.

"I need this walk."

"Don't brood, Vermande. What you did was right."

"Thank you. Goodnight, Madame."

"Till the next."

"Yes."

And she was gone.

The night and the walk he'd walked these last two years with her. The stag-beetle rising and frightening her, the night she took his arm and then his hand in the pitch, them sitting on the bench when Jerome said they should fuck, his mother's funeral, her saying she'd stay, their returning home - all that glorious Time spent here together; he came out of the woods and ahead, moonlit, his empty home.

Where was she now? In a lorry heading to Spain? Where was he - walking into the echoes of love. To do what?

In Tulle the Germans hung a hundred and thirty men in groups of ten, on the stroke of the hours. Making a priest choose which ten, each hour, from the hundred and fifty they'd rounded up. All day barbarity - nothing quenching the Commandant's glee at watching people hope and watching people's hopes dashed. The priest prayed God for His forgiveness and asked for mercy on the soul of the Commandant, and as the hours passed begged forgiveness for the hate welling in his being. It seemed God was deaf, all day, but He is such that when the last twenty men were spared all the left-living believed in Him again.

The Das Reich division moved on to Oradour where it sated itself. The whole village, four hundred and more, locked in the church and the building burned.

The Allies invaded.

eleven

HE CLOSED THE DOOR lest their smell escape.

No noise if he made none.

Simone.

No candle. A man in a moonlit room.

The dog.

But, neither of them.

Gone - to Spain and life.

I sent them away.

I hurt.

She was raped. She's going to where she can't be hurt.

I hurt instead.

Day-light.

He opened the barn. He scraped out the dead flies from yesterday.

These flies saw Simone. Smelt Jacques.

I'm milking cows I've sold to send my family away.

'It was the right thing.'

Whose is this milk?

"When it's over," Duthileul had said.

It is over.

These beasts are his.

He left the herd, went and lay in their bed.

You live and you have him and that's right but ohh Simone Simone...

He beat so hard at the bed-head his hand bruised and then split. Bled.

It scabbed, he barely noticed, a day later.

Will I?

The house was cold.

Alone is cold.

Ardelle looked across that evening. No-one. All day. No light at night?

She'd call in the morning.

She went back inside her own empty house, lit a candle, raked a fire, boiled water, took the tisane and the candle, went to her own cold empty bed, pressed the tiny pile of Arbel's letters to her chest and prayed.

When he noticed he was hungry he shared ham, cheese and water with the dog but didn't even hear the cows. He sat on Arbel's bench. Two-day dead ash at his feet. Rolled a cigarette.

"I don't," she'd said.

A heart-attack of ache. A lead anchor of pain.

The dog looked at him, lay down a metre from him.

No-one released the herd next morning Duthileul noticed; but he watched Ardelle walk round and knock.

The dog barked.

Slow footsteps.

From behind the door a wet, soaked, voice. "Who is it?"

"Me, Ardelle."

"I'm fine..." The voice walked away. A door closed inside.

Ardelle milked Jacques' grateful herd and Duthileul watched her take them to pasture. She brought them back at dusk, milked them, fed the chickens and did the same for four more days. He must let the dog out at night, she thought.

On the fourth evening she knocked again.

The dog barked. Good.

Footsteps, shuffling.

"Who is it?"

"Ardelle, Jacques."

A silence.

"I'm fine..."

"You're not. You're dead inside. Your life has gone and I know and talk to me, Jacques. I'm at my empty home."

And she went home.

Jacques milked his herd for the first time in a week.

Ardelle watched the bearding husk stumble home with the beasts for three nights and then went into the village with her coupons and came round with a bottle she left on the doorstep as the dog barked.

I was wrong. You can stop Time.

Time doesn't exist where there is pig-iron pain.

I hate you Simone love for not staying for not insisting for not telling me I was wrong you just went you took my life you selfish selfish cow you should have gone and left my son I hate him too for being born to bring me heart-ache break me into this and most of all I hate the memory of the Loving that made him I hate the Germans and I would kill those who hurt you with my bare hands I'd rip them with my teeth - but I didn't when I should have. No.

I lay on my yellow gut praying. I hate you God you fucker for letting this all happen. I hate Duthileul and his damned money. Hate Jerome for living - Sara and Ardelle for living - Arbel if he is - I hate everyone who was ever happy. Especially me.
I'm not worthy of my skin.

He took the wine back to Ardelle and sat in her empty silence.
A first shard of comfort, shared despair.
"Do you want a glass?" she asked him.
"I don't want to drink, Ardelle." he mumbled.
"Where are they?"
"Gone."
Silence began.
"I'll go home Ardelle..."
"Why? You can weep here - it's all I do."
"You hope too, don't you?"
"I've had no letter for months."
"They can't kill Arbel..."
"Jacques - please..."
Another quiet fell.
"I can't comfort you Ardelle."
And he left before she could dare to begin to describe her loss.

Time slid under him.
This is what my mother did.
Oh, I envy her her peace.
Did she love my father as I love Simone? She must have. Ohh Mamman, your poor sad soul.
Oh, Simone, ohh, son.
He finished the last of his tobacco.
The idea of going to the village, of stepping into the Tabac, was

macabre. The thought of seeing everyone; anyone, their rancid tittle-tattle or their damned questions, their lying sympathy. Or worse, 'You did the good thing...'

No! Never.

I won't ever look at those grotesques again. They never liked her. Never loved her.

Don't need tobacco.

He washed a filthy cup and stood an hour by the bucket remembering the back of her calves, red with sun. Her bony neck. Beautiful.

Mine.

He stood by the bucket and brayed his defeat.

"Simoooone." I never shout. "SIMONNNE."

"Simooooaaan."

He killed a chicken, lit a fire, boiled it and shared it with the dog. Made soup with the stock.

No bread.

He took kindling, beech clippings and oak from his caves and lit them in the stone-dome oven his grandfather had fashioned - the fournil. Went up to the attic to fetch flour, salt, water - got no yeast so it'll be hard, good - good for soup and his hands heeled away and his shoulders caught the rhythm and at least, at last, he was working. And in the movement and the pressure of his hands in the dough, he forgot.

Till he remembered. Found himself frozen again.

Loaded the tray and fed it into the glowing mouth. A cig now.

"I don't." Her voice clear as a winter nightingale.

Jag. Heart-jag.

Echoes of anguish and echoes in anguish.

Water the tomatoes. Weed. Work...

The bread'll be like rock. Good.

I should go and see Ardelle but I can't face talking.

Everyone knew now.

He'd sold something - everything - to send her and the bastard away. That was good. But then? Nothing. It's genetic. Addicted to grief, like his mother and her fool father. What's he doing? Nothing. Killing chickens.

Time'll rot him.

"You gave me so much, so much Time in Love - tell me what to do with Time with No Love. Please. Humbly."

His house silent as a midnight church.

The dog barked. Hell-fire and damnation! People. Who?

Sara pushed the door open, Jacques looked up from the fireplace seat, and Zoe's nose crinkled with acid distaste.

"You're right," said Sara, "It stinks."

The child pointed at Jacques.

"Yes, and he stinks worse, probably."

She looked at him, at the dead room. "What are you doing?"

"Nothing."

"It doesn't include washing? Shaving?"

"No."

"What are you eating?"

"Food. What do you want? Why have you come?"

Sara left the door open, took the child's hand and taking a couple of steps into the space, put her basket on the table.

"I'm your friend, Jacques. I don't want anything. I came to see you. Now I'm here I'd be glad if you had a wash."

His head swam a little. Different thoughts. Damn. Damn them to hell.

"Sit down."

"Sit down, Zoe?"

The child stared at Jacques.

I must make an effort.

He slowly knelt till he and the child were at eye-level.

"She's lovely, Sara - "

Tears utterly dismantled him.

"I'm sorry, Zoe - you're lovely - but - I'm so sorry..."

The child's face mirrored his, crumpled into floods and Sara picked her up and walked her, raising small clouds of dust, calming her. But the child was now full of his anguish without the reason. Sara took her out of that house and to the garden where her sobs were softer on Jacques' ears. He could hear his own better. He left Sara's basket on the step, shut the door, lay down on their bed and howled.

He was awake for some silent moments or more before he remembered his heart was broken.

"So, what are you going to do?"

Sara. Two days later. No Zoe.

"I don't know."

"What do you know?"

"Every second of this - talking - hurts."

"They're only words."

"Go away, Sara. I can't speak."

"Don't. I'll talk. I have no-one to talk to - it'll be perfect. I haven't seen Jerome for six weeks. Zoe is growing into a world of women and it's unbalanced."

A beat.

"They'll tell me if he's killed. So, I hope and I pray too. Do you? Ardelle doesn't. Not in church, anyway. Have you seen her? You should. She's broken, Jacques - we must hold her together till Arbel comes home. If he comes home. If any of them do."

"Simone won't."

"None of them might. Then we'll know what your Mother felt. Less, forever."

She knew he did not want to hear this, but she spoke anyway. "You did the right thing. And I'm proud to know you."

"I can't speak."

A pause.

"You should be sad. You did the hardest thing. It must be awful. What can I say? My blessings on you."

Two people crying in a sunlit room.

The cows festered when he left them in the field all night and the following day until Dominique Duthileul came and led them back on the second evening.

Jacques heard him milking them. Heard him take the milk across the road. Good. That went on for three days.

Then, Duthileul Pére came across the lane and knocked at the door.

The dog barked.

"Who is it?"

"Me."

"Yes?"

"We must talk."

"Talk."

Duthileul looked at the door.

"Work your land."

"Why?"

"I can't work your land and mine." He was talking to a door.

"It's not mine. It's yours."

There was a pause.

"I said we'd talk when it's over."

"It is over."

"It isn't."

"I shook your hand."

"Are you trying to blackmail me?"

Jacques laughed for the first time since Souceyrac. "No."

"I won't give it back."

"Good for you."

"Vermande. Jacques," the voice gathered some passion, "it will rot - it's ridiculous."

"I spent the money. It's over."

"The land! The animals."

"I don't care."

Duthileul jiggled at the latch. You had to jiggle it just so. The dog growled.

"Let me in."

"Why?"

"I want you to see reason."

"I have no reason to see."

"Someone must work that land!"

"Hire someone, then. Pay."

There was a pause and even through the door Jacques could tell Duthileul was going to say something he'd already considered.

"I'll pay you."

"No, you won't. Your money's misery."

"You'll regret this."

"I do."

"Please."

Silence.

"What did you say?"

"I said please."

Jacques opened the door. The stench passed Duthileul.

"Good God, man." Duthileul felt the chill foolish wind of

compassion ruffle his state of mind.

"'Please?'"

"Look at you."

"'Please?' "

"Jacques. You must work. Look at you. Work the land and when it's all over, when there's peace, then we'll talk again. Eh?"

"About what?"

Jacques watched, fascinated for a second, as avarice squirmed.

"The animals will rot, Jacques. The land will die."

"And so, what will we talk about Jean-Louis? May I call you Jean Louis? Jean-Louis, if you gave me the land back I wouldn't work it."

Silence.

"What when you've killed all the poultry - what then?"

"I'll eat grass."

"Are you mad? My God, Vermande. For a woman?"

"Yes. My heart is in lineage, too."

And he closed the door.

I was wrong. I was wrong. I was wrong. I did the wrong thing.

Jerome came for ten minutes - no surrender, nowhere, never. Not now!

"Capitulation is for Italians!"

"France capitulated."

"Vichy capitulated."

Jacques sunk back into the fireside, tired with the conversation already.

"What do you think about, tramp?"

"I don't want to think."

"Mm, but it's not that easy, is it? What do you think about?"

Silence.

"You did the right thing."

"No. The Germans haven't come back yet."

"What?"

"When they come back and kill me it will be right."

"What are you saying?"

"The truth."

"Godsake man! You did the right thing. She's alive!"

"You didn't get Sara and Zoe out. Send them away."

"I'm not you. You did the right thing for you."

"Oh, Jerome - bollocks! Obviously - I didn't."

"Well, no. You did the right thing for them."

Jacques was silent.

"Tell me about the baby... Tell me about your son."

"Please..."

"He's - alive? Gorgeous?"

"Gone."

A beat.

"If The Germans had killed her, Jacques, and killed him while you shivered in that copse - if you'd come back and found them dead - would that have been better?"

Jacques considered that for the first time.

"I'd have buried them."

"And would you rather have done that?"

And only now did his eyes meet Jerome's.

"Yes."

Silence.

"Vermande - you're a coward. All these years - waiting for you to grow - and you're a thief, a miser." He stood, dust following him, "You'd rather you knew where they were? Than their lives?" He kicked wildly at Jacques' legs, missed. "I'm ashamed of you."

"The truth changes, Jerome. Yours has. You have. I've told you what I feel today."

"And I'm telling you I'm disgusted."

"Then fuck off and leave me to it. Get back to your murder."

Jerome rattled. "It's a purge."

"Is it? Good. Do it."

Silence.

"De Gaulle's to land in France. He'll be on our soil."

"I couldn't give a fig, Jerome, I really couldn't. I'm glad for you. But please don't tell me I'm going to be free."

"You did the right thing. Stand up and be proud. I'm doing the right thing and when my right and De Gaulle's and the Allies meet and the war is really over she will be free - to come back." Jerome walked to the door. "She'll be impressed with this."

He left the words behind.

Jacques opened the door to shoo them out into the garden. And saw her bending at weeds, saw his mother working, saw himself working in a June field two years ago, then saw Simone stopping her work to wave. He closed the door, went back to Arbel's bench and reached for his tobacco. He hadn't any.

I will not be my mother.

I will not grieve to the grave.

I will work.

What work?

In fields that aren't mine? Beasts that aren't mine?

"That is the price you paid."

The dog looked up, startled by his voice.

And when the bastard takes my land?

"I'll have the chickens the garden and this morgue for a home."

The dog's head tilted, puzzled.

Only work can help you forget.
"But do you want to forget? Should you?"
Stop asking questions with no answers.
Work. Just work.

twelve

THE PICTURE MAGAZINE in the Tabac, 'Signal', had been published every month throughout the war. Now the pictures were of De Gaulle and the Invasion and the editorials harangued Laval and Darnand, The Head Of The Milice, and were even critical of the senile Petain. The magazine had sent a photographer to Algiers and there was De Gaulle, tall, erect, correct, superior, secure. Not a doubt in him. And here was The Government in Exile - the Next Republic. Upright, uniformed, determined, pure. The future. Alongside advertisements for perfume and a German toothpaste, "A quality German Product."

Duthileul took it to his window seat and basked in his success. Hot July 1944, much more blood to weep - but not him or his - he had backed the right horse and would continue to do so; go with his son to the parachute drops and let Dominique himself give the next money. Then, and only when it was completely safe, have him join the Maquis.

Captain Phillipe was killed in a botched ambush outside Cahors. Three others with him. The men came down the hillside and made off with the bodies. Phillipe was taken to Montluc where his parents and all the men of his Lotoise Maquis buried him -

daring a German attack - and swore they would commemorate his real name - Jean-Jacques Chapou - in the streets and schools and churches and playing-fields of The Lot he had died to Liberate. Then they went back to War.

Sniping at the German patrols that left Cahors less and less frequently to hopelessly police this land they were losing.

The RAF and the Americans bombed German-held French towns. A wind moves a stick of bombs and the barracks or the factory is missed and innocents are killed. It is hard to forgive, harder still to forget. Hardest of all to live with the irony of surviving the invader to watch family and neighbours taken by the Liberator. It asked God hard questions. And the people of Paris and Milan and Berlin and Dresden could only wait and hope that the sprinkling of His random miracles would spare them and theirs.

Arbel and the men heard rumours of the invasion. Heard the planes that left each night to shoot down the bombers; and heard the first bombs falling on Germany. He walked to the bar on Sunday and asked Lothar which direction was West. The direction the German planes went, the direction the American and British planes came from, of course.

German paranoia accelerated. Police arrived at the mine at night, woke everyone and searched everywhere. For guns, information, anything. They found nothing but letters and an accordion. Next day, a siren, an air-raid, another hour without work.

De Gaulle fretted lest he not be first into Paris when it was liberated. Then, brilliant, gave the honour to General Leclercq. The following day he would walk the Champs Elysee to Glory.

Jacques saved some of the tomatoes and raspberries and trimmed back the exploding courgettes and weeded for two days. Aching, bent all day, hot, sweaty, occupied. He ate some carrots, some of the gooseberries, drank from the well, took half the courgettes and left them on Ardelle's doorstep, came home and, like every evening, dreaded the night.

The Maquis of the Lot united to launch the full-scale attack on Cahors. Rid it of first the Germans and then, as they had been promised, of the attentistes, the collaborators, bureaucrats, all the servants of the vile and shameful Vichy Regime. All those who hadn't refused.

Sniping, scurrying, terrified, it was hand-to-hand now. Every house to be searched; no way of knowing who was in control of what - no way of thinking further than keep the weapon loaded, ready, identify by silhouette - fire. Re-load. Wait. Ignore what you felt. Ignore. Check all around. Again. Make a yard toward the door - look around - step over the moaning youth in the doorway - see the flash, hear the pop in your chest as your lung punctured, fall fall fall no air so quickly black to white and pass over. And that killer killed as he reached the doorway he'd just won. Terrified screaming families barricaded in with Germans, with Maquisards. Smoke and shot and splinters of masonry and glass and bone and blood and brain and the stench and the dogs and the death. Three days and nights.

Jerome, Bernadie, Serge and Michel trapped six Germans in a church and drove them up into the bell-tower, then above the clock, firing through the pigeon-shit covered volets. Serge died and Michel, too. The two surviving Germans surrendered. When they saw there was only Jerome and Bernadie they considered reaching for their weapons; but like their Occupation, that moment had

passed. Exhausted men, tired to death, tired of death, their hands on their heads, were rounded into the emptied schools, fed, and locked in.

The Capital of the Lot was free. Their Department, their beautiful Lot, free.

To rejoice.

He ploughed manure into what was Duthileul's land. He performed the routine - washed the barrow, raked down food, fed the chickens, came back to the house. But no sitting there. Ghosts would swallow him. Work. Change the bed sweep the floor clean the windows clear the cobwebs.

Breakfast. Coffee? Egg? Need hot water. Light a fire? In July? Ham? Got none. Is it July? Cheese? All gone. Make some - churn - that's hard. What day is it? Don't know. Do the washing.

He found a baby bonnet. His heart stalled, teetering immediately on the precipice of despair. He moved, and stalled again when he opened a drawer and saw clothes she'd never wear again. Wash them? He laughed for the second time. Maniac! Someone might be there. At the Lavoir. Someone to have to not talk to. Ever again. Do the washing at night, fool. Wash the floor? The table? I need hot water. Light a fire. In June? Is it June? It's August, surely. I don't know. I should know. I'm a farmer, I know the sky. Herrisson said I knew things.

I don't want to know anything now - that's the difference.

Jerome, so proudly quoting Lenin, bellowed above the bedlam in the bar, "And now we must proceed to construct the New Republic!"

"Fuck that, Josephine! Tonight we drink and fuck!"

"I put it to you Comrades - Sex - or Politics?"

The bar bellowed back, "Sex!"

"I stand down," he said to applause. "And I shall take a leak!"
Cheering.

He went upstairs, took his piss and opened the toilet window onto
the square and watched the party.

He could taste a meanness in the bitter way he scoured the dancing
singing feasting mob and couldn't not think, "Where were you
when there were ten of us?"

A weariness swept through him and he slumped on the cold floor
next to the shit-hole and wanted to be with Sara.

He had survived it.

He had survived it.

He had killed. He had liberated. He had risked and he had doubted
and he Lived.

Someone knocked at the door.

"Come in Comrade," he called.

"Come in?"

"Sure."

The door opened - a man Jerome didn't know stood there.

"Pissed?"

"Probably."

"Toughen, my friend - this is our Party!"

"I did toughen," said Jerome.

"Good. Thank you. Now - could I have my first crap in Free France
in peace?"

"Sure."

He was pulled to his feet, shook the man's hand and went down to
the raucous bar. He would have preferred to leave his bitter blood-
lust in the toilet with the other shit - but he didn't. The survivors,
Jean-Luc, Bernadie and the Basque, Roger De Mendes, roared
when they saw him.

"Jerome - come here and tell us what we should be thinking."

"I want to be with Sara."

"St. Cirgues? Not tonight. Drink - and stop thinking, you fool. You - barman - give this soldier, this comrade, this windbag with balls a drink!"

"Dance, Jerome," said Roger, "dance to oblivion - tomorrow we'll make a Republic – we promise."

Roger danced. No music, just a clapping, stamping ecstatic bar as Jerome and all of them caught the Spanish rhythm. And drank. And laughed. For Joy and Survival and his bloody Mother and Sara and Zoe but most of all for what he'd been and what he'd stayed. Zealous.

And he had to laugh at the arbitrary roll of dice that had spared him, taken his betters and left him here to try and understand Fate. Could almost make you believe in God! And what did God, that indolent voyeur, think of him, Jerome Lacaze?

"What an ant!" he roared into a sudden silence and the bar turned to him, swaying, laughing.

"What a fucking ant!"

"To the fucking ants!" toasted Bernadie and the bar toasted the fucking ants of this world and the inane sound filled, for that moment, that bar in that square of that town in that Department of that Country for the End of That War.

Ardelle and Jacques sat.

He came one night a week and sometimes she sewed and sometimes they talked, but mostly they shared the silence. Neither had anything new to express, it felt enough to connect their lifelessness.

"The German soldiers..." she began and stopped.

"Yes?"

"Raped me."

Silence.

"Simone, too?"

"Yes."

Silence.

"You're not pregnant?"

"No. It's the only thing I've thanked God for in months."

Jacques tried to think of something to say.

"I'm - sorry, Ardelle."

"We manage without words, Jacques."

"Have you washing you need doing?"

She looked at him. It was night.

"Some..." she said.

"I need work you see..."

When he left he walked the dog and his barrow to the Lavoir where he midnight-washed their clothes.

Two nights later when he brought them back, dried, Ardelle had been to the village - and she had The News.

"The Lot is free, Jacques."

He absorbed that, nodding.

"Is Jerome alive?"

"No-one knows. Yet."

Now possibilities swarmed around the quiet room.

And Ardelle's heart quailed.

"He'll be bombed, then..."

"No. No, Ardelle." He stood. "But... It's safe..."

Ardelle's tears dripped on the washing.

He held his till he was outside her door.

She could come back!

He stood on Ardelle's doorstep.

Spain. It's not far. I could go and get her!

He walked towards their home.

I could sell something - sell Duthileul the house - anything - go and get her.

Where? Where is she? Where are they?

The Curé in Souceyrac!

He'll know! He knows where she is!

I must see him.

He marched past his house, down the lane, through the village and out into the empty black night.

He will know, he will know, he must know, he knows...

Senaillac, the Pas d'Aubinies, the endless woods and hills of newly Free France.

As his church clock struck the quarter to four o'clock the Curé was woken.

He opened the door on a bearded, excited, face. "Where is she?"

"What? Who are you?"

"Jacques Vermande. You sent my - wife and son - Simone and our baby - some time ago. I paid. You remember me! I asked could I go. You said 'no'. And you left us in your room. Where did she go?"

The Curé struggled to grasp this situation. "South..."

"Spain?"

"Yes..."

"Where?"

"Where in Spain?"

"Yes!"

The Curé took a tiny breath. "I have no idea. No idea at all. Come in. Sit down. Do you need a drink? I've wine..."

"You don't know?"

"Of course not."

Jacques' ashen face demanded more.

"I never knew. If I were to have been tortured... I could never know."

Jacques' mind froze.

"You don't know?"

"No."

An empty quietness began.

"But the war is over - she could come back now."

The Curé sat. "Perhaps she will..."

Jacques swung to face him. "Do you think so?"

The Curé thought again. He had a war's worth of grief experience.

"I have no idea."

"But she might?"

"The War is not over, my friend."

"But I could go and find her... There is no war in Spain..."

"No-one knows where she is. No-one."

Jacques thought.

"She does."

"Ye-es. And God, too."

"Well He won't tell me."

"No."

Another quietness. The Curé sat forward.

"Do you talk to Him?"

"Yes..."

"And does He respond?"

Jacques thought.

"He gave me..."

"And now He has taken her away?"

"Them - yes."

The Curé offered the chair again.

"When did you last sleep?"

Jacques thought.

"Before I met you. With them."

A small clock struck the hour.

"Will you sleep here?"

Jacques looked at the man.

The Curé looked at him, simple heart-rent peasant.

"She'll tell you when she can, won't she? A card, a letter?"

Jacques Vermande had not considered such a thing.

The Curé poured a wine, fixed it in Jacques' hand, drank one himself and said, "My wife and child don't exist. My wives and children and their husbands have been killed and maimed, deported and tortured. This War, my friend, this is Hell. Don't let the bastards get you down. Keep the Faith."

"In?"

"You."

"And her?"

"Of course."

Jacques walked westward Home. A dawn rose behind him. His eyes saw only the dying night.

She could write! She could tell him where to come to. To meet them. To get them. To bring them back! Home. She'll hear the news, and she'll write!

He would sell something. Else. What had he?

In Ludwigsdorf the food situation became desperate. Eggs were stolen. Vegetables were stolen. Anything was stolen. A bike was stolen. A trailer for a car was stolen. Anything of value that could be traded for food. Then one of the Italians, a butcher, stole and killed a baby pig, cut it up, salted it and hung it from a ladder. The

whole dormitory had a thin feast.

And a new Polish prisoner could play the fucking accordion!

The Director of the mine was replaced by a man with one arm. He'd lost the other in Africa. The Director was sent to the front. Still they had to work. The news outside the pale green hell was good, life inside was pale green and hell.

Late August and De Gaulle walked the ecstatic Champs De Lycee. All France celebrated.

Jerome wrote to Sara, a letter bursting with pride. He had been voted - voted! - onto the panel of men and women of The Resistance who would judge the collaborators. He would sit in the high leather chairs in the Palais De Justice in Cahors! When this work was done he would be home. Till then, he sent his whole Love, but he would keep his heart here, if she didn't mind. He might need it.

The drive for Vengeance and the promised purge was strong. Consuming. Three hundred civil servants, gendarmes, teachers, shop owners, labourers, men and women had been rounded up in an orgy of denunciations. There was a fever in the air.

When the first thirty cases were heard there were crowds teeming inside and outside the Court. The panel were cheered as they arrived, the prisoners spat on. The panel found all but one guilty and they were marched straight to the Place Gambetta and a firing squad rid France of their stain. The Committee ordered they be buried in un-marked graves.

Someone must have cleared away the carcasses. Wives, mothers, husbands, fathers. Buried them. In France.

THE SINGLE SOLDIER

Sara came with the child, who wouldn't enter Jacques' house again. So they stood on his steps and Zoe knocked on the door. It was flung open by a man desperately hoping for a letter. When Sara told him Jerome had lived he flooded with joy, relief and Envy and went back inside, hurt again. They went to tell Ardelle.

Zoe's eyes gaped at the ageing woman her mother said was her friend. Sara failed to find words of comfort as she saw how deep news of Jerome's survival ravaged at the remnants of the woman's Hope.

When Galtier brought him nothing, no letter, no card, nothing for three new days in a row Jacques walked down to his beech copse at highest noon with the big axe and swung and cut and swung and ripped the buried blade out and swung and cut and felled and chopped and split till it was evening and he was exhausted. And had enough fire wood for this winter and the next. He left it there. Not enough. Not enough. No letter, yet. Work. Wait.

The next day the Court tried the men of the legislature, men who had handed down Vichy sentences, enforced Vichy laws.

"What could we have done?"

"Refused. We did."

"What we did was lessen Vichy law. We saved lives. Many more would and could have been lost."

"You didn't refuse."

"I never wanted Germany to triumph."

"You say now! Our refusal is our proof of that."

"You are arguing gradations of Purity."

"Purity has no gradations."

"Now you are judging my heart. There is no legal basis for that. You have no legal means to make that judgement. You cannot look into my soul!"

"You have no soul. You tried Frenchmen under Vichy law."

"You are trying me under yours - and yours don't exist."

"Guilty!" someone bellowed from the packed gallery.

"This is the guillotine again," shouted the man, a prosecutor himself up to a month ago, "You've learned nothing and you can teach nothing."

All over France.

When Toulouse was liberated one thousand two hundred were arrested to be brought to trial. Old scores settled with a fictitious denunciation and plenty of fear-soaked Miliciens lying through their teeth. Shaven-headed women spat on in the streets. French Public life was placed on trial.

And De Gaulle, President elect of the Fourth Republic, saw that if this purge carved through the civil service particularly, as it threatened to do, as he had promised it should, then France could not operate. Whole stratas of Society could not function. The great bureaucratic cacophony that is France, the infrastructure, would collapse. Nothing would move.

De Gaulle, who had claimed only the soul of France, a claim which had found this passionate, proud response; De Gaulle who had lit this fire in his people, fuelled it, celebrated it, enshrined it with this promise of Revolution and the new France - he, De Gaulle, now had to trim this flame. And retain his position. Timing a limited pardon with the announcement of the trials of Laval and Petain, he retained almost all of his charisma, and lost only the zealous. Among them, Jerome.

It wasn't that he didn't understand what politics De Gaulle was playing - it was the fact of more politics. He realised only now, in his stupidity, that he had been prepared to die for a new world without this kind of politics. And now he wanted to see his family more than he wanted to sit in judgement. He had had enough of

death. He wanted to see life.

He shook hands with everyone and was driven home to St. Cirgues. Through eighty-odd kilometres of Free France.

A kilometre from the village he stopped the driver, got out and said he'd walk home.

"But - the mayor... he's waiting," said his driver.

"He would. He can. Thanks, comrade. Bonne route."

Madame Valet.

He had to face her.

He would, but he would not ride into town to glory in her loss. He came in on Sara's mother, shushed her, and tip-toed into Zoe's room where Sara was wrestling with a nappy and two wide-awake legs.

"You two need a man."

There was a second of silence.

"Bollocks," said Sara. She picked up their naked daughter and walked into his arms.

"Chibret's waiting," she said.

"Bollocks to Chibret, what's for supper?"

The Russians advanced from the East, fast and deeply furious.

The Allied armies advanced through the lowlands of Belgium and the American 8th Air Force began to target German aviation fuel supplies.

German workers were called from the factories, from anywhere and everywhere, to defend their land. The specialist miners were taken from the Kalkwerke and Arbel was selected to take their place, do their work. And to select four others.

"I'm a farmer, not a miner." Arbel told the Director.

"It's for the effort. You must."

"Fuck your effort," Arbel said in French.

"What?"

"I said, I won't do it. I'm not qualified. I won't."

The Director looked at Arbel. He was too good a worker to lose. "Get out."

He set a team of Poles in Arbel's place. Within a week one of the men had dropped the thirty kilogram drill and lost a leg. He was replaced by a Ukranian. Who was jealous of the one-legged man, sent home.

Jacques milked the herd, took most of the milk across the road and saw what he had become. Duthileul's farm-hand.

Jerome was invited to Toulouse to receive a medal from De Gaulle himself. Glory Day for the survivors. Galtier spread the news round St. Cirgues. Cause for communal pride or Valet's murderer honoured. Madame Lacaze heard. She hadn't seen her son and he, crippled by the family pride, hadn't seen her. Sara took his best trousers to Feyt who sewed the frayed turn-ups, invisibly mended the cigarette burns and pressed them till the creases themselves deserved honouring.

I will not be that. I will not.

I will not grieve and I will not slave.

I will find something.

Either she will write or I will forget.

Jerome heard that none of the Basques, not Roger, nor the English Tommy, would be allowed to stand by his side - De Gaulle would only honour Frenchmen. He put the trousers away. Stuff the medal. This was not a New World.

I can't forget.

Time to go to Janatou. For what? The winter feed for his cows he won't take? I won't go. He can go.

No! I don't want him there. I don't want anyone there. No-one. Ever.

Zoe was his New World.

And Sara.

And his mother?

And Jacques and Ardelle - he hadn't been to see them yet...

And Madame Valet.

It was unthinkable to knock at her door. Again.

So he walked the village hoping to see her, but she, relieved of her teaching, had retreated into shame. Of having married Gaston, of having loved him only the little she'd managed, and most of all, of not missing him. She needed to forgive herself but the weak Curé failed to ask the hard questions that might release her, so she stayed chained to her shame. Like a goat.

Ardelle's desolate reason broke and she walked into the village, to La Poste, and gabbled that they had made a mistake, his letters must be here. Must. She demanded the office be searched. They refused. She accused Galtier of destroying the letters, of hating the victory and hoping Arbel was dead. Chayriguet and Chibret were called. The doctor gave her a sedative, sat her down and organised the search of the office himself. No letter was found. Chibret drove Ardelle home. He was sure Galtier was not responsible, he told her. There might be a happier explanation. There was happier news. The war was being won now, not lost. And surely, soon, Arbel would be sent back. Ardelle felt the man's warmth but couldn't believe a word of it.

The moon rose, earlier each autumning evening.

Jacques sat with Ardelle.

"They say no news is good news. We know better."

They almost smiled. There is comfort in misery.

There is comfort in anything shared.

Jerome, Sara and Zoe ate and Jerome denied, to his wife and himself, that he was bored.

"Go and see your friends," said Sara.

Jacques looked up, furious, as the dog barked. Not Duthileul again. The latch was jiggled, just so, and Jerome walked into the musty gloom.

"Hello, brother." He waved a bottle.

"Jerome!"

Two men hugging for one of them being alive.

"The hero."

"Bollocks. How are you?"

Rather than articulate an answer, or even try to, or even think about it, Jacques managed, "Tell me about it."

Jerome opened the bottle, poured a glass and talked.

"The war's over. It's not finished but here it's over. Patton and Montgomery and The Russians will finish it and I don't care. I don't care. I'm glad I lived and I hope Arbel makes it home and I hope for your sake she comes back. And I'm glad they're alive rather than dead and I hope you do too..." He left a pause and took the silence for Jacques' confirmation. "And I don't know what to do now."

He left another silence. His friend offered nothing. He poured another glass.

"I suppose we're adults now or something but all I can feel is my youth's been taken. By what I've seen and what I've done. With my youth. In my youth. And I don't know what to do now."

"Neither do I."

"I'm not surprised." He smiled an old smile. Jacques said nothing. "Chibret wants to see me. Arse-licker! He's brown-nosing a murderer."

"An assassin."

He remembered her saying that. Heard her voice saying that.

"In the end its all death," said Jerome, "and when you've done it once it doesn't matter after that. You don't count."

They sat. One of them drinking.

"So - I'll be a father. Like I said I wanted to be." He looked at Jacques. "Sorry - subtlety was never my strong point, was it? But, for the rest of my life? I just don't know... can't see it somehow."

Jerome stood.

Glugged the remains of the bottle.

"I'm going to see Ardelle. Coming?"

"You go."

"Do you see her?"

"Yes."

"O.K." He moved to the door. "You know where we are..."

"I won't go to the village," said Jacques.

"Eh?"

"I haven't since - and I won't. I won't look at them and I won't let them look at me."

"They're all old women - even the men - they always were, you know that."

"I won't go."

"Your coupons?"

"I'm in Germany. I haven't got any. I don't need them."

"Tobacco?"

"I don't."

Jag. How can two words drag so hard at the heart?

"D'you want some?"

"Yes."

"Done." He went to the door. "Keep the faith."

"A Curé just said that to me..."

"Annoying, isn't it? They aren't all full of shit."

And he was gone.

She hasn't written.

Jerome found Ardelle aged, frozen and terrified.

"Ardelle - he's working for them. He'll be fine. You know that! They'll need him - old mule, head-down - It's probably him keeping the bastards going single-handed..."

"Bombers..." she muttered her new fear.

"Bounce off his pig-head, won't they?"

"No. Yes."

He walked home in the chill night.

Some stars - some cloud - good night for a parachute drop. Past Duthileul's place. He'd been told how Dominique Duthileul had 'joined up'. At the very last. The scum. Riding other people's bloody shirt-tails. Him, a Maquisard? I'd have shot him if I'd seen him.

He walked down through the woods. There's something eternal here. It's survived more than us. It knows more than us. Seen more. It dwarfs me and quite right. I am a dwarf. And a pig-headed one, too. And I'm adrift here.

The woods ended, the road dipped and the temperature with it. Jerome opened his coat, unbuttoned his shirt and bade the icy air in. Wake me up. Make me see it clear. What, though?

He could make out the cemetery walls now.

Madame Valet - unfinished business.

And then? I have no idea. Not one.

He came in the door, closed it softly and Sara looked up.

THE SINGLE SOLDIER

"Good gab?"

"No - not really. I need a drink."

He went out.

Sara sat.

thirteen

ARBEL TOOK HIS Sunday drink to Lothar's table. Lothar stood, leaving a piece of paper. Moved to another table.

The paper read, "The child by the bar, he's eight, is posted to seek out traitors. I can't talk with you. Have a good life, eh?"

When the other men gathered in the bar after their whorehouse ritual, Arbel said, "I'm off. You coming?"

"Back? It's not time."

"Not back there - I'm going home."

Arbel had gathered no reputation as a joker.

"What?"

"You heard."

"How? Are you mad?"

"No. How? Walk. Bike. Ride. I don't care. It's finished this war. The Germans have lost - it's time to go home now."

"They'll shoot you."

"They won't, they'll understand."

"I'll come," said Claude, the once-fat Boulanger from Latronquiere. "Anyone else?"

"Me." Figeac, the garagiste from Souceyrac.

Eight left the bar. Arbel shook hands with Lothar, wished him a

future, and they left.

"Do we have a map?"

"No."

Eight men in faded denim suits walked out of the war.

"Arbel?"

"Yes?"

"What happens when you sober up?"

The first sign-post said the next conurbation was eight kilometres away.

"We'll sleep there," he said.

"Arbel - can you speak German?"

"Enough, yes."

Jerome could not knock at Madame Valet's door. He could not. So he sat on a bench where he could see her door. A whole day. His determination stayed. He was genuinely surprised. When night fell he went home and was back there at six the next morning. People said he'd gone mad with remorse. Like Jacques the chicken-killer.

Madame Vigne nodded to him as she went to the Mairie. When she came home and he was still there she knocked at Madame Valet's door.

"Who is it?"

"Severine."

The door opened.

"What is it?"

"Someone needs you."

"Eh?"

Madame Vigne directed the woman's gaze to the bench.

"Lacaze?"

"Yes." Madame Vigne placed a hand on Madame Valet's arm,

squeezed it and left.

Madame Valet closed the door and went back inside her grey world.

Ardelle and Jacques made a first winter-warming evening fire. For the first soup they prepared.

Arbel thought of home. Would anything be there? Had the Germans killed her, burnt his home? Don't ask, Arbel. Don't start thinking now! Just walk into this next village. Only 5 kms now.

When they reached that first village Arbel found the Mayor, showed him his papers, told him the exact truth, and they were given food and beds. Arbel asked for a bike. In the morning it was there. He begged a post-card and a stamp and wrote to her.

Ten kilometres west, the next village, they were told. Take the back roads.

"When we get near, I'll ride ahead and arrange things."

The eight walked home.

Jerome sat on the bench till it was dark, went home, ate, slept and was back there every morning for three days until Madame Valet came out of the house, locked the door, and walked across the road to stand in front of him.

"You were always a willful child."

Silence.

"I only came out because I need to shop."

"Let's shop then."

Arbel rode ahead to the next village and when the men arrived they were lodged in a school. Arbel drank with the Mayor and came back with his arms full of clothes. They burnt the prison

lime-pit rags and squabbled over shoes. He took the worst pair because he would cycle. Outside it rained. Set in for the night.

Lacaze and Madame Valet!
Trailing round the thin shops! Then going back to her house, where they'd parted! No-one had heard them speak and that said more than enough.

The German Mayors Arbel met were the same creatures Simone had met on her walk. Battered, baffled, defeated bureaucrats. Still they found meagre food and lodging for the men. And news, too. Of Arnhem. Montgomery, the Americans and the Poles held and repulsed by the Panzas of The Reich. Oh, God, no. Two of the men panicked and went back. Arbel wouldn't argue with them.

Jerome breathed easier that evening, laying with Zoe.
"Good, husband," said his wife.
"Better - not 'good'," he said, "Can it ever be good?"
"Give yourself a rest. And a pat on the back."
"They all know. They know what I did."
"Well if they didn't, they do now."
"Good."
"That's what I just said! Honestly!"

Galtier read both post-cards, cycled up to Puech, found Jacques and Ardelle together in her kitchen, put the cards message side down on the table, shook their shaking fingers, and rode away.
Jacques stared at a line drawing of some place called Oporto. He'd never heard of it. A wide river, a bridge and a town.
Ardelle's card was plain. Her name and address. The stamp was German. It's official. This is the notification. A post-card. Lying on

the table. On the other side - words to finish her life. Her living.

They looked at each other. He was 26, she 25. Both felt and looked 50.

"Stay with me no matter what it says," she whispered.

"I'll try."

"You first?"

They picked up the cards. Ardelle read "I'm walking home. Arbel."

He read, "Jacques, we sail tonight for America. Your son will be a Yankee. Stay Living. Simone."

Arbel heard, then saw a German motor-cycle and side-car patrol and they spent two hours on their bellies in a ditch. Those Germans were retreating and they, wet, muddied, bedraggled, scared, were going home too.

America.

Ardelle read his card. Then her own, again.

America.

Ardelle shed years.

He tried to say something, failed awfully, and reeled out of her suddenly too-hot house.

Numb.

Numb with horror.

Numb with shame. Jealousy. Envy. Numb with every sin but 'iffing'.

America.

He hated the bitch he loved her bones he wanted her here he wanted her dead the mare the cow the lover the angel the thief the cunt.

One of Arbel's group got ill. His shoes didn't fit, they had next to no soles, and when they levered off the ragged leather one

soaking filthy night, shivering in the pig-pen they'd been billeted to, his foot was livid purple and green. Arbel went to find a doctor. Village peasants stared amazed at the foreigner dripping on their front door-step, talking pidgin German, repeating, "Doctor - pigsty." They told him where the vet lived - and the vet drove him to the doctor and the doctor drove the man to hospital. Five.

Late October. They found a cart. A hand-cart. The wheels and the tyres were good. They took it.

He found the picture of his father in the bottom of a drawer. Under a dress of his mother's Simone had left. He put the picture to one side and gathered all he could find of Simone's. Her few clothes, the child's bonnet, a comb she'd used, the post-card with the dreadful words on it, the cot he'd fashioned, the rocking chair and every other moveable physical memory and cut them, ripped them, bent them and broke them. He put the remnants in his barrow with the long-handled spade and waited till dusk before he walked down to the cemetery, dug out the earth above his mother's coffin, and buried the ruins of Simone.

Arbel, Claude, Figeac, Jean-François and Yannick walked. Pulling their cart. Pushing Arbel's bike. Days of mud and slush and cold, nights of ragged fires, thin vegetables and black bread. Autumn gone and winter coming.

The men had no idea the Allies had liberated Athens, that Tito and his partisans had entered Belgrade, or the France they were walking to was all free. But Arbel could sense in the eyes of the Mayors and the people of the villages and the farmers who housed them that the boil of Hitler was lanced. These people had no fight left in them. The hate so obvious in the youth on the streets of Ludswigdorf had gone. It might still be there, but it was private

now. Good. It should be burnt. Razed like his autumn tares. Hope Ardelle remembered to do them...

Jerome and Madame Valet sat on the bench. Still there was everything to be said. They talked around the unspeakable for days. Until.

"Jerome, I want you to do something for me."

"That would be a pleasure, Madame."

"Go and see your mother."

Silence.

"I could have asked you to come to Church with me..."

"That would be easier."

"To pray for Gaston's soul..."

Silence.

"I don't believe in those prayers, Madame."

"No, neither do I anymore. But I believe your mother has prayers."

"Oh yes."

"And I think Zoe should know her grandmother."

"I don't."

Silence.

"I've intruded perhaps; but you owe me something, Lacaze, and that's what I would like. There are too many holes in this commune."

Silence.

America. The eternity of Loss flooded him.

An awesome noise approached them. Tanks. They dived, sprawling, into cover of the trees. No swastikas. These had stars on their side. American. Another. Another. An army. The men stood. Walked back towards the road. Each tank had a man sitting up

top. When one saw Arbel and the men he threw packs of cigarettes from his tank-top turret. Spread his fingers in a 'V' and turned his thumb up when Arbel copied him. Arbel, pointing West, his voice rusty, shouted, "Vive La France!" The soldier threw his thumb up again and passed them, going East to make war.

They were 200 kms from the French Border. They could be in France for Easter. Maybe.

Of course someone noticed the grave had been disturbed. The Curé came.

Jacques opened the door and the dog sniffed at the priest while the Curé tried not to smell Jacques.

"I told you when your Mother died, that God still has work for you to do."

"What is it?"

"I don't know."

"God does?"

"Of course. Ask Him."

"I have."

"He must answer, Vermande. That's His Work."

They learned their home-land was free of Germans.

From the Germans who were feeding and housing and helping them.

The same Germans who, some of them, clearly hated them.

For their nationality. For the arbitrary geography of their birthplace. As if that were anything to do with one single person walking the planet.

Fuck God's work.

Let Him do it.

The Germans aren't coming back. And neither are they.
Not from America.

Other Americans threw chocolate bars, cans of explosive sugary drinks, and pink bubble-gum that Claude said tasted like inner-tubes. Figeac, the garagiste, asked how he knew what inner-tubes tasted like. Then he tried some and agreed. They walked home. Claude learned how to blow huge pink bubbles. When one popped and they had to dig the gunk out of his filthy beard he abandoned the gum on a post saying Dornstetten 13 kms.

Jerome, in lieu of doing as Madame Valet asked, began to drink. And think. And then drink to stop the thinking. And eventually to re-start the thinking.

America. She could have waited in Spain. Waited and come back - but no - America.
He went down to the caves, brought back his heavy headed axe, stripped the bedding from his bed - the bed they'd loved in, the bed his son was born in - and hacked the oak to matchwood. The dog went out.
America.

Arbel rode ahead each day to charm or demand room, roof, and food for his friends. They all walked together till he rode ahead and they would meet him - and rain, snow, sleet or starry sky - he provided.

Jerome crossed a threshold.
He drank in the café. With shivering, fawning Chibret and Duthileul in his window corner. He had shot Gaston Valet out of

here and taken his place. Some club.

America.
Gone. For ever. Eternity. This whole life.
What's it worth now? What's it for?
'God's work..!'
He stood. A man with a heavy-headed axe in his hand. His life in splinters.
'Stay Living.'
Black black joke.
Die.
Yes.
I can't.
But this - and every single possible moment to come – this can't be Living.
'Stay living.'
Not worth living.
In this. Torture.
Sara and Zoe and Jerome and Arbel and Ardelle and I'm so jealous and so angry and so empty.
What's to live for?
Meet someone else? He almost laughed.
All tears dried now.
Mother, wife, son, blood, love, gone.
'It's a Mortal Sin, suicide. There is no forgiveness.' I told mother once.
I don't care a fig for forgiveness - just an end to this.
Do it.
Hang yourself. Here.
What if Ardelle had to find me?
Good. Serve her happiness right!

See! See? Not fit to Live.

Not Fit.

The well.

Don't think.

Don't think.

Act.

Don't think any more.

The axe dropped. Clattered on the floor.

The dog followed him out of the house.

Ardelle watched him pull the bucket up and lay it on the ground.

Watched him take off his jacket.

Watched him climb on to the open mouth.

Sit on the ledge. Swing his feet into the stone moss-green black hole.

She screamed.

Push forward and be gone.

Push forward, man!

Look down - look how deep and still it is. See? Your head'll hit the sides and you'll be dead before you drown.

Peace. All over. Gone. Peace.

"Jacques!!" She screeched as she ran.

Name of the father and the son and - you can't say that - you can't. Those are words He gave us and you can't use them to justify breaking His Law...

Don't. Don't think. Stop! Stop thinking. Just push.

The dog barked hard.

"Jacques! No!!"

It's Life. Ignore it - it's done.

America.

Push!

"Your son, Jacques - your son!" she came screaming into the

garden -

What?

Nothing! Nothing!! Go! Push!

What? My son? What?

More pain! Jump!

Push now for Peace.

Ardelle enveloped him in her peasant's arms and pulled them both crashing to the ground.

The clock struck in the village.

Quarter to something.

Jacques' head clanged.

It passed.

A deep grey pain replaced it, thudding behind his forehead - a drum – pounding. Speaking. "I know. I know. I know. I know."

He lay his head on the grass. Cool. Needs cutting. Graze a beast. America. Simone.

"Jacques?"

He turned his head to his name and he lay in Ardelle's arms in his garden.

Her hands moved to hold his face, hold his eyes.

"He can never hear his father killed himself. You may not do that. Nothing can ever be that bad."

He studied her eyes.

"I know, Jacques."

"I see... that you do."

"Good."

She loosed her arms and their bodies moved an inch apart.

"I know," she said again.

He waited.

Ardelle said, "You - and Simone. And then your baby. Jacques."

She swallowed and her eyes were like the well; deep, dark death.

"I hated you..." he managed.

Silence in the garden.

The dog approached them low.

Silence.

"I've been a bad friend," he managed.

"We've both had troubles."

They moved a little more. Enough.

"You all right?"

"Yes. No. You?"

"I'm fine." She almost smiled.

Of course you are - he's coming home. Simone's in America.

"What was that thought, Jacques?"

"Not to be shared, Ardelle."

Ardelle sat up, looked at him and a charge of maternalism fired through her.

"And what was that thought?" he asked.

"I don't know..." she said.

He sat up a little. Then lay back. His head did hurt.

"Come and eat," she said.

"I need to sleep."

"Come and sleep," she said.

Their eyes locked.

"Come and be with me."

As they walked up the steps to her door his hardness was full.

"Are you hungry?" she said, at the table, her back to him.

In his silent answer she turned to look at him.

He shut the door and she sat on the bed and unbuttoned her blouse. He stood watching.

"This is need," one said.

"I know," said the other.

Their bodies lay together again - locked again – now naked eyes and arms and legs.

"Don't make me pregnant," she said.

"Then I must stop."

"Stop then," she said and moved him out of her and taking him in one hand and his balls in the other she squeezed and held and squeezed and held till he pumped himself, arching, gasping, out. She was amazed how long it took for his thing to empty.

"Need is good," she said, softly watching his eyes as his bliss diluted with shock towards shame. And now she saw fear...

"Need is good," she repeated.

She held him still, limpening in her hand.

Jacques looked into her square, plain face.

"What about your need?"

Ardelle's eyes widened.

"I don't know..."

His hand warmed her wetness and his fingers found her and she gave a short gasp of surprise and then her groan was deeper and her spine arched and her breasts rose searching for his mouth and she gasped again at his kiss and her thrusting urged his farmer's fingers up her and down and back and harder and round and up and he bit so gently at her nipple and one kind need flowed with the other.

He slept in her bed and she brought both herds in and milked them, fed his dog and the sad straggly chickens and made thin soup.

Arbel would not judge her badly.

No-one would. Unless Jacques did. She stirred.

He didn't.

He slept through the evening, through Ardelle's undressing again and putting her night-gown on and wondering what and if and getting into bed and chastely turning her back and he slept through her not sleeping and through her sleeping and through her wakening, too.

You needed that, she thought. And she laughed in her kitchen at her first little joke in two years. A smile. He's coming home. He's walking home. My fool. My man. He won't judge us badly I'm sure of that.

And I needed that, too.

No.

It was the news you're alive - you're living - you're walking home - that was what I needed. It gave me enough to answer his need. Enough joy to spread. Yes.

I wouldn't have done that before. He's been here a lot and never thought of that, I'm sure. It's Joy that released me.

To betray my husband.

To love my friend.

To be unfaithful.

Yes. Guilty.

No. I won't regret it.

I'm not sorry.

I didn't want to...

Well, when he was - when we were - then I did want to - I was happy to.

How can something good and warm and loving be wicked? Was it? It didn't feel so.

Confession? Oh no.

Ardelle knelt on her kitchen floor.

You saw, so you must have judged. You know why. You saw me sin.

But Lord - when he bit my nipple, and when he made his mess - that was the best of the sin, Lord.

His eyes opened.

"Coffee?"

"Yes. Please. Ardelle."

He was dressed and at the table when she poured it.

"Thank you."

They sat.

She wanted, she needed his eyes. There they were. Read them, Ardelle - and now say it.

"I'm not sorry."

"No. I'm not sorry," he managed, "I'm shocked."

And his eyes lowered. "She's only been gone - how long is it..?"

Ardelle stated, "Neither of them would judge us badly."

He thought about that. "No, they wouldn't."

They took a mouthful of coffee.

A quiet began. Their quiet.

"The dog..."

"Fed, waiting for you."

"The beasts - "

"Done."

A beat of time.

"I should go home."

"Yes."

He finished the coffee. Had to think about standing. He stood.

"I'm going," he said.

"I'm here for you."

"Yes. I know. Now." He looked at her. "I didn't before."

"We must get on," she said and stood.

"Did I have a coat?"

"No."

He opened the door and looked across at his farm. Duthileul's farm. His chest heaved. She turned him and kissed him on each cheek.

"I'm here for you," she said.

Jacques went home. The dog leapt to greet him.

He squeezed deep into the dog's head, running the warm skin, rolling it through his fingers.

He looked at the well.

The herd.

The garden.

The house, the empty house.

The future, the empty future.

I'm hungry.

He ate with Tayo in the empty house.

What does this mean?

Me and Ardelle..?

And Arbel coming home.

And America.

Now what is life? Now who am I? Now what do I do? Now what am I for?

Arbel thought of Ardelle not as she had been when he'd left, nor as she might be when he got back, but as she would be when they would one day both be sixty. Thickened, sturdy, steadfast and with him. And he walked towards that.

fourteen

SARA LOST HER TEMPER when he slouched in yet again from the Tabac.

"Go and see her! Do as you were asked! I don't want a drunk putting my daughter to bed. Maudlin and mean in the head."

"Our daughter," came the feeble riposte.

"Don't make me laugh. I'll go and drink all day tomorrow shall I? I'll sit and maunder and you," she laughed at the thought, "you can dress and feed and clean up after, entertain and amuse our daughter. One whole day. Yes?"

"I could do that," he snapped.

"Done! Where's my drinking money? Or do you have a tab? Just sign my married name, shall I?"

"I can't talk to my mother..."

A cold silence filled the room.

"You could kill Gaston Valet - and I make no judgement on that - you can face his widow, you can walk and talk with her and you can't talk to your mother!" His wife dripped scorn. "What are you teaching your daughter?"

"She's too young to know what - "

"Shut up! Shut up, Jerome. What do you know about children?

You know nothing! Nothing."

The child stirred, turned, mewled in her bed.

"Shh..." said Jerome. Sara exploded.

"I will not 'Shh!' If she wakes you'll deal with her. And I'll go and drink and I'll go and talk with your Mother - and she and I will have the talk about Pride that neither of you have the humility or the humanity to admit to or manage." She leaned a hand on the table, panting a little. "She needs to be taught about Grandparenting as much as you need – agh! you're two peas from the same stupid pod."

Zoe woke. Whimpering, but wakening, too.

"Deal with that - and give me some money," Sara demanded, holding out her hand. "Give!"

Jerome handed her coins and a note and with a martyr's tread, went to his daughter's bedside. He heard the house door close, hard.

"Shhh - there, there - it's just Mamma and Pappa having a row. Shh. All over now. Shh."

Of course the child woke, crying solidly.

"Please, Zoe - it's all right. Where's your dummy? Eh? That what you want?"

Zoe hadn't had a dummy for a year and more. She squalled, a little frightened now.

"Oh, Zoe, please - forget it - it's nothing. Please now - Daddy needs to think - you just go back to sleep now, yes?"

Zoe sat up.

"Where's Mamman?"

"Drinking."

"I want a drink."

"Water?"

"What's mamma drinking?"

"I don't know."

"Go and see, silly."

"Well - we can't."

The child's eyes, bleary till now, cleared instantly.

"Why?"

"She isn't here."

"Why?"

"She's gone out."

"Why?"

"She - wanted to."

"Why?"

"Oh! She's gone out for a walk. O.K.? She'll be back in a minute."

"You said she was drinking."

"Yes. Outside."

"Why?"

"Zoe! Does it matter?"

The pair of them stared at each other.

"I want Mamman."

Negotiation was finished.

"Why?" tried Jerome, pleased for an instant.

"Because I do."

"Why?" His confidence evaporating.

"Because."

"Would you like some milk? Shall I warm up some milk?"

"No."

He scoured his empty mind.

"Shall I read you a book?"

"I want mamma." Her eyes began to fill.

"She'll be back in a minute. Shall Daddy cuddle down with you? Eh?"

"No! I want Mamman."

"Because I'm no good? Is that it?"

"What?"

"Nothing. I didn't mean that."

"I want Mamman."

Jerome looked at his daughter.

"Right! Fine. Come on then."

And he lifted her sharply out of the sleep-warm bed, hoisted her into his arms and walked through the house.

"Mamman, right? Fine. Pappa isn't good enough. I completely agree."

He opened the door with his free hand and the night air covered Zoe's bare arms instantly with goose-pimples.

"Cold, isn't it? Still want to go and find Mamman?"

The child, though frightened by this tone and the cold, nodded.

He looked across the square at the dimly-lit Tabac. What if she weren't there? What if she had gone to his mother's? Oh shit.

"Zoe - let's wait, eh? She'll be here in a minute, I'm sure."

The child stared at the village.

"You said she was outside. Where is she?"

Ohh, fuck all Mothers to Hell and back, he thought.

"Where is she?"

"I don't know."

Jerome stepped back inside the house, closing the door.

"I want Mamman."

"Right. Yes! I understand. But if I don't know where she is then we can't find her can we?" he snapped.

"Why?" His daughter was tensing with fear.

"Because!"

Zoe cried.

Jerome took her back to her bed.

Zoe cried.

"I want Mimi!" howled the grand-daughter.

"She isn't here either. There's just useless me!"

Zoe threw herself face down on the bed and howled.

"You're not Mamman! You're no good!"

"I know! Thank you - I know!"

"I want Mamma. I want Mimi!"

"Well, you can't have them! Can you? You can't have them. They're not here."

"I want - someone..." the child was heading into hysteria.

"Someone else - yes, I know. No can do, Zoe."

"Mamman!!"

Jerome walked out as he felt the impulse to strike the child flood him. Her howls turned to screams as he closed the door and he panicked instantly -would some fucking neighbour come running? Would Sara hear over in the bar? What was he to do? I need a drink. Zoe took a fresh breath and howled.

This is awful.

I'm her father. And I'm worse than useless. Jesus Christ, Sara's been out of the house five minutes and look at it - listen to it! It's almost funny, except - Zoe howled again - it's true. Oh, fuck me, I never felt this helpless in the fucking war!

"Mamman! Mimi!"

Fucking women. They have a stranglehold on children. Colonised them. Men are useless. No! Fuck that. I won't have that.

"Mammmmaaan! Mimmiiii!"

Got it.

He went back to the child's room, opened the door and her terror swarmed out and filled the house.

"There, there - no problem, Zoe - we'll find Mimi," he said as he ransacked the drawers for a shawl. Zoe wept, in a loop of uncomprehending fear.

He found socks, they didn't match but what the hell...

"Where's your woolly bonnet? Eh? Where is the bastard thing?" He ripped clothes out of drawers, strewing the floor - till he found a scarf of Sara's.

Zoe took a breath and looked up at her father, arms full of clothes, a demented look in his eyes and she filled with panic again.

"I want Mamman!"

"Come on then - we'll find a bloody woman - if that's what you need my little precious darling - we'll go and find a bloody woman, eh? Let's get warm, tho' eh? Because it's cold out there in the big world, isn't it; yes it is, we know that because we went to the door and it was freezing wasn't it? But the women are all outside so we know we'll have to be warm, won't we? Yes."

His diatribe quieted the child long enough for him to prepare the shawl and socks and he lifted her from the bed and she squirmed, human plasticine, wriggling away from his hands. Again he curbed the desire to smack her into acquiescent shock and burbled on instead.

"I know - I know - you want them to just be here and for big bad poppa to disappear up the chimney with the smoke but Life isn't that simple Zoe; no it isn't. When we really want something - like you want Mamma or Mimi now - we have to work hard for it, don't we? Yes, we do, we have to put this shawl on, yes, and these socks and we have to go into the cold cold night to find them. Yes. Sit still! You must have socks on. You must!"

The child looked ridiculous. Shawled, scarved, odd-socked, sad and scared, as her father scooped her up into his arms, wrestling away from him now, pushing at his chest with her little strength; and he prattled on, since, thank God, at least his nonsense silenced hers for the moment.

"Mimi - yes - we'll go and find Mimi, shall we? Yes, let's Daddy and

Zoe go and find her. Ready? It'll be cold when we open this door won't it - but we don't care, do we? No, we're determined, aren't we Madame? Yes, we're determined to find a female!"

He opened the door and the cold air wrapped itself around them both and he stepped out with his shocked daughter into St. Cirgues and the black December night.

Sara flicked through the magazines in the Tabac. Drivel. The three shocked men had said nothing but she giggled inside imagining what they must be thinking.

No Duthileul.

Just ragged ancient tares of the religion of alcohol. She nursed the wine and didn't give a monkey's fig what the gossip would say - hell, it wasn't too difficult was it? She'd had a row with her fool man. Correct. And if logic had any courage the bars of France would be teeming every night with frustrated women instead of these old sods. That's it though, isn't it? This is their bloody silly dull church. A man's club.

"What do you buggers talk about?" she asked.

Three heads looked up as though a goat in a wimple had just walked into the bar.

"If I wasn't here," she was suddenly enjoying this, "what would you be talking about? M.Galtier?"

"What are you doing here?"

"Drinking - like you. Like men. What do you lot talk about when you're not gawping at seeing a woman alone in your bar?"

"Why?"

Sara laughed. "You sound like my two-year old!"

"Shut up and know your place," one of them growled.

Sara downed the glass, enjoying the rush of cheap warmth.

"This is your place, right? Mine's in the home, right? I'll tell you what I think, shall I?"

"No."

"Why not? You sit here and drink for the courage to think thoughts you don't have the nerve to think outside this place. It's a coward's watering-hole."

One of the men turned to actually face her.

"Maybe we come here to get away from the likes of you."

"What's so scary about the likes of me? What could I do to upset you?"

"Oh, bugger off!" The man turned away, into the support of stifled sniggers.

"No. I won't. I'll have another please," she raised her empty glass to Janon.

He looked helplessly at the men.

"Don't serve her," she heard muttered.

"Don't serve me, then," Sara said. She rose and walked to the table where the three men sat.

"Need a fourth for cards? Eh? A little Belotte?"

She pulled up a chair, sat down and picked up the cards.

"Leave them alone!"

Sara laughed in the man's face. Shuffled the pack crudely, spilling some. A hand clamped down on them.

"Get out. You're not wanted here. You've no place here."

"Men only? It's not men only in here is it, Janon?"

The old one looked helpless at her.

"I'll get my wife," he spluttered and headed for the back of the bar.

Sara roared. "Get your wife? Get your wife! Oh, come on! A game of cards, a glass of wine - where's the threat that needs a woman?"

Janon stalled, waiting for help from his customers.

"Why do you need a woman? Aren't you men? Aren't you men enough?"

  THE SINGLE SOLDIER

Janon took another step towards his wife.

"What if she agrees with me? Then what? You'll all have to get your wives and then we'll outnumber you - that's a good idea! Get them all, then I can have a game of cards."

"Your husband killed Gaston - that's why you're not welcome," said Galtier coldly. Janon stood still, the men mumbled their agreement. Slowly, in the silence that developed, all the eyes turned to look at her, to see the wound bleed. It didn't.

"Then how can you allow him to drink here?"

There was no answer.

"You're pathetic."

She left.

Jerome walked down through the village, past the Maire, La Poste and the Gendarmerie, out on to the lane to his mother's house. The wind that had only picked at them round the edges of the straggling houses now found its icy way through the crochet holes of the shawl, found the skin above Zoë's ridiculous socks, whipped the shawl from her head.

"Mmm, cuddle close Zoe. Cold, isn't it?"

The child, amazed, wide-eyed, needed no second invitation. He wrapped her into his coat, pulled the shawl tight and rubbed at her little legs as they walked the half-kilometre.

"Look at those stars, eh? The Milky Way. Where's Orion? He's the Hunter. Where is he? There he is! See those three straight stars - those three in a line? See them?" He pointed, making her follow his arm. "Those? You see them? That's his belt and in his belt is his sword. To kill with. To defend with. To hunt with. Orion. And, where's the plough?"

A man and a child, spinning in an empty road, searching the sky.

"There it is! See - see that box with a handle? That's the plough. It's not a plough really, is it? It's more like a cart. But it doesn't sound so good to say 'The Cart', does it? No. Well, bugger 'em, Zoe - for you and me - that's the cart. Right. That's our cart. Yes?"

"Yes."

"Good! I don't know any others. Well - I know there's a bear." They walked on, the child craning its neck to scan the firmament. "There's a Great Bear - like Russia - and there's a little Bear. But I don't know where they are."

"What's Russia?"

"Russia is an ally."

"What's an ally?"

"A friend."

"A bear is a friend?"

"Yes. Sometimes it is."

He walked. The child leaned closer. The forgotten fear replaced with wonder at the adventure.

"Where are we going, Pappa?"

"We're going to see another Mimi."

"Another?"

"Yes. You've two Mimi's. Mummy's Mimi and Daddy's Mimi. We're going to see her."

"Is she nice?"

Jerome Lacaze bit his tongue very hard indeed.

"Of course."

"Will she have ice-cream?"

All round her rancorous heart he thought.

"I don't know. We'll ask her shall we?"

He could see the house.

No lights on. Oh bollocks. Oh fart.

Sara saw the open door, came in and smelt everything in an instant.

In the child's room clothes were strewn everywhere; no husband, no daughter. Oh God - what's happened? Has - her mind reeled into nightmare - have they been taken? Have some straggling Milice taken some ghastly revenge on them all? For Gaston bloody Valet? Surely not? No - that's drink talking. He's taken her. She picked up fallen clothes as her mind rattled. No scarf - he's taken my scarf. Why? Her shawl. He's taken her. Where? Why? What if it wasn't him? What do I do? Her mother was at her sisters in St. Hilaire. What do I do?

She almost snorted with black laughter at the idea of going back to the bar to ask the men to help her look. They'd be thrilled at my distress. So? So? Sit here - wait and hope? He's taken her - that's what must have happened. Must have. Where? To Jacques? What? He's walking Zoe two kilometres in this night to - to what? To sit and whinge about me? Surely even he couldn't be that pig-headed? Ardelle? Feyt? I should tell the Gendarmes. I should tell someone something - God's sake my daughter isn't here, I can't sit and trust Jerome.

He's taken her to his mothers.

He would.

She sat down and let the thought calm her. It made sense. He would. Pride. That's him.

At this time? She'll be asleep. Right. She wrapped Jerome's big coat - the dumb fool's gone out without a coat - round herself and set off.

Jerome and Zoe stood on the door-step.

"I think Mimi's asleep."

"Knock on the door, silly."

God, why did I start this?

"She's not here."

"Knock on the door."

"Her car isn't here."

"Mimi has a car?"

"Yes. And she isn't here. We'll go home then shall we? Yes, eh? Mamma'll be home now, I'm sure."

"I want to see Mimi."

"We'll come back," he promised, and surprised himself by meaning it. "I promise."

A car's headlights approached.

"It's Mimi!" the child exclaimed.

Oh shit, I bet it is, he thought.

Madame Lacaze could make out a man with a child in his arms. Her heart both stalled and melted. Another victim? No, surely, not now. That was over. But, if so, why had they come to her house? Was she known, named, now?

As she neared her compassion took hold. A wee child. But, there hadn't been any children since The Debarquement. As she turned into her driveway and the babe shielded her eyes from the headlamps Madame Lacaze's heart took a sharper, colder turn. It's him. And her. At this hour? What was this?

Jerome Lacaze held his blood in one arm, as his mother stepped from the car.

Madame Lacaze locked the car slowly. She ought to put it in the garage, the night would be cold, but...

"Is this Mimi Two?"

"Yes."

"Why doesn't she speak?"

"She's rehearsing."

"What's rehearsing?"

"Never mind."

"Has she thrown you out, then?"

Jerome had never had a problem being honest with his mother. More that their truths lay at right-angles to each other.

"No. I promised Zoe she could meet her grandmother."

"Half a truth is better than none."

"That's what you taught me. Zoe," he hitched the child higher, "this is Mimi."

Zoe leaned her body and her cheek into her father's neck.

"No, it isn't."

"No, you're right. This is Mimi Two, isn't it?"

Madame Lacaze coloured, visible even in the dark night.

"Is this a Mamman, too?"

"Yes. Mine."

She's cold. The child is cold.

"Come in," she said.

Jerome Lacaze went home.

Madame Lacaze had poured hot chocolate by the time Sara banged at the door.

"I'll go," said Jerome. "Can I leave you with Mamman Two?"

"Yes." Zoe was confused by the question.

Jerome opened the front door.

"You spineless hypocrite."

"No..."

"In half an hour you're at her skirts?"

"Zoe wanted - "

"Blame the child? Jesus, Jerome - I knew you were weak - but..."

She took just enough breath to say, "I want my daughter."

"I was hopeless, I admit - and angry - "

"I want my daughter."

Sara moved past him into the dark corridor, said, "Well?"

"Ahead."

Sara opened the door. A room of lace and heavy oak cabinets, flocked wallpaper, a piano, crucifixes, a portrait of The Virgin, another of The Pope and standing the other side of the table, a long-faded photograph of Jerome's father directly behind her, Madame Lacaze. Zoe turned in her seat, holding her hot chocolate and, pointing at Madame Lacaze, said, "This is Mamman Two, too!" Giggled and then plain laughed.

Jerome came into the room.

"What's funny, Zoe?" he asked.

"This is Mamman tutu!" And she laughed again. Only her father laughed with her.

"She's my mamman, too, yes."

"Zoe," said Sara, "It's time to go home."

"Would you like some chocolate? Sara? It is a cold night."

Sara dithered.

Incomprehension flooded her. Her feelings waved. Swirled.

She felt anger and contempt for the fool behind her, unconditional love for the child at her side and nothing at all for the woman talking to her.

"I know," said Madame Lacaze, "We've wasted years. All of hers."

Sara looked round at Jerome.

"Well?"

"Well, what?" he replied, dumbly.

"What is this?"

"I don't know. There was an invitation to chocolate."

"Jerome!"

He almost jumped. Zoe did.

"What?" he said, "I don't know what. Or why. I know how. I know I'm a fool. I know I'm her son. I know I'm her father. And your husband. Much else is beyond me just at this moment. Though I'd like something stronger than chocolate."

"You would." said both women.

"Two mammans, daddy," smiled Zoe.

Her parents stared at each other.

Finally, Jerome asked, "What am I guilty of?"

Sara laughed. "You think like a Catholic!"

"It's how he was raised," said Madame Lacaze involuntarily.

"Dragged to piety," corrected her son instinctively.

"Not hard enough," said his wife.

Then, surprising herself, Sara said, "Yes, I will have chocolate Madame, thank you."

"Jerome?"

"No. Thank you. Mother."

Sara smiled, swallowed the snort bursting from her and then plain laughed. Madame Lacaze frowned as she went to the kitchen and it was Zoe who asked, "What's funny?"

Sara shook her head, dismissing the moment and the question.

Jerome, reddening, heard himself say, "I don't know Zoe - what's funny, Sara?"

Sara felt - almost saw - the alliances shifting. It made her sick to her stomach. She looked at Jerome, took Zoë's hand, called, "Thank you Madame, but I've changed my mind. Home, Zoe." And lifting the child into her arms she walked out of the room, the house and Jerome's heart.

Jerome and his mother stood.

"Do you want chocolate?"

He could see the effort to keep her smile at bay. The glee. The victory.

"Have you anything stronger?"

"Yes."

Two days later he missed Zoë's birthday.

fifteen

HIS OAK CEILING. Hundred years old. At least. Or it would be. One day. If it wasn't already. No way to tell, now. Now it's a floorboard. A beam. Same tree? The shelf over the door. The door. The bed. The floor. All oak.

And me?

Gnarling. Skin to bark. Impervious wooden man. Rain falls, feeds my roots. I grow, flowering leaves of dry tears. For Arbel, now. Walking faithfully home, like a dog; while I defile the sacrament of his marriage. For lust. For 'need'. For ever.

I've stolen the purity of their vows.

I can't ever look at his face without I'll see me and her in sweat and disgrace and - we didn't kiss - we did not kiss - and - I didn't come - not in her.

But we did what we did with no thought of him. For him.

Or her.

Bound for America.

He no longer saw the ceiling.

Ardelle worked. Tidied. He was coming home. The card was stamped in Germany - where? - a week - a month from the border?

And the bombers? Enough. He was alive and he was coming.
Home.

And he would understand.

When I tell him. Why. Tell him why. And if he says 'was it good?'
I'll lie. Or tell the truth. If I tell him. If he asks.

What was it?

It was an event and it had passed. It had gone.

But it was here.

In his home. He would see it. And if he didn't? Then it didn't exist
- it never happened.

Or - it would be a stone secret between us. If I don't tell him.

Yesterday I was surer.

A week ago there was just the Spanish border between us - now
we're an ocean apart.

Why doesn't Jacques call? I can't go round there. He might think
– anything.

It was near noon when he moved and worked his baffled herd and
felt Ardelle's eyes on him.

He's ashamed. Oh no no no.

The day passed, the earth turned, the night came and the sky
turned. They lay in their beds at Puech - apart and widening.
Silence eats.

I've betrayed everything.

My son? He almost laughed.

What would your mother feel if she knew I'd sucked Ardelle as you suckle her?

What exactly am I?

Well, I'm bereft of prayer.

I'm a sinner.

Against Arbel.

Would I blame Arbel if he'd been with a girl? No.

Do I blame Ardelle? No.

Do I blame me? Yes.

For what? Wanting? Needing?

Yes.

Didn't you try and kill yourself?

Yes.

Were you rational?

No.

And so, tell me, what's so wrong with wanting? What's wrong with need?

Something.

Ardelle said 'neither of them would judge us badly.'

If Simone does with some American - will I judge her badly? Yes!

Would she judge me badly? No.

What does that make me?

Meaner.

I said it. I said, 'Come and sleep.'

It's rotten in two days.

Poisoned. Why? By what? How? Why?

It was warm. It was warmth. It was good.

And if it was goodness in Sin - then - it must be the goodness that makes us sin. And that must be the sin. There's the cruelty in breaking His laws, then. It's good. It feels good.

I bet it felt good to steal from Germans. I bet it felt good to kill Germans.

'I'm here for you,' she said.
I wish we hadn't.
But it was Good. It was.

What is he thinking? To himself? Why doesn't he talk? It was I who said it, yes, but it was we in the bed.

🐑

Madame Valet asked Jerome whether he hadn't gone too far.
"Do you mean, 'why'?"
"Yes."
"I don't know."
"You can't say 'I don't know' in matters of the heart. It's evasion."
"I have no heart."
Madame Valet looked at the slouching wine-soaked youth who had murdered her husband.
"Jerome. Gaston drank - as you know. And the more he drank the further from his heart he drifted. And from me."
Jerome looked at her.
"I never loved Sara. Did I? I always only hated my mother. Didn't I? What's real now? When I was fighting…" he stalled but she nodded him onward, "I knew. I knew everything. Now I can't grasp my mind."
"We're all in shock, Jerome. For one reason or another."
A silence.
"We've all been through a shocking experience…"
"I can't listen to my heart, Madame. It appals me."

"Drowning it won't work. Courage, man. Here comes the hardest part. The hardest thing, for all of us. Re-building."

Arbel and the men walked into Sindelfinger. It had a railway station. The station master put them in the waiting room, lit a fire, found them all blankets. Blankets in a railway station? Don't ask. Be thankful.

"The time-table", he told them over coffee, over fresh coffee, "is fiction. But any train that stops or slows enough will take you to the French border and Strasbourg."

No-one needed any persuading not to walk on and for four days, in return for the station-master's wife's soup, Jean-Luc tidied and weeded the flower beds, Figeac serviced the man's car, Claude the Boulanger learnt strudel and taught croissant, and Arbel and Yannick whitened the platform edge and painted the station roof.

On the fourth day a goods train roared through, ignoring the station-master's flags.

"I'll cut the signal cord," he offered, simply. "I'll deal with the driver."

Two nights later - at four in a freezing morning the five Frenchmen shook the German's hand and clambered into an empty cattle truck.

"A day to the border," he said, closing the sliding door. "Bonne route, eh?"

The people you meet. The train pulled Westwards.

THE SINGLE SOLDIER

He slept in slabs of darkness. He woke frequently, hideously alone; with Arbel in his black vision sometimes even before Simone and his son.

I cannot face Arbel's eyes. I cannot face his forgiveness.

I must leave. I've poisoned this land. His land. He's coming home to a plague.

The dog barked him upright.

"Who is it?"

"Me."

Ardelle.

He pulled his trousers on, shushed the dog, came out of his room, her room, their room, and opened the front door. Morning.

Ardelle offered a wire pannier with a handful of green beans in it.

"Come in..." he mouthed.

Ardelle put the pannier on the table and sat where Simone last sat, at her last meal, that last evening of that last night.

"There's no fire - I'm sorry..." he muttered.

Why hadn't Jerome bought tobacco - I'd kill for a fag.

"Why have I had to come here?"

"I was - afraid..."

She waited.

"I thought we might... Again... I was resisting temptation."

"I don't believe you. But thank you for saying - something. You wish it had never happened."

Yes.

"You wish it away and I remind you of it."

Yes.

"You've even wished Arbel won't come back..?"

"And so did you?"

"Yes," she conceded heavily. She looked up at him, said, "We did something - for each other."

"Yes." Their eyes met. "And now we wish we hadn't."

Silence agreed.

He managed, "I didn't know what to think."

"And what do you think?"

"I've betrayed Arbel."

Ardelle nodded.

"We've betrayed him," she said and again fresh pain as their eyes met. "Jacques, how can good become bad?"

"I don't know."

"Why?"

"Because I'm ignorant."

"No - why has good become bad?"

"Because - " again the eyes met, "of vows."

She nodded again.

Damn him. He was right.

"Do you blame me? Your silence did."

"No! I - " he blushed, "I dread looking in his face, Ardelle. I was a friend."

Very slowly she said, "I'm a friend. I was a friend."

Jacques sat.

"Oh, God, Ardelle. I know nothing. Except, I'm not a friend. Obviously."

"You were three days ago. A week ago. All our lives. What are you saying?"

"A friend doesn't - do that..."

"Two friends did."

The dog lay down, re-assured by the quietness of their talk.

"You were going to kill yourself. There's a war. He's walking home through it and he might still be killed - please God he won't..."

"Simone's sailing away..."

"Yes, with little Jacques - and - these are our lives."

Ardelle struggled.

She'd never thought such things in her existence.

"This is our life. I - bring you beans - and we did - something - because..." she dared herself to think and say, "...it was right. Forgive us, Jacques."

"And it was wrong."

"It can't be both."

"It isn't. It's wrong."

Silence.

"We've abused his faith. In you. And me. We've been unfaithful to him."

Silence.

"It's sin."

Ardelle aged. She'd been young again so very briefly.

"And I will leave. I can't stay here."

Ardelle looked up. His eyes were hard. Faraway.

"I couldn't bear to shit on your joy - and I already have."

"You leaving would change nothing."

Ardelle stood. Left him.

She stood in his garden.

O, Holiest of Merciful Fathers don't let him be right. That can't be your will. No. Christians forgive. She turned and strode back up his steps.

"You're making it bad."

"It is bad."

"It wasn't! Till you - couldn't speak. What part of it was bad? Why?"

"I don't know..."

"You're making it bad. You. Why?"

He was silent.

"Because she's gone to America? Are you taking that out on me?"

"No. Ardelle, no."

She managed the smallest nod.

"But now you're afraid to face him?"

"Aren't you?"

"I wasn't. And I wasn't guilty. But I am now. Aren't I?"

His jaw swung down a little.

"So am I," he said.

Ardelle's eyes ravaged the room. Stone walls and oak. This peasant man, the dog, up now, staring at her. "No! No. I don't accept. It must not be. No."

She stood and stumbled to the door, eyes running.

"You were going to die," she reminded him.

"Don't you wish I had?"

"Not yet."

"I do."

She couldn't imagine any more words.

The garden grass where she had pulled him back to life was freshly frosted beneath her feet, the air late December, the light pale grey, the future -

Sara came with the child.

"I need to talk to you."

He's done what? The world moved off its axis.

In the silence Zoe said to Jacques, "You've stopped crying."

"Will you go and see him?"

"No."

"For me?"

"What could he tell me that you don't know?"

A short sad quiet. "Nothing."

Sara looked at him, placed her thick hand on his. "I'm going to see Ardelle. Do you want to come, Zoe?"

"No. She's sad."

"No, no. She'll be very happy this time, won't she, Jacques? Arbel's coming home. Will you come, Jacques?"

"You two go."

If Sara knew about Arbel coming home - then the whole commune knew Simone was bound for America. Galtier would have told the gleeful ghouls. Damn their wagging tongues. Damn their gossip soaked ears and souls. Damn their lives and damn them to death that they should know of his grief. No wonder my Mother withdrew. Damn them! I will not look at any of them ever again. And bless Sara for saying nothing.

Zoe found Ardelle very far from happy. Her mother and this woman sat and her mother said, "What is it?" about a hundred and fifty-five times and the sad woman shook her head and said "Nothing." And it wasn't true.

He bought the herd in. There was nowhere for his eyes to rest that didn't wound, no thought that didn't chill, no respite. Blackness on darkness. Echoes of anguish and echoes in anguish.

I can't live here. This isn't life. Where is it, my life?

He sat to milk.

The post-card news reached Jerome in his seat inside the café.

"Arbel's walking home? He fucking would!"

But Jacques will be desolate.

The tobacco!

"And two bottles, Janon." Because old Ardelle'll want to celebrate.

Jacques rolled the cigarette. Reverently.

"Have you heard about me?"

Jacques nodded, licking at the paper. Rolled it. Twice. And heard himself say, "Why?"

"I don't know. I do not know."

Jacques lit the cigarette. Pulled hard.

His chest swam, his neck heated, his head rocked and the tiniest perspiration bibbled on his brow.

"Good?"

"Horrible." He hauled again. Everything turned back, dropped inside him, settled. His humming hand rested, fag nestled in the knuckles, on his knee. That. Looked. Better. Another drag. Hand on the knee. "Mm."

He looked up. "Why?"

"I don't know. I wish I wished I did - but I don't..."

Jacques leaned his back into the cold firewall and said, "What about Zoe?"

"I see her. I'm her father."

A beat.

"And you're sleeping at your mother's?"

"Living there. If you can call it that."

"Jesus Christ, Jerome!"

"We don't speak. We'll start that when I've drunk everything."

A beat.

"What's happened to us?"

"War?"

Silence.

"What are you going to do?"

"Drink. Hope Arbel gets here. You?"

"Move."

Jerome stood and looked at his friend.

"Jacques..?"

"Yes?"

"Where to?"

"Don't know."

"Go to America."

He stood there with a grin and the bottle as Ardelle opened the door, eyes red-veined and sodden. When he left an hour later, the bottle still unopened in his pocket, not a word the wiser, he walked the late evening lane straight to Sara and told her she must go and see them both.

"I went, this morning."

"Well, whatever it was, it's worse now. Go, now. Please."

"I'm bathing Zoe."

"I'll do that. You go."

"Now? No. Still want to bath her?"

"Of course. Here," he put the bottle on the table, "get that open. Let's celebrate something. Zoë's bath, we're alive - any damned thing."

Zoë's parents sat at the table and drank the bottle.

Neither spoke, nor did they make much eye-contact.

When the bottle was done he stood.

"You'll go tomorrow?"

"Yes."

He went home, to the bar.

Another evening fell on shattered St. Cirgues.

Sara washed the glasses away. He has no notion of my feelings. And neither have I. It's like I haven't got any. And it's as if that's what we both think. And now he has none of his own. For himself. He's not - himself. And what am I, then? Now? And when will I weep?

Baden-Baden. The train was not going any further. They had 30 kilometres to the border.

The advancing Allied armies were bringing another kind of winter to the people of Germany.
The Third Army crossed the German border.

In the Café Tabac Duthileul sat like an owl, everyone within his sight. Busted Janon shuffling. Galtier and Chibret's circular conversation arrested as ever by the eau-de-vie round. And Lacaze nursing yet another dying bottle. He'll drink her money away if his liver holds out. Now that would be a waste...

I've spoken to everyone, Jerome thought. Madame Valet, Madame Mignon, Madame Herrisson. I've not said anything. I've nothing to say. But I've spoken. Registered my life, my survival, publicly, against their losses. So. I've earned my place as the drunken village hero.
He took a mouthful.
Duthileul troubles me.
Hasn't changed. Just waited out the whole storm. Learned nothing. Not like me - I've learned less!
And still I hate him.
And I've left my family - to go home!
I'm regressing.
Least I don't go to Church yet.
He snorted. I'm not that drunk. Wonder if I ever will be?
My friends are in ribbons. Jacques and Ardelle. Ribbons.
So.
"We won nothing."
The few in the gloom looked up. He was at it again. The talking.

  THE SINGLE SOLDIER

Everyone wondering why it's like this. I don't. People have so much to forget. I don't. I've nothing I should forget. Or if I did, he laughed aloud, startling them, "I've forgotten what it is!" Was. Wasn't. "Don't know. Which. Do I?"

And everyone wants something - their men back, their dead sons restored, a family. The impossible. "Or the highly unlikely."

And, I don't want anything.

He said quietly, "Love you Zoë - but oh dear - Papa's pissed."

Hope Sara sorts Ardelle. If she can't no-one can.

Can't be right. That I don't want anything...

"Closing soon..." he heard Janon say.

Ohhh. The walk. Back there. Noo...

No!

Take Jacques a drink..! Yes - the brain works yet!

"Two more, Janon. Unopened."

"Do you want a lift?" Duthileul asked.

"From a cheat? No." Jerome lurched into the night.

It was cold, sharp and dry.

"Drink?" Jerome felt sobered by the walk.

"You're pissed. It's midnight."

"Am I? Are you sure? I was. Anyway you're not in bed."

"No."

"Not sleeping are you?"

"No."

"Me neither. So?" He waved the bottle.

Two friends at a midnight stone doorway.

"I'm - I was - " Jerome steadied himself, " - concerned."

"Balls. Go home."

"Er - no."

"I don't want to drink."

"You don't have to, misanthrope. I'll drink."

Jacques stood aside. "I wish you'd go..."

Jacques saw Jerome was more than content to drink the first bottle alone. In silence. No rush. Not like Arbel. When he opened the second Jacques rolled a cigarette.

"Do you know you were here this afternoon?"

Jerome looked up, "Did I make any sense?"

"None."

"Thank God for that." He poured. "We're all making it up as we go along."

He took a mouthful, tasted it.

"Oh, this is rank. What did we win a war for? We're French for fuck's sake! This is pitiful."

He pushed the other glass an inch nearer Jacques and his energy suddenly flagged. "Can I sleep here? Worry the crone. Eh?"

"Take the blankets upstairs. I chopped the other bed up."

"Did you? Good."

His body slumped a little more at the table.

As a quiet began he looked up at Jacques and said, "Have a drink please - it's piss - but I've no-one to drink with. Huh? Don't worry - I've nothing to say and nothing to ask and nothing to pry. I can't do a damned thing at the moment - except drink - and it's not long till I fall over now so share a glass in this little life please - old friend?"

Jacques touched their glasses together.

"And - I won't ask in the morning, either."

"Because you won't remember?"

"Not a fucking word. Guaranteed."

Jacques lugged Jerome to his bed. He took some blankets upstairs

and only when he got there realised how cold the house was. He lay down as he had - above her - above that memory and that time. His heart ached.

I want to be in so very many places and none of them here.

Jerome was still asleep when Sara came up the lane, alone.

Jacques watched her knock at Ardelle's door.

"What?" Ardelle was cold as the morning.

"Jerome said..."

"He sent you?"

"Yes. Please talk to me."

Ardelle looked at Sara.

"Jerome sent you?"

"Yes..."

"Then - you're back together?"

"No. He came last night. Worried."

Why doesn't Ardelle let her in?

Will she tell her? I won't. What does it matter? What does it alter? Turn back the clock and I would rather have died than caused this. And what's to come.

"What is it? Don't say 'nothing' again."

They sat across the table.

"I can't say."

"Arbel is coming home, Ardelle. To this?"

"I know."

"What are you going to say when he says 'What is it?'"

"I shall tell him."

Sara nodded.

"Good."

"Yes. Then we'll see."

The two girl-women looked at each other.

"How did Jacques take the news about America?"

"Badly."

Ardelle stood, fetched a handful of beans and a knife and began topping and tailing them.

"He is bad," said Sara.

"What?" Ardelle's eyes scoured Sara's.

"He's dead in his mind." Sara felt a need to defend her choice of words. "He's lost."

"Oh. Yes." She resumed her cutting.

"What can we do?"

Ardelle laughed a single cold dark bark that shook Sara.

"What?" Sara was still. "What?"

"Nothing," she lied.

"What's funny?"

"Nothing." It was true. Ardelle stopped cutting. "What?" she asked.

Sara looked at her evenly. "You tell me."

"No."

Sara stood.

"His pain isn't funny."

"I know."

"He's a friend."

Ardelle wanted to say 'then you have him' - but instead she swept the cut ends into her hand and threw them into the compost bucket. "I know," she said.

Sara went to the door.

"Let us know the news - about Arbel," she said sadly.

Ardelle said, "Of course, yes," whilst she thought 'I won't, no.'

He was sitting on Arbel's fireplace bench in front of cold dead ash.

"No fire?"

"No."

Sara sat opposite him. Where she'd sat.

"We've survived - and we're in tatters."

I don't want to hear this. I do not want to listen to this.

"Ardelle..." she prompted.

Jacques was at one with the granite wall.

"Ardelle, Jacques."

"Mm?"

"What's happened?"

This is nobody else's business.

"I don't know. Nothing."

"That's what we all say now. 'I don't know.' And 'nothing.' All the time."

Jacques didn't move, didn't look at her.

Sara shivered.

"Why are you angry with each other?"

This is Arbel's business. Not Sara's. Or Jerome's. Asleep. In my bed.

"What's happened?"

"Nothing." His eyes met hers, not warmly. "Nothing, Sara."

"What's happened?"

"Nothing."

"How long have I known you?"

"Leave it, Sara."

"I don't believe you."

"Why are you here?"

"Why are you angry?"

"That's a very stupid question."

"I'm here because my friends are in distress. Isn't that the business of a friend?"

They faced each other across the fireplace.

"There's nothing - can be done."

"Till Arbel comes home. When she tells him."

Jacques paled.

But he said, and he meant it, "Good."

He leaned back into the wall.

Sara rubbed the gooseflesh at her arms.

"Hell's cold I see..."

I don't want this conversation either.

"He's asleep - in there. Jerome."

"He came back here?"

Jacques nodded.

"Did he realise he'd already been?"

Jacques shook his head.

A beat of time.

He said. "You spoke?"

"He told me to come here. And then he came. And didn't remember he'd been..."

She looked round the barren room.

"We're all - lost."

A beat.

"Can I talk to you, please?"

Jacques quailed.

"Not now. I understand. And you wouldn't actually have to listen - just... but some time, eh?"

"Talk..."

Sara's smile was as feeble as his gallantry, and she shook her head and stood to go and out it poured.

"Zoe and my mother and that house and he he he used me to get out of his house and what did I do wrong, Jacques? What? Mothered him too well? And now I have to be strong for Zoe and not feel shat on and not show shat on because that's not fair to her and where and what's fair to me? Eh? I've no idea, Jacques. And,

why aren't I truly angry? Haven't I the right? Don't I think I have the right? I was a hook he used - a rope a climbing rope-thing and he's climbed and looked and loved such a little and made his child and gone back down again and I was - nothing. He never - " She stalled on the word 'love'. "No, he never. Did he? It's gone."

Jacques sat, stone.

"And living love-less is cold. Isn't it?"

Jacques couldn't even nod.

"Even if it wasn't Love. And it wasn't, was it?"

Jacques thought, 'Do I shrug?'

"And you know the best? It's not a surprise." She gestured at the bedroom door, "He's from The Big House, and I'm me!"

She almost laughed.

"I keep waiting to cry. I'd like to. But there's no sorrow in it."

Jacques could only tell she hadn't finished yet.

"He'll be Zoë's father and - I think he might even become a friend! And he won't leave here. Big fish little pond. And I won't - so. None of us will. There's nowhere to go, is there? No horizon."

I will have. I must.

"I can't see a thing beyond the child. And I'm frightened."

She heaved a long breath.

"There. Thank you."

She saw a stone man, stripped either of, or to, his barest emotions. She couldn't tell which. And he wouldn't.

"What's happened to us?"

"War - he says..."

"He's right."

Sara sat down.

Oh no, not more.

"Tell me about Simone. And little Jacques."

Horror leaped from his soul to his face.

Desolation.

Sara reached across the fire and took his cold hand.

She rubbed the pads of her fingers over the huge square thumb-nail till she'd made a tiny warmth in that cold house; a warmth she eased gently down his thumb, over the knuckle, into the softer flesh between thumb and first finger - into the calloused layers of his farming. His palm loosened a millimetre. Her fingers and thumb worked into the rough sides. When the warmth made him look up into her eyes she let the hand go and went home.

Jacques walked down to the copse and watched and waited till Jerome left.

Now there was quiet.

Now there was only Puech.

And Ardelle and him.

Till Arbel came home. And she told him.

I cannot - I will not wait for that.

I must leave.

No.

I must wait -

Because - I have a share in that...

The cows groaned, pointlessly searching the iron earth.

He walked to Ardelle's door.

So many memories.

How could a man so young have so many bad memories?

"We'll tell him," he stood at her door.

She waited a little.

"All right. Thank you."

He went home before he might smile. At her face.

One tiny pebble less of the load.

sixteen

ARBEL AND THE MEN watched the flocks of bombers flying east every night, raining liberating death.

They reached Buhl and, for the first time, were refused everything. All Arbel's practised charm and blackmail failed. They starved.

Huddled in the nooks of an empty summer-house in a ragged wintry park.

Dreading Police. Or anyone with the authority and the sadistic will to send them back. Now.

He pulled his wee stool and the bucket up to the udders and thought of what Jerome had said.

"Go to America."

To find them?

How?

He milked.

How could I afford it?

Well, if I was going I wouldn't need anything here. Sell it all.

Then what would you bring them back to?

This is insanity talking. I can't speak a word of American.

But, Duthileul would buy the house. Definitely. And the garden.

The wood.

God! I could afford it...

Had anyone been near enough they would have registered Jacques Vermande's rusty laughter.

I land in America without a word and - he snorted another mad laugh - I don't even know her name! Simone. That's it. I never asked her. Chibret must know it. On some paper. Go into the village and ask those shits my wife's name?

His mind cooled in the instant. I'm milking someone else's cattle.

Arbel and the men went back to the D roads and the tiny frightened farms where they might steal a chicken. Or anything. Root vegetables, anything. They ate like pigs. And walked. Slower. In the cold. But nearer. Every step did feel nearer now.

He marched out of his house, the dog following, crossed the lane and found Duthileul and Dominique in the bigger of their bulging barns. Father and son, alerted by their dogs. The hounds circled each other, sniffing.

"I won't work as a slave. Pay me or do it yourself. Tayo!"

And he was gone.

Dominique said, "Even he was bound to notice. Eventually."

His father scowled. "Must be hungry. Needs money."

"Well?"

"Well what?"

"He's got a point."

"Of course he has. He forgets I offered once. I'll think."

"And I'll do his work?"

"For a week."

"Thanks. Why not pay him?"

"Dominique - if I'm to pay a farm hand I'll choose who I pay."

"Jerome Lacaze?"

Father and son smirked.

Duthileul was right. Jacques needed, or would very soon; candles, matches, soap, flour, grain for the animals, and protein for the human. His winter vegetables and stored maize made plain fare. If the snow came hard and stayed, as it usually did, it would get monotonously so.

Jacques sat in his silent tomb-house. Pay me? Ha! He won't give me a sous. Duthileul couldn't give anything. I'll have put his knobbly nose right out now. Good. Good. Good to be angry. Good to feel some heat.

What the hell am I supposed to do with it?

A sign read France 6 kms.

They had no papers beyond Arbel's from a factory miles and months away. One more tomorrow. One more. Little was said. Until you've been far away you cannot truly know what home is - or means.

Madame Lacaze tidied the damp winter leaves into a pile and lit them. Eventually they took. She stood there, hypnotised for an instant, gazing into the reluctant flames.

Her son, upstairs, asleep.

Another year ending. What would the next bring?

What did she want?

What did she desire?

The word troubled her. The connotations.

She poked at the fire and allowed that she hoped for some future for her son.

Yes - and for yourself? What do you desire?

The fire smoked badly and she turned from it and the thought.

Jacques had no cheese left. Make some. He had no milk.

Thou shalt not steal. He would not steal the milk.

And he would not buy it from the village. No cheese, then.

This might be harder than no tobacco.

Sara, her mother and Zoe edged about the house. There was so much Sara's mother would have loved to have said but didn't, and slowly Sara came to the conclusion her mother chose not to inflict pain and in that belief she gave a daughter's respect and the mother sensed it and the atmosphere in their home softened. Warmed, even.

When Jerome called the mother was as brusque as she'd always been with him. She'd never understood him, liked him, or trusted him. Nor had she ever seen what her daughter might have seen in him. She'd always given Sara more credit than that she'd wanted any part of Lacaze's money - but when there was never any evidence of any of it, what was the point of the waster? All right, yes - he'd fought - and like a lot of St. Cirgues she never castigated him for ridding the commune of Gaston Valet - but since? Decadence will out, Sara's mother thought. Proof of the pudding.

Zoe absorbed the changes. She went with her father to 'his house' for Sunday meals with Mimi Two. There were more forks and knives and different plates. And more food. And more wine.

Galtier cycled up the road with St.Cirgues' first ever letter from America.

And he stood at Vermande's door in the blatant hope Jacques would open it, discuss it with him and let him be the bearer of the glorious gossip.

Jacques shut the door on him, and he thought, 'I knew I should have steamed it open...'

And, 'I will next time...'

The straggling German D road had a border post and a barrier - but as soon as it came into view they could see it was dilapidated.

They ran, sprinted, galloped, laughing.

One by one they recognised they were racing.

They all slowed. Then taking each offered hand they linked arms and finally, as a ten-legged creature, they walked back home together.

He left the letter unopened till twilight. Why, he didn't know. Something about wanting to read it by candle-light. He didn't know why that either. He knew he hadn't forgotten her for a second, ever, or his Jacques; and he knew he didn't hate her, never had, never could. And by the time he opened it he knew the letter must say she was staying there, oceans away.

Dearest Jacques,

You were right, I was wrong. I am teaching. German! In a war. In New York. I have a room in what they call a brown-stone. We have a room.

You don't want to hear this. I will settle here, Jacques. And raise him and the ocean will keep us apart.

What a man - what a giver you are. You gave me so much - and him his life - and I seem to have taken it all. Away. A long way.

He is well - he is alive and well because of you.

May we meet in paradise.

Simone.

He read it over and again and he saw the bones on her neck as her hair fell from it, sitting at a table in the New World while she wrote to him. He read it again. "May we meet in paradise." He poured over her signature. It was the proximity of her hand to the paper that shook him. She, his life's wife, had touched this paper. That was enough.

And they were safe. A part of him had been right, then. It had been A Right Thing.

He read till he knew it. Then read it again.

"May we meet in paradise."

There was something. Something.

He took the letter to bed.

Next morning as a feeble winter sun rose so, finally, did Jacques Vermande's heart.

A deep expanding smile took hold of his soul, radiating through every vein, every pulse in his whole body.

"Of course!"

The dog looked up at the warmth in his voice.

And the smile on his face.

A smile that reached his eyes for the first time in the longest darkest dying time.

"Of course, Tayo! Fool!"

Of course.

I understand.

And Jerome was right. 'He must be proud of me.'

And he will. He will be proud of me.

I know what to do, wife!

seventeen

DOMINIQUE DUTHILEUL took Jacques' herd.

When he came back he saw Vermande sitting on a kitchen chair in the garden staring at his house.

That evening when he walked the beasts back he was still there. Still looking.

Dominique milked the beasts and took the metal vats across the road and reported the madman's latest manifestation. Duthileul Pére squinted up at the news. Something is about to change then. Caution.

Alert.

Next morning he was there, sitting in the frosted morning garden on the kitchen chair, looking at his house with a piece of pencil and paper. And in the evening, still there, now with a daft grin when he looked at you. A grin? What's to grin about?

Dominique complained about his extra work to his father over their food.

"Patience."

Ardelle too watched him sitting there.

What had been in his mail?

Should I ask?

  THE SINGLE SOLDIER

Why doesn't he tell me?

On the third morning Duthileul and Ardelle watched Jacques working on his cart. Servicing it. To last.

In the afternoon he was back in the garden chair writing a list.

A block and tackle.

Wood for the frame. For the frames.

A big ladder. A yoke for the cow. No, there's one in the caves. He ran to check. Solid as the century.

Hammers. Mallets. Chisels. A crowbar.

Stop.

Think properly.

Start where you'll start.

He went inside and upstairs, the dog following.

The roof was gabled at the barn and chimney ends. Two oak A frames supported the huge main beam and the cross-beams. From the apex of the roof to the walls ran thinner beams holding horizontal slats on which the tiles rested, and were pinned. The chimney rose through the roofing, sealed with lead. The A frames, their big wooden pins and the long cross-beams they held, were no problem beyond weight. The main beam, resting on the A frames, though... Damn! I'll need help. Grandfather didn't put that there himself. And the cross slats were pinned with no-headed nails and would probably splinter. Need to replace them. And need to be able to cut wood to fit. He wrote. Nails. A saw. Two. The hooked pins holding the tiles were old. Might need to replace them. The tiles were good. And there were Grandfather's pile of spares. He turned his attention to the chimney breast.

A pick. A pick-axe. A masonry hammer and a metal chisel for the stone - what are they called? Don't know, but a couple of them. Good ones.

The floor boards. Oak. Again, no real problem. A good claw-hammer.

Down the stairs. Oak, nails, simple enough.

The living room.

The fire-place was two oak beams supporting a third, like a goal. The supporting wall between the bedrooms is easy. We will need both bedrooms. I'll have to build another bed. No, he can have mine, I'll build us a proper double. Fifteen oak ceiling beams.

Lime and sand for cement. A lot. When that time comes.

A tool to cut stone?

He went out and stood again in front of the house, Tayo following, animated by his energy. The corner stones. They were big.

Chalk. I'll need to mark them. Charcoal.

Chain - did I write chain? Block and tackle - yes.

Spades! Good ones. A spare long-handled and another. To dig out footings.

He walked into the caves. Fifteen oak beams under the kitchen floor. All the window lintels will be heavy. He came out and walked round the house.

Axe. The heavy-headed and a hand axe. Got both. Will they last?

A chisel to make mortis and tenon joints. A drill.

He sat to consider the corner stones again. Big. The biggest.

No - the lintel, the stone lintel that supported the wall above the cave door - huge. Same as the one over the front door. And over the windows. And the twelve stone stairs! God! He was looking at his home for the first time. Back inside. The dog, baffled, followed. A trowel, a sieve - Scaffolding? I could make that. Use the oak. And there's masses of wood there. What else? What else? He took the list to bed, slept well, and woke thinking, a bache. Of course. Otherwise the floors'll rot. Two? Two, yes. And a third to cover the wood when I get it there. And wood for the frames. Said that.

Written that.

All morning he sat in his winter-thin garden and drew first rough plans.

Rough measurements. Be generous. Can always cut wood. Three saws? A serious one for the oak, one for the pine and another?

And a new plane. Good, Jacques. And a claw hammer? Said that.

He wrote till he was satisfied with the list.

God's sake! Food! For me and the cow and the dog.

And a pair of horse-blinkers.

Galtier rode past, delivered to Ardelle and cycled slowly back. He'd report the grave-digger-upper was now drawing pictures. Or something. Sitting in the December cold with paper and a pencil. Cuckoo.

"Now, we price this," he showed the completed list to the dog. The beast cocked his head. "Then. How do I sell it and keep it?"

Ardelle came, her face flushed.

"Jacques - it's Christmas!"

He was surprised and not surprised. Time was irrelevant now. "Is it?"

"Yes. Look."

He read, "I'm in France. My feet hurt. Arbel."

It was postmarked Strasbourg.

He looked up at her square fearful grinning face.

"You're right, Ardelle. It must be."

She took the card and read it again. And again.

"He lives."

Jacques' heart surged with joy and dread.

"Perhaps there'll be a train..." she said, letting her tears just roll.

"Tell Chibret. He'll go and fetch him."

A smile. A beat. He'd joked.

Jacques was glad for her and now he wanted to return to his thoughts.

"Jacques - what are you doing?"

He covered the paper like a schoolboy who won't be cribbed from. "I'm thinking."

It was bright, cold and nearly noon.

"Can I ask what about?"

"My Christmas present to me," he said finally.

"Good." She nodded, agreeing with herself.

Please go now, Ardelle. Please.

"Will you eat with me tonight?"

"I won't talk."

She smiled and shook her happy head a little. "I didn't ask you to talk."

"Then - yes."

"Good. Good." And she left him.

This is a sign.

Her Joy. And he's Home.

This is a Good Sign. I'm doing a right thing.

At last.

He and Ardelle ate her bread and cheese.

"May I borrow Arbel's bike?"

She smiled at the pedantry of his politeness. "Of course."

"Thank you."

"Is it part of your present?"

He almost grinned, she noticed.

The last time they had shared this house was present in the air, yet both felt strengthened by neither mentioning it.

He took Arbel's bike and at dawn cycled the long way down to Maurs, avoiding St. Cirgues. He spent the whole day in and out of shops and stores and wood-yards and had his list priced. He spoke to a Notaire and an estate-agent to get an approximate valuation for his house and garden. Cycled back up the same long and private way.

He sat in the house looking at his numbers. Figures. What his list cost and what Duthileul would know to pay. He would be ahead, just.

Next morning he woke and checked the list.

And, his heart pounding with a future at last, at last, he could think of nothing new.

Nothing he'd forgotten.

Add more for food. How long would it take?

Years.

He dressed.

What - he had to face this moment - what if it doesn't work?

Then –

there is this life.

He went over the plan.

Still he stalled.

Waiting.

Fearful.

And as if by magic, Co-incidence, Fate, Luck, The Hand of God; whatever we call serendipity - Galtier arrived with another envelope with an American postmark.

Again he hovered. "Any reply?"

Jacques glowered at him. He who'd snarled 'foreigner' at her. "Fuck off."

He held the envelope.

What is this?

Is she coming back? Is there no need?

He gently eased the gummed lips of paper apart.

A picture post-card. A coloured photograph of a square, pencil shaped tower.

"I never left an address, did I? Write to us, please. I'll send photos when I can. This is the tallest building in the world. Simone and Jacques."

And an address.

Her address.

An address..!

Well, of course!

Oh, risk it Vermande and risk it now!

Everything's to gain.

Now?

Yes, now. Greed never rests.

"Vermande..?"

Jacques stood there.

"When you finally hire a man - since you won't pay me - you'll have a problem."

Duthileul straightened, alert. "Yes?" Cold eyes, searching.

"A problem where he'll live..."

A grunt conceded the truth in that.

"He should live in my house." Jacques watched Duthileul hooking into the drift of the unfinished thought.

"Ye-es," he allowed that he too had thought that far.

It's like fishing.

Timing the strike to get the barb in good and deep.

"How much will you pay for the rest of my land?"

A quick, sharp, pregnant morning silence.

"For the house?"

  THE SINGLE SOLDIER

"For the land, the garden, the earth, the wood."

"I'll think."

Jacques named his price.

More than he needed and less than the Notaire in Maurs had said. So, it was low.

And Duthileul, greedy greedy greedy, accepted it. His head nodded sharply, once, his eyes locked on Jacques.

Jacques Vermande offered his hand and Jean-Louis Duthileul shook it.

"When it's over, eh?" Jacques said.

"When the war's over?"

"When it's over."

Jean-Louis Duthileul nodded. Their hands parted.

"Where will you live?"

"That's not your concern."

Duthileul took the rebuff, went off somewhere deep inside the house.

Jacques breathed. Stay calm. Breathe.

Calm. Breathe.

Duthileul came back, leaned over his kitchen table, carefully counted and then handed Jacques another roll of money.

Jacques took the money, shook hands again and went home.

I did it!

I avenged Grandfather!

Mamman, I did it!

It is Christmas!

He sat and wrote the first letter he'd ever composed.

"I understand. Perfectly."

eighteen

WINTER COMING. Snow. Ice. Cold. But I can't wait till Spring. There's no waiting now. I'd wait forever. I must get it ready.

He lay his longest ladder against the chimney wall of the house, climbed onto his roof and walked its length to the barn. The gap between the barn and the house was a half-metre. He could stride across though the barn roof was marginally higher. He checked the corner stones of the barn roof for where he could attach masonry pins. Easy. He almost slid back down the ladder.

Before dawn next day he yoked the strongest cow to the cart. This isn't my cow any more. Oh, fuck that thought - and he walked through sleeping St.Cirgues, seeing no-one, rode the cart down to the Maurs wood-yard and bought and loaded it with six six-metre lengths of weathered oak, a plane, two wide heavy chisels, the huge tarpaulin covers, rope and a pair of horse-blinkers. And posted his first letter. Walked back. It was evening as he approached St. Cirgues. Fifty yards from the square he stopped the beast. It grazed the hedgerows while he cut a length of string to crudely hold the blinkers either side of his face. Then he walked through the village, taking them off only as he passed the cemetery. Home, he unyoked the beast, fed it, left the wood on the cart, stored the

tarpaulins and the tools in the caves.

Duthileul was not alone in noting everything.

What was this? Is he going to build? A house? A shack? Where? Not on land I've just bought he's not.

Who could he ask?

Who would know his mad mind? The drunk in the café was his best bet.

The drunk squandering his mother's old money...

At mass on that Sunday before Christmas, the Curé asked God to accept their prayers for the imminent deliverance of Europe from the Hun; to be, by inference, thankful for the death and destruction the Allies were now visiting on Germany. And the good people of St. Cirgues, who had suffered vilely at the hands of the enemy, encouraged their Lord with a collectively righteous vengeful heart.

Jean-Louis, more than thankful for the bargain price of the house he planned for Dominique, waited in the square for Madame Lacaze and quietly said, "Seasons best, Madame."

She swallowed her genuine surprise, he noted, and replied in kind. Jean-Louis, putting his most sincere face and voice together, added, "I'm glad your son survived."

"Likewise, Monsieur."

He smiled at her, tipped his hat and went to his car.

Madame Lacaze walked slowly home. What was that? He could have said that at any time in the last few months.

Sara was not the only one to notice the conversation. She would have loved to have asked her ex-mother-in-law - but she'd tell Jerome when he came to take Zoe down the road.

"What did Duthileul want?"

Madame Lacaze registered her son's aggression.

"He says he is glad you're alive."

"My God."

A little quiet began.

"Pappa?" asked Zoe.

"Mm?"

"What is a God?"

"Not a God, Zoe. God." Madame Lacaze simpered, deliberately.

"No talk of God."

Her father's voice was sharp and Zoe looked up, startled.

Madame Lacaze, feeling a warmth beyond the soup and wine, demurred.

In the quiet Zoe thought.

"You said it. First."

"I shouldn't have."

"Is it a bad word?"

"The worst."

"The best," said Mamman Two, then turning to her son, "Sorry." Eating continued.

He still hates, then. Good. I feared he'd drunk himself beyond that.

"Who is God?"

"Zoe!"

She poked her tongue at her flustered father and Mamman Two giggled. So she did it again.

"No, no no." said Mamman Two.

Zoe pouted.

You just never knew where you were with grown-ups.

"What does that senile gangster want?" Jerome snarled at his mother.

"Who?" said Zoe. "God?"

THE SINGLE SOLDIER

Her father laughed and then he shushed her. Great.

Madame Lacaze looked up at her son, "What possible interest could it be to you?"

"I could ask you the same thing."

"No need, I already have."

"And what did you conclude?"

"That it was my business."

Jacques measured the width of the oak lengths. Took the new narrow spade and dug two sharp metre-deep holes a half-metre out from both corners of the house wall furthest from the barn. He strode down to the beech-copse, bringing back some of the wood he'd cut. He split and planed it to line the holes till they were the same dimensions as the oak. He tipped one of the huge oak lengths from the cart. It lay, long and heavy at his feet. A few centimetres at a time he dragged the great weight till one end rested on the lip of the hole. I need the block and tackle. Damn. Think, fool. Should have thought of that. It would have saved time. He snorted. Why, what's Time got to do with anything now?

Fixing his blinkers with a belt this time he rode Arbel's bike through the village, back down to Maurs, knocked up the Sunday-lunching shop-owners and store-yard keepers and paid them to deliver the pulleys, chain, rope, hook, the block and more wood. And masonry pins.

It was evening when he cycled, blinkered, back through the village again. He killed another of the starving chickens, lit a fire, ate well, slept well.

Next morning two men drove up in a lorry. The last lorry through St. Cirgues had been German. They delivered the materials and drove away. Jacques spent the morning constructing the frame for the block and tackle.

"What are you doing?" Duthileul suddenly stood in his garden.

"Working."

"What are you doing?"

"Working."

"Working at what?"

"When it's over, neighbour."

"This is my land you're digging into."

"Yes, when it's over."

Duthileul watched Jacques thread the rope through the pulley, tie the hook on, check the stone counter-balance, make a loop of chain which he slid under and around the oak and round the hook, spit on his hands and pull on the rope and the oak lifted a half-metre. He locked it off there, checked the beam would fit the hole and lifted it a metre more. It slid in, against the split beech, threatening to shatter it and ruin the hole so now he pulled fiercely and the beam slid down the beech, filling the hole so the chain slackened and swung madly free, but the piece tottered upright. With a hammer he whacked more splinters of beech into the sides of the hole till the beam was secure.

Duthileul walked away.

Good. I don't like people watching me work. Makes sad memories.

It took him the rest of the day to do the second but by food-time he had both towering posts in place.

The village said he'd finally gone mad.

Chibret drove up. It was true. He'd covered the roof of his home with a tarpaulin bache, and was carefully sealing the hole he'd cut for the chimney stack.

"Vermande?"

"Monsieur Le Maire?"

"What is this?"

"Is it illegal?"

"No. I don't think so."

"Then?"

A pause.

Chibret puffed. Shouting up to a man on a roof. Pff.

"I heard - and was wondering - that's all."

"You mean Jean-Louis asked you to find out?"

"No. Yes. Among others. What is this?"

"A bache."

"Yes, but why?"

"Is it illegal?"

"No..."

"Then - I can't stop and chat. I'm sorry."

"What are you going to do?"

"Anything else?"

"We - people are worried."

"No, they're not. They're not worried. Not about me." He stopped working. "You once said, when mother died, 'Whatever you want - ask.' Remember?"

Chibret didn't, but said, "Yes."

"I want to be left in peace. Thank you."

And he went back to work and Chibret drove back and everyone said he was a fool and they should get a new Mayor.

With his roof covered, the bache attached and secure, Jacques was rewarded with a crystal-clear evening. He loaded the cart with the remaining four posts, beech cuttings to split, his chisels, plane, hammer, spades, bolts, the biggest ladder, the block and tackle and the other tarpaulin bache and food; yoked the cow and walked into the village. As he approached the square he put the blinkers on. Everyone stared. He couldn't see them. He took the Maurs road. Took the blinkers off. Sara was not in her frozen field.

At Janatou, in near-freezing moonlight, he picked his spot by the edge of the pine wood, offering the only shelter. There he dug four more holes, lined them with beech, constructed the block and tackle and through the night and dawn and morning built a house-sized frame, covered it with the bache and secured it. No-one watched, no-one knew. He walked back early the next afternoon.

Jean Louis Duthileul, reading war-news in the snug of his Café corner saw him walk, blinkered and bearded, past. And considered the direction from which he had come. Folded his paper, drove to the letter-boxes, walked the dirt track, pushed aside the last branch and saw the bache, framed, and ready to take the house he thought he'd bought.

Jerome came with Zoe.

"Madman!"

"I'm not mad."

"Digging up graves? Blinkers in the village? This - "

"Are you in a position to judge sanity?"

"Certainly not. Why have you sold the house to Duthileul?"

"I haven't."

"Eh?"

Jacques bent down to Zoe.

"Zoe, is Pappa a bit slow?" he asked her. "A bit dim? Bad luck."

He turned to Jerome. "I sold the land to Duthileul."

Jerome's mouth dropped in respect.

"Be a friend and tell everyone."

nineteen

ST. CIRGUES WAS THRILLED. Duthileul has been bested.
The grave-turner with the blinkers and the bache wasn't mad.
He'd bested Jean-Louis. At Church they would wait gleefully for
him to drive up so they could nod their heartfelt sympathy. And
if he didn't come it would prove it true, and they would hug the
news tight as they knelt to pray. Such a nugget. Such a Christmas
present.

Sara and her mother were knitting and darning when Jerome
came in the back door.
"What do we give our daughter for Christmas?" He was drunk.
Sara looked at her husband. Put down her work. Sara's mother
excused herself.
"You speak to me…" She couldn't finish her thought for the taste
of her anger.
"You treat me - "
Sara took a breath to calm herself.
"You speak to me - and you think of me - like you have no need to
consider my emotions. You think like your Mother. You're better
than me. Us. And yet you're guilty enough to try and drown your

emotions. If you said 'sorry' and meant it, we could get on with being friends. And parents."

Behind the kitchen door Sara's mother flushed with pride.

"You were always smarter than me," she heard him say.

"How much is that saying?" the mother thought as her daughter said it.

Silence fell.

"Got this one wrong, too, then."

"Drunken remorse is less than nothing, Jerome. I've already got a child to care for."

He shifted in his chair, one leg wrapped hard over the other and his hands white, clenched. His knuckles purpled a little. His brain scraped for truth.

"I'm trying to learn how to live."

"Apologise to me Jerome."

He looked hard at his fists.

"I can't. Yet." He left.

He began. Taking off his grandfather's tiles. Claw back the ancient pins gently, pile the tiles till he'd an armful, down the ladder, stack them. Back up the ladder, another armful. His back began to ache. A slab of sunlight warmed the bache. Work.

By hunger-time he'd taken off an eighth of one side of his roof, leaving the struts bare. A wind lifted the edge of the bache, but it held secure, and the breeze would chill the house all through. Good.

He stacked the cart with the day's tiles and sat on the house steps with his round-headed hammer and beat bent pins back into shape, bagged them and put them on the cart. A day's work. Tomorrow, work till I've filled the cart, then take them.

The dog slept by the fire. A candle on the table. Two peasants in a stone house. Drinking soup.

Late December 1944.

"Jacques? What's the bache for?"

"To protect the floor."

He nodded with his eyes to the ceiling. Ardelle looked blank.

"When it rains," he added patiently.

Ardelle shook her head to indicate incomprehension.

"I'm taking the roof off. First."

Ardelle's brain stopped trying to understand.

"I'm moving. The house."

Her eyes dilated.

"To Janatou..."

He's mad.

"To wait."

Years ago she'd read a phrase in a book; 'crazy as a wedge'. She'd never known what it meant.

She dared herself to ask.

"For - them?"

His face glowed.

"Yes."

She saw his tears form as he mistook her shock for understanding. Agreement, even.

I don't know what to say, thought Ardelle. I don't even know what to think.

The room fell silent.

"Jerome's gone back to his mother," Jacques said.

"Sara told me. He's mad, too."

Jacques thought.

"As mad as who else?"

"Haven't you noticed? All of us." She looked at him. "No. You haven't."

They finished the soup.

Jacques rolled a cigarette and looked at her.

"Jerome said you were dreading Arbel coming home..."

She didn't reply, didn't deny.

Her square stolid face.

"What are you thinking to yourself day after day, Ardelle? What are you thinking of yourself?"

She stood, her hands on the table.

"I have to face his God."

"We. We have to face that. And His God didn't strike us down dead."

"The soup was good." She walked to the door.

"You've changed your tune."

"We both have."

He came to the door. Opened it, freezing night came in.

"Ardelle - whatever you need."

She left.

At Janatou the view was misty. Bleached and bare. Like me. For now.

He stacked the tiles and their pins in the furthest corner of the huge bache-tent. The bache isn't big enough to take the whole house.

Fool. It's for the wood, the glass, bed, your pathetic furniture. The stone can wait outside - you can't get colder than stone. And the tiles! They're weather-proof, too! The dog looked up at his laughter. Stop worrying, you might be doing it wrong - but you're doing the right thing. He turned the empty cart for home, checking for his blinkers.

Jean-Louis Duthileul strode over the road.

"Vermande!"

"What?"

"Come down here."

THE SINGLE SOLDIER

Jacques chilled a little. He'd thought of something. He came down the ladder, stood in the garden. Tayo growled a little, catching his fear.

"You duped me."

"You duped yourself."

"Don't use my cows to pull your cart."

He walked away.

Chibret received the phone-call the whole commune had been waiting for. Arbel. From Strasbourg. Their train to arrive tomorrow, some time, at Maurs. Tell Ardelle.

He bustled into the Café Tabac, self-importantly spread the glow, and drove up to see her. Jean-Louis Duthileul drove up a minute behind him.

Neither Jacques nor Ardelle had ever seen two vehicles on the lane. Not since The Germans.

Jacques heard Ardelle's scream of joy.

"I'll drive you there tomorrow," Chibret announced proudly.

Ardelle, in shock, must have nodded because he drove back beaming.

She came straight round and he was waiting for her.

"Tomorrow. At Maurs."

"We'll go together," he said, shortly.

"Yes, please. Oh. No. Chibret said he'd take me."

Jacques revolted against the idea but what could he offer? Ride her down on the bike? How would the three of them get back?

There was a soft knock at the door. Tayo barked.

"Shush. It'll only be Jerome."

It was Duthileul. The cold house chilled further as the door was jiggled open.

"Yes?"

"I wondered - Ardelle - might I offer you a lift tomorrow?"

"Er..."

"I'll explain to Monsieur Le Maire."

"We were going to ride down on cows," Jacques heard himself say.

"What?" Ardelle said from the table.

"But of course, we can't use mine. Yours. I was just about to suggest using Ardelle's. Ardelle?"

"What are you talking about?"

"Nothing." He flushed and felt irredeemably stupid. He stalked to his empty fireplace, turning his back on his anger and embarrassment. Ardelle came to the door.

"What is he talking about?" she asked their neighbour.

Duthileul squinted at Ardelle. He'd no memory of when he'd ever spoken to her before. To nod on her wedding day. Now she was asking his business. He looked at her and nodded at Jacques and said softly, "He's mad."

"He's not that mad."

"Do you want to be driven? Tomorrow?"

Ardelle could smell the glory-trail connecting Duthileul and the Mayor.

"No, and explain that to Monsieur Le Maire, too, would you."

"Now what?"

They almost laughed as she closed the door. "Walk down? And ask him to walk back?"

Jacques thought.

"Wait here!" and taking his blinkers, he left her.

Jerome watched a blinkered Jacques cycle past the café and down the long lane.

"Madame," he gasped when she opened the door.

"He's in the bar."

"I came to see you."

Madame Lacaze's body eased towards inviting him past her and into the house but she left the action incomplete. "Oh?"

He told her. She smiled.

"I'd be happy to. Do you want me to tell him," she paused for the briefest second, "and her?"

Jacques imagined forward to what he and Ardelle needed to tell Arbel.

"But - how would they get there?"

"Of course. Well, I'll tell him anyway, shall I?"

"Yes, Madame, tell him. He'll be glad."

There was something so simply caring in his tone that made her relieved they were not now inside her house.

"Tomorrow morning?"

"Yes."

He rode back, told Ardelle.

She told him it was Christmas the day after tomorrow.

Their thoughts met in the black sky above their homes.

Tomorrow he'll be here. Home. My Arbel.

Tomorrow we'll find out if what we did was good or bad.

By whether he forgives us.

So, it's nothing to do with God?

If Arbel doesn't forgive then it was wrong? Yes, of course!

And if he does?

What will be will be. You plant and sow and reap.

🐏

They were at Maurs by eight in the morning, Christmas Eve. The bleary-eyed station-master knew nothing.

"A train from Strasbourg? Bollocks! Pardon me, Mesdames - but there never has been nor ever will be such a thing."

Ardelle quailed.

"Connections, dolt." Madame Lacaze smiled.

The man's manner changed.

"I'll phone Aurillac."

"Thank you."

Other cars arrived.

As the day grew conversations began between Ardelle and Jacques and the parents and wives, children and friends of Jean-Louis, Claude, Figeac and Yannick. None of them knew anything about anything. Just the phone-call they'd all been allowed from Strasbourg. So only now they gathered there were five of them. They all wondered how many more were lost en route. But this was no day of mourning.

This was a Day of Returning Home - having survived - the most profound mutual feeling humans can know. Outside childbirth. And Madame Claude had a two year-old in her arms all day to meet her father for the first time. Maurs station teemed with latent, simmering emotion.

Trains were scarce. They all leapt to their feet at the first bell and the station-master, now dressed in his best since his Mayor had telephoned, straightened his uniform and peaked cap, marched himself in front of them and as the train clattered past behind him, and bellowed, to their deafened ears, "Goods, Mesdames, Messieurs!"

He phoned his spouse and she brought food for them all at lunch-time.

A branch-line train after lunch.

Another at four.

THE SINGLE SOLDIER

No-one's patience, beyond Claude the Boulanger's daughter, wavered. They concentrated on the track and waited. And would wait all day. Positive stoicism.

At six they all stood as another two-coach train steamed in.

This was the one, Ardelle knew.

She strode further to the front than she had yet and everyone caught her certainty - as they had caught someone else's all day - but now there was a scream as the carriages slowed and hands waved and there was a crush at the doors and now tears and weeping and the out-pouring of years of anguish and still the damned fucking doors on the train had not been opened but there was never any mistaking the two-toothed grin beneath the aged eyes of Arbel Jammes. Jacques stood back from the scrum - as, strangely, did all the brothers, fathers, sons and uncles. This first touching was for the women. God knows why - but it was.

Five men enveloped in a wave of Love, in the arms of rewarded faith - the warmest place they'd ever left and would ever find. You could hug all day - you could hold those bones and feel that skin and smell that forgotten smell and stay there rocking and crying till eternity froze.

"Thank you very much, citizens - best of the season, very pleased, sincerely - but we have a timetable beyond all this, you know..." The station-master herded the scrum of weeping humanity towards the waiting men so he could release the train.

Jacques stepped forward. She still held him in a grip. Let her - she deserves it. He stepped back. Arbel looked away from her eyes and saw him. Fresh tears leapt to his eyes, and to Jacques', and Arbel wrapped the pair of them in his bony grip.

And there they rocked.

All four men made a point of telling Ardelle none of it would have even ever been considered and most definitely never accomplished

without her husband; that he was a diamond and her heart flooded as he grinned, bashful and daft and deflecting their compliments.

"And Claude with a child, a daughter!" he said as they drove Home. "I wondered if..."

"No." Ardelle squeezed his arm even tighter. "Plenty of time for that."

How easy it was to Love. Everything forgotten.

"God! How are Jerome and Sara and - "

"Zoe," Ardelle said, watching Madame Lacaze's back and neck straighten. "They survived," she said, squeezing him, "like you..."

Jacques, in the front, said to Madame Lacaze, "Please don't drive through the village, Madame. Would you take the back road?"

"Forgotten your blinkers, Vermande?"

Arbel looked up from his wife's eyes. She shushed him and signaled 'later'.

"If you wouldn't mind. If not - I'll walk."

Arbel looked directly at Ardelle. What was this? She nodded towards their driver. Not here, not now. O.K...

Madame Lacaze drove the back way. It was dark and Jacques was grateful Arbel wouldn't see the bache over his house and so wouldn't ask questions tonight. Not those questions anyway.

They all thanked her and stood watching the headlamps drift down the lane. Arbel couldn't breathe deeply enough. This air. The air of Home.

They stood in his kitchen.

Arbel looked around. How could very little be so exquisitely precious?

Ardelle still held his hand.

"Happy Christmas Arbel. Both. Happy Christmas," Jacques said and left them.

I faced his eyes, then.

Now will we tell him on Christmas Day?

My God! That's sadistic.

And will he give us the present we crave?

Should we even ask him? Do we dare? Have we any such right?

Let it pass Lord. Let it pass.

And why should The Lord listen to me, now?

Because He's The Lord and us fools are only human, that's why.

Arbel had no desire for words or talk and Ardelle was only too happy to meet and share the desires he did have. Right into Christmas morning.

twenty

HE OPENED HIS EYES. The sun was winter-high.

"Mass!"

"Too late," Ardelle lied. "Leave it. We are Christmas."

"I've never missed. Not even there."

"Well, you have now."

"My God!"

She reached down into the bed and distracted him.

"My God," he groaned and rolled onto his back.

Do I work? On Christmas Day?

He rose, pulled his filthy clothes together.

No eggs. He'd forgotten to feed them so very often their eggs were pale green and putrid now.

He pulled water from the well.

Lit a fire.

Throttled the last three chickens and sat and plucked them.

Went to his store in the fournil and found potatoes, Ardelle's winter beans still in the panier, and some straggly brussels in the garden.

He boiled water and cooked a chicken feast casserole for his friends and it smelt so good when he used the pepper for the first time since Simone left he laughed and told himself he hoped they didn't come.

At church everyone guessed why Arbel and Ardelle were not at Mass and everyone smiled forgiveness. Madame Lacaze nodded to Sara and her mother and passed muslin-wrapped bonbons to Zoe, taking the kiss Sara prodded her into giving. Duthileul Pére again cracked his starched face open to smile at her and it raised a curious nausea in her. And, as the Curé invited them all to celebrate Arbel's deliverance, Madame Lacaze fleetingly wondered whether he, the Curé, felt either a hypocrite or simply a coward for still being here when so much of his flock had been taken. And then knelt for ten minutes after the 'Go in Peace' to beg His Almighty forgiveness.

Sara, Zoe and Mamman One cooked and ate their thin celebration. Beyond the innocence and health of the child they hadn't a great deal to celebrate. But they toasted Arbel's return and Ardelle's relief with full hearts.

Jerome drank a bottle of good red, more than his share of a bottle of port and was into the brandy. His mother sipped at her glass.
They had eaten Christmas dinner.
They had not spoken.
The silence suited them both.
They had exchanged neither presents nor touch that morning. And she had not told him about Arbel.

It was ready and he would have to go round.
He had an idea. He crossed the lane, wished Jean-Louis the

season's best, paid for a vat of milk, came back and was churning for cheese, when he heard Ardelle's clogs on his stone staircase.

"I've cooked us dinner," he said.

"Smells good."

"You'll both come?"

"I think we should tell him in his house, don't you?"

Today, then.

"Yes."

He rose, sudden dread in his thighs.

He left the dog in a house smelling of cooked chicken and gravy.

"How is he?"

They walked the few metres.

"He's - he's home Jacques."

As they neared the house Jacques said, "Must we, do this? Today?"

Ardelle said, "We said he wouldn't judge us badly. I can't live with this a secret."

They came in.

Arbel was older now than both of them. His hair had thinned and seriously grayed. Jacques' beard and uncut mass of curls felt like mockery. The two men shook hands, hugged again and Ardelle moved round the table to sit next to her husband.

"We missed Mass!" Arbel laughed and poured them all a glass.

"So did I."

"Shame on you."

Jacques sat opposite. He looked at Ardelle.

She expects me to speak.

O.K.

Speak, then.

Speak.

"What?" Arbel grinned.

THE SINGLE SOLDIER

"Simone..."

He stopped. Wrong. Wrong place to start.

"Of course! Where is she?"

"Oh - America."

Change the subject, quick now change the subject.

"Is that - good news?"

"It was the worst. I - wanted to die."

Silence for one second.

Not a pause, nor a beat - but ocean-deeper - a whole second of total silence.

The preface.

Speak.

"Ardelle - comforted me - and I - I comforted her."

Arbel tasted the change in the air. "And is this good news?"

"It was. It was."

Ardelle saw Jacques' mind stall.

"Husband - he and I shared your bed once. That one time."

Silence much much longer than a second fell.

"Pass me that wine."

He drank the glass she poured, then reached for the bottle, to hold it, to have something to squeeze. Water, dripping somewhere, could be heard.

"Are you pregnant?"

"No."

"We - didn't... I didn't..." Again his brain seized.

Again silence.

"Husband?" No sound, no movement. "Arbel?"

"Wife?"

The word seemed to scrape through his voice-box as he looked round at her. When his gaze shifted Jacques' eyes fell to an examination of a knot in the wood of the table-top.

"Friend?"

Arbel poured another glass and let it stand.

"I've spent two years learning how not to think - and now..." he thought, "Now I can't think."

"I'll leave," said Jacques.

He opened the door, tried to say something.

"Arbel. It was – friendship – not desire. Not Lust."

"It was penetration," Arbel said quietly.

He left them sitting at their table.

A candle guttering.

Two glasses, one empty, one to be emptied.

A bottle.

A man.

A woman.

The sound of his clogs left them.

With a private silence now. Ardelle froze.

"Is this why we missed Mass?"

"Yes."

Jacques ate the tiny amount he could force past his emotions and the dog demolished everything else. Groomed itself, licked Jacques' draping hand gratefully and slept like a baby next the dying fire. The milk had curdled. Still no cheese. And now I do feel a Judgement on me. And this is mine.

Sara came with Zoe. Christmas evening.

Jacques made the supreme effort, focusing on the child. He and Zoe sat close on Arbel's bench in the fireplace and she showed him the candied bonbons. Five left. Jacques could hear her brain working out how to offer them round so she would surely get two. He kept his focus on the child, because anything was so preferable

to talking. Sara saw he didn't want to speak, respected it, took it as his thinking of his family on this day.

"Are we going to see the sad woman?" Zoe looked anxiously up at Sara.

Before Sara could respond Jacques said, "I think you should leave them for today." He even managed a kind of tortured wink for Sara to misread.

"No, they won't want to see us, not today. So, eat up."

Jacques and Zoe breathed an inch of relief.

"And she must the happiest woman in the whole world, today. Isn't that so, Jacques?"

"Of course she is."

How simple lying is.

Sara's eyes rested so fondly on his he had to ask in a desperate hurry, "And why isn't her father here with Zoe?"

"I don't know."

He watched his hand reach to rest on hers. Two of her fingers gently squeezed his.

"I thought I was mad. He's certifiable."

Zoe didn't understand either the words or the context but she recognised he had paid her mother a warmth. She smiled at him.

It took a minute or more in a house with half a roof for either adult to realise.

New morning and weather for ducks. A veil of thin rain.

Arbel emerged to breathe this, the fresher air he'd dreamt of.

To taste the view he'd held in his mind's eye.

The reality he'd clung to. That fool's mirage.

Jacques' house was covered in a tarpaulin and Dominique Duthileul

was walking Jacques' herd to the pasture behind Duthileul's house. What?

He'd walked all that way, imagining home.

And it was this. It didn't fit. Nothing fit.

And now Duthileul Pére came to his doorstep, saw Arbel and waved. Called inside the house and the old woman shuffled out beside him, gazed across at Arbel, nodded, sniffed the rain and shuffled back inside. Duthileul raised his cap.

By reflex Arbel tipped his finger to his brow and turned.

And went back inside to -

His roof?

Simone in America?

Him and my wife?

He opened a bottle and had drunk it in the time Ardelle walked ashen through the house, out to their beasts, milked them, walked them to their mudding pasture, and returned, wet.

In the awful silence she laid a fire and lit it.

She went back out into the sodden grey for water.

Puech has been raped, she thought.

Like me.

Oh God - I haven't told him that. I won't. That wasn't my choice.

The wife-robot made coffee.

"Do you want some?" She dared to offer.

To break the iron silence.

He looked up at her. "You haven't been to confession, have you?"

"No."

Silence. Worse.

Nothing he'd held in his heart - nothing he'd anchored his soul to - nothing remained. Nothing. You keep the faith - and it all goes shit.

In a conversation.

The bowed head, the aged shoulders, the heart-break in him.
Why?
Why had they spoiled his life?
Why hadn't they carried that weight?
It was theirs - their Sin - their lie - their stone, hers and Jacques, and they'd loaded it onto a man freshly returned from a Hell they couldn't begin to even want to imagine. Why had they been so selfish, so guilty, so eager? So needy?
And what now?
This silence is choking.
I deserve it.
Where is warmth? Gone.
I don't deserve warmth. He does and I'm neither worthy nor capable of offering it. Not fit to. I'm where I deserve to be.
I accept. But him? Where's his comfort?
"I'm going to church," she said in a silent voice.
Nothing. No movement.
She took her coat and beret, wrapped a scarf around her throat and walked to the door.
He sat at the table - the nothing man.
She walked into the drizzle.
Half-way down the lane she saw Jerome, Sara and Zoe coming towards her.
Jerome waved a bottle in each hand and she could feel Sara's smile.
"No! No!" she screamed, waving her arms, shooing them back. "No! No!"
They stopped.
"Go back! Not today. Please!"
She watched Sara turn the child and take her ex-husband's arm

and force him to turn too. Dragging him. Ardelle stood in the drizzling lane and waited till they'd turned the corner. She waited till she was sure they were not going to return. Then she knelt.

The crude tarmac bit into her knees. She welcomed it. Had always associated prayer with pain. She put her hands together. Looked up into the spitting grey.

"Guide me. Comfort him. Save us all."

Her head sank down. Rested on her chest. Water dripped down her neck.

"You know I'm sorry. Penitent. Forgive me for telling him. Forgive me all my trespasses. Please."

"Name of the Father..." she intoned and crossed herself and pushed herself upright.

She stood in the lane.

Turned. For Home.

Headed back up the lane.

As she walked past it Jacques' house felt as silent as her own. As leprous. Disturb it? She couldn't. For what? Bear your cross, woman.

What had happened? Jerome had wanted to see Arbel. Ardelle screaming 'no'? Sara didn't know. So, he vaguely kissed his daughter and headed to the bar. Sara wanted to talk with her mother but didn't.

Jacques sat in the wreckage.

I hate myself.

And I regret. So much, too much.

I won't have to look into his eyes, now.

So. The sooner I'm away from here the better.

A beast. I need a cow. Oh, no.

THE SINGLE SOLDIER

I should have asked them to lend me one before we -

Ugh! Agh! Damn and silence on this rancid selfish brain!

Buy one.

I've enough. Or barrow it all. Hand-barrow your house.

Take the rest of forever – what does it matter?

Isn't it plain insane anyway? Aren't I trying to turn back time? Is that what the rest of my wretched life is for?

If it is for anything.

God's work? Ha!

I will deal with it as it comes to me.

But I can't go towards people anymore.

I'm poisonous for others.

He stood.

He went upstairs.

He started on the horizontal cross strips. The no-headed nails were a pain - who'd invented them? His grandfather clearly never imagined anyone would ever have reason to remove them. Ha! Too many of the slats split before he thought of taking them out from above, by loosening the hole round the no-head with his penknife and lifting the slat out whole. His back pressed against the bache, rain lashed at him and he did not care. There was nothing nature could do to him. He split another slat with this thinking and cursed the damned thought that had wasted that strip of ancient wood.

Madame Lacaze checked her cellar. At this rate her son and his alcohol needs would be back in the Bar Tabac by early April.

Jerome too counted the stacked summers and wondered what, if anything, he might have learned by the time he had finished them. Which, he accepted, had become one of his very few objectives. And he knew he drank rather than consider any others. He

thought about Zoe, but only carnally did he recall his wife and he owned up, to himself, that he had used her as a red-rag to the sow sitting reading by her expensive Dutch stove. Why? He had absolutely no idea.

As the day ended she marked her place in the book and went to her room, placing a hand on the back of her son's chair for an instant as she passed. She knelt and prayed continued thanks to God for her son returned. Prodigal he was, but home. And in bed she wondered where His will would lead them. And as these days moved into weeks her bed felt warmer. The blood in her thighs warmed, and one night reminded her she was only 47 years old.

THE SINGLE SOLDIER

twenty-one

ARDELLE FARMED IN THE RAIN.

Jacques Vermande took his roof off.

Arbel drank as Ardelle worked around him.

Jerome drank as his mother cleaned around him.

The Allies advanced, as implacable now as The Hun had been.

The priests of The Allies gave thanks as The New Year dawned.

Simone went to Cathedral in New York.

The main beam. Nine metres of oak. At least two men put it there.
And it was never meant to come down. It couldn't of course, till
he'd dealt with all the tiles and slats and cross-pieces, but still.
And snow soon.

Is this impossible?

Mad.

Am I like Louis now? Is this my mushrooms?

It's your work. Do it.

I have no beast to take my home to Janatou.

What moon is it?

Mad moon season.

I miss her. Him. Them. Life.

Warmth.

The chimney must stay till last. And I'll need heat there. For the dog. And the beast. What beast - I have no beast. A stove. A pipe running outside the bache. Why not?

Despair, that vicious Arctic wind, enveloped him in an icy grasp.

No, don't!

Think, quick!

A beast. Deal with it.

Start digging out a garden at Janatou.

If I were to buy a beast where would I graze it? Janatou. Duthileul won't let me use what was mine.

He went outside to piss. The dog followed. The cart waited, half laden.

Arbel sat in his silence. Poured a glass. Sipped at it. His eyes looked round, again. Another day, then. Nothing has moved.

Should I go to confession? Do I confess. To feelings of - what?

He drank the glass and poured another.

My God.

That I lived for this.

The snow came as he'd known it would. A metre and a half. He'd never get to Janatou now before the thaw. If he'd been there he'd

THE SINGLE SOLDIER

never have got back. He wasn't sure which he'd prefer.

So day by day he dismantled his roof. The tiles, beams, struts, nails were stored on the cart or in the caves. Dominique coming and going with his herd became as unremarkable as dusk and dawn. He became cocooned in his dwindling building. He'd step out to toilet or fetch vegetables or wood for a fire when he was truly perished; but otherwise, climb the stairs, remove the roof, don't think, store it, climb the stairs.

Sara struggled up the snowbound lane to see Arbel. Her galoshes were soaked and her skirts sodden. She found Jacques' house colder than the walk and him, lean, stinking and unwilling to stop work. Or talk.

Ardelle and Arbel had a fire to dry by but no other warmth. Though she hugged him and kissed and rubbed his hands and he smiled, the effort was not disguised. Their lips were set thin as string. Yes, they talked and nodded and listened but they wished her gone.

The sky darkened winter-quick. Sara sloshed home and Zoe had a painting of a man made of tomatoes to show her.

Ardelle and Arbel came to Mass for the first time together, but they did not stay to drink. They did not stay to talk either. They were the first out of church and no-one was given the opportunity to shake his bony hand, tell him how very glad they were he'd returned. Even though his return made their own loss the sharper. Mass was the ritual of Sanctity and nodding. Sara to Madame Lacaze, Madame Lacaze to Sara's mother and Duthileul and Dominique to Madame Lacaze, which she, curious with herself, began to return. If God did look down on St. Cirgues He must have wished them a Spring.

Chibret sat in his office and thought of his responsibilities as a Mayor. To his commune. He took a piece of paper and doodled. By the fourth attempt he was satisfied and passed it to Severine.

"Print this and have Galtier deliver it everywhere."

He went out, pleased, to find who could plough the snow off the lane up to Puech.

Severine read, 'New Year's Night. A Feast! Salle de Fetes. 7.30. Celebrate!' There was a half-way decent drawing of a champagne bottle and a cruder one of a roasting duck. She dusted off the printer.

Chibret returned, phoned the commune of Grézes and arranged that their musical troupe would play. He had the lane cleared of snow and drove up with a first copy of the poster.

He stood, beaming, on their doorstep, whilst Arbel scanned the paper.

"I won't come," said Arbel.

Chibret rocked on his heels.

"I've printed the posters…" he spluttered.

"I won't come."

It was snowing again. The Mayor and Arbel looked at each other.

"This is a commune, Arbel."

Snow and silence.

"A commune of ruined lives - "

"I know that."

"And you're a reason to celebrate something."

"No, I'm not."

Chibret looked at Arbel's set jaw and stony eyes and righteousness exploded in him.

"Damn you! You won't come? Damn you."

Arbel stared at his Mayor. Snow on his flat cap, fury in his tiny eyes.

"I don't understand. It's selfish, selfish. Why won't you come?"

"I've nothing to celebrate," Arbel said coldly.

"We won! You're home! You've come back to us! Think of other people who lost loved ones, won't you?"

He looked hard at Arbel. He hadn't budged.

"It's pathetic I know, but we need something."

"I'm sorry." Arbel closed the door.

Chibret drove back to the Mairie, wrote his resignation letter, took it to La Poste and went home. Outside his home stood the stripped birch tree with its weathered tricolour bandages and the sign reading "Honneur à notre elu." Chibret took an axe and felled it and everyone in St. Cirgues knew by the time Galtier delivered their invitations there would be no New Year Celebration.

Jacques nursed his swallows' nest down to the caves and wondered, a tiny warm thought, whether they would find it in the Spring, or whether he should take it to Janatou - when he had a beast. When the snow had gone.

He removed the roof's lead in strips and the dog huddled against the chimney breast for the memory of the last fire.

Jean-Louis Duthileul learned about Chibret.

He thought for a long, very fruitful New Year's Day and first thing in
the morning telephoned his lawyer, who drove up from St. Céré. For an hour-long consultation, a look at Jacques' near roof-less house, and the drive back down the white hills to draw up Duthileul's action. Two days later Galtier delivered it to Jacques after reading and re-sealing it.

By his third brandy that evening Jerome knew too. So everyone knew.

Jacques read the accusation, burnt it and worked till he slept.

Arbel had drunk everything at home.

Now the pain was in waves instead of constant. He walked to the Café Tabac. Yes, he could buy wine and drink at home but why drink in Hell?

He found nothing much changed there. No Gley or Valet. But, drinking inside, Jerome.

They hugged each other for having survived and then drank together, silently.

For two nights.

On the third Jerome said, "Chibret's resigned."

Arbel's hands warmed the wine glass.

He nodded.

The next night he asked, "Why are you drinking?"

"I've always drunk," said Jerome.

Then considered the question more thoroughly.

"I'm pissing my life away," he said evenly.

Arbel looked at Jerome properly for the first time in four days. The bloated face, the reddening nose and cheeks. No, he realised, I'm looking for the first time in three years.

"Why?"

"You don't know?"

"Know what?"

Jerome took a glass, emptied it down his throat, poured another.

"I know you left your daughter and Sara. To - be at home."

Jerome nodded. Voila.

Arbel nodded. Reason enough to drink.

"And what's your excuse?" the bloated face enquired.

"I've always drunk, too."

"And the rest..." scoffed Jerome.

"You don't know?"

"No."

Arbel thought, took a mouthful, finished the glass, poured another.

"Does Sara?"

"No."

Arbel rolled a cigarette, passed it to Jerome, rolled another, lit both.

Next night there was the two of them and Duthileul.

"Where are the bovine?" Arbel nodded at the empty bar.

"The what?"

"It's what you used to call them..."

Jerome remembered Gaston Valet for the first time in a long time. The two young-old men looked at each other.

"How was your war?" Jerome asked.

"Pretty fucking awful."

"A-ha."

"Yours?"

"Yeah."

Another glass. Another quiet.

"You know that twat," Jerome nodded at Jean-Louis, "is suing Jacques?"

"No..."

A pull on a cigarette.

Another mouthful.

"I left Sara..." Jerome began.

Arbel nodded slowly.

"I know. Why?"

"Not sure. Yet." Another mouthful. "It's why I'm drinking. I think."

Arbel tried to think.

"Why?"

"Why what?"

"Why is he suing Vermande?"

Jerome relished raising his voice just enough, "Made him look like a cunt. Can't have that."

Arbel nodded. Just.

There was a quiet now even Jerome registered as cold.

He lowered his voice. "What?"

Arbel shook his head. The quiet waited.

Shook it again. Looked up.

"Jacques. And Ardelle. While I was away."

Silence.

Jerome wished Sara were there.

He heard himself say, "Right."

He felt unutterably feeble.

He hauled hungrily on the cigarette for inspiration, for a sentence, then blew the smoke out so loud Jean-Louis' head turned. Jerome leant back in his chair in a parody of relaxation. Poured himself a glass, controlled his voice and said, "How often?"

"Once, they said - but who's to believe anything?"

He drank his glass, searched Arbel's desperation, felt so very helpless and said, "I've left Sara."

Arbel's faced managed to darken. "I know. I knew," he said. "You said."

Jerome felt the contempt.

He said, "Let's walk you home."

A hundred times Jerome thought of something to say and a hundred times dismissed it. One of Dominique's dogs barked, woke the other, which, uncomprehending, joined in the echoing racket.

Arbel looked round at Jerome, left his front door ajar.

Jerome stood.

Ardelle came to the door to close the draught, her dressing-gown pulled tight. She and the swaying Jerome looked at each other and she knew he knew and that was a change. He'd told. He'd spoken. Something had moved. Thank God. I don't care now who knows. I'm past shame. I don't care about outside this house. She closed the door on Jerome.

He walked into Jacques' garden. Should I call? Why? What with? My worldly wisdom? He won't want to talk...

Dominique Duthileul found Jerome snoring in the hay next morning and left him there.

The commune met outside and inside Church. But religion is essentially grave and Chibret had rightly seen the need for something lighter, positive. Fun. Distraction. Now he realised his resignation was to be that. An election. New Mayor. "Fuck 'em," Chibret thought as they prayed. That should be on every Mayor's tree, that. Not "Honneur à notre élu" - 'Fuck 'em.'

Jean-Louis lay in his bed, warm. His body warmed so much he felt his ancient balls stir. And why not? Someone has to win.

Arbel betrayed no change but Ardelle understood waiting, and she would wait and see this through. The difference now was a candle of hope.

Madame Lacaze sat with her morning coffee.

Chibret was gone.

Duthileul and this action against the Vermande peasant.

And he will surely push his son forward for Mayor.

And mine? She almost snorted into her cup. My son.

Dear God, she placed her hands together, I beg you give him purpose.

Madame Valet went to the Café Tabac, took two cups of coffee to Jerome's table and said, "Remember when you sang La Marseillaise and Herrisson arrested you?"

Jerome stared at that zealous naive back in Time's fog. "Yes."

"Chibret's resigned, hasn't he?"

"Yes..?"

"Think, Jerome. Soberly."

She sat opposite him.

Jerome and Sara sat at her kitchen table. He told her what Arbel had said.

"Ahh," said Sara slowly. The jigsaw made sense now she saw the picture. "What did he say?"

"That."

"What did you say?"

A pause.

She looked at him. "Nothing?"

"Right. I said 'right'."

"Right?"

"Just like that. As pathetic as that."

Sara sat, arms on the table and looked at the wreckage of her husband.

"If I was the new mayor I'd ban alcohol," she said.

"You'd never get elected."

"Neither would you," she retorted unpleasantly, and whilst she had that tone fresh in her voice, "and neither should you be."

Next morning his mother told him Duthileul's lawyer had applied for a court order to stop Jacques' working whilst the case was pending - and she was certain Dominique Duthileul would stand for Mayor.

twenty-two

THE NEW CHEF DE GENDARMES had arrived New Year's Day. He'd missed the first Sunday Mass and felt suspicion as tangible as the mountain frost. In his first weeks he introduced himself, as The Chef With No Gendarmes, to most of the outlying farmers; shopped on market days and did a night or two in the café. He had no family - killed in an air-raid on Dijon. A town cop farmed out. The lawyer's letter informing him of application for restraint on Vermande's illegal dismantling of what was contestably Jean-Louis Duthiluel's property lay on his desk. He read through it again, looked at the high white sky. I'll walk it.

Jacques had only the barn-end gable of slats to take out and then he would have to face the problem of the main beam. Without taking it down he was stymied. He couldn't move the A frames till that monster weight were lifted and he couldn't start on any brick work for fear of weakening the whole structure. And the worst thing was he'd need help and that meant asking. Talking.
Like Jerome yattering on now about this letter.
"You need a lawyer, Jacques. An avocat."
"I need a cow. When it thaws."

"Vermande! You have to face this."

Jacques stacked slats by the top of the stairs.

"He's a shit, Jacques. He'll have you for breakfast and laugh about it."

Jacques pocketed the pins, piled the slats along his arms and went downstairs. Jerome made to follow.

"No, please," Jacques said, "a minute's quiet."

He went down to the caves and Jerome sat in the attic skeleton, the wooden rib-cage, the bache-lungs breathing noisily with the wind. Wee stones everywhere on a carpet of gritty dust.

When the robot re-appeared he said, "I'll help you with that beam if you'll listen."

Jacques' body went back to removing slats and pins.

"You'll never see Janatou - or anyone else there or anywhere - if you don't resist this."

"I'll say what happened. To anyone."

"You need a lawyer to say it."

Jacques laughed. "Listen to yourself, Jerome." He stopped moving. "I need a lawyer who wasn't there to say what I said when I was there?"

He turned back to the slats.

"Oh! Fucking grow up. I'll be fucked if I'll let that shit take this from you because you're too damned mule-headed to not stop him." Jerome was stunned at the sound of passion moving in him. Jacques stacked wood.

The Chef de Gendarmes rapped hard at the door.

Tayo barked. Jacques went downstairs, jiggled the latch and Tayo sniffed at the starchy smell of the man.

"Vermande?"

"C'est moi."

"May I come in?" the man said after five seconds staring.

Jacques stood aside and the man stepped into the dust.

"Terses. Paul." He offered his hand.

Jacques shook the fingers and gestured towards the empty fireplace.

Jerome listened till The Chef mentioned Jacques' need for an avocat then he came pouring down the stairs.

The drunk from the café. The Maquisard who shot the schoolteacher's wife. Left his own. The son of the old money.

"See?" Jerome said to Jacques, brusquely shaking Terses' hand.

Jacques looked from one to the other.

"Monsieur," he settled on the flic, "do you believe what I've just told you?"

"That's not the point!" Jerome leapt in.

"Do you?"

"Monsieur Vermande - my opinion doesn't count."

"Give it anyway."

"I haven't heard M. Duthileul's side of this story."

"I told you. I duped him. Do you believe me?"

"I'm not making judgements."

"Then you don't?"

"I came to advise you of your legal position. When I have all the information I am required by the court to submit a report."

"Oh, whoopee..."

Terses' eyes moved slowly across to Jerome.

Jerome looked evenly back. "Right." He stood. "I'll get him a lawyer."

Terse stood and said to Jacques, "You must stop work if this application is granted."

"Till then," said Jacques and headed upstairs.

Whilst Jerome walked home the Chef sipped a cognac and was introduced to Dominique.

"Give me the money to help him," Jerome said to his mother.

"What will you do for it?"

"What? What scheming is this? What do I have to do?"

"Go back to her. Before she goes to Vermande, where she should always have been."

"What! I can't. And you can't possibly want me to. You never wanted me to - you can't now."

Madame Lacaze looked even and silent in her son's eyes.

"And I don't want to."

There now. He'd said it out loud. And it felt true. Still she gave him nothing. Anger rose.

"Don't manipulate me! Help him."

"It's you I want to help."

"Good God mother - where did you ever learn to be so devious?"

"Stop drinking and he'll have his lawyer."

"Right." He sat. "I will."

Dominique and his father both nodded ostentatiously to Madame Lacaze at Mass. She smiled slowly at both of them. Everyone knew about the letters and the lawyers and the Gendarme and the shrewd wondered why Jean-Louis had taken so long to do it. The rest weren't surprised but took the madman's side - for all that was worth in a battle involving money and its' protector, the law.

On the last Monday in January, as the bombing raids on Berlin were stepped up and the Allies landed at Anzio, Bernadie arrived with the Prefect to organise the election. Normally the council members would have elected one of their own, but since May last year there had only been Chibret and his secretary. They printed

posters with the date of the election and welcoming nominees. 'The losers can make up a new council,' they agreed.

Jerome had the shakes.

He'd spent a first day in bed and now the second at Puech.

"I'm getting you a lawyer," he said, the thought crossing his mind he was trying to make Jacques feel guilty. Except Jacques showed no evidence of being grateful.

He would finish the gable end today.

"It'll take three of us," Jerome said, nodding at the beam.

Nothing.

"I'll go and ask Arbel, eh?" Nothing.

Jerome left.

Returned.

"He'll come tomorrow."

Jerome sat back down in the dust, pulled his coat round him.

"That house is Hell. Too."

Jacques worked.

When Jerome trudged home, his galoshes and trousers soaked with fresh snow he certainly felt sober.

Next morning his mother drove them both down to Maurs and her lawyer, who was deference itself. A small cake was produced. Jerome wolfed it.

M. Hubert folded his arms happily, "And M. Vermande accepts the charge?"

"Yes."

"Madame Lacaze, the case will be a pleasure."

They drove home.

Jean-Louis drove into the village with a good bottle of red for Chibret. Then drove them both to the Mairie where Chibret seconded his nomination of Dominique Duthileul. Bernadie

scowled and crossed the road to Sara's house. Spoke to her mother.

"Where is he?"

"Lives with his mother now," her head gestured down the village.

Bernadie rocked slightly.

"What?"

"You deaf?"

"He left her? And the child?"

"He lives with his mother now." She folded her arms.

"Jesus Christ."

"He may even get to Him."

"God forbid. Madame - my condolences."

"No need."

The door closed.

Bernadie strode down to Madame Lacaze's house and rapped hard on the door. Jerome answered it.

"Bernadie!" His face warmed with joy.

"You twat."

Madame Lacaze opened her living-room door to see Bernadie's hands close round her son's throat and the two of them falling hard onto her polished hall parquet. She winced as Jerome buried his knee hard in Bernadie's groin and the older man groaned balefully onto his side. Jerome stood. He nodded to her and Madame Lacaze went back inside.

Jerome watched Bernadie rise to his knees then helped him gingerly stand.

"Let's walk," he said.

At the front gate Bernadie shrugged off the helping hand and by ten yards up the road his back had straightened.

"You left your child?"

"Yes."

"Man who turns his back on his family is no good."

"I'm not."

"You were."

"I must have changed."

They walked. La Poste up ahead, then the Mairie, then the café.

"Why?"

"It happened. I's easier."

Bernadie looked at Jerome. The fattening face, the nervous eyes.

"Do you want a drink?"

"More than anything."

Bernadie stopped walking and snorted, "And I thought you should stand for Mayor."

Jerome stopped. Two men in a snow-slushed street.

"I'll buy 'em," he said.

Jerome took two coffees and two cognacs and thought of Jacques and the lawyer and his mother and Madame Valet and sobriety and this election and sipped at his coffee and wondered if he dared have just the one kiss of cognac.

"Mayor?"

"I thought about it. But as you say - you've changed." Bernadie nipped hard at his alcohol. Jerome watched it warm Bernadie's mouth, watched him savour the taste, the heat, the lift.

"Duthileul'll have a clear run."

"Jean-Louis?" Jerome was genuinely astonished.

"The son, clothhead!" He downed the rest of the cognac. "They'll be building statues by Easter. Should have topped them when we had the chance. First time he came to a drop."

Jerome remembered how he had first feared, then respected and had finally come to love this man. He did his very best to think.

"The fight - that war," he managed, "that was my politics. This kind of politics is institutionalised corruption."

Bernadie, the ex-Mayor, leaned pugnaciously forward.

"You always did talk shit. There are lights on the streets of Senaillac - for the old ones at night. There is mains water to every house in the village that wanted it. The school has books and papers and pencils. Next year there will be sewers. That's not Politics - that's being a Mayor. You make things better for your commune. Are you drinking that? Come on Lacaze – why did you fight? Eh? For Dominique fucking Duthileul - that arriviste - to do his father's will?"

"Who else is there?"

"Never mind that - where's your responsibility gone?"

"Ask Sara - I'd vote for her."

"Ohh. Are you drinking that?"

Jerome shook his head and his drink vanished.

"Lacaze - you're not fit. Forget I mentioned it." He rose and was gone.

Jerome sat in the café with Bernadie's coffee and a whirling head.

The beam! He'd forgotten.

Oh Jesus.

Jacques and Arbel managed the beam. They tied two long lengths of the heaviest rope a half-metre from each end. Then nearly broke their backs lifting and holding one end of seven metres of oak from the groove in the A frame to be resting on the side of the frame and tying it off. Then the other end and hold that weight on the rope and tie it off before it fell. Neither spoke. It was scary. When they had the weight held on the rope they lowered it down the north side of the house and out into the lane. That took two hours. With it finally laying on his cart, and them both wasted, hands ripped with rope-burns, Arbel said, "Was it just the once?"

"Yes."

Arbel nodded.

"And was it good?" He looked hard at Jacques.

"It was need, Arbel. Answering a need is good."

Arbel nodded.

The bache was sagging between the A frames now, snow gathering above his attic floor.

"You'll need to prop that."

"I know."

Arbel nodded and walked to the village, bought two bottles and drank one on the walk home, wondering should he tell her he'd spoken with Jacques. He drank the other at his kitchen table and by the end of it knew he couldn't. Or wouldn't. He recognised that it saddened and hardened him, and the hardening made him sadder yet. Ardelle sensed only some shift. She'd wait. All change was for the better now, no matter how tortuously silent and slowly it came. Things can't get worse. And perhaps she'd get pregnant...

When Jerome arrived Jacques was glad of the guilty help with the A frames. Oak is serious wood. He would have got them down but this was safer. Three hours later the bache rested on the walls.

"You'll need to prop that," shivered Jerome. Jacques had timber ready. His wigwam roof.

"Can I light a fire?" Jerome asked.

They sat and smoked either side of it.

"Dominique's standing for Mayor."

"He'll win."

"We've got you a lawyer."

Jacques looked across the fireplace.

"That make you feel better?"

"Yes."

"Good."

His eyes went back to the flames.

"Bernadie thought I should stand," said Jerome.

Silence.

"I haven't had a drink in four days. This is your fault, I'll have you know. And Madame Valet."

"Make you feel better?"

"No. Neither."

"Then don't do it."

"Dominique Duthileul, Jacques..."

"Irrelevant. Going to bed. Sleep if you want. There's blankets."

Simone posted him a first photograph of his son.

Jerome walked back to Sara's. She sat there in her night-gown. Offered wine. It was refused.

"What is this? Are you thinking at last? Good God."

"Maybe. Might be."

"Madame Valet wants to see you."

"Can you see me standing for Mayor?"

"You're sober..." she offered, as though that were both a miracle and a first qualification.

"Temporarily. While I think."

"Oh. Then, no."

A quiet.

"What do you think?" he asked.

"What do you care what I think?"

"A lot."

"When did this start, caring what I thought?"

"Don't, Sara."

"Why'd you leave us?"

"I don't - know."

"Will you come back now? For the election?"

"No. I'm weak – but not a total hypocrite, remember?"

"Will you come back?"

He looked at her. "I don't think so. Sara. I am sorry."

"You are sober. I am, too. Sorry."

"Don't know what you've to be sorry for."

"I'm sorry for the loss. I wasn't apologising."

"Neither should you."

They shared a little grin.

"Friends?"

"Parents."

"Where is she?"

"Jerome - it's nine o'clock - she's in bed."

"I think you should stand. I'd vote for you."

"I think you should think more."

Jerome stood at Madame Valet's door and couldn't knock.

He stood there three cold minutes before Severine Vigne came out of her house, knocked on the door for him and went home.

His Maternelle teacher opened the door. Again a cardigan over a cotton blouse. Her slippers and warm eyes.

"Come in, Jerome."

He hesitated. She took his elbow.

"I've changed the furniture."

He walked into Gaston Valet's house. Into that room.

She offered him an armchair.

"If you don't mind, Madame..." he gestured to the other.

She nodded understanding.

"A drink?"

"Coffee?"

Madame Valet raised an eyebrow. "Good, Jerome."

"You used to say that over my mathematics."

"Don't make me feel old, please," she said, moving in the kitchen.

"You're not, are you?"

"Ha! You wait, young man."

Jerome sat down by the fire. "I feel old," he said.

"Feeling and being are two separate things."

He thought about that and called through, "I'm not sure I agree, Madame..."

She poured two coffees and giving him one, sat opposite, across the fire.

"Sugar?"

"No. Thank you."

He looked at the coffee, then at her and realised she was waiting.

"I have been thinking," he said. "As you suggested."

"And?"

"When are you going back to teaching?"

"I - "

"The school needs you. The children need you."

"I have been - considering it."

"Good, Madame."

They almost smiled.

"And you?"

"I don't want to be Mayor..."

The sentence was ended but not finished.

"But..?"

"Dominique Duthileul..."

"That's not a good enough reason."

"No, I know. So I can't. Won't."

"What would be a good enough reason?"

Her fire was grand.

"I don't think I care enough about other people to care for them."

"That sounds lonely, Jerome."

"It is."

A beat.

"You don't want a real drink, I take it."

"I do, but I won't. Thank you."

"Well..."

A quiet began.

Jerome eased his back into the chair, the cushions. Madame Valet uncrossed her legs, kicked her slippers looser.

He looked up - she was almost smiling.

"What?" he said.

The smile vanished as she leaned forward unnecessarily.

"Nothing – no."

"You were…"

"More coffee?"

"Smiling..."

Madame Valet sat back. Conceding the point.

"Yes. I was."

The warm quiet began again.

"Well," she offered, "I'm pleased you've thought about it."

He nodded. "Me too. Thank you."

Warmth and silence and now something else entered the room.

When they both smiled again, sensing and accepting this new something, Jerome stretched a little and Madame Valet could openly look at him.

His childhood, adolescence, marriage, war, baby, murder.

Murder here.

And the truth is I was smiling because Gaston is gone.

I'm smiling because he's not here. I never smiled with him.

And now this boy, this pupil, this young man, the murderer, my releaser, is utterly confused, and that makes me smile too - and -

Jerome loosened in the blaze from her fire.

I don't think I want to be anything but drunk again.

Mayor is ridiculous.

I have possibilities but no momentum.

I'd rather be Jacques - no possibility and all momentum.

I'd rather not be Arbel.

I'd rather be more than I am.

What am I meant for?

To oppose. But I've nothing left to oppose. I don't even oppose my mother!

Captain Phillipe appeared in his thoughts. He'd order me to stand. Duty. Bullshit. It's paper-pushing. Committees. Compromise. Street lights!

I need a drink - I can't have a drink.

He looked up.

"Penny for your thoughts?" she said.

"I have to stay sober for Vermande's sake."

She nodded. "I see. So, you do care about other people."

He shrugged. Leaned forward, put the coffee on the floor by the chair and said, "And a penny for yours?"

This quiet began very quickly. And into it Madame Valet stood to answer.

She took his hand, lifted him to his feet and placed his fingers on the top button of her blouse. Jerome froze.

🐏

The first wall. Barn end. Double thickness of bricks and rock separated by an insulation of sand, small stones, lime. Big keying stones laid across. The mortar had dried a century gone and he'd have no need of the hammer or chisel yet. He took the first stones out.

Jerome and Celine Valet made love four astonished times, slept like babies, ate bacon and sausage for breakfast and went down to the Mairie where Bernadie seconded her nomination of Jerome Lacaze, and she re-registered to teach.

twenty-three

"WILL YOU VOTE FOR ME?"

The stone-man stopped dismantling his wall, turned.

"Will it make you feel better?"

"Yes."

"Then I will." And turned back.

"Thanks."

Jerome stood a moment longer, watching the automaton, thinking, 'And does this make you feel better? Or is it that it stops you feeling at all?'

"Will you vote for me?"

"As what?"

"Mayor."

"Chibret's Mayor," said Ardelle.

"He resigned."

"Why?"

Jerome looked at Arbel.

"What?" said Ardelle, turning to him.

"I'll tell you later."

Ardelle accepted that. Gratefully.

"Will you vote for me?"

"What will you do?"

Jerome's jaw sagged a millimetre. "What d'you mean?"

"As Mayor. What will you do? Why should I vote for you?"

"I haven't a clue. What do you want done?"

Ardelle thought.

"Nothing."

"No problem, then. I'm your man."

Ardelle shifted her stance. "Why are you doing this?"

Jerome looked at her. Old adversary, old bull-shit sniffer. "I don't know, Ardelle."

"Don't you think you should?"

"Of course, of course. But I haven't time. The vote is next Sunday. We'll talk politics afterwards, yes? Will you vote for me?"

"Who else is there?" Arbel said.

"Dominique Duthileul."

They both nodded.

"Thanks. You can tell her now."

He left Puech, that campaign a triumph.

Arbel told Ardelle why Chibret had resigned.

"If he wins you should change your mind," she said, "have the feast."

"I'll change my mind when I choose."

"Yes, husband."

Ardelle went to bed and waited.

Arbel sat and fought with his thoughts.

I needed.

Madame Lacaze drove her son round all the outlying farms and Jean Louis and his son did the same.

Jerome was relieved of postulating the practical or political

THE SINGLE SOLDIER

initiatives an incumbent Mayor might indulge in as he dealt with questions about his broken marriage, his drinking, and his relationship with the swindling Vermande. Since Jerome had next to no concrete ideas beyond his abhorrence of the Duthileul's he cheerfully encouraged the campaign to descend into murky personal waters instantly and Dominique and his father found themselves answering awkward pointed questions about the length and depth of Dominique's Maquis adventures and exactly why Jean-Louis was so vindictive, and how that reflected on the family character.

Bernadie organised a public meeting, Friday, in the Salle de Fetes. As that neared, following Madame Lacaze's lead and initiative, the two candidates' war-records became the axis of the argument.

On Thursday Galtier let it be known that Jacques' court appearance was set for the following Tuesday. In Cahors, in the self-same court where Lacaze had been honoured to sit in judgement; and had then wilfully walked away from that civic responsibility, as he had his marriage, never forget.

Galtier delivered the letter to Jacques, who burnt it when evening got so cold even he couldn't function. He also burnt his lawyer's letter informing of the hour M. Hubert's car would arrive to take him to Justice.

Dominique talked sadly that Thursday, as he toured the village, of the curse of alcoholism. His rival had only been apparently sober perhaps ten days.

By Thursday Jerome was exhausted. Disgust clogged his will to rise and trade more slander and innuendo. He shaved and looked hard at his face and didn't much like what he saw. But, even that's better than a Duthileul, he told himself, again, and dressed.

"Have you a speech ready for tomorrow?" his mother asked,

pouring them strong coffee.

"No. I shall ask for questions and try, and doubtless fail, to speak my mind."

She passed him a cup. "I believe you might win."

"I know I could. Isn't it ridiculous?"

A moment passed between them resembling warmth.

Jerome had the fleeting urge to describe to his mother Celine Valet's luscious saucer nipples. Instead, surprising himself, he said, "What on earth do we do, if I win?"

Madame Lacaze was kissed by the sweetness of the word 'we' - it ran right through her body. I have something to lose now, she thought. And I don't want to. "If you win," now she dared say this, "If you win - you should go back to Sara."

They shared a smile, Mother and son.

"I think she's got far too much sense."

She nodded another smile, then bustled away at the breakfast crockery.

"He'll have something, Duthileul, up his sleeve." she warned, "He'll have thought this right through."

On Thursday night Jacques found a piece of paper and a pencil and wrote, "I, Jacques Vermande, vote for Jerome Lacaze." and walked the midnight snowy lane to the Mairie where he posted it and walked back.

All day Friday Bernadie, The Prefect, Chibret, Dominique, his father, Jerome, Sara, Mesdames Valet and Lacaze drummed up for a full appearance at the Salle De Fetes that evening. No problem. Since the cancellation of Chibret's feast and the toppling of his tree the commune had waited all too eagerly.

Bernadie and Monsieur The Prefect, flanked by the candidates, sat at a table clothed with the tri-colour as the hall filled.

There were a surprising number of men. So, some had escaped both the Germans, and, thought both Bernadie and Jerome, any war-effort. Hidden in the woods and survived.

At 7.30 as Arbel and Ardelle squeezed in to stand, jammed at the back, Bernadie called the meeting to order and asked the candidates for opening remarks.

Dominique Duthileul, shirt ironed, stood.

Jacques worked.

His hands were changing from a man dealing with wood and slate to a man dealing with stone. A layer of lime formed seemingly beneath the skin itself and protected and calloused the hand. After two days he never cut himself on a stone again. You feel the weight. Of the stone and in the stone. They were individual, surprising, personal. His. Theirs. He became confident as he worked towards the corner stones that he could re-build as his grandfather had built. This was possible. He worked.

"I am concerned for the political state of the commune," a man near the front said, "when we are meant to be involved in nothing so squalid as a battle between its old and new money."

Madame Lacaze and Jean-Louis Duthileul nodded a wry acceptance of that. Shared a glance across the floor of the meeting, even.

"Your point being?" asked The Prefect.

No answerpp.

"You should have stood then," someone called.

Agreement.

It became clear natural sympathies rested with Jerome. For all his

enumerated faults he was a human-being. Dominique was bland, a creation of his despised father. The election was there for the taking. Sara wished The Prefect could close it, produce the urns now, and he might be saved. As a Mayor. Ridiculous, but. As the tide against them rose Jean-Louis stood from his seat. The meeting stilled immediately. Madame Lacaze straightened. Here it is.

Duthileul waited for silence and then addressing the Hall said, "Is it right, I ask our commune, to elect someone who - we must call a spade a spade - robbed us, criminally, of one of its most valued members?"

Quiet.

Jerome froze.

Dominique, he later dimly remembered, did not.

The meeting turned to Jerome.

The election, the future, was there for the taking. Right there. Sara, Arbel, Madame Lacaze, everyone, could feel it. Get this answer right and ride home.

Jerome went to stand and stopped, arrested, as Madame Valet rose to her feet. Immediate silence.

"Point of order, M. Chairman."

"Madame?" said Bernadie.

"I was widowed, was I not, by the politics of war?"

"In my estimation," Bernadie unhesitatingly replied, "yes, Madame."

"Then as I have nothing but respect for the character of M. Lacaze, may we not keep now to the politics of peace?"

The election was won. Vote now. He'd done nothing - she'd won it for him. Vote now. It was done.

Dominique Duthileul scraped back his chair and stood.

The babble in the hall dropped again. To curiosity. What could he possibly have to say?

"I rebuke both my father's question and its inference."

The room hushed deeply.

Madame Lacaze stiffened with apprehension. Dread.

"We must live in the future, not the past," he said. "What has been done should have no bearing on what needs to be done, or why."

Everywhere necks strained to see Duthileul Pére reddening.

Dominique paused.

"Further, I have to say, and publicly, that I take issue with my father's action against our neighbour, Jacques Vermande."

Absolute silence.

"What's done there is also done and I ask my father now, as a gesture of goodwill for the future of this commune, to publicly withdraw from his action."

He looked to his father. Everyone did.

Immobile.

As the meeting waited Dominique seemed to turn the screw.

"We have been at war. We need to heal and wounds kept vengefully open can only fester and cancer us all."

Silence.

"Well, father?"

Silence.

Jean-Louis rose, gathered up his hat, almost inaudibly growled, "As you will," and elbowed his way out of the meeting.

Dominique stood whilst his father made his way through the stunned room, then as all eyes returned to him, nodded to Jerome to speak, and sat down.

Too late. No need.

The election had just been won.

Madame Lacaze's jaw hurt. She couldn't help but admire the tactics.

Jerome drank hard all day Saturday and on the Sabbath Dominique was elected Mayor. Jerome was invited to stand on the council but as he chose not to be able to stand at all, that chance, if indeed chance it was, was gone too.

Sara watched as her pissed ex-husband weaved about the platform. "Vive Ma Pauvre Republique!" She took Zoe home.

Madame Lacaze shook Jean-Louis's hand.

"Congratulations."

"Madame." He even motioned to bow. "May I introduce my son?"

"In a moment. May I ask a personal question?"

Jean-Louis Duthileul's eyes registered surprise. "Of course, Madame..."

"Why do you go to Church?"

Jean-Louis allowed what he trusted was a private smirk to calm his briefly rattled spirit. "Oh, hope?"

She arched an eyebrow.

"Show?" he offered.

"Form?"

"Voilà."

They nodded.

"And yourself?"

Madame Lacaze flushed with outrage and Jean-Louis took the woman in for the first time. Strong shoulders, petite breasts, neat waist, thickening legs – and, of course, money.

Madame Lacaze stared hard into the walnut face, plonked on rounding shoulders, above the paunch, and the good legs.

"We have so very little in common, Monsieur," she said, whilst hearing herself think, 'And I will have such revenge on you for that – and all of this.' And she smiled.

Jean-Louis sensed Something.

An impulse moving in her. He returned her smile, "I'm sure

neither of us meant any offence. My son."

His arm beckoned and Dominique abruptly left off his conversation and appeared at his father's side.

He offered his hand.

"Monsieur Le Maire," Madame Lacaze took it, almost bobbed, but held herself.

"Vive notre Pauvre Revolution!" her son droned from a chair somewhere.

"Madame Lacaze - would you please consider being a member of my council?"

"Yes."

The bare-faced cheek of them!

"I will consider it."

"I'd consider it an honour." He let the hand go.

"You flatter us both, sir."

"Thank you, Madame."

Dominique Duthileul smiled. It was warmer, more generous than his father's but she returned it, thinking, 'And I will take revenge on you both for my son.'

He could feel grit with each blink.

He had a day left on this section before he would have to lift the first of the corner stones. He would need to strengthen the stairs. Assuming he could lift and carry the stones, he certainly could not afford for the stairs to give. And there's the lintels over the two windows. And the two beneath them. They're bigger yet. Fix the stairs. No. Finish the wall first.

"What did you find to talk about with M. Duthileul and his Mayoral fils? And where's the brandy?"

"Politics. There, sot."

"He wants your money. Are you blind?"

"No. Are you?"

"Am I what?"

"Blind. Perhaps I want him in my bed."

She relished the chaos on her son's face.

"This village should be quarantined. There's no-one sane it."

"Sara?"

Jerome poured a tumbler full. Half way down the glass he thought of going to see Celine Valet.

Galtier cycled up with the photo. This'll break his heart. He left the envelope lodged in the door and went across to Duthileul for another celebratory glass and a pre-council talk. Immigration - that'll be the new world problem when the Nazis surrender...

Jacques found the letter when he next slung a sack of the small stone over his shoulders. He dropped the sack on his top step and it tottered over and spilled a pebble cascade slowly down his steps as he gazed at the stamp, took the letter inside, closed the door and took out the black and white image that begged the question how many times can one heart shatter?

He sat and read.

"Here he is, here we are and where are you? I have two jobs, he has two teeth and you have two loved ones. The war is over isn't it? Japan seems mad..."

The letter detailed their lives, the buildings, smells, noise, speed, everything but any notion of return.

It ended "Write to me, please, tell me what it is you understand so perfectly,

Your friend and much much more
Simone."

Dominique Duthileul's council consisted of Madame Lacaze, Galtier, Severine and in a temporary advisory capacity, Bernadie. There should have been ten but there weren't.

He exposed the huge square granite corner stones of the barn-end wall. If I push them off, spose they break? 'And much much more' And much much more. He took the photo from the envelope and kissed it again. Strengthen the stairs.

In a drawer he found the photo of his father. He wrote on the back, "Show him his grandfather. He should know his history. You are mine. Jacques." He wiped an envelope dust-free and sealed it. I won't go to La Poste - I'll wait for Sara. And work. Strengthen the stairs. But something in him said this was wrong. If he was taking the house down surely there was another way than building bits of it up. It was wrong. He began on the stone of the north wall.

Arbel worked. Ate and swapped the platitudes that pass for meal-time conversation in a wounded house and they began to make love again. Not intimately but Ardelle waited and held him and hoped.

Dominique's one rebellion from his father's vision of the new St. Cirgues was to take the flat above the Mairie. So his father need only place a man in Dominique's job.
Jean-Louis went to the family LaCroix.
He offered Renée the position of working his farm and a wage he couldn't, and didn't, refuse. Meanwhile, and more pressing, his mother was approaching senility fast and couldn't be trusted

to cook any more. Jean-Louis went to the Tabac, took his corner throne, stared at the mid-day-sloshed Jerome and thought.

The Conseil General had called for nominations for medals for war-heroes. Such as Arbel Jammes, offered Monsieur Le Mayor. The tiny council nodded.

Or, Galtier moved, Jean-Louis, who had given money and helped with the parachute drops, wasn't that so, M. Bernadie?

Bernadie left the council at the end of that meeting.

"You've no need of me. You're absolutely fine. In control. Bon courage."

He had a last drink with Jerome.

"Some you lose. You risk your life for a standard, a faith, you turn around and it's gone. Like yesterday." He drank. "When they start with the statues we'll blow the buggers up. I know where there's some dynamite..." A grin came and went. "Should have executed them both. Too late."

"Too late," Jerome agreed and smiled emptily.

"Go back to her. Get back to them both."

He was gone.

Jean-Louis suggested to the new Mayor that it might be an idea to invite the council members round for an aperitif, ou quoi... One night. When Spring came. Or the surrender, the Armistice.

twenty-four

ST. CIRGUES SMOOTHED ITS FEATHERS and sat to cackle. Of course they'd voted for the wrong man. Of course they'd been duped. Jean-Louis had control of the village now via his mouthpiece son. God knows what they'd get up to. Mind you, Lacaze revealed his true colours, hadn't he? The drunk. People shrugged. The rich always win, isn't that so?

The Allies were on course for making twenty million Germans homeless. Laval was arrested and to be executed. Petain too, when they found him. De Gaulle nationalised the Renault factories.

Madame Valet prepared lessons.

Arbel ploughed. And Sara and Renée. The cycle re-started. The hibernation of winter and war was ending.

Mayor Duthileul had Severine print letters announcing the re-opening of school

The letter to America with the photograph of little Jacques' grandfather waited for Sara to call. He left the two pillars of corner-stones and worked on the windowless north wall, under his tarpaulin wigwam. The rubble of the house began to fill what had once been a garden.

The Maternelle re-opened. Sara packed Zoe's bag.
Madame Valet took five children - Alexandra, Arno, Cara, Marie and the youngest, Zoe, into her school-room.
And she took the drunk into her bedroom.
In the newly silent house Madame Lacaze suspected he might have gone back to his wife and daughter but some instinct knew that wasn't so.
He was missed in the bar, but no-one cared to question why. It was quieter and that was better.
Celine accepted it was insane.
Time would reveal them and what then?
But she lead him upstairs again, and willingly embraced their sensual oblivion again, thinking - whatever happens it cannot be as good as this.
She could become addicted, like him to alcohol.

Why doesn't Sara come? The letter to America remained unposted.
Why don't you go and see her?
Or walk to La Poste?
What have you become?
He worked on dismantling his walls rather than consider that.

Celine's tidy home rotted around them as they spent more and more time exploring sex. Every position, any fantasy - their appetites unending, it seemed.
They made love on the table, under it, on the stairs; the whole

house became a lust-sack. Between her years of emptiness and his desire to never think again, they created an empire of exploration. It was so total only school and food interrupted them. And at meals they would bargain potatoes for buttons undone, wine for underclothes removed and the plates and cutlery clattered and congealed on the floor as they swept a place clear to lay one or either down for the other to feast on. Both brains transferred wholesale to their loins and answered only those questions, those cravings. And each week-day morning she would dress prim and tidy and hope the facade held. Till she could get home.

"I think I'm pregnant," Ardelle said at supper, serving soup.

Arbel cried.

She waited, afraid to touch him, and he wept and wept and left the soup and took her once in his arms, stepped back and went out to the village for a bottle.

In the café he read that Dresden had been obliterated and 130,000 were dead.

And he would be a father.

He walked back up the lane, a full early Spring Moon casting his shadow sharply, knocked on Jacques' door, jiggled it just so, petted the barking dog quiet and when Jacques stumbled, gritty and clothed from his sleep Arbel said, "You'll need a beast to pull that cart now it's thawed. Help yourself."

And went home to his family.

Two men came back from Germany.

Jauliac, aged terribly, and George Gley. The rest were dead.

Madame Jauliac folded the wretched shocked body in her arms, as did Gley's sisters, consuming them with tears of grateful horror. Dominique, encouraged by Madame Lacaze, decided to re-instate

Chibret's feast for returning heroes. But to wait for VE day. When his father suggested the same idea over their thin Sunday meal Dominique was pleased to say, "It's already in hand," and then felt anger at his father's condescending, "Good, son."

It took Jerome a week of sex and alcohol to realise he was akin to a sexual prisoner. And a more than willing one. Craving even. This oblivion of flesh was perfect. Barring only that it be acknowledged. He dressed.

"I have no-one to talk to," Sara said to Jacques' back.
She sat in the attic grime, watching him.
He swung the bag of stone over his shoulder, took it down the stairs, loaded it onto the cart, came back upstairs, opened the bag, laid it on the floor next to his wall and prised out the next stones. A minute or two passed.
"How are you going to take those corner stones down?"
Jacques turned slowly, his back bent beneath the sagging bache and his eyes passed from her to the stone columns.
"You don't know?" Sara was surprised. A fragment of Time passed.
"How did I get so old so quick?"
He had the bag filled. Swung it onto his shoulder and as he passed her at the top of the stairs she asked, "Would you miss me if I didn't come?"
"Yes," he said and went down the stairs, loaded the stone on the cart, came back upstairs, opened the bag, laid it on the floor next to his wall and prised out the next stones.
"Thank you," she said.
The bache drooped on the shrinking stone-work.
She lit a fire, pulled water from the well, boiled it, took the winter vegetables she'd bought in her panier, covered the pot with the

clean muslin she'd bought to counter his dust, and the soup smell eventually penetrated even his grit-loaded nostrils. She sat stirring, tasting, as Jacques went in and out of the house with bag after bag of stone. Finally he stopped in the doorway and said, "That's ready."

He swept the top layer of stone and grit off the table with his gritty sleeve. Found two bowls and blew a cloud from them.

"Wash?" she said.

He rubbed his hands on the arse of his trousers - more dust - and sat to roll a cigarette that was one quarter grit to three of tobacco.

"How is Zoe?"

Sara looked up. Grey man speaking. Grey man asking.

"Surviving..."

They ate. She ate, he savoured. Every nuance, every possible flavor he filtered around his grimy mouth, but most of all the heat. Hot food.

Madame Lacaze now felt for certain wherever her son was he had descended. She also knew who she blamed and the idea, the possibility and the compulsion of revenge took a more serious grip in her.

The school-teacher wished the mothers and children a good weekend and on the way back from shopping saw Jerome in the bar.

Her blood stilled.

He looked up. "Celine!"

Ancient raddled heads turned.

He waved her to come in.

"I'll carry the bags home."

That was enough.

He'd said enough. On purpose? What was the difference now?
She came to sit with her lover for a drink.

A fire, a fag and Memory.
The dog rolled over in a dream, his feet twitching, running, chasing; snorting through his nose.
Jacques looked across the fireplace at his woman-friend. Sitting there. Where...
She was right. She had aged. And saddened.
Still earthed though. Rooted.
He heard himself say, "Sara..."
"Jacques." She didn't look up. "What?"
"Nothing." He dropped the fag-end in the ash. "I was telling myself your name."
She laughed.
"What?"
"Is this Life?"
When she left, taking his letter, she said, "Lay some hay beneath the corners of the house and push the stones off. One at a time."
She couldn't be sure but he might have smiled at that.

On Sunday when Celine returned from Mass she and Jerome sat perfectly still. Waiting. Talking of what each would do to the other. Zoe forgotten. Hours of dirty luscious endless talk. As dusk came they went upstairs, where she tied him naked hands and feet and beat him with her clothes till he spurted all everywhere and she licked the love up and then lay as he tied her and licked her to screaming bliss.
Severine Vigne heard them, again.
A week ago she'd been mortified. Horrified, shamed, disgusted. And had thought of complaining. Of denouncing. This abomination.

She wasn't altogether sure to whom. The Mayor? The Curé?

But a fascination had overtaken her as the sheer constancy of the sounds beyond the wall became a ritual and now, her secret.

And in her worst moments, like this Sabbath evening, she felt almost complicit. And envious. And, didn't they say men who drank a lot – couldn't? This one could. Did. Endlessly.

Then, finally, over some Sunday dinner somewhere, some husband mentioned Lacaze had said he'd take their shopping 'home'...

Sara reasoned with Zoe that Papa must be poorly to miss his Sunday walk.

She was not prepared to walk down to Madame Lacaze's house - she had her pride yet.

On Monday there were no other children at the school gates.

Sara stiffened. As did Madame Valet. The two women looked at each other and their separate blood ran cold.

Sara left Zoe with her mother and went straight to the other children's houses, hoping there'd be talk of a bug or head-lice or similar. And, yes indeed a disease had taken root, but not physical. And not curable.

Dominique sat with Severine.

"You knew?"

"I hear them. Every night. All night. All week. It's - incredible..."

Dominique Duthileul needed to think.

"And disgusting," Severine added.

I need a drink, he thought.

"I thought you should know."

I need a walk. "Yes. Yes. Thank you."

"Madame Cantagrel is coming back this afternoon."

"Coming back?"

"She was here, she went to collect signatures."

"She doesn't need signatures."

"She's gone to get them anyway."

"I need to think, Severine. I'll be back in an hour."

He left.

Madame Valet locked the school, went home, sat on the bed, woke him, and told him.

He sat up. She smelt the booze waking in his body.

"Well…" he said, "O.K. What is this? What are we?"

"Need?"

"I'll drink to that."

"Aren't you afraid? Of what will happen?"

Something to oppose.

"Not a bit."

He opened the buttons of her blouse.

"To us? To the village?" she urged.

Through the cotton he urged her big nipple upright and the conversation went on hold.

Dominique walked quickly away from the village, taking the road to the Roc D' Etang, the cold wrapping itself around him.

Think!

Obviously, she can't teach.

They can't stay in the village.

They can't - carry on. It's an obscenity.

Why aren't I going to talk with my father?

Oh Jesus - what did I even agree to all this for?

I don't want any of this.

This - this is him. Father.

No, this is me! I did want this.

Fucking Lacaze. And her?! Is he mad? Is he certifiable..?

He looked up and there was Lacaze's house.

O Christ! I've come to see her.

Well, someone must. This is Responsibility.

What are you going to do?

First things first. She's a councillor and you need her counsel.

They sat around her stove.

"I'll come directly to the point Madame, if I may..."

Madame Lacaze nodded.

"Your son..."

Madame Lacaze admitted Dread. Again. It was part of her motherhood.

"...is living - in sin. With Madame Valet."

A silence.

"So."

Another quiet.

"I think I came to ask your counsel, Madame."

Silence.

"I've been denying something of this kind, you must give me time to consider, Monsieur Le Mayor. Though I wonder how much time there can be."

"Quite. Madame Cantagrel is collecting signatures."

"Signatures on what?"

"A Condemnation. I imagine. A Denouncement."

"She'll get them all." She said, then added, "And mine."

Dominique nodded. That was most of what he'd come for, he realised. He even relaxed a millimetre.

Madame Lacaze looked at her Mayor.

"How old are you, Dominique?"

The Mayor looked at Madame Lacaze.

"A year older than your son, Madame. Why?"

She hesitated, and then chose to tell the truth. "Because your fear touches me."

Something in him moved, which she saw, and it warmed the coldest part of her. They both managed a certain smile.

On an instinct she asked, "What does your father say?"

"I haven't told him, yet."

"Which doesn't mean he doesn't know..." she said.

The son agreed silently, ruefully and then tried to cover the inherent betrayal. Madame Lacaze was too quick for him.

"I'm flattered," she said.

Oh, but she Loved this seedling wedge sliding between him and his father.

"I'm very flattered."

Dominique was distracted by alien movement through his veins. Attraction.

He stood.

"I'll be very grateful for your counsel, Madame - and I apologise for bringing such news..."

"Rather you than anyone else, Monsieur Le Mayor," she said, standing.

They walked to the door.

"It will end very badly," she said.

"I fear so. I'm sorry, Madame."

There was a tiny silence in which he wanted to say more.

She opened her door and said, "Perhaps not. God willing."

God might be willing to allow Jerome Lacaze and Valet's widow to fornicate in his sight but Mayor Duthileul doubted his commune would.

He walked back.

And what was that?

With her?

Madame Lacaze poked at her stove, poured a nipper of brandy.

  THE SINGLE SOLDIER

You two duped my son.

Yes, he is a bloody fool. So I shall have to take his revenge for him.

The brandy ran clear and hot down through her chest.

At Puech the silent subject that had divided Arbel and Ardelle was dropped. They might still trip on it - it hadn't gone, just been dropped.

Their child was coming. A healing thing. They began to speak. Immediately she wanted to tell him she'd been raped but she daren't do it to that fragile wafer of peace. So now they came hand in hand to Sunday church and stayed for one drink inside the café. No Sara. No Jerome. They declined Duthileul's offer of a lift home to walk the spring lane together, up past Jacques' bache, his north wall down to the ceiling floorboards.

Arbel made a mental note to help with the window lintels.

He bustled at their garden and sold his thin cash-crops on a Wednesday. They got along. To the point where Arbel forgot.

When he remembered he was silent again.

Ardelle waited. He came back, slowly forgetting again, to this new marriage.

The bache withstood a fearsome storm, the worst of the winter, and he lay in his grit and lime studded bed, listening.

Next morning, after Renée Lacroix had taken what had once been his herd to what had once been his pasture Jacques Vermande helped himself to four bales of what had once been his hay. Lay them at the bottom corners of his house, went upstairs and one by one pushed down his huge corner stones. Arbel watched. When all of them were down he came across and said, "Let's do the

lintels, eh?"

By the time Ardelle called Arbel for lunch the bache rested flat on his oak ceiling and all the huge stones were on the cart. Arbel asked would Jacques care to come and eat and Jacques said he thought not but thanks and they shook fingers and parted.

"I've moved. In. With Celine."

Silence.

"Valet..." he added.

"I know her name," Sara managed.

Silence.

"I'm not sorry, Sara. I've done enough apologising for one life."

Silence.

"Don't. Ever. Take Zoe there."

He stood, desperate to go. Home.

"Don't ever take her there..."

A righteousness rose in him. "I should be ashamed?"

Sara looked at him. Shoulders moving. Foot tapping.

"If you could be - yes."

Silence.

"There's nothing left of you," she blurted, "what are you doing?"

His head fell on his chest and an arm flung itself around it. As abruptly he straightened. "We've had our lives, now we have to exist. You know?"

"Yes, I do, Jerome. Don't take my daughter there."

"Might take mine..."

"No. You've shamed her family enough."

He couldn't meet her eyes so he left.

Madame Cantagrel rode her bicycle down to St. Hilaire and rapped hard at the Curé's door.

Righteous bile poured out of her and she showed him the signatures. He reeled.

"But what do you suggest?" he quivered.

"They must be moved."

"Banished? St. Cirgues is hardly Eden, Madame..."

Madame Cantagrel nearly slapped him. "They flout God's Laws, sir!"

"True," he sighed.

"You're useless. I'll see the Mayor."

The Mayor had gone to see his father.

Who knew.

"Prefect doesn't anticipate problems with a replacement teacher," offered Jean-Louis.

"You called him?"

Dominique wondered if his father even registered the outrage in his voice.

"He's a friend." Duthileul shrugged.

Apparently not, concluded Dominique; resentment quiet in him.

"She'll get a month's wages," his father snorted. "And her pension!"

They sat across the table.

Dominique's grandmother muttered into her crochet work in the gloom of the fireplace.

"Is she dying?" Dominique said softly.

"Her brain, yes. Her body, no. She's peasant stock," his father almost snarled.

Silence.

"Councillor Madame Lacaze?" Jean-Louis enquired.

"She'll vote for whatever's worst for her son."

Duthileul nodded. "Good, my boy."

There was a silence.

"Well?" Duthileul finally said, "Do you want my advice?"

Dominique straightened his pride. "I'll take your counsel, father."

Duthileul absorbed the rebuff. "When you need it, then..."

The room chilled and Dominique left, tipped his hat to Renée and went back to the village where Madame Cantagrel seethed in his waiting room.

Jean-Louis Duthileul cursed. And now I must cook for Lacroix. Again. This can't go on.

"It could be arranged," The Mayor said, "that she be given an alternative posting..."

"Teach more children! Are you mad?"

"You suggest eviction. On what grounds, Madame?"

"Moral!" Madame Cantagrel shook.

"There's no law. No moral law."

"You're as bad as that water-lily priest."

Dominique eased his chair back a millimetre.

"Madame Cantagrel, I agree with you. Their behaviour is - beyond description. It disgusts me."

"Does it really? How much?"

"But what can I do - within my powers?"

"Tell them to go! Tell them their shame is our shame - the disgrace..." She was too full to complete the sentence. She stamped her foot once and began afresh.

"Tell them they're not wanted. Because they're not." She shook her sheath of signatures. "It is a stain before God."

"You could tell them that."

"I will! But you, Monsieur Duthileul, are our Mayor. Our servant. I have a hundred signatures - and you agree! God! Go and DO something. Something must be done! I don't know what - I'm no-

THE SINGLE SOLDIER

one - but you reach a point where - "

Words failed her.

He stood quickly before she started again.

"Leave this with me. And thank you, Madame Cantagrel - for your..." he ransacked his brain for a flattering word. "...vigour. And your faith in us all. Sincerely."

Madame Cantagrel went home to her sickly husband.

"He's got a problem."

"Who?" he asked, wearily.

"Never mind."

He didn't.

Jerome was trying to shave. With the early morning shakes. Celine took the razor from him, lathered the brush and shaved all of him, his head, eyebrows, chest hairs, armpits, every o so very carefully pubic hair; until he, bald and hard as bone took the razor and shaved off her clothes and they fucked standing there in the bathroom, fucked with her sitting on him sitting on the toilet, ran a bath and nearly drowned fucking in that.

Curé Phillipe sat in his cold house and considered his duty.

To God. To His flock. To his commune. Should he not talk to the Mayor? In his genuine panic the one thing he never considered was asking The Almighty's advice.

She read the letter.

"They've sacked me."

"On what grounds?"

"Morally unfit..."

A beat.

"They'll send my pension book."

"D'you need a drink?"

"Yes, and I need to know we'll love tonight."

"Fuck all self-appointed arbiters of morality Celine, we'll love now!"

He was smoking on his front door-step. Sara noted the corner-stone laden cart and sat with him. They looked out at a dust-grey cold spring garden, bleak as a picture of my heart, she thought. Piles of stones everywhere. Wreckage - things in bits and pieces.

"Jerome's moved in - with Celine Valet."

Silence.

A one-story house with a chimney stack and a tarpaulin roof behind them. Late February sky above them.

"He's gone. This time."

She wished she smoked.

He was so tired of the madness involved in thinking.

He scraped together, "How is Zoe?"

Sara heard the effort, smiled gratefully for it and said, "Bad. She thought she'd be teacher's pet. Now no-one speaks to her."

He nodded, smoked.

"She's been sacked. Best thing for Zoe. New start. I - "

She gulped for some air to speak with.

"I can't show my face, Jacques. I never knew I needed to before this. My mother can't go out. Zoe doesn't understand. We haven't seen him since he told me. I want to leave. Like you. Can I come with you?"

She felt him stiffen and added in a rush, "I wasn't serious, Jacques. Well, I am, but you know what I mean."

He said, "Bring Zoe here."

She said, "To bake some bread?"

"Could do."

They sat there.

Time crawled by.

Sara took pity on the dog hopelessly trying to groom even an inch of it's wretched matted coat. She laid and lit a fire, warmed some water, found a chunk of grimy soap and broke a comb and bent a fork untangling the months of dried slime on the beast. A part of her wanted to do the same for the bearded, hairy man but the thought didn't last.

The whole garden was grey with dust, the trees prematurely aged. We all are, she thought. God, what's it like in Germany if we're winning the damned war?

When she left Jacques borrowed a beast from Arbel, yoked it, set his blinkers and he and the dog walked the evening through St. Cirgues to Janatou, unloaded the cart, and slept under his other bache till the morning frost woke him and he walked, blinkered through the village, home. To half a home. Half his home here. Half there. Now, prop the bache and take out the floorboards. Then the beams, then the ground floor stone work. Move my bed to the caves? Yes. Work.

Mayor Dominique watched his grandmother talking to herself of 1914 and Vermande's grandfather, and saw his father struggling with food preparation and moved out of the Mairie and came home. He gave Renée the option of his own home every night but the fool only grinned and ate at their table and went to the spare room his Mayor had furnished for him. Across the road, the other fool walked his cart of rubble blinkered through the village twice a week now and Lacaze's wife, if she could still be called that, came to see him once a week. Arbel and he nodded when they saw each other. And the rank, rising pus of the village boil waited to be lanced.

"Come to Mass with me? Please?"

"Celine..." the bald man laughed, "Please."

"Weak as piss," she said and went to dare to take The Holy Sacrament.

Jacques heard the Sunday bell calling the commune to celebration as he levered up his ceiling's oak floorboards.

It was brisk but not overly cold and Ardelle and Arbel walked, nodding to Duthileul and his mother and son as they slowed to over-take them on the lane. Ardelle was not yet showing but they had decided this was the day to share their news - to re-join their community. To announce their child. They held hands as they came late up the slope into the Church Square.

The people were gathered in the sight of the Lord and no-one spoke. There was only one topic of conversation, and it was fast moving beyond words.

As she came in and took a pew the congregation took one collective intake of breath and held it for the next hour. Arbel and Ardelle, ignorant, only sensed the palpable chill. They looked round. Neither Sara nor her mother would make eye-contact. Zoe looked fearful. The Mayor and his father stared straight ahead. Madame Cantagrel's jaw ground outrage. Madame Lacaze, Jauliac and his wife, Chibret and his wife, the whole commune seemed charged with something...

When the Curé gave Madame Valet Christ's body and blood Arbel thought he heard a gasp, two, or was it tears? He looked round but no-one looked at him. They'd ask Sara.

But at the "Go in Peace," Sara, her daughter and mother bolted from the place. Arbel frowned. He and his new-found wife had good, happy news to spread. In the church square, two yards from the big door, they watched Madame Cantagrel spit in the schoolteacher's face. No-one moved to censure her, no-one moved

to comfort Madame Valet.

The teacher moved away through the crowd.

When the Curé appeared Madame Cantagrel raged in his face about ex-communication, fired a fearsome volley about spineless ineptitude at The Mayor and had to be dragged away by her husband. Arbel took Ardelle's arm and they left the coven buzzing.

The Curé and The Mayor looked at each other.

Madame Lacaze nodded to Jean-Louis Duthileul.

The village dispersed.

twenty-five

CURÉ PHILLIPE didn't need to scour his bible to know there was no passage, no wisdom on the subject of a woman fornicating with her husband's murderer. A man who'd left his wife and child.

Dominique and his father sat across their silent Sunday table.
Dominique thought, I am to go to the house and what? Tell them to leave. Ask them? Lecture them on morals?
Is that my job?
Yes, it is.
Do I take the Curé? Waste of space that he is. No. Take him. He won't speak, will he?
The father watched his son and wondered what he was thinking.
Jean-Louis Duthileul, a man without trust, never thought to ask.
His own thoughts, however, warmed him.
"I'll take a drive, I think."
'What's he up to?' thought Dominique.
Duthileul drove the long way round - avoiding the curtains and wagging tongues - and came to the house from The Roc road.
"Madame, I hope..."
"Come in, Jean-Louis. If I may..?" she demurred.

"Please."

He took off his best hat and followed her through to the dining-room. Heavy furniture. Old. Serious.

He sat in the proffered chair the other side of her stove.

"Drink?"

"Ah – perhaps a small cognac?"

She nodded. O, he feels celebratory does he?

She poured two glasses, placed the decanter back in the walnut cabinet. Leaded glass doors, hinge-drop moulded handles. Crystal glass.

"Your health."

"Santé."

Nice. Rich.

She sat, waiting.

"Your son…"

"Yes, Monsieur Le Maire spoke of it. Them."

"Oh," Jean-Louis was momentarily stalled. Madame Lacaze watched surprise pass fleet across his craggy dial.

"Children…" she sympathised.

"Your child, Madame."

"My God, you're prideful."

Duthileul blinked at such directness.

"I am," he recovered. "Aren't you?"

"Not about my son, no."

Suddenly Jean-Louis didn't want to talk about Jerome. He took another mouthful of his drink.

"This is better than mine," he offered.

Madame Lacaze nodded. Waited.

His eyes came to hers.

"I wanted to know how you felt…"

"Why?"

Jean-Louis stalled. There was something delicious in this. Something ancient.

"I wondered what would hurt you least. I imagine."

Madame Lacaze turned the glass in her hand.

"Why?"

"Respect?"

"You know nothing of me." Not even my name I bet.

"Enough..." he ventured. God, I haven't done this for forty years.

"I'm rich."

"So am I."

"Respect for that, then?"

"You know I've respect for money. This isn't about coin."

Madame Lacaze nodded her appreciation of the honesty, the tiny raising of the stakes.

"How could you affect what hurt me least?"

"If I could I would, is my point."

"That's a kind thought."

"You sound surprised."

She took a first sip. "I am. You're not a man to do things from the goodness of your heart are you, Jean-Louis?"

"This is a small community. An injury to one - "

"Oh, piffle, sir. We're as feral as cats."

"True."

He dared a smile.

She registered it and played back with, "And what, in your opinion, would hurt me least?"

"That your son should somehow - remain within reach?"

"Do you mock me? Again?"

Again Duthileul blinked. "No."

"My son could hardly be further from me."

"Of course. I meant - geographically."

"We know what you meant." Madame Lacaze placed her glass on the table and asked, "What business is this of yours?"

The question came direct and uncluttered by anything but curiosity.

Jean-Louis spread his hands just a little too wide. "My son - your son - our commune. Taste. Tone. Tact."

Her head nodded whilst she thought 'Nonsense. And your commune, you mean.'

She swirled the liquid and watched it settle.

He wants something.

What?

If I lift my eyes in one second, in one more second, I shall see.

One more.

O My God! He does.

Weight lifted from her.

A wary Delight moved into her.

Jean-Louis, no fool he, sensed change and stood, gathering his hat. "Madame, perhaps I have said too much. And as you say - what possible business is it of mine?"

Madame Lacaze said, "You won't have another?" And could have kicked herself.

"Another time - I'd be delighted. When our hearts are less burdened perhaps."

She followed him to the front door, watched him to his car, tip his hat and drive away. She closed the door.

His mother must be senile. He needs a cook.

And I have my idea for the revenge.

Jacques worked.

Sunday afternoon, warming sun, The Mayor and the Curé stood

outside Madame Valet's house. Severine pulled up a chair, edged aside her curtains, and flattened her face against her window. Jerome opened the door.

Dominique Duthileul gawped. Shaven head, no eyebrows, sunken eyes. Wearing what must be her dressing-gown.

"Fuck me," it said.

"Who is it?" came from upstairs.

"Everyone but the law," he called. He raised his nose at the Mayor and asked, "Where is the flic?"

"May we come in?"

There was a smell. A stale smell.

Jerome called, "May His Holiness The Mayor and God's boy come in?"

"What for?"

When they didn't answer Jerome offered over his shoulder, "Moral dressing down I imagine..."

"Then, no."

"Gentlemen?"

"We need to talk with you both," said the Mayor.

Madame Valet came down the stairs and joined Jerome at the door. Squinted at the sunlight.

"Afternoon, Severine," she called.

The smell was doubled. It was both of them.

"May we talk?"

"Go ahead. If you bore us we'll close the door. Fair enough?"

Talking on the doorstep? This wasn't Mayoral. Wasn't respectful. A pace behind him Curé Phillipe shifted helplessly. A few seconds of village history passed.

"What?" Madame Valet snapped.

The schoolmistress tone made all three men almost jump. Jerome laughed.

"Your cohabitation is - " Dominique hesitated, "upsetting people."
Jerome really laughed.

He stacked the last floorboards on the cart. My stairs lead nowhere.
Take them down now. My back hurts. All the time. He counted the
oak beams holding his bache up. Fifteen. I haven't washed. Sara
washed the dog. I'll wash when I get there. What's the point?
The bedroom walls are only light brick and plaster. The doors and
frames no big problem. Prop the bache through the beams, take
the walls down. Then the beams, put my bed in the caves, then
this floor.
I'll need help with the steps. Arbel? And the door and window
lintels.
And how deep are the foundations?
Work.
He rose, his hand catching at his spine. Straightened.

Ardelle was almost showing. Life was quiet in this lull. The
excitement to come throbbed. The surface of their life was not what
it had been - before - but it was as near as they could remember
without remembering everything. A deal had been done. Was
being done.
They were sitting in the thin spring sun and Arbel watched Jacques'
bache raise from its sagging flat shape back to a wigwam point.
He's on the bedroom walls, then. Arbel could wait till he reached
the lintel of his front door before he need call again.
"He'll be gone by summer, rate he's going. Jacques."
Ardelle went cold. It was the first time they'd spoken of him. In
any way.
'Will you be glad?' she thought. 'I will.'
But she said, "You think so?"

Arbel looked puzzled. "Yes."

"Oh."

He rolled a cigarette.

"He might freeze to death before that," she offered.

'And do you care so very much about that?' he thought, and reproached himself. She was right.

"No," he said, "we wouldn't let him do that..."

Ardelle's heart flushed. It was the nearest to forgiveness she'd been. Stay there. Never go back.

She smiled.

"What?"

"You."

"Oh, me," he lit the cigarette and went to do something.

"Is that it? No threat? No legal position at all? Just gossip, immorality and envy? Not good enough for me Monsieur Le Mayor." Jerome tasted every savage nuance. "You must have some strategy! Christ! What did your father tell you to think?" This was fun.

"I asked your mother instead."

"I know what she said."

"I'm sure."

"And so?" Madame Valet had had more than enough. "We are outcasts. Social malaria. Fine. We accept. We agree. And now?"

This was going as badly as Dominique had expected.

"In God's eyes..." Curé Phillipe sensed an opening here, "In God's eyes you are both His children still and He loves you..."

"Shall I tell you something, priest?" Madame Valet barreled into his watery eyes. "I have a new God. Here."

And she held Jerome warmly and firmly at his crotch.

He relished the electricity of shameful delicious disgusting joy.

Dominique and the Curé stared for a second. Severine Vigne too.

Then they turned and walked away from that place.

Jacques loaded the cart with the bedroom doors, the wood of the staircase, the nails.

Monday morning.
"Severine?"
"Monsieur Le Mayor?"
"You will tell no-one what we saw."
"No Monsieur."
"Not while we work together."
"No Monsieur."
He wanted to ask 'What do you think I should do?' but thought it would be weak.

"I'm nearly sixty and we have no income."
"I need a drink."
"I know."
"Have we any?"
"We won't soon."
"One day at a time. Where is it?"
Celine realized she would have to think for him.

Jacques, blinkered, walked his loaded cart through St. Cirgues.

The replacement teacher arrived. Mademoiselle Noyes.
She began teaching the children English.
The children, given a secret code only they and the Mademoiselle could speak, no parents at all, were thrilled. Engaged. The parents filled with a parochial fury - but they daren't complain about another teacher.

"We've a month's money."

"So much?"

"You've never worked. And you won't now, will you?"

He was 26, looked 36, smelt 56 and felt ageless in the warmth of the brandy and the oblivion in her body.

"You're not to be troubled by life, are you child?"

"The worst it can do is end. And if it's to be penniless and starving - an end'll be better."

"I'd prefer to live."

"You could eat me when I'm dead."

"I'd prefer to live with you."

"You are. This is us."

"Then I think I'm a little frightened."

"Daddy hold you?"

A bearded blinkered man walked his empty cart back through the village.

Madame Cantagrel hammered at Sara's door.

"Bring him to his senses," she demanded.

"He hasn't any."

"Refuse him access to his daughter."

Sara's bile rose. "And tell her what?"

"He's not fit."

"That's for her to decide isn't it?"

A vein throbbed in Madame Cantagrel's temple. "She's a child, you fool. How can she decide? What does she know?"

"You're a bit diseased, Madame," Sara heard her voice almost cheerful for the first time in she couldn't remember how long. "She knows what she knows. If she can't decide for herself about her own father how can she decide on your opinion of him?"

Madame Cantagrel rocked slightly on her heels. Her jaw flapped a little. "You approve?"

"No. But I trust my child."

"She's four!"

Sara's mother appeared. "She's not three," she said. "Get away from my house."

Madame Cantagrel went.

To tell the shopkeepers not to serve Jerome or Celine. Starve them out of the commune.

Fifteen oak beams.

The dog rested his head on its paws, fixed him with his eyes.

Jacques stood on a chair beneath where the first beam rested on his north wall. He nestled his shoulder beneath its weight and straightened his legs. It lifted from its stone groove. He bent his knees and it re-settled. He took the chair to the opposite wall and repeated the action. It rose. Good, grandfather. Right.

He stepped down. Think. Lift it, push it along till it's clear of the wall, lower it. Can I take the weight? 'Iffing'. Reap and sow.

Jacques stood back on the chair, back to the wall, cupped his hands under the beam, took the strain at his wrists and back and lifted by straightening his legs. He had the whole weight. He pushed forward. Across the wreckage of the room, at the other end, it resisted. He took a breath and pushed. It shifted, wee stones splintering. Wait. Breathe. Push. Enough! His end was clear of the wall. He had the whole weight now. Lower it. The dog watched.

He eased the oak down into his shoulder.

Wait.

Adjust.

Breathe.

Don't drop it - it'll go straight through to the caves. Take you with it.

Don't think.

Breathe.

Right. He took the whole weight on one leg as he stepped down, a desperate foot reaching for the floor. There. There. My back, my back! Breathe. One foot on the chair, one on the floor and half an oak crucifix on his shoulder. Don't think! He stepped down to the floor. I can't lift this off my shoulder now. He pushed the chair aside and slowly bent his knees till he knelt, the oak warm against his cheek and crushing his shoulder. The end was less than a metre short of the floor. Pray. He knelt lower, the wood following. Prostrate yourself Jacques. When he slid his knees and legs beneath him the beam finally came to a rest on the kitchen floor. The man beneath it. He rolled away. One.

There was a knock at her door.

She heard herself think, is it him?

And then, almost giggling at the notion, which one?

Madame Lacaze straightened her blouse, allowed herself one glimpse at vanity in the hallway mirror and opened the door on Madame Valet.

"Will you pay us to go away? To another commune?"

Madame Lacaze held the door tight in her hand, took in the odour and said, "But you must consider his pride. There would be no-one to know his story. No-one to disgust. It would kill him."

"They'll kill him soon."

Madame Lacaze considered her choice of words. "And, in another commune he'd eventually see you for what you are. Are you sure you'd want that?"

"You've money you wizened bitch - give him some so I can save his life."

"No, I won't finance that."

"What would you finance?"

"You're insane woman."

"I'm doing your job. Pay me."

"If you ever call here again I shall get the gendarme."

The first brick through their window was placed by Jerome on Chef Terses' desk.

"No problem, Monsieur Lacaze."

Christoph, the gendarme of whom Terse was now Chef, stood his shifts outside their house for a week; listening, sweating, hardening. Battered by shock, disgust and a bizarre respect.

Nothing else was thrown and Jerome and Celine didn't replace the glass. When it rained in they pushed a cupboard against the hole and lusted behind it. Christoph returned to the Gendarmerie one evening and five minutes later a brick smashed through their other downstairs window and a voice said, "Fire next..." and then it went quiet.

twenty-six

CURÉ PHILLIPE walked up the stone stairs to his pulpit.

He knew he was no orator.

He accepted he had no genuine relationship with any member of this parish, nor indeed any of the other two he ministered to. He accepted also that each and every Sunday of his calling he had hoped, with always disappointed breath, for just a sliver of God's passion and wisdom to speak from or through his heart, his soul.

He knew, as he grasped the front ledge of this pulpit, that when he raised his head and looked out at these people he would see, again, that he was tolerated and heard only because it was form and he was a part of that and not, in their blatant opinion, a great deal more.

To quell this rising fear in him, he turned a page of the big, embossed Bible. And he felt he saw St. Cirgues for the first time ever.

Rows and pews of unexpectant faces.

Tight jaws, and decided minds.

And he knew the prevailing feeling in this church. In these people. In this village, and, he believed, in Heaven too. He was sure he understood their feelings better even than they - for he had seen

her hand on his person. His bald person.

"Today is no ordinary Sunday..." he heard his voice ring in the stone acoustic.

"You and I are about to meet a miracle. We will witness, in our midst - here - a living saint."

Curé Phillipe took his hands off the front pulpit edge, looked right round every single, shocked face. Then he shook his head a little.

"Well, I don't recognise you."

He laughed.

"And, why would I, a poor sinner like the rest of us?"

His congregation began to gawp somewhat.

"You see - Our Lord said, 'Let he who is without sin cast the first stone.' So, please stand now - that we may feast our eyes on your sight. A being without sin!"

He gestured - offering, as it were, the floor of his church, to be taken.

The church shuffled.

Someone coughed. Curé Phillipe felt his first full flushing intoxication of Attention.

"Someone here is without sin. We know this - because someone here was so offended by the defamation of our codes of conduct, of the Holy Scriptures and of Our Lord God himself - that he cast the first stone. And even a second."

His church had become very quiet.

"Because our belief in decency, and morality - even our imaginations - have been profaned. Our Holy Mother Church itself, profaned."

Murmurs.

"Our understanding of what is human and what is inhuman."

He heard someone say, under their breath, "Yes."

He was also sure everyone else had heard it.

"We are soiled. Abused and angry."

"Righteously," Madame Cantagrel was clearly audible.

"Righteously," he repeated. "But - what is righteous? What is right? Might is right? God is Mighty. In fact, He is Almighty. What does God think?"

"Shame," a voice muttered.

"Disgrace," called Madame Cantagrel. Her husband coughed, ashamed now and horrified to his bones. Where would this end? Curé Phillipe gripped hard now at the stone of his pulpit's edge. The stone was warm under his touch.

"I'm not a brave man. As you all know. I would never have been brave enough to throw a stone if Christ himself had stood between me and the act. I wouldn't. And He is everywhere, people. He is right here, now. Amongst us. Now. Or. Or, He doesn't exist."

The congregation didn't move. He was that close to sacrilege.

"And now you have to decide you know what God thinks. Because I'm not brave enough for that, either. But somewhere here is a man - or a woman perhaps - who is without sin. So, let them, or God, in the words of his son, be your guide."

The church was as silent as if it were empty.

"In the name of The Father, The Son and The Holy Ghost."

He crossed himself, felt Pride and asked God to forgive him. He felt relief and thanked Him for that. He felt fearful and asked for strength. As he turned and fainted gently down the three steps of his pulpit.

Madame Lacaze and Sara were the last ones to leave. They had so much and absolutely nothing to say to each other. And the church square had been silent.

For that Sunday.

  THE SINGLE SOLDIER

Another stumbling day.

"Write to me," came from across an ocean on the back of a picture postcard. Of a bridge.

He found paper, blew the grime from it.

I can't tell her what I'm doing.

I can't tell her why.

To come back she has to want to come back.

His arm swept a space at his table.

Not feel she ought because of my madness.

He sat at a chair, licked at the pencil.

But I can't lie. He flattened the paper pointlessly. And I have no other truth.

The end of the pencil found his mouth, like a schoolboy.

Tell her about myself and Ardelle?

That faithlessness? Give her an excuse to not come back?

Tell her about Jerome and Sara? The election? Madame Valet?

Tell her about the cancer in the world now she's gone?

Jacques bent over the paper and wrote to his son.

"I know what it feels like to have your mother all to myself - I know how you glow. Your turn, n'est-ce-pas? You are the love we shared. Simone, it's all been arse about front for me. I've had my rewards. Now I have to earn them. So, I work. Taking things down. To write is to think and I daren't think any more than this. That's this life."

They were marked, surely, to die. One way or another. Her month's money was going, there was no sign of the promised pension and only the cheese man who came Wednesdays would sell her food. And Jerome, she dreaded, was no longer afraid to die. The blackmail of Zoe was past. He was beyond all recall but the alcoholic and the physical. And Celine was even more afraid, for herself, that the sex would stop. That there could be some hideous

kind of realisation. A different, worst of all kind of death. Alone.

And she thought all this as he was inside her. Pounding and circling and reaching and knowing and finding and there there I am, that's me, that's Us; Oh! Love again - again - don't ever stop - and, with each crashing orgasm she knew exactly, she knew oh so precisely how much she wanted to live and wanted him to live. She held him panting on her chest.

They'll *have* to pay.

She kissed the top of his hairless head.

She dressed in something long ago resembling clean clothes whilst he snored. And walked down the lane, turned right and strode into the Mairie.

Curtains moved everywhere.

Severine's eyes ballooned.

"I want to see The Mayor."

"I'll - ask."

"He's in? Good."

She stalked out of Severine's office, down the short corridor and, opening both doors, strode into Dominique's office, where he and Madame Lacaze looked up, startled.

"You look guilty," she told him. "The pair of you."

Madame Lacaze stood. Gathered her bag together.

Dominique simply stared at the creature who'd taught him to read and write. It was a shocking sight. Torn clothes, angry sunken eyes, lank skin.

"Pay us to leave," it demanded. "Buy us a house. A room. Rent it. Anywhere."

Dominique Duthileul blurted, "What? You've got a pension..."

"Have I? Where is it? It won't buy a room, will it?"

Madame Lacaze waited.

"The commune - " said it's Mayor, trying to grasp this fog, " -

should pay - for you?"

"Or you. Your father." She flicked her head in Madame Lacaze's direction, "Her. She's got money. You've got the money. Spend it you squirrel-minded fools or there'll be death - murder perhaps - in this village. It's money. That's all it is. Get us out of here."

Madame Valet turned and left. Severine darted back to her papers. When Celine stepped back into the sunlight there were more than a dozen in their doorways. One standing in the road. With a broom handle.

She turned for home.

Her house was a hundred yards down the street and left by La Poste. She'd have to pass the ones in front of her and the man in the street.

Her steps became instantly heavy. They made no distance - was she in cement?

Somehow she was now alongside the man with the broom.

"Fat cow."

Some woman laughed from a doorway across to her right.

"Fat ugly cow."

Two more came out of doorways ahead of her.

"Filthy whoring tramp."

There were voices gathering behind her.

She stepped into the road - the pavements were claimed.

"Shall we teach you a lesson, Mistress?"

She walked, hard.

"Leave us, or else." she heard.

'You touched my child!'

Then, "Fetch my scissors!"

She reached La Poste, saw her house, and ran.

A stone overtook her, skidding past and splintering against a wall. Another passed her ankles. A few yards. Her huge chest hurt.

Another stone.

She reached her door.

"Inhuman!" She recognised Galtier's croak.

"Cage her! Cage them both!" Gley.

She had no key.

She battered at their door. If his drunkenness sleeps him through this?

She banged again.

"In-HuMan."

More voices, joining into a chant. "In-human, in-human, in-human," a mantra excusing and generating violence. Nearer, up the lane they came now, their hands finding missiles. She banged till her fist hurt and turned to see Galtier, Gley and three other men approaching, hands loaded, the women crowding behind to see the justice done.

"Jerome!" Her terror eachoed. She turned and hammered at her door.

"In-huMAN!"

Run to the Gendarmerie? They'd catch me.

She kicked the door.

"JER-OME!!"

Her voice shocked her cold as Christmas.

"IN-HU-MAN!!"

They'll stone me.

All of them - her, the men, the women, nearing a primal state.

She turned to face her fear. Face the eyes. Face the stones.

The men slowed.

Then there was no movement, except the women, sensing denouement, pushing for the best view.

An oil-black, irreligious, violent hope in the air around a house with two broken front windows, and a raggedy school-teacher

facing a classroom of adults.

Jerome, naked, opened the door.

"What?" he squinted at her back.

Those who'd voted for him recoiled furthest.

A totally naked man. A smooth man.

Madame Valet moved to his side and he saw the mob, struck quite perfectly dumb by the sight of him.

As they closed the door a brick hit it.

They stood in the hallway; he naked, she panting, sweating and waiting.

A beat of silence.

Another.

A third.

It was past.

Madame Valet allowed a full screaming breath from her twitching body.

Her back crashed against the wall as her legs gave. As her head hit the wall

one foot stamped involuntarily. She doubled forward and fell over her knees to retch but couldn't, just spittle and violent shaking.

Jerome stood, watching.

Jacques worked.

From The Mairie Madame Lacaze and the Mayor had heard. And, leaning as far out of the window as possible, Severine had seen some of it. Then she'd listened at her connecting door but it was old wood and she had to return to her work.

Madame Lacaze re-seated herself at her Mayor's invitation.

This was Trouble.

Madame Valet was right. It had been there in the church, the

Curé's fine words had not lasted, and now it was in the street. They had to act.

Madame Lacaze waited.

On her own agenda. Monsieur Le Maire would have to consult his father. And as there was no advantage for Jean-Louis in parting with his money then he wouldn't, would he? But surely she could use this?

What had been said? "Whatever hurts you least..." Waffle. Conniving balderdash - but the fool had said it. Her gaze rested on the son, lost in his response to his responsibilities. A child really... So, there's opportunity, too.

Dominique looked at his farmer's hands and this desk and the papers and Lacaze's mother, sitting there; prim, tight, composed...

She looks at me like my father does.

She weighs me. For what?

As what?

He's looking at me just as his father looks at me.

How perfectly can this revenge go?

He picked up the phone.

Severine leapt to her extension, heard him ask the Chef De Gendarmes if he were free; then he telephoned Chibret to ask his advice.

"Can't have mob rule..."

"Quite so, sir." He hoped his voice sounded deferential.

"Best for all if they went."

"I agree."

"Mind you, can't make them go."

"Seemingly not."

"Problem."

Dominique waited for the old man to consider. He offered Madame Lacaze a tiny 'in-a-moment' smile. She returned it.

THE SINGLE SOLDIER

"Personally," Chibret had done with consideration, "I don't give a fig. Sex is it's own master sometimes. Bad for the commune, though."

"Yes..."

"Well," Dominique heard the old man snigger, "good luck."

The line went click. The Mayor put the phone back in its cradle. He looked up.

"Waste of breath."

"He always was."

"I meant mine."

She folded her hands on her lap. Waited.

"What is your counsel, Madame?"

"Speak to your father."

He nodded.

So, she's not going to stump up a sous.

Why should father?

We. When I inherit. When he goes. If he ever does.

He nodded, hoping it looked like responsive consideration.

She stood.

"And will you speak to your son?"

"To say what?"

Dominique watched her mouth thin at the idea.

"What you feel. Whatever that is."

"My son knows my feelings."

"May I?"

Madame Lacaze blinked. That was direct.

"About my son?"

Dominique listened to the silence before he said, "Yes please, Madame Lacaze."

"I don't think they affect - " she gestured around the office, " - this."

Dominique needed another breath to say, "It wasn't as Mayor that

I asked."

That was a request for an intimacy.

She crossed one hand over the other so neither could tremor.

"They are not wholesome," she allowed.

He nodded, but his eyes asked if there were more.

"And yours?" she asked.

Dominique hesitated.

"Don't spare my maternal feelings. I have none."

"Then..."

he ventured forward into coded areas in which he was a virgin, "perhaps..."

the resonances of what he was about to say hummed in his reddening ears, "...our feelings might be mutual?"

She felt sure she'd heard that correctly. Careful, now.

"I wouldn't be surprised if they are."

And then she smiled.

"Then I shall speak to my father."

Madame Lacaze, herself feeling her way through this new minefield, smiled again. Slowly.

Dominique momentarily toyed with suggesting she came to speak to him too, but was astute enough not to. I'm no match for father. Yet. I'm no match for her, come to that. Yet.

He stood. "I must talk with the Chef."

"Of course."

She placed a warm hand on his, "Courage. Dominique."

But when The Mayor had walked home for his supper her car was parked next to his father's.

His father had phoned her? What? Was he interfering in my Mayoring again? Were they both?

Needing to gather his thoughts he stepped into the barn. Renée, looking up from his milking, tilted his head towards the house. A

wink, a dirty grin. His thought was transparent - and the same as mine, thought the Mayor.

He shook Renee's gnarled hand, slapped at a cow's buttocks, inhaled the warm hay-shit smell and wished he'd never left it.

I knew this.

I know this.

This - Mayor business. It's a fucking fog.

And this – other thing.

This flirting. With her... That's beyond belief, surely?

Her...

He slumped a moment - his body leaning hard onto one of the cow's stalls.

No. No.

Genetic pride and weak arrogance straightened him.

I am Mayor.

Only me.

My father thinks I'm his toy.

I don't know what she thinks.

I'm not sure what I think.

He wants her - I do know that.

He tasted that. It was true.

And - he gave truth a centimetre more rein - I want her.

Why? For herself or to fix father?

He snorted a laugh that turned Renée's head.

And, if we did - she and I - then what would be the difference between Valet's widow and Lacaze and his mother and me? Eh?

Jesus Christ - what is this in the air?

Peace?

"Ha!"

Renée looked up again.

The son was barking mad laughter in the barn, by himself. He

shrugged – bourgeois turds.
And why haven't I got a car?
I'm the fucking Mayor, walking home.
Into this. Some plan, some concoction.
What's my plan?

Across the lane Jacques Vermande stood like stone.
He hadn't seen Madame Lacaze's car since driving to bring Arbel
into hell. And before that?
Don't remember.
Don't remember!
"Work," he said. The dog looked up at the sound of the rusty voice.
In what had been their living room there was now only enough wall
to support the two window frames and their lintels, a comically
free standing door frame with its huge lintel, and, above an inert
fireplace, a chimney stack.
He stood, looking at it, living in it, the insane grief-soaked
wreckage of his Plan. The Future.
"I am mad," he said and the dog cocked its head and waited. No
more. The ears subsided.
Can't go back. Can't go on. I'm mad.
She's gone. They've gone.
Back to that again. Never went anything like away, did it.
Won't weep. I will not weep.
He took his shirt collar and twisted it into his gritty mouth and bit
hard to hold back the flood. Spat the grit out.
"Work." The dog sat up.
"Work."
He didn't move.
"Work."
The dog lay back down.

You reap you sow you reap you sow you pay.

He ordered his back, his knees, to bend, ordered his hands to pick up a stone, just a single stone. They all disobeyed him. The soul ruled and his soul grieved afresh. Hell is inside us.

Heaven is outside us then.

I wish I was outside us.

Is their attraction to each other that they're both misers?

What's mine to her, then?

Never mind her, he snapped to himself - what about the village?

No, fuck St. Cirgues - what do I want? You can't make a plan without being honest about what you want.

I want - her.

Because it would break my Father - and - and because I do.

I do. I want his mother. Her.

Fact.

I want Lacaze and that eyesore out of harm's way. And harm's way are the members of my commune! Fact.

I want my father and her to sort it. To pay.

And I want a damned car.

And I'm very afraid I may be out of my depth.

Renée heard him sigh. He milked.

What's going on in there is them deciding. What they'll tell me to do.

Time to go see then. Time to influence my life.

He snorted an encouraging laugh - stood free of the wooden stall - turned and hooked a punch into the wood. Another. His hands hurt. Good. He laughed. Renée stood and watched...

Dominique grinned at him.

"Right, Renée - right."

Renée waited for more information.

All he got as Dominique turned in the barn door-way was, "Right."
He milked.

Jacques Vermande finally moved. Feet of lead, hands of stone,
heart of glass.

twenty-seven

SERENDIPITY HAS THE CHARM of appearing profound, when it could just be one more random factor, one more admirable evasion. Either way, the magic is - it works.

Dominique opened the door to see his father, red-faced, elbows on the table, leaning forward at Madame Lacaze. "Why?"
She turned to see The Mayor. The father, ignoring the son, continued, "Why should I pay?"
Madame Lacaze stood to greet her Mayor. Perfect timing. She smiled gratefully at Dominique. He gestured for her to sit. She did. And as Dominique sat she turned to answer Jean-Louis.
"Because," and she said it so quietly, "without your carefully planned dupery my son would be Mayor."
Jean-Louis could say nothing.
Dominique thought, 'Well, that's true.'
And now she wondered what, if anything, she truly wanted for Jerome. That he leave her sight? Did she want revenge on him, too? Was she on the point of winning the wrong battle?
One glance at Jean-Louis' gnarled greed and she was set on course again.

"I'd share some of the cost."

Jean-Louis exploded. "He's your son!"

Dominique had never seen his father so rattled.

Tasting it, timing it, he spoke, "Very fair Madame."

The look of untrammelled fury his father shot him confirmed all he'd ever doubted about the priorities in his father's mind. He raised an eyebrow to say, 'Don't you agree, father?'

Madame Lacaze saw the wedge between them and knew now the perfect way to twist it. The fleeting look she shared with the triumphant son was but the first seed of it.

As her car found its gears and rolled down the lane Jean-Louis lashed his fury on his son.

"You never do that. Never! Not with my money."

Dominique wanted to grin, but asked politely, "Isn't it our money?"

"Bad tactics. Bad! Done now. You fool," Jean-Louis snarled, ignoring Dominique's ridiculous comment. "But I'll make the best of it..." he muttered.

'And I father,' Dominique thought, 'might do even better.'

Jean-Louis telephoned Madame Lacaze the next day and they agreed to meet to discuss the detail. The money. When he arrived she had the Godin warm and the cognac served.

They had both had the night to think. Gather their cards, sort their hand.

"Of course," she said, "they may refuse. He surely would."

Especially if he knew I'd paid even half a sous, she thought.

"Yes, a possibility." Is she trying to wriggle out of this?

"And," Madame Lacaze took the tiny extra breath with which to lie, "I can think of no means to force him to leave."

Jean-Louis knew dis-ingenuousness. He could taste it. Here, right here now, in the room. Ah.

"No," he agreed. She means beyond shaming him out. So what is

she driving to? "No means beyond the physical. Heaven forbid," he added, beginning to warm to this.

She sensed his confidence.

A beat.

Two people thinking the same thing, but saying nothing. Sexy.

"No legal means, either. Alas..." Jean-Louis sounded at a loss.

Madame Lacaze put her glass down on the table and lowered her eyes to it. She placed her hands together, feeling his eyes following her, straightened a minute pleat in her dress and then slowly raised her eyes to meet Jean-Louis Duthileul's. Yes, she could read him like a book.

"What are you thinking, Jean-Louis?"

A pause hung as he gathered the nearest plausible lie. She watched all this.

"Of some way - some action to - to..."

"Hurt us all the least?"

"Voilà. And save our money being w- spent."

"Quite." Shifting her voice towards a tone of sublimation, "And so, how?"

She pressed one hand into the other to stop any show of the adrenalin flowing through her.

"I - " he genuinely hesitated, "I don't know," he said, finally.

'Liar,' she thought.

"I'm not sure I believe you, Jean-Louis," she said.

Jean-Louis Duthileul blushed.

Damn her, she's got some part of me.

"Exactly," she smiled, "We do know."

Silence.

Spring light spread.

Jean-Louis and Madame Lacaze looked at each other.

Jean-Louis rolled his glass in his hands and she picked hers up,

locked eyes with him, poured the warmest smile down deep into the fissure of his vanity, watched it sink to his ancient walnut privates probably, she thought - and clinked glasses with him.

She sipped, he drank. They warmed.

"I came to discuss money," he said, surprised at himself.

"We will, Jean-Louis, O we will." And she smiled.

Jean-Louis' antennae rose. She thinks she's won something. What? What have I missed here?

"You haven't missed anything," she said.

Jean-Louis Duthileul gently gasped.

"Of course I can read your mind."

She offered a reassuringly warm smile. "And if you'd stop trying so hard to guard it you could probably read mine..."

Jean-Louis' feet seemed to slip on ice. Out on a frozen lake, with no blades beneath him. Only her. For support.

"Mm, trust. It's so hard, isn't it?"

"The hardest," he agreed.

"Must come slowly - "

" - or not at all," he agreed.

Their bodies settled a little more into their chairs.

He knew he'd been out-manoeuvred and that he'd enjoyed it too, and he'd even sensed a glint of the true meaning of Respect; but his mind swirled with the possibilities of the larger hand they were playing. Get back to that.

"What is it, exactly, that we know, Madame?"

She blinked at his directness. He enjoyed that.

She saw it and said, "We know that you want me."

He blinked hard and she enjoyed that. "N'est-ce-pas?"

The game was speeding now - the cards were to be thrown. Fine. What could he lose when she played like this? Nothing.

"True."

  THE SINGLE SOLDIER

She was surprised.

"You're surprised," he nearly gloated.

"You see, I told you you could read my mind."

"We're not so very different?"

"I don't know that. Yet, sir."

"Do you hope not?"

"I hope for the best."

Jean-Louis put his nearly empty glass on the table.

"This - flirting - is delicious, Madame," he conceded, enjoying again her surprise, "but what else do you think we both know?"

Madame Lacaze had prepared her hand and she played it.

"That the most painless way to rid our commune of the danger of my son and that slattern is to provide them with an escape route, a room - at our expense - and then…" she paused, "to consider some action that would convince him they should take it."

"And that, in your opinion, would be..?"

The air waited.

"What we both know," she smiled, "surely?"

Jean-Louis said, "Won't you say it?"

"Won't you?"

She watched him falter. He didn't even trust himself.

Madame Lacaze raised a hand from her lap to her hair. She lightly touched the brooch at her neck, straightened a button and slowly re-placed her hands together again. Jean-Louis' eyes followed her movements and rested one second more on her breasts as he heard himself whisper, "That we'd be - one?"

"Voilà."

The air moved.

Madame Lacaze and Jean-Louis Duthileul looked at each other.

He foolishly heard himself think, what do I do now?

And she read it and thought, ask me my name. This once. Anything

might happen if you showed just that glimmer of Grace.

Silence.

Jean-Louis could sense it right there, in the room.

The something she wanted him to say. So he said it.

"And do you want me?"

Poor sap. "You know I do," she said.

God, lying was easy.

And fun. Fun!

She smiled intimacy at him. Nailed to her chair.

She stood and gathered their glasses together. The faint ting of crystal.

"Perhaps we ought to speak with the Mayor?"

Duthileul surfaced.

His eyes dilated with question, suspicion, acceptance, glee and he said, "Of course, of course."

"I'll see him at council tomorrow," she said.

"I'll see him at supper tonight."

"No. Say nothing Jean-Louis."

She placed a hand, warm and promising, on his.

Oh, but she relished this physical power.

"You know how impetuous he might be..."

Jean-Louis smiled. She was sharp. She missed nothing.

"We must speak to him together."

"As you wish, Madame."

Ask me my name. Now. I'll make it easier on you. Just ask me my name.

Jean-Louis' blurred antennae read something but he couldn't translate it, and she was leading him to the door.

Where she said, "And you'll find a room - somewhere - for them?"

Jean-Louis had to think who 'they' were, so warm was he; then said, "Of course." He looked down into her face, "My dear."

   THE SINGLE SOLDIER

"Good. Then - till we speak with your son."

She opened the door to distract him from the idea of kissing her and pressing her cheek against his, handed him his hat.

She waved a tiny gesture as his car drove away, shut the door, walked back to her room, downed the dregs of his cognac and allowed herself one fierce slap of congratulation on the table top.

She rose next morning, bathed, sat at her mirror and watched herself comb her hair, apply a little rouge, a hint of powder. It was sharp outside. Madame Lacaze saw for one cold instant her son lying in that gross slut's arms and still she determined to take a vengeance for him that he would be disgusted by. Good. Two birds with one stone, then. Three. I no longer care.

Arbel looked up from whittling the bars of the infant's cot.

He nodded across to Jacques' wigwam house. "I'll be all day, I think," he said and went for his cap

"Ask him to come for supper?"

"He won't."

They looked at each other.

"I just wanted to tell him..." she gestured at her softly rounding stomach.

"I'll ask. And I won't tell him."

"Thank you, husband."

The day was sweaty and silent under the first real blast of what would be the summer of Peace. All morning they de-mounted windows. The lintels and their big stones, Jacques chalking and numbering them for the re-building, and humped them on the cart. As the sun rose past dinner they spat on their hands and inched the huge door lintel to the point where it would tumble. They laid three hay-stacks in front of the door and dared push the granite beast on to them. It grunted and fell. They tipped it end

on end down the steps; end on end to the cart, then spat again, bent their knees, straightened their backs and found strength and leverage to inch an edge over the lip of his cart, gather two quick snatched breaths, and push the bastard fucking thing to a resting place.

"You won't get that back up by yourself," Arbel grunted.

Jacques only set back up the stairs for the door's column stones. Arbel followed.

By mid-afternoon the cart was loaded and there was only a bed, a table and Arbel's bench on the floor of his house. Arbel saw the futility of inviting him to eat, shook his hand and went home to soup and a wash.

Jacques laid his creaking carcass down in the dust and filth that was his bed and cried inside for Arbel's having forgiven him. No tears fell, but their source, their spring, moved still within the grey man.

The bache flapped all night against the chimney and his bed.

Move the bed down to the caves tomorrow.

And take down the pointless chimney. No need now of heat. The dog? Sleep with me down there. Need the warmth. Both of us. Eat the gritty bread and ham. Sleep. Work. His back hurt.

Dominique plugged away at questioning his father, who shared a half bottle of Pernod - so something was definitely up - and gleaned only from his smugness that he and Madame Lacaze had agreed on something that pleased Jean-Louis very well.

Finally his patience snapped and he demanded a car.

Jean-Louis grunted. Which meant he'd already thought about it.

If and when he grunted again, it would happen.

As for her – well, he'd ask her.

"I believe," she said gently, "we agreed to share the cost of re-housing." She stalled on Celine's name.

"I see."

"Your idea..." she reminded him.

"Yours Madame - I only showed enthusiasm."

"You did. You do."

She spread him a smile and watched it pick at his hide, his defence - his wounded youth. "It's the rarest quality." She sat down.

Dominique steepled his thick farmer's fingers together, rested his chin on the point and his thumbs, looked at her and said, "I don't like this."

A delicious alarm bell rang in her.

"Monsieur Le Maire?"

"Your son."

Conscience? Surely not. Not in that blood. "Yes?"

"I accept there is danger..."

"Yes?" He's been thinking.

"And I endorse the commune's outrage."

"But..?" she prompted.

Dominique looked up at her. He wanted so to trust her.

"The War is nearly done. A matter of weeks. Perhaps days."

"So they say..."

"I suggest a celebration. A public healing."

As she nodded she thought - Sweet lamb. I wonder if he's a virgin?

"Go on. Please." I hope he is.

"A meal. The meal Mayor Chibret wanted when Arbel Jammes came back. A chance to heal."

And invite my son and that thing?

"It's a bold idea," she conceded, waiting for his detail.

"Yes?" he edged forward. Eager for her support. Especially hers.

"It's a noble idea, Monsieur Le Maire," she said and almost meant it.

"Thank you, Madame."

"But then, are you suggesting..." she gathered the words, "that my son and that woman continue to co-exist. Co-habit?"

"Madame Lacaze," he leaned back in his chair, to her surprise. "Why not?"

The spring air in the office stilled.

Severine at the door strained to hear.

Madame Lacaze pushed back her chair and stood.

"His wife?"

"I understand that marriage could be annulled."

Playing at the corner of his mouth was a twitch of triumph. Of some sort.

Intrigued, Madame Lacaze put a hand on the back of the chair.

"It offends everything."

He nodded, agreeing.

"But," she asked, "it should be accepted?"

"Or killed. Yes."

Madame Lacaze blinked.

"That seemed to me," said the Mayor, "what the Curé said."

Madame Lacaze nodded slowly.

"And it seems to me what our commune must consider."

"They were throwing rocks at her last week."

He leaned forward.

"A meal Madame. Together."

"And they should come?"

"If they choose."

"It could end in hell..."

"Let it then."

Madame Lacaze blinked hard. He had been thinking.

"If that is what we are. So be it. Animals? So be it."

"Why are you angry, Monsieur Le Mayor?"

"Oh, but I'm not. I'm afraid, Madame."

She felt a flash of respect for him.

"Will you help me? Dare it?"

That question relaxed Madame Lacaze.

"Yes, of course."

"Good."

He stood.

"I feel a fool saying such things - but we must prepare for Peace."

She smiled at the sweetness. She felt patronising. But perhaps he would be right. Either way it couldn't but help her.

"I agree."

Wednesday broke and Jacques hitched the beast, gathered his blinkers and rode through the dawning village to spend another day unloading at Janatou. He didn't look once at his view, saving that for another, sweeter Time.

By that Wednesday the last of their liquor supply had run out and Jerome was prepared to dress and go and search for more. He was not yet so brainless as to imagine anyone would give him a thing on account. But alcohol is its own master and he dressed.

Celine dressed. The pension book had still not arrived. She gathered their coins.

"Food," she said.

"Drink is food."

Celine was prepared for this, the probably penultimate stage of their insane existence. She would not buy alcohol, despite it's being the conduit that glued their bodies together. She would risk even that - to dry him out. She considered it some sort of duty - that

she attempt to save his life rather than be ruled by her compulsion for their sex.

"No. It isn't," she said, firmly.

The cheese-man was delighted to see them both. He served her cheerfully and could now report, in graphic detail, not only on them but of the comically furious frozen mouths and folded arms of the St.Cirgues women. Their infamy had spread throughout the canton and his customers in the surrounding villages would be eager for news - and a report of an actual sighting of the bald eagle and his lecherous aged barn-owl.

He worried about the customers here, though; the women who walked away from his wagon.

No, it was worth it, even if next week they were the only two he served. And they wouldn't be. This was France - any cheese is stronger than no cheese.

Janon wiped his outside tables and refused even his version of conversation. When Jerome, undaunted, asked for a bottle of brandy on account there was cold laughter from those reading the endless good news in the papers. She pulled at him and he came, swearing.

"I need..." he said and headed to Jauliac's. She followed him, stood there as he was refused in the curtest terms. He swore there, too.

"Feyt - he's a pal..." and he headed that way.

The old man had only tea and next to no sympathy.

"Arbel! He's never without."

He turned towards the church square and the road down past the cemetery to Puech. But word of their appearance in the streets had spread and four men from the bar were outside God's house.

"Get off our streets. Now."

It brooked no argument from a sane man.

"Where were you when we were resisting?" Jerome asked. "Hiding in the hills?"

Celine yanked at his arm as one of the men moved forward.

The crack-pot wearing blinkers walked through the evening village leading his dog, Arbel's cow and his empty cart.

It was the first night they hadn't made love. She sat on their bed as he lay there shaking and swearing and threatening to walk to Puech now, at three in the morning.

She was awake before him and ready with coffee. He swore vilely at her and refused everything.

That evening he threatened her with a punch if she tried to stop him going to the café.

"They won't serve you."

"I know that."

"Then why go?"

Jerome laughed. "You don't know me at all do you woman?"

"They'll attack you, Jerome."

"Just don't say I can't go to a bar. Okay?"

"I care about you."

"There's the difference between us then."

The bar froze, again, as they walked in. They were refused any service.

She sat them down. Jerome shook. Angry men watched, waiting.

She pushed the paper with the headline "Huge Russian Advances In The East." towards him. Hoping some spark might ignite anything left inside him.

He glanced at it, looked at her, read her thought and rejected both with a smirk. She could have slapped his wastrel's face and realised she was surely not the only woman to question whether he was worth the loving. She pushed her chair back and everyone but him watched her walk. To the bar. Their bar. Her.

"Two coffees?"

"No."

"Good, it's piss anyway," she said and sat back down with Jerome. His head swung up heavy to look at her, stared hard at her and then fell, heavy to the table.

"Why are you here?" Galtier.

George Gley said, "Why don't you fuck off, properly?"

Madame Valet fixed the mason with a look that had pinned generations of 8 year-olds. "You disgusting slug," she pointed at the door and ordered, "Get out of this room."

Gley actually took a step. Jerome snotted a glob of laughter at him. Wet with instant shame Gley snarled, "Write out one hundred times 'I must not fornicate with my husband's murderer.'"

"Or I'll cane you," said Galtier.

"Pull you up by your ear-lobes, eh?" a voice from the bar said.

"Enough."

Jean-Louis. Quiet.

"Take that wreckage out of here, Madame, please."

He was icy polite.

"I will leave," she stated clearly, "when there is quiet."

Again, involuntary, there fell a moment's silence.

Then a vicious burst of movement. Galtier hauled Jerome to his feet and Gley and the man at the bar took a hunk each of her and they were both through the door and in the street very quickly indeed. Any resistance and they would both have been beaten. Certainly her.

"I'll be back with a Gendarme."

Deep laughter greeted that.

Jacques stripped his bed, shook off the top layers of dust and grit, rolled the bedding and walked it down to the caves. The dog followed. He went back upstairs, wrestled his bed upright and step by step down the stairs and, like a one-stick marionette, corner on corner, walked it into the caves. Set it down, dragged it to the wall beneath his chimney, and threw the bedding on the frame.

It was dank and grim in there and it would be worse tonight.

Worse than what?

Don't think. Work.

Work.

The chimney. Tomorrow.

Arbel watched him place his longest ladder against the chimney stack. Jesus, he thought, I hope it doesn't give.

Ardelle came out to their door and watched Jacques wrestle the cowl off the chimney and come back down the ladder with it. Place it in the cart.

"He needs a hod."

Arbel laid a hand on her stomach, and went to his barn.

Rhythm.

Up the ladder, pick stones, down the ladder, stack the cart, up the ladder, pick stones...

It was warm noon when he heard Sara's footsteps, without the child, come up the lane but when he came down the ladder it was some other woman.

His momentum stopped for only that half-second. He loaded the cart and went back up the ladder. Madame Valet stood in the garden, watched him, raised a hand to shield her eyes against the sun and waited for him to stop.

Pick stones, down the ladder, load the cart, up the ladder... When his foot touched the bottom rung again she said, "Vermande?"

Jacques, grey, grimy, bearded, matted hair like plaster, paused a second, then - up the ladder...

"Monsieur Vermande?"

Who are you, he thought, I don't know you.

"I need your help," she said.

Jacques' took the two steps back to earth, turned and settled his weight over his heels. Damn. Damn this. What?

"I need your help," the woman repeated.

Other people, other people.

"It's Jerome."

Other people. Jerome?

"Lacaze."

He said, "Jerome. Yes."

"I'm afraid." Madame Valet was about to flood with tears and slapped hard at her hip. Jacques' eyes followed the action, came back to her.

"Please help."

Jacques thought. Of money.

"I need it all. For them."

Madame Valet shook away her incomprehension.

"He needs a friend. You're his friend."

"I need all of it." Jacques' mouth hung stupidly loose.

"Please, come and talk to him. Please."

Other people.

"I don't come."

"Vermande - he is killing himself. Help me to help him. He's not very much now, I know, I know, but he's all I have - and - he's worth so - " sobs gathered behind her chattering teeth, "Don't - want to - them - kill him." Her left arm reached out and he took it. Stone hand holding fat flesh. A fat stranger puking. Crying. Sad

for Jerome. Jerome.

"I don't. I won't go there." he gestured east. "I don't."

Madame Valet brought her jaw bones together and ground her teeth. She leaned into the strength in his grip, straightened and released herself.

"I don't think he'd get here," she said simply.

Jacques thought.

"I go to Janatou." He looked at his cart and the sun. "I'll be there tomorrow. Somctime."

Madame Valet saw that was all.

"Thank you."

Jacques turned, up the ladder, pick stones...

Celine considered Arbel but she dreaded his arrival with a bottle, so she turned to walk the lane back down through Duthileul's woods and home.

Arbel waited till Jacques was at the top of the ladder, occupied, to leave the hod. When the stone-man came down he thought he was hallucinating. The neat mortise and tenon joint told him its maker. Work. Up the ladder, with the gift, pick stones...

Madame Valet saw Sara walking towards her. Impulse told her to scuttle into the brush and logic told her Sara had seen her.

Her feet slowed.

Sara didn't want to believe what she saw - but it was. Her.

What to say?

What to think? What to do?

Sara stopped.

What do I think? What do I feel?

She's stopped. I'll go back round the long way.
This isn't Life. This is something less. She walked. Forward.

She didn't steal him. She's entitled to him.
Sara walked.
I know what it is to need him. And she knows what he is. Now. I can see.

I won't speak. We can't speak.

Has she been to see Jacques? Or Duthileul?

She's coming to see Vermande.

Jesus but she looks awful.

A nod. A nod.

I survived.

She didn't attack me.

Their breath rushed, cheeks flushed. They both felt stronger. Not much - but some.

"You can't sleep in there. You'll get pneumonia."
He loaded the cart, picked up the gift, up the ladder, pick stones, load the gift, down the ladder...
"You might as well sleep in the grass. It'd be warmer."
Up the ladder...
Sara waited till he came down and had stacked the cart.

"What did she want?"

Up the ladder...

"Jacques!"

Her tone registered distress.

"Jacques..."

Other people. He stopped.

This wasn't other people, this was Sara.

"What did she want?"

Jacques thought.

"Simone?"

"No, Jacques, Madame Valet. Was she just here?"

Other people.

"Who?"

"Madame Valet!"

Jacques put the gift down. The dog looked at both of them. Jacques straightened his back. He looked at Sara. Distressed. Distressed animal.

"Food?"

"What?"

He looked at the sun. "Shall I make food?"

He left her to fetch some kindling. Took an armful past her and up the stairs, pulled the propped bache aside, strode the rubble-strewn floor to the fire, kicked the dead ash to one side and laid the wood. Lit it and went out for a couple of bigger pieces. The smoke rose up the remains of the chimney and Sara still stood, still distressed.

"Work helps," he said and went past her into the caves. When he came out she was in the garden pulling up something that must have self-seeded.

"I think I said I'd be at Janatou. Tomorrow. Will he come?"

"I don't know!"

The soup was gritty. But warm.

"This," she almost laughed, "is like the last supper, isn't it?"

He didn't understand. That last supper with Simone?

"Well, you won't be cooking here much more, will you?"

She sat there in the fireplace, on Arbel's bench, where she'd sat. When there was a ceiling. And a grenier. And a roof. And walls. When it was a home.

"How's Zoe?"

Sara gulped back tears for his caring. "She'll be fine. I swear it."

"You don't need to," he said.

The smoky tent warmed.

Jerome shook. The hatred had him now. It was so private, this sink of a bed, sweat and filth inside and out. No thought could enter the pit of his brain without it stabbed and scoured, scraped at what remained of his putrid and useless, vile, worn-out, proud conscience. He was all bad and finally desserts were to be paid. Good. Good. This was correct then - bring it on - come on, come on in you evil truths and realities. He shook, all of him.

She watched.

The Western and Eastern Allies raced for the new borders of what would become Churchill's Iron Curtain. Hitler, as bunkered as Jacques Vermande and as raddled as Jerome Lacaze, shook too. Not long now.

Dominique listened avidly to the radio and had Severine prepare to reprint a version of Chibret's posters.

The shakes throughout his body, inside his head, in his attempts at

speech. The shame was a dark shake in itself. His head thrummed, he felt deeply sick and couldn't and wouldn't move from the reek of the bed. Every move, every thought brought waves and oceans of shame with it, threatening to drown him and the only thought was of a drink but that gave him the dry heaves and he wilted down into a no-mans-land of numbing pain and terror.
She watched.

Jacques had the whole chimney stack at Janatou. Jerome hadn't come that day and Jacques had forgotten about him anyway. He set to work ripping out the floorboards. He'd never step inside that room, that house, again. Not till he'd re-built it. Oh, just work!

Spiders crawled over his face, oblivious to his frantic hands. They were swarming the ceiling if he opened his eyes and on his chest if he closed them. He itched all over with the lice of imagination.
She stared. Scared.

Dominique, sure of the imminence of Peace, called his tiny council together to plan and distribute the labour. Galtier was to organise tables and benches; Severine to inform the village; Madame Lacaze, having a car, would drive to the outlying farms delivering the invitations when they had a date and he would organise food, wine and music.

Duthileul sat with his gibbering Mother.
It was days since he'd seen Madame Lacaze. Their proposed meeting with his son hadn't materialised and when Dominique returned in the evening it was Jean-Louis' turn to pump for information. He received the same stony, smug treatment he'd meted out, without recognizing the irony. When he dared ask what, if anything,

Madame Lacaze had said on any subject, Dominique's bland "Oh, nothing much," followed by the blatantly disingenuous, "Why?" served only to rouse the old man's suspicions further. And how Dominique enjoyed that.

Jean-Louis hadn't phoned her. He didn't know how he'd phrase what he wasn't sure how to say.

And across the chess-board of their village, Madame Lacaze worried about the silence too. She considered going to see him but in the flurry at the Mairie her judgement was he could wait; it would do neither him, nor, more importantly her, any harm.

The Mayor, on the other hand, had begun to creep under her guard. She still thought this meal was a potential disaster, but she couldn't help but admire his determination and energy. She - rather liked him.

Which was no bad thing.

It could be used.

Mussolini was captured and hung.

Jerome reached the bottom of the darkness and from that deep despair some passing-out happened; something lessened, and in this new grey limbo a light insinuated itself into the farthest reaches of his consciousness. And he knew he had this one chance to follow it.

Celine sat there.

Hitler voided himself. It was done.

The wounds would heal. The scab would form. The diseases interred, again. The infections would wait and one day break out again. History.

THE SINGLE SOLDIER

twenty-eight

ON MOMENTOUS DAYS it is possible to look at the sky, or at the common-place, just the people around you and seriously imagine a new tomorrow.

A brighter future. Hope, the greatest human quality.

Jacques Vermande struggled from the damp cellar beneath what was left of his home, stepped out into another morning. The last beams. Fifteen more of the fuckers.

Those with radios knew. Those without would read the papers tomorrow, or be told today. Dominique and his council shook hands and settled to work.

Saturday, announced the Mayor.

Severine, hesitated, wrote it in her pad and then rattled her teeth with her pen. Dominique raised an eyebrow.

"No. I was just thinking..."

Madame Lacaze, her Mayor and Galtier turned to her.

"If - 'they' come..." she tried not to catch Madame Lacaze's eye.

"Yes?" prompted Galtier.

"Well, mightn't it be better on Sunday? After a Mass? Just..."

She left it for the Mayor to pick up.

"Excellent, Severine. Sunday. Any objections?"

Galtier had plenty - but as Lacaze's mother pointedly waited for him to speak, and as this was a day of the greatest celebration, The War being over, he said, "None."

"Print Sunday 7.00 on the posters then."

Noted.

That was the only reference to her son all day as, armed with the posters, she drove the canton to deliver the wonderful news and the invitations. Galtier hustled potential carpenters, driving up to Arbel to ask him to help, and was rewarded with the promise of a bench, or two. Galtier saw that Ardelle was well on the way, but when he nodded to her blossoming, she was cold with him.

When he left Arbel said, "What?"

"I don't like him," was all he got.

Fair enough. He went to his tools.

Galtier had a quick celebratory drink with Duthileul and blithely rattled on about not being able to stop, what with the preparations for Sunday. Assuming, quite naturally, that Jean-Louis knew all about it.

Dominique phoned all morning before finding the music troupe in Gréze who would happily come and play for a meal, free drink and some cash. Other Mayors agreed to have meat, wine, vegetables delivered; anything to help. And bon chance.

Dominique's confidence grew with the rising freedom sun.

Severine would deliver an invitation to them, and Jerome would come, his mother was sure. So, she had need to speak with her intended. To get their timing right.

At five o'clock the council reconvened.

"And now, a drink, don't you think? Or two?" The Mayor stood, beaming.

Agreed.

Dominique made one last round of phone-calls and by six the Café Tabac was as full as at the last village funeral. One person he didn't call was his father and Madame Lacaze, waiting with her cognac for the toast, found herself both intrigued and grateful.

Terses the Chef, Christoph the gendarme, Gley and his sisters, Chibret and his wife, Jauliac and his, a weeping-eyed Feyt, twenty others and the St. Cirgues council and its secretary all raised their glasses.

"To Victory and to the memory of all who died for it," said The Mayor.

"Balloons for the children," said Galtier.

"I did that," Severine repeated. Why do drunks go deaf?

The bar had settled into groups, Janon and his wife bustled between the tables, serving.

"To Peace and to Sunday," said the Mayor, raising another.

"You said that," muttered Severine.

"I know I said that and I shall doubtless say it again," Dominique grinned lopsidedly, "every day till Monday."

At the bar someone began a slurred and sentimental singing of "La Marseillaise." It was taken up. By "Aux Armes, mes citoyens!" where the tune married the surging melody with the driving lyric the rafters rang and the sound carried as far as Celine's broken windows.

"The last person to sing that in this village was you," she rubbed his sweaty emaciated hand.

"Why?"

"Because you believed."

His head sank deeper into the mangy pillow. Scorn dribbled out of the side of his foul-smelling mouth.

"In what?"

"A future," said the school-teacher.

"And what do they believe in?"

Celine imagined they were singing because The War was over. Hers wasn't.

"Their future?"

"The fuck-wits."

"Allow me, if I may besobold," The Mayor weaved to his feet, "to escort a free woman home..?"

"Enchanté, Monsieur," replied a merry Madame Lacaze.

He made a clumsily gallant bow and giggled.

She stood, gathering her bag.

"Goodnight one and all."

Two final heads lurched a nod.

"One for all," Dominique repeated foolishly.

He held the door open and sucked the evening air deep inside.

Madame Lacaze dipped under his outstretched arm, bobbing out into the square.

Freedom.

Victory.

There was both a nip and a warm breeze.

They set their steps for her house.

"A good day," he slurred, "No. No - A great day."

"A very good day," she agreed.

"Madame Lacaze, as I must be so damned bold, but what is your name?"

So.

He was the one, he was the first. He would be well rewarded.

"You may. It's Elianne."

"Elianne," he purred. It sounded like an approval. She approved of

his approval.

"Dominique," she added.

They walked. A curtain or two moved.

As they passed The Gendarmerie and the last light he took her elbow in his hand and she leaned into it. They walked.

"I appreciate your support," Dominique said. A slight shiver ran through his mouth and it wasn't the cold.

"Likewise," she pressed into his arm and almost giggled.

"It means - a great deal," again his lips and jaw trembled.

Don't kiss him, she ordered herself. No matter what, don't.

"Thank you," and her voice just trembled too.

"You're cold."

"No."

His coat was round her shoulders in an instant. He stretched his arms high above his head and bellowed "Peace!"

His voice careered off, swallowed in the night.

"I could do anything," he heard himself say.

"I'm drunk, too," she said.

"I know - I'm enjoying that."

Defences were lowering. Caution.

"Are you? So am I." She laughed and imagined she'd recovered herself.

"We should do it more often," he gushed.

"We will."

"We will?"

A beat. Careful, Elianne.

"On Sunday?"

"Oh! Yes, Sunday - God! I'd forgotten! Yes. That will be..." He paused. "I was going to say magnificent but I'll settle for fine."

She said nothing and he blurted, "No, I meant you and I."

"I know you did."

Oh, taste the power.

"And you said, 'we will'?" His feet slowed as his heart sped.

"I did, didn't I?"

Ten charged, silent, strides and she peeled his coat off, folded it into his arms.

"My door, thank you young man," and she curtsied.

"My pleasure. My pride, Madame," he bowed.

"Elianne," she reminded.

"Elianne."

She kissed him three times on the cheeks, hesitated and the drink had her lips on his for a touch, a genuine kiss of contact and gone and through her gate. "Good night."

Dominique stood there, everything racing round him. Everything. She walked into her front room. Deliberately, drink focusing her actions, she turned a single side-light on. Placed her hands flat on the iron-cold Godin, felt the shiver run right through her, and her feet moved in an almost forgotten jig.

One and two and a one and a two and a turn and two and a kick and spin. One and a two...

Laughter belched from her and her hand stifled it and her feet stopped lest somehow the love-struck Mayor should hear.

Hell, no.

Dominique, walking, whirled between the taste on his lips, a cold dread of Vermande and Sunday, the warmth of the alcohol, Peace, the night, his father and - the taste on his lips.

He'd sleep in the Mayor's flat tonight.

The dog slept in his arms with Jacques' coat on top of both them and the blankets. Wet warmth.

'Jean Louis' she thought as the hang-over bit.

Jean-Louis, today.

It was moving fast now.

"A party dress? What's that? What's a party?"

"A special day."

Sara's mother had cloth, scissors, measures, edgings, cottons, wee buttons, two magazines, their patterns and a mouthful of pins.

"Wait and see," said Sara.

"Will papa be there?"

Sara and her mother glanced at each other.

"We don't know," said Sara, "I wouldn't be surprised."

"Is that why it's a party?"

"Shut up and stand still," Sara's mother managed without swallowing a pin.

Would 'they' come?

As the hours to Sunday passed the whole commune came to that question. Sara and her mother cut and sewed and didn't discuss it. What was to discuss? Pray to God for the child's sake they don't. Sara's mother briefly considered, and she was not the only one, calling round to beg them to stay home; but she wasn't at all sure she wouldn't attack him if he stood in front of her.

He will, I know him, Sara thought. I'll leave. I'll take her home. Why are we making this dress? It's to be spoiled. By her own blood. This is a world I'll never learn.

Dominique's nerves too were rattling hard. By Saturday afternoon he was in his father's kitchen.

Jean-Louis was not best pleased to see his son. But his invitation to Madame Lacaze's house 'to discuss their detail', gave him reason not to display any negatives.

Dominique came straight to the point.

"Can we move them tomorrow?"

"Move who?" Jean-Louis looked puzzled.

"Lacaze and her," stating the blindingly obvious. "Haven't you a place in mind?"

"Of course not!" His father gurgled with buried laughter. "Are you mad?"

"I thought - I understood you and Madame Lacaze had agreed..."

"So we did."

Dominique registered the guarded gloat.

"So?" His father asked.

"On a place? A house - a room?"

His father laughed openly. "On him? My money on him? You are mad, boy."

"Then what have you and Eli - she agreed on?" Dominique cursed his damned slip of the tongue, but pressed on. "She said she'd split the cost..."

Jean-Louis absorbed the snatch of her name. They were talking money.

"We will pool our money - but not on vermin."

Something in Dominique chilled. His hands came to the table-top. He pressed them down. Behind his father his grandmother nodded and grumbled from her dark fireside corner.

"On what, then?"

"The future..." Again the nauseating smirk.

"What future?"

The old fox arched his back, preened and took a long breath.

"Whose future," he corrected.

Dominique cracked. "Sunday, tomorrow, is my future! And if they come - it will - it could all just – go..." he finished lamely.

"Have the Gendarmerie place them under house arrest as a potential public nuisance."

"We're celebrating Peace!"

Father and son looked at each other.

He shouldn't have raised his voice. Weakness and need were apparent. And would be punished.

Jean-Louis settled back in his chair.

He'll say nothing now, damn him.

I know him.

Fine, neither will I.

Five seconds passed.

"Father, please - what do I do?"

"You'd like my counsel?"

The old bastard was like a rancid elephant - he forgot nothing.

"Yes." Dominique's teeth ground.

"Please..?"

Dominique cracked again. "I'm the Mayor. I'm the fucking Mayor!"

"Language."

Both men looked at her.

Jean-Louis composed himself. "Of course you are, and my counsel, for what it's worth, is that they will come - and then they will leave."

Dominique blinked.

"And what's that idea based on?"

"Oh, you know - experience?"

That bloody smirk.

"I don't trust you, Father."

"Neither should you." And said with approval.

"What have I got," Dominique leaned forward again, "that you want?"

"Absolutely nothing. Son."

"Oh. Are you sure?"

When Jean-Louis smiled again Dominique had to leave.

He stood on the doorstep and watched his neighbour, grey as November, loading his cart.

He strode across to Arbel's house.

Arbel had made a bench and he wouldn't hesitate this second time. A booze-up, Peace - and to spread the joy of her pregnancy.

"We'll be there," he told Dominique.

"Good man. Is there any point asking him?"

Arbel looked past him to Jacques.

"You can try."

Dominique stood in what had once been a garden.

On the cart oak beams and floorboards were stacked. The bache was now a shallow pyramid that would run any rain off it. The house was a stone staircase leading nowhere, and the remnants of his cave walls. From which Jacques picked more stone and tossed it into a barrow.

The longer Dominique stood there the more he was sure Jacques wouldn't and couldn't share. Anything.

"Vermande."

Jacques loaded stone into his barrow.

"It's over."

He'd heard those words before. Used them.

"The war. It's done."

He straightened, caught at his back.

"Well, not in Japan - but here. We won."

Jacques turned back to his work.

"There's a celebration - a meal - in the village. Tomorrow. Please come?"

Jacques took a key stone out, chalked it, placed it in the barrow.

"So, it's not over?"

"For us, yes. But it - no."

Work.

"But soon."

"Tell me then."

He bent to his barrow and walked to the cart, unloaded it, walked back, ripped at the stones and it seemed to Dominique he worked faster.

Soon.

'Soon?' What's soon? Six years ago it would be over 'soon'. Work. Soon.

Work. It gets soon if you work. Obviously.

Jean-Louis wondered if Eli meant Eleanor. Like The Yankee President's wife.

He would check the register in Severine's office.

He formally requested her hand.

"Jean-Louis - I'm flattered and honoured."

"You're neither, my dear - I'm not a fool. But I'm delighted you accept."

"I haven't," she reminded him.

"You will, though."

"When we've agreed the detail, yes."

"Money?"

"Voilà."

She produced cognacs.

Jerome got out of bed. He stood.

She waited.

The single light, that fluttering candle of possibility he'd seen at the bottom of his bleakness beckoned. He considered it.

"Where's the drink?"

Celine Valet blanched.

"There is some little difference in our ages," she said gently, "What if - heaven forbid - I should survive you?"

"Then a percentage of my estate would go to my son."

"Naturally. What percentage?"

"Well. If, heaven forfend, I should survive you - a percentage of yours would go to your son?"

Elianne Lacaze thought for one cold second before she said, "Of course."

"What percentage?"

"Whatever you had planned for your son I'm sure would be just, Jean-Louis."

He smiled. She was neat.

"What was it?" she prompted.

"Half."

"You lie."

He smiled. "I do."

"I know."

"I know you know," he added, "But you think I won't always."

"I'll hope you won't," she countered. "Meanwhile?"

"Forty per cent?"

That wasn't a lie so much, she saw, as the first time the man has even considered the idea. Of giving money. It almost tickled her.

Then he said, "How much would you leave your son?"

"Nothing."

Jean-Louis nodded respect.

"A woman after your own heart?"

"I hope so, but I doubt it."

"Oh, but I'll prove it to you, sir. I promise."

"Really?" Jean-Louis' old balls rustled.

"Why, yes."

Jerome felt like shit.

He was shit. Inside and out. Refuse. Rank. Worthless.

He turned to Celine.

"Sex?"

Her eyes lit.

"Get a bottle."

"Where will we live?"

"Wherever you wish. Elianne."

Oh, but I will punish you for using my name without ever asking it.

She smiled.

At Janatou he'd noticed blossom, Spring's calling card. At Puech there was none. "It's because we're higher here," he told the dog. That and his trees choked with months of dust.

They would live in his house, then.

"What will you do with this?" Jean-Louis asked.

"Oh," she demurred, "we'll think of something."

The dress was ready, the child was completely over-excited and Sara considered going to see her husband. And didn't. Couldn't trust herself. She'd seen her, yes; but him and her, no.

"And - the place, the room? For - them?"

Jean-Louis dared glance round the room.

She laughed at him. "You don't imagine I would allow that creature over this doorstep?"

"No."

"Then?"

"In hand," he said.

She laughed again.

"Dear one, you can't lie to me."

"I can't, can I?"

They laughed. "We're more alike than you dared think," he said.

Jerome dressed.

"You won't get any, anywhere."

"I know that," he snarled.

"I'll come with you."

"I don't need a nanny." In his poison he almost added 'goat'.

"Really?"

They walked to Feyt's house and were told the news. Of The Victory and of tomorrow's celebration. He shook the old man's hand in a parody of joy and stumbled back.

Celine led him back to bed where he shook such dry tears for the memory of Captain Phillipe, his lost comrades, lost hope, lost youth and his lost soul.

They talked all afternoon, settling details and avoiding, till last, the real issue. When do we tell our children?

Jean-Louis, warmed through by cognac, money and the promise of something he hadn't considered in so very long said, "We tell him, Jerome, tomorrow, at the meal, surely?"

She took her time to nod; no mistakes now.

"You think so?" she said.

Jean-Louis had gathered enough of her ways. Here was the nub of all this, he was quite sure.

"When you said," he leaned forward, demanding and receiving eye-contact, "you could think of no means to make him accept a room - away from here - you meant beyond disgracing him. Driving him away. Repulsing him. Didn't you?"

In the beat of her silence he was suddenly nervous. Had he misjudged all this?

"That's what this is, isn't it?" He pressed.

"Yes."

"That's been your plan all along?"

'Partly' she thought as she bowed to his perception, "Yes."

She watched her flattery warm his Pride.

"It's a good plan."

His voice was not patronising.

She demurred, surprised. Where was he driving now?

"I'll go and see them."

She blinked.

"Tell them I've rented a place in Lacapelle." He fished in his pocket. "Here are the keys."

She was genuinely surprised.

"You see," he smiled, "I can lie to you."

She smiled at his pleasure.

"How long have you rented it for?"

"A month. They'll be finished in a week."

She nodded. "He'll be back and living here, probably."

He nodded. So that was her plan, eh?

"And her?" Madame Lacaze asked.

"Who cares?"

"Perhaps he does."

Jean-Louis snorted. "He won't once he's away from his audience."

"Exactly," she said, tasting the bitter sadness of agreeing with his contemptuously correct analysis.

"We understand each other."

A quiet began.

"And your son?" Madame Lacaze hoped she sounded curious and almost disinterested.

"When I get home. Happy news shouldn't wait."

Elianne Lacaze and Jean-Louis Duthileul smiled at each other and sat back.

Finally he said, "I'm glad I met my match."

"You old fool," she said.

He placed a surprisingly warm, soft palm on the back of her hand.

"I'm old - I'm not a fool."

Jacques worked.

"Have you found them a place?"

"Yes."

Dominique was surprised. And genuinely grateful. And then suspicious.

"Thank you," he managed.

"When will you tell them? Today?"

"I won't. You will. You're the Mayor."

He placed the keys and an address on the table.

Dominique looked from the keys to his father.

"Why are you doing this?"

The kind of question his father liked.

"You asked me to..."

"No. Why are you doing this?"

"Oh, you'll see."

"Has she paid?"

A gesture that read 'none of your business', but the old man thought, 'She will.'

Sunday dawned.

Jacques rose, worked.

Sara worked.

Dominique scoured the clear sky for clouds.

Jean-Louis rose, beamed.

Arbel and Ardelle worked. She warmed an iron for their clothes, he took the beasts.

Jauliac began to sort wine.

Madame Cantagrel gathered her cooking things before meeting the other women at the Salle De Fetes.

Severine fretted.

When the bell tolled everyone but Jacques, Jerome and Celine Valet headed for Church.

Galtier walked to Mass, to pray Lacaze would dare show his face tonight.

Gley, too.

Chibret avoided his wife's eyes. The word bitter didn't cover her feelings. Arbel mule-head Jammes had cost her the highest female position in this community.

Curé Phillipe prayed with them all, and then, as if he had God's ear, prayed for them all. They went, finally, after six long dark years, into Peace.

Madame Lacaze laid out her dress for the evening ahead. Excited, nervous.

Feyt creased his best trousers.

Zoe put on her dress. Sara's mother took it off her, told her to go and help her mother pick vegetables.

Terses and Christoph did not discuss the possibilities of tonight's event.

Janon closed the café when the post-Mass slurping was done. Night off, get drunk.

The commune prepared.

Trousers, shirts, dresses, even socks, were ironed.

Celine ate old cheese and waited for him to come downstairs.

He did, at three in the afternoon.

"Please say we won't go."

Jerome said nothing.

"I don't want you to go."

Nothing.

"You'll drink..."

"And then we'll fuck," he offered indifferently.

"Exactly. I won't come."

"I don't care." He recognised the truth as he said it.

"So, you'll go - where they all hate you - only to drink. And then come back here and expect me to love you?"

"I don't care."

A beat.

"So, what's the point of us?"

Jerome looked at her.

"I've no idea."

Silence.

A shred of conscience moved in him.

"Why have you let me get to this state? Get a bottle and let's go to bed."

"You're fu- loving the bottle, not me."

"That is true," he agreed.

"How do you think that makes me feel?"

"I don't."

"Try!"

"I need!"

"What about what I need?"

"You can have what you need - "

" - after you've had what you need?"

Jerome was baffled.

"Yes! What's the difference?"

"Poison is the difference. You're a cup, not a man. And I need more than your cock."

Someone knocked at their door.

What? Stones? Threats.

"You going to answer that?" she suggested.

"No-one I want to see."

Celine opened it. The ex-Mayoral candidate, stinking, lurked in the hallway. The Mayor, shaved, stood in the doorway.

"Yes?"

"You asked me to find you a room. Here's the address and the keys."

Celine faltered.

"Who paid for this?" asked Jerome.

Dominique had had enough of these two. "I did. The commune - we all did. We all coughed up to get rid of you."

Jerome came to the door, held out his hand for the keys.

"What's the condition?"

"Don't come tonight."

"See you at seven," Jerome grinned. Bad breath. Worse than bad.

"You'll regret it," said Dominique, resisting a profound urge to smack his stupid face sideways.

"I regret everything," the prat smirked.

Dominique cast one cruel glance at Madame Valet. "I don't blame

you," he said, threw the keys on the floor and walked.

Celine aged.

And then went to beg, steal, find a bottle. Two...

Five o'clock. Tables and benches were laid outside The Mairie. Food was cooking in the Salle de Fetes. Jauliac had the wine ready. The musicians were on their way. The evening would be warm and the sky was high.

In the Mayor's office Madame Lacaze owned that nerves were getting to her, too. "Will they come?"

"He's your damned son! What do you think?"

The Mayor shocked himself with the snap in his voice but hell, he was the Mayor - fat lot of good it did him.

Silence.

"Exactly, Madame. Silence."

Dominique looked at her. "Why did my father say 'they'll come and then they'll leave'?"

She almost blushed. "I don't know."

"Madame - I'm not sure I believe you."

Her back straightened. "Ask him."

"D'you think he'd tell me? He talks in smirks and riddles."

"Yes," she nodded, "that's so."

"And so - Elianne - I'm asking you."

"And nothing, Dominique. Nothing I know."

"I don't believe you."

"But do you want me?"

He was sitting, she stood.

"Yes."

"Then whatever else happens tonight - so will that."

The Mayor's pulse raced.

She picked up her bag.

"6.30? To check the arrangements?"

His mouth opened and closed, soundless. "6.30. Yes."

"Till then, then."

Gone.

At six-thirty Arbel, spruced and combed, took Ardelle's hand and hooked the new bench over his shoulder.

They looked at each other and decided to waste their breath.

The bache drooped over one and a half walls, a staircase and a bed. And him, dismantling a wall, loading the barrow, then the cart, then back to his dismantling.

"Jacques," Arbel said softly.

Jacques lifted his eyes from the barrow, saw Arbel's clothes, looked at the sun and asked, baffled, "Is it Mass?"

"No," he laughed. "The War's done." He added hopelessly, "Won't you come and celebrate?"

Jacques stared at Arbel. Is he mad, he thought?

His eyes drifted to Ardelle, clearly pregnant and his heart jagged.

"Yes," she said, "Come and celebrate this, too."

Jacques said without a trace of self-pity or sentiment, "I've nothing to celebrate. You have." And turned back to his work.

They waited one second, turned and walked to the village.

At six-thirty it was as if she, Elianne Lacaze, had not said a word.

And certainly not those words, the ones she had said.

No sign, no smile, no intimacy, no code, nothing.

He scoured her face as she and Galtier, Severine and himself folded napkins, counted plates, glasses. Nothing.

Jean-Louis looked in the mirror. The shave was good. He dabbed eau-de-cologne behind his ears.

"I'll be back later, Mamman."

"Who are you? Who are you?" she squinted.

"Your son."

"God, you're old."

Sara and her mother and Zoe sat.

Zoe watched the clock.

Sara watched the child and her mother silently prayed. Again. In case God had been out the first time.

The Chef closed the Gendarmerie door, locked it, looked at Christoph.

"Wish us luck."

Jauliac placed three bottles; one champagne, one red and one white along with a carafe of water on each table. Uncorked the red to let it breathe. A delicious smell swept into the air every time someone opened the Salle doors.

Dominique greeted the musicians.

Madame Lacaze invited the Curé to sit at the top table, The Council table.

The people began to arrive - smiling, shaking hands, kissing three times, and looking round. To see. If they were here.

Not yet. And maybe not.

Jerome and Celine, at five to seven, were too occupied fucking themselves to a frenzy.

Jacques worked.

twenty-nine

THE CHURCH CLOCK struck the hour and Dominique stood. He welcomed them one and all, had each table uncork the champagne; the children squealing at the explosions. He poured a glass, waited while his commune had done the same, invited them all to raise their glasses and perfectly sincerely, said, "To Peace."

"To Peace."

He's not come. Please, Lord, keep him wherever he is.

When the entrées had been served Curé Phillipe stood. Hats came off.

"In the name of The Father, the Son and The Holy Ghost, we thank you Lord, for the reason for this meal and we ask your blessing on this our food."

"Amen." Hats were replaced.

And that those two haven't come, he wished he'd added.

The foie gras was demolished and the champagne began its merrying work. There was some laughter and time for a quick smoke.

Dominique caught Madame Lacaze's eye and again she smiled at him as if she'd never offered any intimacy.

While the soup was being served Feyt stood.

Silence.

"You people," he took the breath he needed not to weep, "could have betrayed me. Many many times. You didn't. I'm proud to be one of you." He raised his glass and toasted them. "LeChaim!"

"LeChaim!" Laughter.

People began to feel good.

Better.

Jauliac smiled, he'd make a packet on this.

By a quarter to eight the tense atmosphere was dropping away.

They hadn't come.

Galtier passed the word of Jean-Louis' generosity. He'd paid, from his own pocket, for a place for the two filthy wretches. And for the champagne.

And the soup was delicious.

And the one sad person was Zoe.

He hadn't come. He hadn't seen her frock. He hadn't come to see her. Sara felt sad, glad, stressed and relieved.

Jean-Louis smiled at his intended, his great capture, and waited his moment.

"You did tell your son?" she whispered.

"Of course," he smiled. Like the confident liar he is, she thought.

Soup plates were pushed back, the cooks were to be seriously complimented, napkins dabbed at smacked satisfied lips; and Zoe's scream of joy cut clean into the evening air.

"Papa!"

Jacques worked.

When Jerome took off his hat to greet his commune he was freshly shaven. Those who'd only heard of it gasped.

Madame Valet removed her headscarf and now she too was egg-headed.

Only Arbel and Renée Lacroix laughed.

Chef Terses put down his glass. Christoph too.

Zoe stared. Her teacher. Papa.

It was very quiet. Very.

Time sneaked by.

The child thought. Everyone hates him.

She looked to Sara.

My mother hates him.

And Mimi One, look.

And Mimi two, see.

Zoe swung her legs over the bench and ran home.

Sara followed.

The commune watched his child leave their celebration.

Arbel stood.

He rapped his glass on the table, once, lightly. The quiet swung its attention, and its disgust and simmering rage to him. What?

"Mayor Chibret, I apologise." He raised his glass. "When I came back Mayor Chibret suggested this celebration and I refused. I was wrong, Monsieur, you were right. But it was snowing..."

Chibret laughed. His wife didn't.

Arbel looked round, specifically taking in Madame Valet and Jerome and said, "No-one needs me to say this - but there is a need for some good news here. Ardelle and I - we're having a child."

He sat down. Blushed. So did Ardelle. Blushed crimson for him, for herself and for the embarrassment of being smiled at. She slapped Arbel hard and people laughed. Then Chibret stood and toasted their baby.

So the commune did.

Bread was picked up.

A glass re-filled.

A mouthful taken.

Was the evening possible again, somehow?

Terses motioned Christoph to relax.

Jean-Louis sensed if the focus swung back to Lacaze and her now there could still be disaster.

He tapped his glass with a soup spoon.

She pulled once on his sleeve.

"You haven't told your son," she hissed.

"Our son," he gleamed and stood to address the village.

Stone, barrow, cart. Looked up at the dusk. Another hour.

Sara held Zoe tight in her arms, rocking them both for some shred of comfort.

"I know I know I know I know I know I know."

Zoe joined in, "I know I know I know I know I know..."

Simone sat at the Formica-topped table, slurped her instant coffee and placed two photographs in an envelope. One of their son in her arms, standing in front of their brownstone, and the other of him staring at the single candle on his first birthday cake.

She wrote, 'You said you were afraid of forgetting. Don't. I don't and I won't and I can't and I shan't. Ever.'

The biro rested on her mouth.

She wrote, 'You know, if you sold the house you could be here.'

She crossed it out and threw the paper in the pedal-bin and began again. When she reached '...and I shan't, ever' she added, 'What are you taking down?'

"My good friends."

That brazen lie gathered almost all their attention.

Madame Lacaze braced herself. Watched her bald son drink.

"This is our celebration," the pompous fool continued. Dominique's eyes were fixed on Jerome. "Our commune, our country, our peace."

Elianne glanced up. Saw a bead of sweat.

"But I know you will all want to join me in celebrating something even closer to my heart..."

Dominique stared at his father.

Everyone did.

Including, and Duthileul waited for the eye-contact, Jerome.

"Please raise your glass and join me in celebrating," he was talking directly to Jerome, "Madame Lacaze agreeing to become my wife." And he raised his glass, inviting.

Silence.

Apart from the sound a hundred dropping jaws makes.

Elianne Lacaze fixed her eyes on a single crumb of bread on the table. Dominique Duthileul's jaw closed and dropped, like a fish.

A whole empty second passed.

Nothing moved.

A second and a half.

Two.

Sara's mother stood, climbed out of the bench and walked home.

Five silent seconds, in public, Madame Lacaze reflected, is a very long time.

Jean-Louis, glass in his hand, arm outstretched, unshaking, still dared smile at Jerome.

Galtier muttered, "Congratulations."

Jauliac looked around, repeated, "Congratulations."

The Mayor felt people's eyes settling on him. His brain, flooded with fury, shock, contradiction and humiliation, had seized.

'And then they'll leave...' came into his head.

He looked to see.

Au contraire.

No. He watched Jerome Lacaze's body organise itself so well, so capably, co-ordinated enough to push itself first upright, then to stand and to move firmly, determinedly, past Madame Valet's restraining hand. He navigated the bench. He was walking towards them. How does he do that at this moment? Dominique was scientifically fascinated. Look. His whole body functions, moves. My mouth doesn't. Look at him, striding.

Forward. To...

As Jerome launched the punch designed to smash his mother's nose across her face so his jaw met Dominique's fist travelling no more than a half-metre and light and heavy bedlam exploded as his neck cracked back, his spine arched involuntarily, an instant wet bloody warmth ran from a pain in his mouth and he folded into the square.

The sound of bone hitting bone so very crisply stilled everything. Until Celine ripped the night open with her scream and climbed straight over the table, towards the top table, the Council Table. She was grabbed by Gley, bit him and he thumped her nose hard. It split. Spilt a lot of blood. Women, for that instant sisterly murderous, screamed. Gley's sister lashed an elbow at him. The blow splintered his glasses and his hands leapt to his eyes. He lashed back at her. Another woman set on him. The man next to Arbel rose to help Gley. Arbel put out an arm to calm him and took a punch. Celine ignored the mess of her face and came on for Dominique. She stepped over the groan that was Jerome and Terses blew his whistle so hard everything stopped. Everything but Celine. Her nails were at The Mayor's face, ripping for his eyes and Madame Lacaze was on her and the whistle was forgotten. Arbel, tasting blood in his mouth, calmly motioned Ardelle to leave, took off his coat and dived

on the man's back, his wiry arm first cutting off the windpipe, then spinning him to receive the full intent of his fist. It hurt, Arbel reflected in the instant, but it was a nice hurt. Severine launched herself at the bald banshee of Celine Valet and a fat left arm swiped her in the stomach and she doubled over, retching instantly. Still she clawed at the Mayor. Arbel felt strong arms pin his from behind. It's not Ardelle was all he thought. Galtier kicked the prone Lacaze hard in the ribs. Madame Lacaze brought an empty champagne bottle down on Celine's bald head. Neither broke, but the thud released the tension in Celine's hands and Dominique pushed her away from his ravaged face and back into the chaotic developing mayhem. Arbel trod hard on the instep of the man holding him, spun and buried his knee neat and hard into the Chef Des Gendarme's crutch. Terse whitened. Arbel, fascinated, watched the Chef's new cap roll to a slow-motion halt as he only felt and heard the sound of people wading into the mêlée, the glasses and bottles smashed, plates broken, tables and benches scattered as everyone either got out of the way, got into the way or moved for a better view. Madame Chibret spat in Arbel's face. Ardelle screamed. Blood welted and seeped from beneath The Mayor's eyes. Elianne Lacaze lied, "No real damage done." Jean-Louis sat down, looked at the glass in his hand, drank it. Rank. Ardelle got in one good punch that flattened Madame Chibret before Christoph grabbed her. The Gréze musicians hid their instruments in a doorway and went back into the brawl. Celine recovered her screaming voice.

"He was the only one of you - shits! - who risked anything to win this War."

People moved away from her, almost kneeling on him, the lepers re-identified. The circle widened. The brawling was held.

"You are the worst people to have won anything. What have you

won? You lot. What are you?"

Terses rolled onto his knees.

"Collaborators. Cowards. And Traitors. He was the only ONE!"

She went to lift him. He groaned from everywhere.

The Curé moved through the crowd.

"Don't help them," Galtier commanded.

The Curé stopped, afraid, physically afraid.

"Or what?" Madame Cantagrel's voice.

"Mind yours, bitch," snarled the postman, "Or, he will regret it," he informed the Curé, personally.

"Threaten a priest?!" Madame Cantagrel screeched.

"Don't!" ordered her husband. When she turned, furious, to him he added, "I'm going."

"Go, you spineless wimp!" She span back to her target. "Threaten a priest?"

Galtier's hand was on her throat.

"Threaten you in a minute you tight-arsed sow."

He pushed hard and she sprawled splay-legged into a table, fell, gathered a knife in her hand and stood. Christoph unholstered his pistol, and fired into the night air, stilling everything.

The square emptied slowly.

Galtier walked Severine home.

The Mayoral party gathered in his flat.

The musicians gathered their instruments. One of them thought of their not being paid and pocketed a bottle. So did the others. Then they thought of the food too...

Arbel was led away down to the Gendarmerie.

"What do I have to do to get arrested, too?"

"Shut up, Ardelle," Terses said warmly.

"He didn't know it was you!"

"He does now."

"Shut up, Ardelle," said Arbel, warmly.

"Who's walking me home? Chef?"

"Oh, for God's sake."

There were rising, violently purpling, welts under his eyes and another under his bottom lip. Madame Lacaze bathed his face in warm water whilst his father rocked on his heels, helpless.

"I'm all right," The Mayor said. His head hurt but not as much as his memory.

Celine gathered Jerome upright.

Home for one more night and then get away. From it. From them.

Jacques and the dog went to their bed. He had to help the ageing creature up.

The ruins of celebration were left as people reeled homewards.

Elianne turned to Jean-Louis.

"Go home," she whispered kindly.

"He'll be - ? Yes. And there's my mother. What about you?"

"I'm a grown up, I'm sure I'll cope."

He left.

Care was not his forté she was not surprised to find.

Galtier hurried back.

To find Gley. Waiting for him.

"You're marrying Father?"

His mouth hurt. The words hurt worse.

"Yes," she said, calmly unpinning the cameo brooch at her throat.

The Mayor gulped.

"And..?"

"No need for that talk now."

She led them to his Mayoral bedroom and closed the door behind her...

Arbel and Ardelle slept like spoons in the same cell.

"There'll be an investigation," Gley whispered hard.

"Why?"

"It's murder!"

"So was what he did to Gaston." Galtier said.

"Gaston was a pain. Ask her."

"Go home."

A naked Elianne Lacaze watched The Mayor's smile fade towards sleep.

Celine and Jerome stumbled terrified, down the stairs, through the worst of the smoke and flames, coughing hideously and naked but for their desperately gathered bedspreads. In the street they watched, fascinated by the speed the flames licked through the broken windows, then gathering to a roar so quickly, as it burst through the roof. By the time the rafters fell in there were fifty and the helpless St.Céré Pompiers watching as they drenched Severine's house to save it from catching.

The Curé said, "Come to my house."

Jerome accepted the offer on their behalf.

"A Good Samaritan's bound to have some wine. Man needs a drink."

THE SINGLE SOLDIER

Elianne dressed. She looked at the sleeping lover, opened the bedroom door and smelt it. Heard it. Was he all right?

She took two steps and her rational brain panicked.

'It's two in the morning and if I should be seen coming from here...'

Disaster.

Unanswerable questions.

Her mother's brain shouted, 'But is he dead?'

Voices. Footsteps running. She froze.

I dare not be seen.

And I have to know.

If I can reach the turn by La Poste without being seen - I can say I came from my house. She ran.

At the turn she saw.

She walked now, gathering herself.

People watching.

At the edge of the crowd Severine saw her.

"He's alright," she said, comfortingly. Then, cold and disappointed, "So is she."

"Where are they?"

"Gone with the Curé."

Madame Lacaze nodded her grateful thanks and walked home.

Terses and Christoph left the Pompiers kicking at the smouldering stone-work.

"This was attempted murder."

"Sir."

"Serious."

"Sir."

"It wasn't Arbel."

Dominique was wakened by the sound of iron wheel-rims smashing crockery and glass. He stood naked at the window to see Vermande, blinkered, walking the cart round broken tables and spatterings of blood.

Jacques turned the beast down the Maurs road. No Sara. And there's been some fire, then.

Dominique looked at the bed and a smile started at his crotch and spread.

She must have gone home after -

He opened the window. Breathed as deep as only a new Lover should - and smelt it.

He never dressed quicker.

When Sara woke she smelt it, and like his mother, knew.

She threw a coat on and ran, her feet ignoring shards of splintered celebration, ran till she saw the grey embers.

She approached the two Pompiers.

"They're alright, mademoiselle. Getting pissed with the priest," one said.

"Decent wine there, I bet you," said the other.

Sara walked away.

Someone had tried to murder them? Him.

Dominique was almost the last to talk with the Pompiers, bored now with their glamour.

He robotically shook their hands and walked away.

Where? Where am I going, first? Her house?

Must tell her. This happened as she and I were -

"I know. Does your father?"

"No," Dominique said, "What's it got to do with him? Now?"

She pulled the dressing-gown tight around what had been naked. Kissed, naked.

"May I not come in?"

"You have things to do, sir."

Dominique said, "So do you, Madame."

She let his hopes hang there for one whole second.

"I've done enough. Go and do your duty."

A fire is a bad wound in a community. Especially when so very few cared. They were alive, wouldn't wish anyone dead, but after that - nothing. Beyond relief. They'd go now.

The first to move to tidy the square was Galtier.

Jauliac appeared. All his wine broken, drunk or stolen. His wife joined them.

"Terrible, terrible," it was a mantra. "Terrible, terrible."

Arbel and Ardelle were released. He with a warning. They walked up to the square, helped a little, walked home.

Dominique walked into the kitchen. No Renée, pissed probably, but his father was dressed.

"You didn't congratulate me. Us."

"I congratulated her."

Jean-Louis smelt some tinge of relish. Why?

"Where will you live?" asked his son.

"Here."

Dominique nodded.

"Well - that's good."

He nodded again.

"Congratulations, father."

And told his father about the fire.

The Pompiers found the charred keys; the Curé organised them both some clothes and Terses drove them to Lacapelle.

"It was no accident," insisted Madame Valet. Again.

"I agree, Madame."

On the drive back Terses thought.

I ought to call brigade in Cahors.

His car hummed through St. Medard.

Was it one of them from the bar?

Who else? Anyone! They all hated him. Them.

Could be an unpopular arrest.

Talk to The Mayor.

He checked his mirrors and concentrated on the road.

It was early evening.

Galtier, Dominique, Madame Lacaze, Severine and Chef Terses sat round the table.

"I haven't yet phoned my superiors," he began.

They could all hear the clock ticking.

"Talk to me, people," the Chef ordered sharply.

All four straightened. They looked round and responsibility settled on Dominique.

"Chef - you know it could have been almost anyone."

The clock ticked.

Terses nodded.

"I'll make a start here, then. Have any of you alibis for two in the morning?"

The clock ticked raucous.

Dominique blushed; no subtlety, no reserve - he blushed. Madame Lacaze opened her bag, took out a handkerchief, and snapped it back shut. Terses turned to her. She dabbed at her top lip, looked him square in the face.

Galtier straightened his back against the high wooden chair.

"Well - I was puking." Severine said.

Terses nodded, waited.

"Madame?"

"I was in bed."

Monsieur Le Maire?"

"Likewise." His ears crimson.

"Monsieur Galtier?"

"Burning Gaston's house."

Quiet. So quiet the clock hushed.

"Alone?"

"Alone."

Quiet.

"Would you come down to The Gendarmerie with me, please?"

"Yes."

He stood, his chair scraped their ears.

"Give her this."

He threw Madame Valet's pension book on the table. "Lead on, Chef."

Dominique wrote his resignation letter. They watched Severine type it.

Madame Lacaze witnessed it.

He locked the door of the Mairie, gave Severine the key and watched her walk away.

Elianne put a hand on his arm.

"Monsieur Le Maire," she said, "Let me drive you home."

Dominique looked at her, his head swirling.

"Thank you."

Jacques walked back up the lane. The beast, gorged on a day at Janatou, slumped in its stall and Jacques slumped onto his bed.

The steps. Cave door lintel. Surrounding stones. Ground level. Foundations.

I'll have done it.

"Iffing."

He called Tayo and again had to help its old hind onto the bed.

"We're getting old," he said. He was twenty seven.

"My dear!" Jean-Louis was unctuous, "How kind of you. Of course, I have to buy my son one of his own."

"I've resigned. Forget the car."

Jean-Louis aged.

Madame Lacaze watched it happen.

This won't need the wedding, she thought.

By the time Dominique finished the tale Jean-Louis had recovered.

"And so?"

"I'm home."

A silence.

The three of them, and the mother, nodding in her rocker.

Jean-Louis stood, went to a walnut cupboard, took out three glasses and a bottle of good red.

"All for the best," he said, sounding self-congratulatory.

He opened a drawer for the corkscrew.

As Dominique fitted the corkscrew into a third bottle, Jean-Louis led his mother to her bed.

"Who's she?" she demanded as she passed Elianne.

Jean-Louis resisted the urge to say 'My bride'. Or 'your successor'. Or any of the wonderful things she meant to him now.

"Who's she? She won't help."

Left briefly alone with his lover Dominique was tempted to ask how she saw their future. And what last night had been. He didn't. He did enjoy the silence and the smile at her lips – a smile he longed to share but their eyes didn't quite meet.

"This is very pleasant," said Elianne. Of the wine.

Jean-Louis sat to join them.

"When is the happy day?" Dominique wondered.

"My dear?"

"Soon. Don't you think Jean-Louis?"

"Well - that'll be very pleasant. Too." The ex-Mayor raised his glass to them both.

"It will," his father agreed.

"It's also very pleasant to be drunk. Together," Dominique said. "Again."

Jean-Louis' antennae buzzed. What was that? And, did she smile? 'Relax' he told himself. She's yours. Forget your paranoia.

"What about Lacroix?" he wondered aloud.

"Sack him," said his son. "Pay him off. I'm here father. No more wages! No more Mayor."

His father settled his eyes on his prize. "Seems you'll be taking on more than me, my love."

"I realise."

She smiled her warmth at him. This is real.

She turned the beam to Dominique. Really real. And really easy.

"Would you care for an evening tour of your new estate?" Dominique asked.

"No, thank you."

"Well, the house?" said Jean-Louis.

Elianne looked him in the eyes.

"Now?"

"Why not?"

"What had you in mind, Jean-Louis?"

Jean-Louis rubbed a hand over the blush racing over his craggy cheeks.

She smiled. "The bedroom?"

"Well - yes," he managed. Ancient rising lust blatant on his face.

"Oh no, Jean-Louis."

She ran a metaphorical thumb across the razor edge of her blade.

"Tell him, Dominique."

Silence.

Dominique's mouth too dry for speech.

"No?" She sounded disappointed.

"What? Tell me what?"

"I sleep with him," his intended said. "I have since Peace broke out."

Complete silence.

Only the vibrations of Jean-Louis Duthileul's world breaking.

"Watch, Jean-Louis."

He watched her stand.

She offered the ex-Mayor her hand.

He watched him take her hand.

He watched his son stand.

"Good night, my dear."

"Stay there, boy." The words barely grated out of his throat.

"Whatever would hurt me least, Jean-Louis." Elianne smiled. "Recall?"

Dominique led her up the stairs, into his bedroom and closed the door.

Jean-Louis Duthileul died inside.

No-one will know no-one can know no-one can ever know.

The insane rhythm of his love-making.

Elianne Lacaze took the thrusts and his hands on her.

Prepared to fake the orgasm Jean Louis would definitely hear.

Jean-Louis was sitting there.

Morning sun rising.

He was dressed the same.

Perhaps he'd never moved.

Madame Lacaze gathered her handbag and car keys.

"I'm going home, now."

Jean-Louis said nothing.

Dominique felt inside for the place where compassion for his father should have been. Empty.

"Goodbye, both."

The words pierced the smug sensual victorious heat within the son. It began to drain. Drain away.

"You're not - staying?"

"I most certainly am not."

No shred of doubt.

"But - " Dominique attempted a whisper, "Us?"

"You and I? Done, boy. You and him? I don't give the tiniest damn."

She went to her car.

She drove home.

Walked into her house.

Well, she thought. And poured a drink.

Well, Revenge *is* sweet.

She toasted herself.

Sat down by herself at her table.

Mmm.

She poured another...

Arbel and Jacques worked all day. The twelve steps.
The lintel. The door. The stones, all loaded.
"Come and eat. You don't have to talk."
Silence.
Jacques reached for his coat.
"We'll have those foundations tomorrow" Arbel said. "If you like."

thirty

THE VILLAGE REELED INTO PEACETIME.
Galtier. Gone.
Them. Gone.
The blinker-man gone.
No Wedding banns.
No Duthileul either.
No Dominique.
Just her.

Galtier's replacement rode up to Puech and found no house to deliver to.
Arbel took the letter to Sara and asked if she'd take it.
She and Zoe walked there.
Jacques was digging foundations.
He took the letter, put it in a pocket and dug.
"Can we go home, now?"
"Yes Zoe, we can."
He dug.

Sara said, "I'll come alone next time."

He said, "Thank you. Both."

He dug.

He'd read when he'd dug.

THE SINGLE SOLDIER

THE SINGLE SOLDIER

George Costigan has been a motor-parts storeman, a trainee accountant, another trainee accountant (both failed) a steel-worker, an insurance clerk, a wood-cutter, a bookseller, a record salesman, a book-keeper for a wedding-dress business – and then someone asked him to be in a play.

College followed and a career that started in children's theatre, then took in Butlins Repetory Theatre in Filey and eventually landed him at the Liverpool Everyman theatre. It was here he met some hugely influential people – Chris Bond, Alan Bleasedale, Alan Dossor and above all, Julia North.

His acting career has included working with Sally Wainwright, Willy Russell, Alan Clarke and Clint Eastwood. He has directed Daniel Day-Lewis and Pete Postlethwaite, and his writing for the stage includes several Liverpool Everyman pub shows and 'Trust Byron', for which he was nominated for Best Actor at the 1990 Edinburgh Festival.

He and Julia North have three sons and one grandson.

The Single Soldier is his first novel.